BREAKER

Stay magical!

Amy Campbell

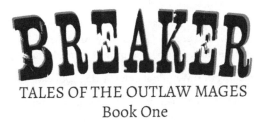

BREAKER

TALES OF THE OUTLAW MAGES

Book One

AMY CAMPBELL

This is a work of fiction. Names, characters, places, and incidents are the product of the author's imagination or are used fictitiously. Any resemblance to actual persons, living or dead, events, or locales is entirely coincidental.

To any librarians reading this: We ride at dawn! Bring your cardigan.

To anyone else reading this page: The librarians are up to nothing. Nothing at all.

For my parents.

Mom, who never shied away from the ridiculous number of books I checked out at the library as a child.
Dad, who taught me the joy of reading together by curling up to read the Sunday Comics with me.

Sorry in advance that some of the characters I write about are jerks.

IPHYRIA

SEA OF HERMEIA

PHINORA

OSCEN

Duskgarde

Izhadell

UMBER   ARGOR

UNTAMED
Greylight ⊛ TERRITORY

Salt-Iron Lake

THE GUTTER   Asylum

Itude

Rainbow
Flat

PETRIA

Ironrun   Fort   Bristle
Courage

MELLA   Morton

DESINA

Ondin

Sable Point

GANLAND

Seaside   Etla

GULF OF STARS

Nera

N
W   E
S

CHAPTER ONE
Mavericks and Magic

Blaise

"Keep your hands where I can see them."

Blaise startled at the voice; its edge dangerous as the strike of a rattlesnake. He kept his gloved hands high as he walked into the Black Market. The speaker loomed in the pale blue glow of mage-lights that lined the long, narrow room.

"Sorry. First time." Blaise winced at the hesitation in his voice. He had every right to be here.

The man leaned his forearms along the top of the bar, dusty bottles lining the shelves at his back. His eyes were little more than slivers above a black bandanna pulled over his nose, his shoulders broad like a bull. "Who sent you?"

"Marian Hawthorne." Blaise's heart raced. Like the other man, he wore a bandanna to conceal his face. Blaise considered the bandanna helpful on the dusty road, but he chafed at the anonymity of it for this transaction. According to his mother, the proprietor was a wanted man. It was safe to assume that anyone setting foot in the building was in similar straits. Anonymity kept all involved from swinging from a tree.

All the same, the cotton bandanna tickled his nose. It was irritating. He was hard-pressed not to twitch or rub at it. Blaise reminded himself appearances mattered at the Black Market.

"Monthly delivery?" the man asked, not bothering to identify himself. Blaise didn't see anyone else in the building, so he presumed the man was Tom Slocum, proprietor of the Black Market.

"Yes." Blaise stepped closer when the silhouette of Slocum's shoulders relaxed.

"Good." Slocum's eyes glittered as he got a read on Blaise despite the bandanna. "You bring a list?"

A list. Right. His mother needed more supplies for her alchemy. The Black Market specialized in hard-to-find items. "Y-yes." He lifted a hand to the pocket at his chest.

Slocum watched him with an air of boredom. Blaise pulled the list out and laid it out on the bar. Slocum picked it up, scanning for a moment before looking back at Blaise. "Unload your wares. Set 'em on the bar."

"Right." Thankful for the guidance, Blaise turned on his heel and walked to the door. He pushed it open with his shoulder.

The blazing sun was a harsh contrast to the interior of the Black Market. Blaise tugged his hat lower to protect his eyes from the glare. The family pony, Smoky, ignored him as he walked over and opened the tailgate of the cart. Blaise adjusted the fit of his gloves and then pulled out the first of the wooden crates.

The contents of the crate sloshed with the movement. Soft linen protected the glass vials from damage. One at a time, he carried all three crates inside and set them on the bar.

Boots creaked on floorboards as Slocum moved in the back room. Blaise looked around, taking the measure of the interior while he had the chance. The bar stretched across most of the room; a few barstools butted against it. Someone had shoved broken tables and chairs into one corner. The dusty remains of a billiards table sat near a window. Blaise supposed the Black Market might have been a saloon, once upon a time. Or perhaps it still *was* a saloon. He wasn't sure.

Aside from his nervousness at dealing with Slocum, the worst part of the place was the lack of airflow. It was stifling. Between his hat, bandanna, and gloves, a steady trickle of sweat beaded his face. He mopped the sweat on his forehead with one sleeve, causing his glove to ride up.

An ominous click sounded behind him. He turned to see Slocum on the other side of the bar, rifle trained on him. "Keep the glove on. I know what you are, Breaker." His tone was low and brooked no argument.

"Sorry," Blaise squeaked, cheeks burning with shame. He tugged the glove to cover the exposed skin on his hands. *How does he know about me?* Had word of his magic traveled this far? Had one of his parents told him?

"I'd hate to put Marian's kin in the bone orchard," Slocum drawled, his tone cool as he settled the rifle beneath the bar. Blaise shivered as he realized the man meant *cemetery*. "So you get the one warning."

Blaise nodded stiffly. He hadn't expected to have a gun pulled on him. Now he knew better. Someone with the savvy and experience of Slocum would be ready for trouble. Even if it was accidental.

"Supplies are here." Slocum hefted a crate onto the bar and shoved it toward Blaise. "Coin will follow in a moment."

Blaise hesitated before pulling the crate closer and peering inside. Brown paper bags obscured the contents. He plucked them out one by one to be sure they were the correct items. Delicate purple mushrooms clustered in one bag. *Check.* Bright yellow moss in dried strips in another. *Check.*

Slocum used a crowbar to pry the lid off one of the crates. He watched as Slocum rifled through the contents, a greedy smile twisting his lips.

"Your mother's quite the alchemist. You have her talent?" Slocum resealed the crate and set it aside.

Blaise shook his head. "Not with these hands."

Slocum grunted. "True enough." He picked up a crate and carried them one at a time to what Blaise supposed must be his storeroom. The proprietor returned with a clinking leather pouch. He set it on the bar in front of Blaise.

"Normal monthly pay." Slocum settled his bulk atop a nearby barstool.

Blaise opened the pouch, spilling the coins out to count. *Trust no one to hand you the right amount the first time,* his parents had cautioned him. Alchemy was not an inexpensive profession or openly practiced. Slocum's eyes tracked him as he counted. Blaise's muscles tensed in response. He would be glad to leave this place.

"You a maverick?" Slocum asked after Blaise finished counting.

Blaise startled at the question. It was blunt and came out of nowhere. "What?"

Slocum gestured to Blaise's gloved hands. "You're the sort the Salties look for. Mage. What happens if they come calling in Desina?" He jerked his chin toward the door. "Mavericks are the ones that get away from 'em."

"Did something happen?" Blaise tried to keep the quiver from his voice.

For hundreds of years, the Salt-Iron Confederation pushed their ideology across the face of Iphyria. Their goal: to bring mages and magical creatures alike under their control. Geography and a stubborn Consul kept Blaise's homeland from the Confederation. Had something changed?

Slocum gave a slow shrug. "I hear gossip."

Of course you do. Blaise didn't know the full story on the Black Market, but rumor had it each day of the month it moved to a new location. On the fifth, it existed in this ramshackle building near the border of Desina. Slocum's peculiar magic allowed him ample opportunity to collect news from all over.

The Black Market proprietor intimidated Blaise, and though he wanted to ask more, he didn't. "Thanks. I'll be on my way, then."

Slocum nodded. "Nice doing business. Keep your hands to yourself, Breaker."

Stress knotted Blaise's neck. He shoved the pouch of coins into his shirt pocket. Blaise grabbed the crate of supplies and balanced it against his hip as he headed for the exit. His goal was to put some distance between himself and any further uncomfortable conversations.

He loaded the supplies into the back of the pony cart, securing the crate to prevent jostling during the journey home. Blaise pulled an empty bucket from the back of the cart. He walked over to a well located a short distance from the Black Market and filled it with fresh water, then carried it over to the parched gelding.

Smoky dunked his muzzle into the bucket and drank his fill while Blaise weighed his options. He was hungry. His choices were to either picnic where he was or eat as he drove back. Smoky knew the way better than he did and would need little guidance. *The sooner I get home, the better.*

Once the gelding had his fill of water, Blaise emptied the bucket and stowed it in the cart. He untied Smoky from the hitching post, then stepped up to the driver's seat. Smoky didn't wait for him to settle into his seat and disengage the brake before starting on his way.

"I know. I want to get home, too," Blaise muttered to the pony.

Blaise pulled his lunch out from beneath the seat. Smoky had things under control. As he ate, he reflected on the outing. It had been a success. He ticked off his accomplishments. Represented his family's business at the Black Market. Sold their wares. Successfully returning home with pay. True, his parents had laid everything out for him to make failure difficult. All he had to do was follow their directions. Blaise was going to declare it a victory regardless.

Hopelessness washed over him as he looked at his gloved hands. He had endured scorn and ridicule about his magic for most of his twenty-two years. It was difficult to feel betrayed by his own flesh. *Walking disaster. The reason we can't have nice things. Ruiner. Sorcerer. Heretic.* He had heard every name in the book. Every single one of them felt true. Because of his magic, he wasn't just an example of a failure to launch—he was a burned-out boat at the bottom of a river.

But today might change things. He had a measure of success. A smile ghosted Blaise's lips. If they let him go to the Black Market again next month, he stood a chance of convincing them he could move to another town. He could seek an apprenticeship.

Blaise could start a new life.

Only if he could hide his magic. He had tried to do that before. And failed.

It was worrisome that Slocum knew of his magic. But other than treating him with caution, the man hadn't seemed upset by it. Not like the townspeople in Bristle. Anyone who knew Blaise in Bristle would turn and walk in the other direction if they saw him. No one wanted to be around to see what destruction his magic wrought.

He noticed a hole developing in the palm of his right glove, exacerbated by his nervousness. His magic was always at its worst when he was out of sorts. Blaise poked at the hole with his index finger. Before too long, his skin would be visible. He made a mental note to check and see if they had leather at home for patching.

Smoky laid back his ears and whisked his tail, nudging Blaise from his rambling thoughts. The gelding rumbled a warning nicker. Blaise cursed. *I'm an idiot.* He had forgotten one of the most important rules of the Gutter and Untamed Territory.

Always keep an eye turned to the sky.

A golden speck in the clear cerulean sky bore down on them as

Blaise drew Smoky to a tentative halt. There was no sense trying to outrun them, not now. Only a fool would try to outrun an outlaw on a pegasus.

Blaise drummed a rhythm on his knees, trying to recall the old nursery rhyme about appeasing outlaws. His mind was a blur as he tried to think. *One gold coin? Two? Two sounds right.*

He pulled the coin bag out of his pocket. With luck, the outlaw wouldn't perceive him as a threat or a more valuable target than he was. Blaise shook two coins out of the pouch and pulled the laces taut. He hoped the outlaw didn't consider the crate of alchemy supplies worthwhile plunder.

The pegasus landed on the road, hooves striking the ground with a thunderous impact. A dust cloud swirled around steed and rider. As terrified as Blaise was, he had never seen a pegasus this close. It was *stunning.* The equine's coat glistened the same color as the golden coins in his palm, its mane and tail as pale and fine as gossamer. The afternoon sun glinted off the pegasus's wings as they splayed open, banded like a hawk's. Blaise inhaled a breath of admiration as the steed arched its neck.

The rider slipped down from the modified saddle, boots striking the ground with a sharp staccato. Blaise jumped, startled back to reality. The grizzled outlaw used his knuckles to tip back his hat, locks of blond sticking out like straw. He pulled up his flight goggles, snapping them into place against his forehead. The breeze tugged back the man's tan duster. In the blink of an eye, Blaise stared down the gleaming barrel of a sixgun.

Things had been going so well.

Jack

THE MORNING WAS RIFE WITH FRUITLESS LEADS AND FRUSTRATION. No one would blame him for hankering for trouble by spooking a random traveler. Even outlaws deserved some of the simple joys in life, Jack reasoned.

The pony cart trundling along on the road from the Black Market to the Desinan border was too much of a temptation. Jack tried to leave his antics for more deserving targets. A Salt-Iron baggage train or stagecoach was a prime target. He left the smaller merchants unharried out of common courtesy.

But not always. Outlaws weren't known for being *polite*.

His palomino pegasus snorted, prancing in place to block the pony's path. Jack cocked his head as he assessed the slack-jawed driver. Even with a bandanna covering his nose and mouth, Jack knew he was young. He didn't have the demeanor of the more experienced Untamed Territory merchants, who traveled with a rifle close at hand. *This kid is as green as a new blade of grass.*

Jack slipped down from Zepheus's back as the kid goggled at him. He pulled out his revolver in a fluid motion—he meant business. He liked the way a greenhorn's eyes went all white-ringed like a spooked colt when his sixguns came out.

Zepheus's nostrils cupped as he inhaled the unfamiliar scent. <I would leave him alone if I were you.>

Jack cast a furtive glance at the stallion, lips taut in response to the telepath's suggestion. *Another mage,* Jack mused. That was the only time Zepheus would suggest caution. The kid was young, not even worth calling a man. Jack had dealt with worse.

"You travel in the Gutter." Jack's voice was gruff and dangerous. "You got the toll?"

The young man kept his eyes averted. His terror at facing a flesh and blood outlaw froze him in place, like a rabbit in a hawk's shadow. A momentary pulse of satisfaction zinged through Jack. Yeah, he still had it. The kid stood before him, gaping. Jack cleared his throat to remind him he was waiting.

"Um," the kid mumbled as his brain caught up with the situation. He rubbed at his hands as if they itched. Then the kid looked down at them, uncurling one hand. Golden coins flashed in the sunlight. "Yes."

Jack's lips quirked. He took a step closer, but Zepheus snorted and shook his head. <I don't like whatever his magic is. I've not come across anything like it before.>

Jack scowled at Zepheus; the stallion minced backward like a spring colt. The pegasus was no coward. He flicked his eyes back at the young man. "What are you?"

The youngster fumbled over the question. "What?"

"Magic," Jack clarified, annoyance creeping into his voice. "What's your *magic*, boy?"

The boy's lips clenched into a thin line, his eyes downcast. "They call it Breaker."

Jack ignored the magical designation and clung to a single word in the sentence. "*They?* You know other mages?"

The kid blanched and shook his head. "N-no." He looked ready to throw the coins and bolt.

Jack studied him, the familiar wave of disappointment washing over him. *Another day without another damn lead.* He gave the young man a curt nod. "Get out of here then, kid."

Sparks lit the young man's eyes at the epithet. "I'm not a kid. Take your gold."

The kid was a dunderhead to think he could talk like that to an outlaw. Jack's right hand tightened against the engraved grip of his sixgun. Zepheus nickered a warning. Jack huffed out a breath and waved a hand in dismissal. He walked over to the pegasus and prepared to mount, turning to address the kid with one boot in the stirrup. "I don't take payment from greenhorn mages. Now get off my land."

"This isn't your land," the young man shot back.

Jack narrowed his eyes, moving away from his steed. "The Gutter belongs to the outlaw mages. Who do you think you're talking to?"

Zepheus snorted, fretful. <Knock it off. You're going to make things worse.>

"Then take the damn gold," the young mage ground out, jumping down from the cart and walking towards him with his hand extended. The golden coins winked in the afternoon sunshine.

Jack didn't fully register what happened next. The kid either tripped or took a bad step in a divot in the road—the cause didn't matter. His arms pinwheeled comically for balance. Gold coins arced into the air, chiming as they clattered to the dirt. The force of the fall sent the young man tumbling into Jack and they sprawled to the ground in a jumble.

A yelp of full-throated horror split the air as the young mage disentangled himself from Jack and crab-walked away, face pale. "Take it off, *take it off!*"

Jack rolled into a sitting position, staring at the young man. *Is he addle-brained?* What in Perdition was wrong with him? "What in Faedra's name are you caterwauling about?"

"I touched it. Your gun. Take it off. Throw it away. *Something!*" The young mage trembled, every muscle taut. His hat tumbled away in the breeze, knocked off by the collision.

Jack rose to his feet, glowering as he replaced the sixgun in the hip holster. No one in their right mind would demand an outlaw to disarm himself voluntarily.

<Jack—!> Zepheus never had the chance to say more.

Jack was accustomed to the sound of gunfire. But nothing prepared him for the discordant concussion of his sixgun meeting its maker. The revolver at Jack's waist exploded with a deafening crack, the cylinder and barrel ripping away from the grip. The force of the explosion shredded his holster. Faedra must have given him the grace of her protection because he wasn't hurt, but his ears rang from the force of the blast. Jack's mind raced, grappling with the unexpected event.

He howled, a feral combination of rage and fear. Zepheus moved closer, protective, ears pinned back as he pawed the ground in warning. Jack unbuckled the gun belt and dropped it like it was a hissing snake. The shattered revolver tumbled out of the ruined confines of the holster. The barrel struck the ground with a pathetic metallic clank.

Aside from the mangled mess of the gun, they were fortunate it hadn't done damage to either of them. Though Jack didn't feel charitable about the situation.

Jack pulled a small pistol from his boot, his arm quivering with rage as he pointed it at the young man's head. He said nothing. There were no words for the anger that clawed through him. Only actions.

Golden wings burst in front of him. Zepheus stood before the young mage. The stallion's ears were back, teeth bared. <No. *Your* fault. You didn't listen. You do not get to claim vengeance.>

Damn pegasus. Jack glowered. With a snarl, he holstered the pistol. Zepheus folded his wings and sidestepped.

"Get out of my sight." Jack's voice was cold and flat. It was so tempting to put a bullet right between those wide, frightened eyes. But Zepheus would interfere again. "Get away from here, before I rethink the mercy I show *kid* mages."

Swallowing, the young man staggered to his feet, scuttling to the pony cart. The stolid little pony had stayed put the whole time, indifferent to the debacle. The mage clambered into the cart, urging the pony off at a brisk trot. Two golden coins glittered on the road behind them.

Jack watched until the pony cart was only a dot on the horizon. Then he stomped his boots in the red dirt, growling as he balled his hands into angry fists to threaten the sky. After dealing with that mage, an old-fashioned hissy fit felt good. Annoyance prickled the back of his neck as Zepheus watched with mild amusement.

He felt a little better once he got it out of his system. Jack reached down and picked up the ravaged revolver. He turned it over in his hands, assessing the catastrophic damage. He needed to empty the rounds, but with the hammer missing there was nothing left to cock. Jack thumbed open the gate and discovered only pulverized shrapnel in the chambers. That half-grown colt had done *this?* It was laughable. It was *ridiculous.*

Jack turned to glare at his pegasus. "Never get between me and my target."

<I told you to leave him alone,> Zepheus pointed out, one hind hoof relaxed. The impertinent stud was calm since the threat had passed.

"Don't be a smart-ass. How was I to know he'd blow my sixgun to Perdition and back again? My *favorite* sixgun." Jack clenched his fists as he surveyed the surrounding area for the missing bits of his revolver. He wasn't foolish enough to leave anything behind that someone could later use against him.

<Maybe next time you'll listen when I say someone smells dangerous. You know, instead of going over and poking the rattlesnake in the snout.> The palomino shook his silver mane.

"Yeah, yeah," Jack grumbled. Zepheus *had* warned him. And he hadn't listened. But in his defense, the young man was about as threatening as a day-old kitten.

<Even kittens have claws.>

"Shut your trap. I don't want to hear it."

Jack should have paid more attention when the kid identified himself as a Breaker. He knew of Breakers, by historical reputation only because their line of chaotic magic was allegedly extinct. They were a breed of mage no one with any sense wanted to have on their side—or on the enemy's. They were a danger to everyone. As this encounter had proven.

The kid's presence bothered Jack. With the news he had learned earlier that day, things didn't bode well for the kid. Jack presumed Desina was his homeland, judging by the direction he had headed. He was sure to be in jeopardy soon. The Salt-Iron Confederation already knew the locations of all the mages in Desina. They were coming for them.

<You always say we could use more mages,> Zepheus observed.

"Stop spying on my thoughts," Jack grunted. He gave the stallion's shoulder a half-hearted shove. "We don't need mages like him. How in Perdition do you train *that?*"

Zepheus arched his neck, looking away with tacit disapproval. Jack picked up a chunk of shrapnel, tucking it into his shirt pocket.

"He blew up my damned gun, Zeph!"

<They will kill him if they can't use him,> the pegasus reminded him.

Jack gritted his teeth. "He's young. Believe me, they'd love to train that up. If they can." The Salt-Iron Confederation would use him. Oh, how they would use a power like that. At least until it blew up in their faces. That thought cheered him. *Would serve the damn Salties right.* "I'm not allowing magic like that in Itude. Don't even think of mentioning it to the other Ringleaders."

Zepheus lifted his tail and made a deposit on the road, a commentary of his opinion. Jack grunted and turned his back, scanning the ground for more bits of his revolver. He stowed the broken remains in his saddlebag, tucking a handkerchief around the cracked pearl handle. The corners of his eyes stung; he swiped away the wetness with one hand. *Damn dust.*

Wildfire Jack, Scourge of the Untamed Territory, *didn't* cry.

But *she* had given him that sixgun. And now it was beyond repair.

After fastening the buckle on the saddlebag, Jack swung into the saddle.

<Back to town?> Zepheus asked.

"Yeah. Need to update the other Ringleaders on the Salties' movements." Jack glanced over his shoulder. Too far away for the naked eye to see, Jack knew the Salt-Iron Confederation was coming.

CHAPTER TWO
From Shadow to Shadow

Blaise

"I'm sorry. Repeat that. The part where you did *what* to the outlaw?"

Blaise winced at his mother's incredulous tone as she stared at him from her place across the table, curly brown hair framing her face.

Everyone else at the table stared at him too, their reactions mixed. His thirteen-year-old sister, Lucienne, shook her head as if she couldn't believe how stupid he was. His five-year-old brother, Brody, thrust his hands into the air and yelled, "Boom!" at random. Their father rested his chin on one hand as if exhausted by all of them.

Blaise hadn't wanted to tell them. Upon arrival, he saw by the drawn expressions on his parents' faces that something was wrong. He pretended that everything had gone well on his trip to the Black Market to keep everyone at ease. But Blaise had found it difficult to dodge further questions at dinner. He had never been a good liar. So what else could he do but tell them?

"It was an accident." Even he wasn't convinced with that argument. *Everything* around him was an accident. He took a frustrated breath as his parents traded concerned looks. "I paid the toll. We should be fine. Right?"

His father, Daniel, steepled his fingers in front of him. "It's hard to tell with an outlaw. They're unpredictable. And dangerous."

That describes me, too, Blaise thought, glum. He pushed the food around on his plate with his fork, his appetite gone. Things had been looking up. He should have known better.

Marian glanced at her two younger children. "Luci, help Brody get ready for bed."

"Mom!" Luci wailed. "Brody can get himself ready!"

Their mother shook her head. "If by *ready* you mean neglect to brush his teeth, sure. *Go*. Help him get ready. And don't either of you skulk around listening in." She pointed emphatically toward the door.

"I don't want to!" Brody howled, fighting banishment to an early bedtime.

Luci rose from her seat, taking him by the arm. "C'mon, kid. Adults are talking and don't want us around."

"I'm not a kid!" Brody shrieked, defiant as he flopped out of his chair. Blaise winced. Had *he* sounded like that to the outlaw? Probably.

Brody's protests forced Luci to pick him up. "You owe me!" she called over her shoulder as she shut the door behind her.

Once the kitchen was quiet, Marian returned her attention to Blaise. "I'm sorry, I didn't mean to sound so harsh about the experience you had today. I know you were hoping for it to go better."

Blaise sighed. "I didn't fall and skin my knee, so don't talk to me like it's nothing. My magic got me in trouble. Again. With an outlaw."

She used a fingernail to scrape a sticky spot from the tabletop. "I'm not saying that it's of no consequence. But I am trying to do my duty as a mother to make you feel better."

Oh, he was aware. But didn't she realize that words did *nothing*? He still had to live with his magic and its repercussions. Maybe it was easier looking at it from the outside when you weren't the one with the magic. What was that even like?

"I'm sorry. I mess everything up." Blaise stared at his cold plate of food.

"Oh, son." Marian's exhaled words softened. "I know you didn't mean for it to happen. One of us should have gone with you."

The muscles in Blaise's shoulders and back tightened. That was what he had been trying to avoid. He hated the constant hand-holding required to keep his magic from ruining their lives. This had been his big chance to prove he could contribute as an adult. He had been *so* close.

"It's been a hard day for everyone," Daniel murmured.

Something in the way the words caught in his father's throat didn't sit well with Blaise. Stirred from his melancholy, he looked up at his father. Lines of stress pulled at the corners of his mouth and eyes. "What happened?"

His mother shook her head. "Do we have to talk about this now?

Daniel pushed back his chair, picking up his plate to clear the table. "It's necessary. He needs to know. We have to make preparations."

What? Blaise looked from one parent to the other. His stomach wrenched at the look of misery on his mother's face. "What's going on?"

Marian shook her head, eyes downcast. His father spoke as he picked up Luci and Brody's plates from the table. "Courier brought word that Desina has officially entered the Salt-Iron Confederation."

"What?"

"They've been courting the Consul for decades." Marian crossed her arms, her voice bitter. "And word came that Consul Stewart died. The new Consul has caved."

Blaise gulped. "What . . . what does that mean for us?" *For me?*

His mother's jaw clenched. She turned away, making a vague gesture to her husband. Daniel rested his palms against the counter. "I saw a broadside posted in town today. Next week, a company of soldiers will arrive to register all the mages in the area."

"But you won't be going," Marian said, steel in her tone.

Blaise's mind reeled. The Salt-Iron Confederation was a forbidden topic in their house. The little he understood about the Salt-Iron's stance on mages made him fearful of ducking out of the rule. Registration was a requirement for *all* mages. They hunted down those who avoided it.

"Marian . . ."

His mother's lips pulled back from her teeth, fierce as she stared her husband down. "I know what they would do with him, Daniel. Don't *Marian* me. Our child will not be a weapon."

A weapon? How could his awful magic be a weapon, when he couldn't even control it?

"Registration isn't an option. They'll send Trackers to search for any mages they miss. But we have time. We'll make a bolt-hole." She nodded as she worked through her idea aloud. "The basement—no, too obvious. The hayloft. That could work."

Blaise rubbed the back of his neck, a tension headache coming on. "Won't I have to hide all my life?"

His mother breathed out a deep sigh. Her distress made him wish he hadn't asked. She felt guilty for his birthright, too. "They can't have you. If that means we spend the rest of our days hiding you when the Confederation threatens . . . then yes."

Blaise understood, but he didn't like it. It wasn't fair. His cursed magic prevented him from having a normal life. His age-mates were getting married and having children or taking on prosperous apprenticeships. And here he was, stuck at home hiding from the Salt-Iron Confederation. He had no prospects. No future. No hope.

"I picked up more flour when I was in town," his father said, changing the subject to something more palatable. "You can take the time to bake some things to keep in the loft when you have to hunker down."

"Treats would put everyone in a good frame of mind," Marian agreed, though her heart wasn't in it.

"I can make a cobbler and some bread." Blaise humored them. He knew what they were doing. He loved to bake—it was one of the few things he was good at. The opportunity should have made him happy. But all he felt was a cold pit of despair.

He hated that his life was comprised of jumping from shadow to shadow, afraid of what he was.

"CAN I LICK THE SPOON?" LUCIENNE SHOT THROUGH THE KITCHEN, heading toward the door that led to the small mudroom.

Blaise looked over his shoulder as he kneaded dough. "Right now I'm making bread, so no, that's disgusting."

"If you make a cake, I call dibs!" she shouted back.

Blaise cringed. "Raw eggs. No. Stop being gross." She cackled as she sped out the door.

He had to admit, he was in a better mood and it had everything to do with baking. It was one of the few activities he knew without a doubt would help him escape the destructive force of his magic. Blaise found freedom in the simple act of combining ingredients to create something delicious. His magic broke down and destroyed anything else he touched. It was a mystery why his magic had no impact on his baking.

Gloves were a necessity normally. It was liberating to feel the grit of flour against bare skin and the stickiness of the dough as he worked the heels of his hands into it. He kneaded the dough for several minutes, content in the simple task. It was its own sort of magic.

Blaise set aside the dough to rise. He washed his hands and moved to the cupboard to check on the sugar supply. Hard gingerbread was next on the agenda.

His mother swept into the kitchen, sniffing in appreciation. "Smells good in here. You're going to make us jealous that you get to hide away with snacks."

He smiled, shrugging. "I need some perk, right?"

Marian nodded, the corners of her dark eyes creased with worry. "Your father hauled a few jugs of water into the loft. I want you to have a go-bag packed."

Blaise put down the bag of sugar. "What?"

She moved over to the kitchen window, peering out. "When we moved to Desina, we made sure our home was as close to the border as possible. I had hoped we would never need to worry about that precaution."

Blaise frowned, tapping the counter with a clean wooden spoon. "Does . . . do they want you too, Mom?"

She bowed her head. "Probably. If they still remember me, that is. If they do, then yes—they will want me. But they can't have the both of us, Blaise."

"Why?"

Her shoulders slumped as she released a pent-up breath. "It's twofold." She clenched her jaw.

For a few minutes, Blaise thought she wouldn't say anything else. She knew more about the Salt-Iron Confederation than she had ever told him or his siblings. He wished she would just tell him. He wanted some idea of what was dropping on their heads.

She must have decided the same, for she finally spoke. "When a mage registers with the Salt-Iron Confederation, they receive a tattoo. Powerful mages receive a tattoo that has a binding—a geasa that compels subservience to the Confederation. At that point, the bound mage become a theurgist."

Blaise frowned. That didn't add up. "How do outlaw mages fit in? Aren't those tattooed mages who broke free?"

Marian shrugged. "Yes. Not to be confused with mavericks. Mavericks escape before receiving a tattoo." She was quiet for several heartbeats. "We can't allow them the chance to tattoo you. The alchemists work to constantly improve the formula used in the geasa and—" She clamped her mouth shut.

"Oh." Blaise looked away, unsettled. *The alchemists work to constantly improve the formula?* He wanted to ask more, but he knew she had already said too much.

"They *can't* get you. Promise me you won't let them take you. If you have to run, run to the Gutter."

The Gutter. Nothing good came from there. It was a harsh, dry region of sandstone canyons carved by the Deadwood River, inhospitable to all but the most determined survivors. Blaise had been as close to the Gutter as a Desinan could comfortably travel when he had gone to the Black Market, and that had been far enough for his taste.

The idea of fleeing to the Gutter for safety filled him with dread, but his mother's fear was palpable. She rarely spoke of her past. And she avoided mention of the Salt-Iron Confederation. If it came up in conversation, she either walked away or changed the subject. Blaise had the horrible suspicion she had fled them, but he was too afraid to ask.

What else could he say? "I promise."

Placated, she wiped glittering tears from the corners of her eyes. Blaise wasn't used to seeing her so upset. She was their rock, solid and everlasting. The one they could rely on to have a cool head in any difficult situation.

"After you finish baking, get a bag together," she said. Then she paused, frowning at the flour-covered counter. "After you've cleaned up this mess."

He smiled. There she was, her old spirit back. "Right. After I clean the kitchen."

Marian took a steadying breath, then clapped her hands

together. "Good. I'll be down in the cellar. Those potions won't mix themselves."

Blaise turned back to his work, gathering the ingredients for gingerbread. His mother was off to work on her alchemy, and he could settle down to his own version—baking. Before too long, he could take out the bread to see if it was ready. That was a pleasant thought.

It was nice to have something in life that he didn't destroy with a single touch.

CHAPTER THREE

Timber

Blaise

The week of the Salt-Iron Confederation's arrival came and went. Blaise's father made several trips into town and reported that the company had arrived. One hundred soldiers, all dressed in the resplendent scarlet and gold of the Confederation. All on the lookout for mages.

The other mages in the area completed their registration. For most of them, their daily life wouldn't change even with a theurgist's tattoo. Their abilities were too weak. Blaise knew at least two other mages his age. Crispin specialized in finding lost chickens. Josephine commanded weak fire magic. The last Blaise heard, she could keep something warm, and that was the extent of her power. Neither mage boasted magic like his.

Each day, Blaise saw to his chores around the house but kept a vigil for threats. Every time hooves plodded down the road, his pulse sped, and he edged closer to the barn—just in case. He grew more paranoid by the hour. Tension knotted his muscles.

At night, his mother recommended he sleep in the hayloft. She worried the soldiers might make a surprise visit after dark. It wasn't a pleasant situation for Blaise, but he agreed with her reasoning.

The hidden compartment above the hayloft wasn't comfortable. But given the circumstances, Blaise didn't complain. The space was tight, with a low ceiling. His mother brought up quilts to cushion the rough-hewn floor. There was jerky, jugs of water, and the fresh bread and gingerbread he had baked.

Things could be worse.

Two weeks after the Salt-Iron Confederation arrived in Bristle, Blaise sat on the floor of the hayloft. He flipped through one of his cookbooks as the natural light waned. The hayloft didn't have any lighting of its own. Before long he would be alone in the darkness.

His situation gave him time to think more about his future. If he kept his magic under control, he had a chance to leave home. Maybe secure an apprenticeship in another land. One not under Salt-Iron Confederation control—perhaps Oscen. Even better, no one there would know him by reputation. And if he worked hard, someday he might have a bakery of his own. That was the dream, anyway.

To even have the slightest hope of that, he had to rein in his magic. Gloves only did so much. He flexed his fingers, looking at his hands. *Traitors.* With a sigh, he settled down on the pallet of quilts and stared into the darkness. Blaise felt detached from everyone he cared about. Was it always going to be like this? Kept at arm's-length from everyone he loved to protect himself—and them?

It was a terrible thought. True, he wished he could have independence apart from his family—but they were his *family*. He cared about them, and even in the worst of times, he never felt alone when they were around.

But in the loft, he was all alone with his thoughts. And his thoughts were terrible company. He had ample opportunity to recall all the times his magic had embarrassed or created havoc in the past. Blaise's earliest memory was that of his favorite stuffed bear coming apart in his hands, simply because he had hugged it after falling down and skinning his knee. When he was eight and the children in his class had pressed up against the windows to look at a rainbow outside, his touch had shattered the glass. And there were more. Before he had been asked not to return to school, he had been bullied for his magic. Blaise absently rubbed at his long-healed left hand. A bully had broken it "to stop your magic, sorcerer!"

Tossing and turning, Blaise growled in frustration. The warmth of the day receded, but it was still humid and intolerable. In the darkness, he pulled his gloves off. It was too warm. He usually tried to sleep with them on—otherwise, his magic ended up destroying his bedding. Blaise set the gloves aside and angled his hands so the palms faced upwards, not touching any of the quilts. He sighed. It was worth trying if he could get some respite.

It must have worked. His eyes flew open to the sound of a dog baying. The voice belonged to Chester, the family terrier. Blaise rubbed the sleep from his eyes with one hand, trying to remember where he was. Dawn's light filtered through the cracks between the walls, casting the hayloft in a surreal glow.

Chester continued to bark, insistent and frantic. Blaise imagined the little dog's ruff bristling with agitation. Something had set him off.

Hooves crunched on gravel. *Many* hooves. In the distance, the unmistakable snort of a horse punctuated the night.

Blaise untangled from the quilts and frowned as he looked down. The fabric had frayed during the night, a gentle rebuke that his hands hadn't stayed put. He shoved the quilts into a lumpy pile in the corner. If he had a chance later, he made a mental promise to mend the damaged quilt. Blaise found the indistinct pile of his fresh clothing for the day and pulled on pants and a shirt.

Smoky whinnied a query. The steady rumble of hooves came closer. Blaise fumbled around for his gloves in the dim light, pulling them on. He crept closer to the wall and peered out of a knotted hole.

Soldiers. The majority rode regular horses. But the telltale gleam of a horn proved they had at least one unicorn. The riders kept a tight formation, their uniforms dark in the haze of dawn. Blaise couldn't tell what color they were. Were they the scarlet and gold of the Salt-Iron Confederation, or some other uniform like the local militia? They drew to a stop between the barn and the house. Chickens clucked, drowsy. The few hens that had braved the outdoors hurried back into the safety of their coop with a flap of their wings. Chester darted around the riders, continuing his barking frenzy. More than one steed lifted a hoof to threaten him away.

Blaise's gut twisted.

A rider mounted on a white horse beside the unicorn dismounted. He cupped his hands to his mouth. "Hawthorne!"

They know who we are. Blaise crouched on the balls of his feet. The soldier braced his arms behind his back as he waited for a response.

Lights came on in the house. A moment later, his parents filed out of the house, still in their nightclothes. His father carried a lantern and tried to catch Chester. The little dog dodged away, still yapping. Blaise's mother had her arms crossed. She was the very picture of someone woken from her bed too soon and was none too happy about it. Pastel sunlight caught the glinting edge of a bottle carried in the crook of her elbow.

"I don't know who you think you are, but you had better have a good reason for waking us so early. I was up half the night with my child." Marian's voice was full of righteous anger.

Her mood didn't impress the soldier. He led his mount closer, waving the soldier with the unicorn after him. "I am Commander Lamar Gaitwood of the Salt-Iron Confederation. My company and I are in Desina registering mages. It's come to my attention we missed one."

A finger of ice crawled down Blaise's spine. He froze.

Daniel managed to catch Chester, and he carried the little dog back toward the house. Chester flailed in his arms, whining. Lucienne poked her head out the door, eyes wide. Daniel thrust Chester at her and told her to get inside and not come out again. She took the dog without protest. In the funereal light of dawn, her face was etched with fear.

She only had to be afraid because *he* was a part of their family.

Blaise's mother addressed the Commander once Chester's yapping ceased. "That doesn't tell me why you're here interrupting my family's sleep." As she spoke, the unicorn leaned closer to the Commander, teeth bared as if to nip him.

Gaitwood didn't so much as glance at the unicorn. He reached behind him and grabbed the reins, giving them a savage jerk. The unicorn squealed, head snapping up in anguish. "As I understand it, there's a mage in your family, ma'am." In the dim light, Blaise saw a trace of malice in the man's eyes. He knew that look. Gaitwood was a bully. "Are you aware that it's a crime to harbor mavericks from the Salt-Iron Confederation?"

Blaise's father put a restraining hand on his mother's shoulder. She shrugged it off. "I'm aware." Her voice was as dry as deadwood.

Daniel leaned in close to whisper something. Blaise pulled away from the peephole and fumbled in the darkness for his boots. He rammed his feet into them, then pulled the go-bag closer. With regret, he shoved the stack of books into the corner. They would have to stay. Books were too heavy and would only slow him down if he had to run. Blaise opened the satchel and felt around inside to check on the essentials. Canteens of water. Jerky. Bread and gingerbread.

Blaise moved back to the peephole and peered out.

"—don't know what you're talking about," Daniel finished. His father had taken control of the situation while Blaise finished his preparations.

Gaitwood scowled at him. "You're lying. Five different witnesses verified a *Breaker* lives here."

There it was. Betrayed by the townspeople. Not surprising. He clenched his fists, torn between anger and the memory of his mother's words. *Promise me you won't let them take you.*

In the hayloft, he was a sitting duck. It was only a matter of time before they discovered him. Blaise eased open the hatch and slung the bag over his shoulders. As he found the top rung of the ladder with one foot, he strained to hear what they said.

"We'll find the mage if we have to tear your entire house apart," the Commander snarled.

"You will *not!*" Marian's voice rang out like the peal of a trumpet. Glass shattered. Then the soldiers coughed, gasping and cursing as they struggled to breathe. She cried out, "Blaise, *run!*"

No time to climb down the ladder with caution. Blaise pivoted on the rung and jumped down to the floor, aiming for a bale of hay. He missed and his leg crumpled beneath him. Blaise gritted his teeth. *No time to think about pain.* He bobbled to his feet, racing past Smoky's feed barrel. Blaise ducked into the gelding's stall.

"Find the mage!" Blaise recognized the strangled voice as the Commander. It sounded like he was having difficulty breathing. Blaise didn't have time to think about what that meant.

Hooves pounded a sharp staccato on gravel. Blaise bolted through Smoky's stall door and into the adjoining paddock. He slowed down long enough to slip between the wooden slats of the fence. Blaise didn't spare a moment to peek behind him. He didn't want to know anything about the pursuit. *If I don't look, they're not chasing me, right?*

Blaise knew the woods behind their home like the back of his hand. His parents had made sure they lived as close to the border as possible. That didn't mean it was without its share of perils. But if he could get through the woods, he had a chance at whatever safety the Gutter could offer. At least he hoped it could offer safety.

Whistles and shouts sliced through the air as the soldiers urged their mounts after him. Blaise headed for the densest section of the wood. Tree limbs hung low, covered with the curling green bipartate leaves of invasive krakenvine. His father had intended to burn the krakenvine out for years. That procrastination worked in Blaise's favor.

Blaise ducked under a low-slung branch, slowing as the footing became treacherous. Armadillo holes littered the ground, concealed by tall grasses, bushes, and shrubs. Blaise hoped it would hinder the soldiers.

Ahead, he saw the rusty barbed wire fence that marked the border. Blaise floundered through a tangle of krakenvine. Panic fluttered in his stomach as a curling green tentacle edged with dual-bladed leaves wrapped around his right hand. He plowed forward as fast as he could, his hand snapping back when the tendril tightened its grip on him.

"Don't have time for this." Out of the corner of his eye, a blur of dark shapes moved through the trees. There were gruff exclamations as they caught sight of him. Blaise jerked his hand back, feeling the krakenvine's barbs digging into the leather of his glove. He wrenched his hand free of the glove, bare skin brushing against the plant.

The krakenvine jolted away from him like a startled fish. His glove disappeared into its tangled depths, out of reach. The plant writhed as the tendril he had touched collapsed on itself. His magic ate through the shoot, destroying it.

"Stop right there!"

Really? I'm not stupid. Blaise didn't stop. He dodged through the worst of the krakenvine. An oak that had died years ago to a lightning strike stood near the barbed wire fence, naked branches towering high above the neighboring trees. Blaise crouched beside the massive trunk as he considered his options. Reaching the Gutter was no guarantee of safety. He rested his bare right hand against the rotting wood, catching his breath. Magic rose to his palm, the familiar itch of his power seeking something to destroy. *Oh no.*

His pursuers were almost on him. They cursed as the kraken-vine snared their fellows. Sabers clattered as the soldiers drew them out to hack at the offending foliage. Blaise spun and ran for the border. He held down the lowest strand of barbed wire with his gloved hand to make enough room to wiggle through.

The middle strand of wire clawed at his clothing and bag, but he ignored it. Blaise slipped through the fence, pausing at the tell-tale groan of snapping wood. The ground trembled with the shuddering impact as the oak slammed into smaller trees. There was a rumble as it crashed to the ground in a tangle of deadwood and soldier. Shouts rose from the men. Blaise winced at a startled scream that cut off abruptly. *Don't think about that now.*

He had made it. He was in the Gutter! Blaise hazarded a glance behind him. The oak tree was down, a haze of dust clouding the area, the soldiers little more than haunting spectral shapes. The Commander barked an order. They were still after him. If they were mad before, now he had infuriated them.

Blaise broke into a run. The muffled throbbing of hooves rang behind him. Over his shoulder, he saw the unicorn rallying after him, this time with Gaitwood on its back. Panic flooded him. *I can't outrun a unicorn.*

The air crackled around Blaise. A glittering cage of silver magic coalesced around him. He came to a sudden stop before he crashed into its bars. Blaise gasped for breath as the Commander trotted up to him on the unicorn, one arm extended.

"Well, well, well. Aren't you full of surprises?" Gaitwood paced the unicorn around the trap, assessing him with the air of someone scrutinizing a prize-winning pig.

It was over. The hiding, his mother's attempts to stall them— all for nothing. Blaise stood in the radiance of the early morning sun, bowing his head as his hands itched with magic.

He didn't want to belong to the Salt-Iron Confederation as a theurgist. Blaise didn't want to be a weapon. Would they turn him into someone cold and cruel, like this man?

The warm breeze played over his naked right hand, a reminder that he had lost his glove. Blaise's magic was unfettered.

Gaitwood dismounted, pulling salt-iron shackles from his belt. Blaise trembled, afraid of what his magic might do. He closed his eyes and slammed his bare palm against the bars of the cage.

Even with his eyes shut, the world exploded into a corona of light like a miniature sun. Gaitwood roared in pain and the unicorn squealed. Blaise's eyes flew open. With grim satisfaction, he realized his magic had ripped the ephemeral cage apart. Gaitwood doubled over, hands covering his eyes as he whimpered. The unicorn shied away, quivering near the barbed wire fence.

Heart hammering, Blaise ran as fast as he could to the north. He wouldn't stop running until he had some assurance of safety. Though Blaise didn't know if there was any such thing.

CHAPTER FOUR
Hope for the Hopeless

Blaise

*B*laise's priority was finding the road that led to the Black Market. Disoriented and exhausted from his headlong run, he didn't stop until he was on the verge of collapse. He found a small stand of scrubby trees to hunker down in while he waited for signs of his pursuers.

As he fled from the border, he heard a single gunshot in his wake. Gaitwood likely fired out of sheer frustration more than the hope of finding his mark. After that, his only company was the whistling wind and birds flying overhead.

It was around noon, judging by the sun's position. With the sun overhead, it was hard to know if he was going in the right direction to find the road. With only one previous trip, he didn't have a grasp for the lay of the land. In the distance, red-tinged plateaus cradled the Deadwood River. All he knew was that if he reached the canyons, he had gone too far.

Reassurance washed over Blaise when at last he found the road that led to the Black Market. He was hot and tired, his skin sticky with sweat. Without his hat or bandanna to protect him, his face was burning to a crisp in the relentless sun.

Blaise focused on his physical misery; he didn't have the strength to think about anything else. It was too much.

Mid-afternoon, he stopped for a longer break beneath a gnarled copse of mesquite. He wasn't hungry, but he forced himself to eat a piece of jerky from his bag. Blaise had eaten nothing since the previous night. When the shock of his situation wore off, he would collapse with no food in him. But the jerky was little more than ash on his tongue.

Blaise rubbed his forehead, wincing at the latent heat on his skin. The sweltering weather sapped his strength, rendering him unable to walk any further. The tenuous shade of the mesquite provided little safety, but at least offered him some protection from the sun. There were no signs of dangerous wildlife.

Or outlaws. Although at this point, he would welcome an outlaw.

His rest gave him fitful dreams and he awoke when the sun was setting. Blaise ate another piece of jerky to keep his strength up. Go-bag slung over his shoulder, he took to the road again. He focused on putting one foot in front of the other, breaking his life down into the basic things he had control over to keep his emotions at bay. Otherwise, the enormity of his situation would become overwhelming.

The moon rose overhead, low and full, providing enough silvery light to guide his path. As he walked, he tried to make a plan, but it was a struggle. This was outside the realm of his life experiences. He didn't know what to do. *If I get to the Black Market, then what?* The Black Market itself should have traveled to another location. He hoped the abandoned saloon was still there—he needed shelter and food.

But then what? Where would he go? He thought back to Slocum's question. *You a maverick?* It seemed like it had been ages ago, not little more than a week. Such a ridiculous question.

To the Salt-Iron Confederation, he was a maverick. *Maverick.* It sounded like someone who forged their own way in life, living on the outskirts of society. A rough-and-ready scrapper. The word fit him like a small child stepping into their father's boots. Blaise was a scared young man far from home, nothing more.

But this wasn't the time to dwell on that. Ahead, he saw the silhouette of a cedar with a tattered cloth flapping from its branches in the evening breeze. An intrepid person had tied a bandanna to one of the skeletal limbs to serve as a marker— a sign that the Black Market was close. Blaise quickened his steps. *Almost there.*

He crested a hill and almost wept with relief when he saw the ramshackle saloon. The building appeared haunting and ethereal in the lambent moonlight. No surprise, the windows were dark.

Blaise walked up to the door and pushed it open. "Howdy?" His voice echoed through the emptiness.

The interior was dark, none of the mage-lights on. Blaise wished he had something to make a light.

"Mr. Slocum? Are you here?"

Nothing. Not even the skitter of a mouse. In the inky darkness, Blaise found one of the empty tables by stumbling into it. He fumbled along its edge with his gloved hand and slid his go-bag off his shoulder, then found a chair and sank into it. He didn't realize he was shaking until he heard the rattle of the chair legs against the floor.

Blaise rested his chin on his hands, shutting his eyes. He was all alone. But a building with a roof and walls provided protection, and that was a much-needed respite. Blaise exhaled a soft breath, tension receding from his shoulders.

He must have fallen asleep. When he opened his eyes, grey light streamed in through one of the Black Market's dusty windows, illuminating the cracking surface of the table his ungloved hand had rested against. Blaise rubbed the side of his face, grimacing at the scraggly growth of his beard. He rose from the table, taking in the room.

It appeared different from only days before. Dust coated the bar, a sign that the building had lacked visitors. Debris—glass shards, bits of broken wood, ripped newspaper, a discarded billiards ball—covered the floor, the tracks from Blaise's boots the only sign of recent life. A musty smell permeated the building, as if it had been closed up for ages.

"Howdy?" Blaise called. "Anyone here?"

No one answered. He ventured into the back room, into which Slocum had ducked on his visit. In the faint light, it appeared empty. A wooden countertop lined one side of the room, and bare shelves stood against the other walls.

It was as if the Black Market had never existed.

Blaise glanced around, uncertain. Was he in the right building? Exhaustion had seized him the previous night when he had stumbled upon it. He walked outside and looked around, recognizing the area where he had tied up Smoky. It was all the same, save for the aura of disuse inside the abandoned saloon.

It would be almost another month before Slocum returned with his nomadic Black Market. Blaise couldn't wait that long. He thought about his next steps. As he saw it, if he wasn't planning to stay at the Black Market, then his only option was to keep walking. There were two outlaw towns he knew of on the western side of the Untamed Territory: Asylum and Rainbow Flat. A journey on foot to Rainbow Flat would prove perilous because of the wildlife of the Untamed Territory. Asylum was his best choice. That was fitting. According to stories, Asylum was the gateway to freedom for outlaws and mavericks.

Blaise had a vague sense that it was to the northeast. If he headed for Asylum, he could skirt between the Gutter and the Untamed Territory. That route would keep him clear of the worst threats. Or so he hoped. It was his only plan since he couldn't go home.

Home. He climbed onto a barstool, slumping as he put his face in his hands. Blaise hadn't allowed himself any time to think about his home or his family. But now, in the questionable safety of the Black Market, he felt like he could—and should. It wasn't healthy to keep it bottled up forever.

What would happen to his family? No doubt Gaitwood would consider whatever his mother had unleashed on him and his men as an attack. Had they taken her, imprisoned her? A sob caught in his throat. No one could stop his mother when she had something planned. He shouldn't blame himself for her actions.

But he did. She had only acted to buy *him* time. It was *his* fault.

"I'm sorry," he whispered, a tear rolling down his cheek and dropping to the dust below.

Would they imprison his father, too? What would happen to Luci and Brody?

Blaise chewed on his bottom lip, murmuring a prayer to Faedra as he thought about his loved ones. He didn't think the goddess of magic was listening. Why would she have allowed this to happen if she cared?

After a good cry and wallow in misery, he felt a little better. He had needed to endure those raw emotions, as hard as it was. Those feelings would rise up to batter him again and again, but for now, he could lay them to rest. He needed to plan his next steps.

The Black Market had potable water and shelter; it was a suitable location to regroup. Blaise decided to stay another day or two. He had wrenched his ankle in the jump from the hayloft and needed time to heal. It was a miracle he had been able to run on it. The adrenaline had likely kept him going, but that had taken a toll. He couldn't help but cling to the hope that maybe someone would stop by the Black Market and help him.

BLAISE STAYED AT THE BLACK MARKET FOR ANOTHER WEEK. HIS ankle took longer to heal than he liked. The delay allowed him to scope out the lay of the land, though it spread his meager food supply thin.

The road from Bristle to the Black Market extended beyond the building, meandering to the northeast. It was a road merchants used between the Untamed Territory and Desina. That made sense—the well made the Black Market a prime location for a layover.

Despite that, he hadn't seen signs of anyone else. Not even an outlaw. On one hand, that gave him a sense of solace. It meant Gaitwood hadn't followed him into the Gutter. But on the other, Blaise didn't like the odds of surviving on his own.

Of his supplies, Blaise only had two strips of jerky and three small chunks of gingerbread left. He foraged around the scrubby woods and found questionable berries to add to his cache. Blaise tasted one; it had a bitter, tart flavor. He didn't have any reactions from it, so decided they were harmless enough to gather and take with him.

For the best chance at success, he needed to leave for Asylum soon or double back to Desina. He wasn't sure which had the greater risk—he might die of dehydration or exposure on the way to Asylum. Or he could face whatever the Salt-Iron Confederation planned to do with him. There would be repercussions for fleeing. Neither option was appealing.

He pulled out his go-bag and rechecked his supplies. He wrapped the berries in a linen cloth to keep them together. His canteens, full of fresh water, made a pleasant sloshing sound. Blaise scanned the interior of the Black Market for anything he might have forgotten. Once he was certain he had what he needed, he shouldered his satchel.

Blaise struck out on the northeast road. He still lacked protection from the sun, so he relied on the occasional tree for respite. By the time he made it anywhere, his face would be a permanent shade of apple red.

He had walked for more than an hour when he heard a piercing cry. It was a strange sound, a cross between a horse's whinny and a songbird's warble. The tone trilled with an edge of pain. Blaise knew in his gut that whatever creature was making the sound was calling out for help.

Blaise paused beneath a young cedar. Should he see what was making the anguished call? Indecision warred within him. Whatever it was might be dangerous. He had been fortunate to not come across any predators so far. Although the distressed creature may not be a threat to him, its cries might attract predators. As it was, an optimistic pair of buzzards circled overhead.

But Blaise knew what it was like to need help—and for it to never arrive. It wouldn't hurt to investigate. A quick look, nothing more. And if he felt the slightest bit uneasy, he could be on his way.

The cry came again, and Blaise angled his head to pinpoint the direction. *A little to the west.* He turned off the road, walking with care as the ground became furrowed and uneven. Late summer wildflowers peppered the terrain with pops of yellow, magenta, and violet. Eventually, the terrain plummeted into a ravine. Cautious, he strode to the edge and peered over.

A black pegasus stood in the middle of the gully, its glossy wings, iridescent purple in the sun, fanned out at its sides, its ebony coat lathered and soaked with sweat. The equine held one of its forelegs at an awkward angle, caught in something. It lifted its head and shrilled another plea for help. Triangular ears rotated, searching for a reply. The pegasus took an awkward step forward and stopped, lowering its head.

The pegasus had something tangled around its leg. Blaise squinted, trying to figure out what it was. The equine sank into the brown grass, the snared foreleg outstretched before it.

Where was the pegasus's flight? Aside from carrion birds keeping a hopeful vigil overhead, nothing else was visible in the sky.

The equine was trapped. It had no access to water. Unless

something changed, it would die. Blaise chewed on his bottom lip, thinking back to the little he knew of pegasi from library books he had read as a child. They were supposed to be intelligent. *Will it understand me if I try to help? I hope so.*

Decision made, Blaise navigated the steep side of the gully. Midway down, he lost his footing and slid to an ignominious stop at the bottom, his back bruised and the elbows of his sleeves shredded by rocks. The pegasus snorted in alarm and pinned back its ears, but it didn't get up.

Blaise shrugged off his go-bag with a pained wince, careful of his scuffed elbows, and set it by a clump of yellow, bell-shaped wildflowers. He was going to regret that entrance later. He raised his hands to show the creature they were empty. "Howdy. I'm here to help if you'll allow it."

The pegasus gave a skeptical snort, white-rimmed eyes rolling. Blaise didn't blame it. He'd be dubious of his help, too. It wasn't like he had a pristine track record so far.

Crouching down, Blaise squinted at the pegasus's foreleg from a respectful distance. Now that he was closer, there was definitely a rope tangled around it. But it wasn't like any rope Blaise had ever seen. Dark beads glinted at intervals along its length.

Blaise frowned. "Is that salt-iron?" The equine's nostrils dilated as it snorted. Was that assent? Blaise crept closer, watching the pegasus for any signs of protest. He crouched an arm's length from the tangled foreleg, relaxing when the pegasus didn't move.

Creeping closer, he realized he was right. Polished dark metal beads twinkled within the braided rope, a pattern of sharp barbs worked into the mix. The barbs dug into the thin skin around the animal's leg, causing blood to seep from the wounds. Flies buzzed around, eager to feast.

Anger surged through Blaise as he realized someone had laid a trap—the nefarious rope hadn't appeared from nowhere. He didn't have much experience with salt-iron, but like any mage, he knew to avoid it. It was renowned for its use against mages and magical creatures. His eyes followed the trail of rope to a stake. The trapper had concealed it in a cluster of tall grass.

"It's okay," Blaise murmured, wondering if the animal would understand him. A calming voice had always helped with Smoky when the farrier came to trim his hooves. The pegasus rolled its eyes again, flailing onto its side. Blaise rocked back out of the way in case it lashed out with its hooves. It stretched out on its side, one wing pinned beneath its bulk.

The pegasus thrashed its hind legs, frightened and in pain. Blaise paused, cautious as he thought through the best way to handle an unpredictable, injured creature with hooves the size of dinner plates. A kick from one of those would be the end of the road. He needed to earn the animal's trust.

Smoky liked treats . . . would a pegasus? Blaise inched to his satchel, trying not to startle the equine. He knelt and opened the bag, rifling through the remaining food until he found a piece of gingerbread. He clutched his prize in his gloved hand, rising to display his open palm.

"I know you're scared. You don't trust me. Consider this a peace offering."

The creature made a hesitant rumbling sound. One ear flitted forward, then backward again.

Right. The pegasus suspected poison or drugs. After being caught in a man-made snare, it would be difficult to trust a strange human. "Okay, watch. I'll have a taste." Blaise broke off a tiny chunk and popped it into his mouth. He chewed and swallowed, then held up the rest. "See? It's good."

Step by careful step, he inched closer to the trapped pegasus. He held his gloved palm out as far as he could. The creature lifted its head enough to snuffle at it, then wiggled velvety lips to snag the treat. The pegasus crunched, tongue flicking out with satisfaction. Its ears swiveled forward as it rested its head against the ground again.

"Are you thirsty?" Blaise asked. He didn't expect an answer, but the pegasus made another rumble. He pulled a canteen out of the bag, settling down beside the equine to trickle water into its mouth. It sighed in relief.

"Okay, I'm going to see if I can get that thing off of you. I promise I'm here to help."

Blaise put away the canteen, then sat down by the equine's leg. The pegasus raised its head to watch him. Blaise frowned at the tangled rope.

"I need you to stay still. I have to pull out the barbs first." Blaise counted at least two that he could see had ripped into the flesh. He shooed away the flies, annoyed when they circled back for another pass.

The pegasus snorted. Blaise decided that was consent. He reached for the rope, then remembered he had only one safe hand. With a grimace, he curled his right hand into a fist and shoved it into his pants pocket. If he didn't keep it out of the way, he risked his magic lashing out.

He worried at a barb with his thumb and index finger and pulled it free of the pegasus's flesh. The animal's shoulder spasmed with a twitch, but otherwise, the beast didn't move.

It was slow, frustrating work with only one hand. To make matters worse, the rope tangled back on itself. Blaise wished he had a knife or anything sharp. He could have cut the pegasus free. Why, oh why, had a knife not been an essential part of his go-bag?

Something to think about for the future. If he survived his predicament.

Blaise lost track of time as he worked on the snare. The sun roasted them as the day wore on. He took frequent water breaks so that neither one of them became dehydrated. The pegasus looked miserable, tongue flopping from its open mouth. Blaise suspected it might not survive, even if he freed it.

Late in the afternoon, Blaise had made very little progress. No matter what he tried, the rope tangled back on itself. He blew out a frustrated breath. What was this, some kind of magic? Maybe just bad luck. Whatever the case, it kept him from his goal. He had promised to set the pegasus free.

"I don't know what to do," Blaise admitted. "It keeps tangling. What in Faedra's name *is* this?"

The pegasus snorted. Blaise was uncertain if it was an answer to his question or the animal's own show of frustration at the situation.

Maybe working one-handed was too slow. Blaise gritted his teeth. He could untangle it much faster with two hands, but at what cost?

"I'm going to try something. I don't know if it will help. Can I try?" Blaise tried not to think about what could happen if something went horribly wrong. He took a breath to calm himself and paste on a façade that he knew what he was doing.

The pegasus lifted its head to look at him but gave no other response. It laid its head back down with a sigh.

"Here goes nothing." Blaise rubbed his hands together, magic itching beneath his skin. He laid both hands on the rope to work at it again.

Pain sizzled through his naked palm. Yelping, he snatched his hand back, rubbing at an angry red welt that arose from his brief contact with the metal. The salt-iron sapped away the magic that itched beneath the surface of his skin.

The pegasus watched him. Blaise glanced from the rope to his hand. Now he knew why magic and salt-iron didn't mix. It blistered his skin, neutralizing and leeching away his magic. He cocked his head, thinking. Blaise's magic was still there, so the brief touch hadn't drained it completely.

Blaise rubbed the welt with his gloved fingers. Salt-iron was rare. The rope's crafter had spaced the beads a hand's width apart, no doubt to save coin for whoever this trap belonged to. If he was careful, he could avoid touching the metal while he worked. Could his magic break the rope as it had broken through the krakenvine? *Worth a try. I don't have any better options.*

He grasped one of the beads with his gloved hand and touched a length of harmless rope with his right. His magic boiled up as if offended by the earlier attack. Blaise felt it jump from his hand to the rope, degrading the fibers. The bolt of magic slammed into one of the salt-iron beads and died with a hiss.

The salt-iron may have nullified his magic, but not before it had undermined the fiber of the rope. A section sloughed away, falling to the ground with a soft thump. Blaise's heart thumped a nervous beat.

"Got it," he told the pegasus as he held another of the beads with his glove and assailed the rope with his bare hand. Hemp fibers shredded and fell away.

Blaise repeated the process until he broke down all the tangles, using his glove to unwind the remaining bits of rope that clung to the animal's leg. The last piece fell away, and he tossed it as far as he could. His hands trembled with nerves, teeth chattering from the fear of blatantly trying to use his own magic. Blaise wished he had a glove for his hand.

The exhausted pegasus lay stretched on the ground, unmoving. Blaise sucked in a breath, reaching out to rub the equine's damp neck. "We did it. You're free."

The pegasus stayed down, sides heaving. Its nostrils flared in the dry grass.

Tears stung Blaise's eyes. After all that, the pegasus *had* to get up. *Had* to live. "Come on. Get up. Please?"

With great effort, it lifted its head and gathered its hind legs. Blaise scooted back to give it room to move. The pegasus remained down for a moment, unfurling its wings.

<Thank you for saving me. I would have died without you.>

Blaise blinked at the exhausted, masculine voice in his head. "Wait, what? You can talk?"

The pegasus stallion clambered to his feet, unsteady as a newborn foal, injured leg held off the ground. <Mind to mind.>

Blaise canted his head, puzzled. "Why didn't you say something sooner? Or you could have called your flight to help? I don't understand."

The stallion snorted. <My mental speech is magic, and the salt-

iron suppressed the ability. So even if I had a flight, I could not have called it.>

"Oh." Blaise rubbed the back of his head. That made sense, after his experience with touching it. Nasty stuff. "Well, I guess you'll want to be going wherever your home is since you're free." As tempted as he was, he didn't ask the pegasus for a ride to civilization. He didn't want the traumatized creature to feel beholden to him.

<And where will you go?> the pegasus asked.

"Um." Blaise looked around. The sun was setting, and he didn't know if there was a safe place to bed down for the night. He gestured vaguely to the northeast. "That way."

Blaise hadn't known an equine face was capable of an incredulous expression. The stallion's ears pointed in opposite directions and his lower lip hung loose. <You have no idea where you're going, do you?>

"Not really."

The pegasus bobbed his head as if he had reached a decision. <That settles it. You have saved me. Now it's my turn to save you.>

CHAPTER FIVE
Wings and Such

Blaise

The stallion's name was Emrys. He needed time to recover from the snare, but he knew of a place nearby where they could find shelter and rest. Blaise walked beside the pegasus as he favored his right hoof.

"Are you going to be okay?" Blaise cast a worried look to the west. The last crepuscular rays of the sunset fractured over the peaks of the distant mountains. Leg injuries could be life-threatening for horses. He wasn't sure if that was the case for a pegasus.

<Once I have more of my magic back, I can fly and that will serve me better.> Emrys shook his thick mane. <The salt-iron sapped my magic, and I can't fly without it.>

"I didn't realize magic makes pegasi fly. Birds don't have magic." Blaise understood the impact the salt-iron had on magic after his brief touch, but the concept of magical pegasus flight made little sense.

Emrys snorted. <When was the last time you saw a bird that weighs as much as a draft horse?>

"You make a good point."

Emrys hobbled beneath a sandstone outcropping, Blaise following in his wake. Was that true for other flying magical creatures? He had so little knowledge about anything related to magic. If he asked questions, would Emrys think he was ignorant? "So what you said earlier . . . you don't belong to a flight?"

The stallion's wings rustled against his sides, reminding Blaise of the chickens back home. <I'm a bachelor stallion. Colts are driven out of our flights once we're old enough to survive the wilds alone.>

Blaise scratched at his chin, thoughtful. "Just the colts? Not the fillies?"

Emrys blew out a derisive snort. <As if any guardian stallion is going to allow a filly or mare out of his flight. No, only colts.> He swished his tail. <But to answer your question, I don't have a flight in the traditional sense, but I do have a place I belong.>

A place to belong sounded nice to Blaise. He had to admit, he was jealous. "And that's where we're going?"

Emrys bobbed his head, turning off the trail and threading his way through red yucca plants. <Yes. I work with the outlaws of Itude. Look, here we are.> He led Blaise down an incline to a shallow cave.

Blaise followed him inside, shrugging his satchel off and peering inside at the sad remains of his supplies. His stomach rumbled. "You said you work *with* the outlaws?"

<Yes. Most often sentry duty. That's what I was doing when I was . . . distracted.> Emrys glanced away, and Blaise detected embarrassment in his mental voice.

"Pegasi get paid?" It hadn't occurred to Blaise that non-humans might receive or need a wage.

<What, I should not collect a fair wage because I'm a quadruped?> Emrys twitched an ear, head tilted askance.

"Sorry, that's not what I meant. I guess I'm not sure what use you would have for coin?" Blaise knew that sounded flimsy.

<A roof over my head and delicious food, the same as anyone else.>

Blaise winced. He was out of his depth. It was anguishing to not have any concept of life beyond the tiny world he had lived in.

<Oh, don't beat yourself up over it.> The stallion nudged him with his velvety nose. <Tell me about you. What is your magic?>

That was the last thing Blaise wanted to talk about. Tension pooled in his shoulders. Would Emrys abandon him if he knew? "How do you know I have magic?" It never hurt to stall a conversation.

The stallion snorted. <Seriously? What you did back in the ravine was obvious.>

Blaise winced. "Um, right." He rubbed the back of his head. "Breaker. That's what people call my magic."

Emrys's head swung up in surprise. <I've only heard of that magic. It's . . .> He trailed off, and Blaise suspected Emrys was trying to avoid hurting his feelings.

"Dangerous," Blaise finished for him. "It is."

The stallion swished his tail, thoughtful. <And that was what you used to free me.>

"Yes."

Emrys surprised him by stepping closer, nuzzling his shoulder. <Then perhaps your magic is merely misunderstood.>

Blaise blinked. He had never thought of it in that context. A brief memory of the magical cage exploding at his touch played through his mind. Escape would have been impossible without his magic.

Emrys bowed his head to examine the healing puncture wounds on his leg. Blaise wished he had thought to bring one of the first aid kits from home. His mother had potions that would aid the stallion's healing. "How did you get caught?"

Emrys swished his tail and made an embarrassed rumble. <Ah. Pegasi use a lot of energy to fly, and sugar is one way we recover. I should have known better. I was greedy.> He hung his head. <I was as gullible as a spindle-legged colt. A poacher set the snare with a stack of sugar cubes for bait.>

Blaise blanched. "People trap pegasi?"

<And worse,> Emrys affirmed. <It's the way of some humans. They do not care if they find their prey in time. Some want us dead because we work with outlaws. Others want to use our flesh, bones, and feathers.> His mental voice oozed with disgust.

"There are a lot of terrible humans out there," Blaise agreed, thinking of Gaitwood. "I'm glad I found you in time."

<Me, too,> Emrys said, drowsy.

Blaise smiled as the stallion's eyelids drooped. If Emrys could rest, then more power to him. Blaise adjusted his position, lower back tender from his earlier descent. He crossed his arms and listened to the relentless screech of cicadas in the distance.

THE NEXT MORNING, EVERY MUSCLE IN BLAISE'S BODY COMPLAINED about the lack of rest and comfort. Emrys looked better, at least. He could put more weight on his foreleg. He declared he was fit for a rider.

Blaise was hesitant. He had ridden Smoky sometimes, but always with saddle and bridle. Emrys had neither. Blaise wasn't confident in his horsemanship skills or how to stay out of the way of those broad wings. But he had less confidence in his supplies lasting until he reached a town.

<I'll stay on the ground until you dare to fly with me,> Emrys told him, magnanimous.

The concept of flying on a pegasus made Blaise's empty stomach churn. He decided not to burst the stallion's bubble by

telling him that would never happen. Besides, his only other
option was walking, and Blaise had lost track of where he was and
where to go. Emrys had a much better sense of direction.

The stallion knelt, allowing Blaise to climb on his back. His
legs hung down behind Emrys' wings, which the stallion tucked to
his sides as he walked. Blaise tried to not interfere with the pegasus's wings.

<It's easier with a saddle. Keeps you in place,> Emrys
commented as he set off deeper into the Gutter.

As they traveled, Blaise understood why the area had the
strange moniker. A network of canyons and gullies crisscrossed
the land, carved into the rock by the Deadwood River. Emrys told
him that in the stormy season, the gullies would be quite dangerous. But they were safe enough now—the Gutter didn't see much
rain in summer.

As the landscape changed, so too did the colors all around
them. Behind them, the distant hills and woodlands of Desina
melted away into the parched grass and low scrub of the grass-
lands. The orange and crimson sandstone of the Gutter rose
around them. After a life surrounded by trees and green grass,
Blaise spent much of the time gawking at the scenery. Desina
didn't boast landscape like this.

Emrys enjoyed his fascination and pointed out features as they
traveled. He detoured down a trail, trotting up to a delicate arch
hewn from the rock. He explained how wind and water carved
the arch into the stone over thousands of years. In another
canyon, Emrys slowed down and bade Blaise to look up. The
walls of the canyon had worn into spire-like towers that Emrys
called *hoodoos*. Blaise had never seen a natural feature like them.
They were inspiring.

<You should see this place at sunset,> Emrys told him as he
picked his way up a perilous trail that led to the upper rim. <I'll
bring you back sometime when you're ready to fly.>

That wouldn't happen. *Too bad.* Blaise imagined it must be an
amazing sight.

Late in the afternoon, Emrys rounded a corner and Blaise saw tiny man-made shapes atop a distant cliff. Buildings. A speck launched off the side of the cliff and flew in their direction. Another pegasus with a rider.

<We'll stop here so the sentry can clear us,> Emrys explained to Blaise, halting along the side of the canyon.

"Okay." Blaise didn't feel as certain as he sounded. He tried to distract himself by glancing over the side of the ledge. The Deadwood River roared below, capped with white foam. The muscles at the base of his neck tensed with nerves as he lifted his eyes to the approaching pegasus. After over a week without human company, he worried about what someone new might think of him.

The incoming pegasus landed and trotted over, rider bobbing in the saddle. Windswept blonde hair poked out from beneath the rider's slouch hat, though most was contained by a braid. He realized she was a teenager—she looked a year or two older than Luci. His heart ached as he thought of his sister.

"Identify yourself—oh, howdy Emrys." The girl tipped back her hat, looking from the black stallion to Blaise. Her pegasus boasted a white coat covered in dark brown spots and mottled wings that reminded Blaise of a falcon. The spotted stallion whinnied and bumped noses with Emrys.

"Who're you?" she drawled, examining Blaise as if he were a particularly interesting lizard.

Blaise supposed he made a pathetic sight, with his beet-red face, scraggly beard, and timeworn clothing. "Blaise. Blaise Hawthorne. From Desina." His voice trembled with the effort. Never had he imagined that talking to another person would be so difficult. He had underestimated the impact the last few weeks had had on him.

She tapped the pommel of her saddle with one hand, brows knitted as she looked him over. "Well, Blaise Hawthorne from Desina, I'm Emmaline Dewitt, and you're approaching Itude. Emrys vouches for you. He says you have no place else to go."

That was an understatement. Relief crashed through Blaise and his shoulders relaxed. He would have to thank Emrys later. "I . . . I don't."

"Right then. I gotta settle a few things with you first." She gave a dutiful nod. "Newcomers to town have to surrender their weapons at the saloon. You got a problem with that?"

Blaise shook his head. "I don't have any weapons."

Emmaline's eyes telegraphed teenage disbelief. "Really?"

"Really."

She frowned, eyes roving as if searching him for weapons. Emrys must have told her something in private because her eyes shifted to the stallion. She tilted her head. "Okay then. Another thing to know is the offensive use of magic is discouraged in town. That a problem?"

That was a big, big problem. His stomach sank. "What about magic I can't control?"

Emmaline's eyes widened, then she shrugged. "That's not my call. We'll let the Ringleaders sort you out." She chirped to her pegasus and the spotted stallion turned away. "We'll fly on up to Itude and make introductions."

"Wait, wait, the who? And fly?" Panic seized him. He wasn't ready to fly with a saddle, much less bareback.

The teen made a soft scoffing sound, and Blaise knew he'd lost any credibility he might have with her. "You're new to this whole thing, aren't you?" Her voice was incredulous, like she didn't think someone so ignorant could exist in the world. "The town is on a cliff. And you're not on the right side of the canyon to take the merchant trail up. *And,* if you didn't notice, you're on a pegasus. Wings and such." She brought her hands together and made a little flapping motion with her fingers, in case he wasn't clear on the concept.

Emrys shifted beneath him. <I'm sorry. I should have considered that. But the flight won't be very long.>

Emmaline cocked her head. "Well, you coming or are you going to go back to whatever fancy-pants place you came from?"

Blaise looked at the distant cliff. He had come too far to turn around. He had nothing to go back to. "I'm coming." He closed his eyes and wrapped his hands through hunks of Emrys's thick mane.

Emrys bunched his muscles and leaped into the sky. Blaise tried not to scream.

CHAPTER SIX

Always Bet on the Jack

Jack

*L*aughter and music roared through the Broken Horn Saloon. Jack nursed his drink, monitoring the game of Wild Dragon in the corner. All but one of the players were regulars, a visiting merchant with more money than sense. Their rowdiness grew with each round, and Jack figured he was going to shut them down before too long.

He *hated* Wild Dragon. Why didn't they choose a different card game? Brag or Three-Card-Monte were better choices. Wild Dragon was the worst game—cheating abounded, and it was never long before a cry went up and fists flew.

Clover, the Knossan bartender, ambled over to where Jack sat by the bar. "Can I get you a refill?" She leaned one of her furry elbows against the smooth wood as she awaited his answer.

Jack pushed his mug over to her. "Maybe later. I'm done for now."

She grabbed the mug with one hand, the dark skin thick and calloused. "Are you thinking of joining the game?" Clover's brown eyes twinkled.

Jack grinned at the Knossan. At his full height, Jack's head came up to her shoulders. Clover was the tallest citizen in Itude, and she often scared newcomers shitless. She looked like an insane wizard had married the concept of a cow and a human into one creature. The hide that covered her body was the same color as the polished brown wood of the bar. Short horns crowned her head, though one had broken off years ago. A brass ring glinted in her nose. With her sheer bulk, Clover cut an imposing figure, and to be sure she could use her mass if she had a reason. She was also the kindest person Jack had ever met.

"I might," Jack agreed, "if only to save you some effort."

"Thanks. Brawls do cut into my business," Clover chuckled as she moved over to check on another client.

Jack rose from the barstool, rolling his shoulders as he paced over to the gamblers. He plucked an empty chair from a nearby table and pulled it over. "Howdy, boys. Deal me in."

"You're sassing me, Jack," flame-haired Vixen Valerie grumbled at him. She was acting as the dealer which pointed to her as the biggest cheat.

"Always, darling." Jack snickered, placing the chair next to hers. He was glad to see Vixen was wearing her smoked-lens glasses. That meant she wasn't planning to cheat with her magic, at least.

The other players paled when Jack joined them. That was fine with him. Let them squirm. Everyone was aware he was the one who took care of any *problems* in town.

"Why won't you let us have our fun?" Vixen complained as she slid cards over to him.

"If you want fun, pick a different card game." Jack watched as the others gathered their hands and started placing their bets. Vixen had spread thirteen cards face-up on the table. Once they finished, he laid his yellow chip on the Jack of Hearts.

Vixen sighed at him. "Really?"

"Always bet on the Jack," he deadpanned.

The other gamblers shifted in their seats as Vixen flipped the first card from the deck. Seven of Clubs. The ranch hand at the table hissed as he realized his bet on Seven of Hearts was a loss. Jack's eyes whipped to the others as Vixen displayed the winning card.

Jack of Clubs.

"Well, what do you know?" Jack settled back in his chair as the others glared at him. Violence telegraphed through the tightness in their shoulders and the slant of their brows. None of them would act on it. *He* was Wildfire Jack, and this was *his* town.

Vixen was about to speak but stopped. Her gaze shifted to the entrance, and Jack realized something was up. He turned and saw his daughter peering around the clusters of people in the saloon.

"Good game." Jack rose from the table. He pushed his cards and chips away, shooting a threatening smile at the remaining players. Just to make sure they remembered who they were dealing with.

Out of the corner of his eye, Clover clopped towards Emmaline. The Knossan had a soft spot for his fifteen-year-old daughter, and there was no one in town Jack trusted more. If Clover had abandoned the bar, something was up.

Then he saw the young man standing behind Emmaline, the kid's unease making him stick out in the saloon like a sore thumb. *The Breaker.*

Jack's world constricted to only his daughter beside the dangerous mage. The mage who had *broken his damn gun*. What in Perdition was *he* doing here?

As Jack flowed forward, anyone standing in his path scuttled out of the way, like birds fleeing before a storm. A roar of approval came from the dart game in the corner, ignorant of the change of atmosphere in the saloon. In the other corner, the pianist played a buoyant drinking song.

Emmaline noticed his approach, her face lighting up. It was a short-lived expression, though, as she read the thunderous look on his face. "Daddy!" she called to him. She didn't have a clue why he was angry. Jack had told no one about the incident on the road, not even his daughter. He hadn't wanted to.

The young mage gawked at the busy interior of the saloon, once again showing how out of his depth he was. He didn't see Jack coming until it was too late.

Jack pulled his arm back and slammed his fist into the Breaker's face. The kid made a satisfying squeak, and his bones crunched as the outlaw's knuckles found their mark. His head snapped backward, and he spun around, slumping to the floor. Emmaline covered her mouth with one hand, staring in horror.

Jack's hand was going to hurt like the dickens later, but he didn't care. He wanted that mage away from his daughter and out of his town, as soon as possible.

The noisy saloon grew quiet. Voices murmured and mugs clinked as nervous townsfolk set them down. The brittle clatter of Clover's hooves shattered the tableau as she clamped her tough hand on Jack's upper arm.

"*Out!*" The Knossan's melodious voice was curt as she steered him around the fallen mage. Jack snarled at her. She ignored him, dragging him out unceremoniously. Clover was strong; there was no breaking her grip. He'd more likely break his own arm if he tried.

Jack let her escort him outside, though he felt justified by the shenanigans. He would do it again if he had half a chance.

Clover shook her horned head at him. She had taken him behind the saloon where they had a modicum of privacy. "What was that? You of all people *never* throw a punch first in my saloon."

The worry in her voice grounded his anger. She knew he was acting out of character for a reason, and she was wary, wanting to understand. "That man can't be here. He's a Breaker." And he was with *Emmaline*.

Even though he hadn't said the last part, Clover understood. Her nostrils flared. "I see. And how do you know this?"

Jack glowered, rubbing the tender knuckles of his index and middle fingers. "We had an encounter."

She canted her head, a classic Knossan *tell me more* mannerism. Jack returned the look, impassive. When he didn't expound, she wiggled an ear. "And does anyone else know?"

Jack opened his mouth to tell her *no*, but boots crunched on the ground as Vixen came around the corner. "You're a hypocrite, Jack," Vixen said, her tone cutting. "Sticking your nose into my game and then you do that? Honestly?"

He crossed his arms. "Had nothing to do with your game."

"Obviously," Vixen agreed, looking at the both of them. "Thought you should know your daughter is madder than a mule chewing on bumblebees. And that kid you tried to squabash got dragged over to Nadine's clinic."

Jack set his jaw. At least that meant the Breaker would be out of the equation for the time being. He would have to deal with his angry daughter later. He turned to Vixen. "We need a meeting."

She scowled. Evening had fallen. The other Ringleaders wouldn't take kindly to a meeting so late in the day. But this was important.

Vixen shifted her weight from foot to foot, considering. "This about that greenhorn?"

Jack nodded.

She pursed her lips. "I'll send word." Vixen glanced at the Knossan. "Clover, Emmaline's hanging out in the kitchen."

Clover inclined her horns, ever gracious. She and Jack watched as Vixen spun on her heel and walked off to notify the other Ringleaders. "I'll keep Emmaline occupied," Clover assured Jack.

Jack rubbed his forehead. "Thanks, appreciate it. I don't know how long we'll be."

To Jack's annoyance, the Ringleaders refused to decide on the matter of the young mage until he spoke for himself. It didn't matter that Jack told them they were dealing with a Breaker. And that, Jack decided, was one problem with trying to have *fair* leadership. Sometimes it wasn't fair, like in a case such as this where he knew what was best for them. Personal experience proved it.

Nadine was unavailable to attend their meeting, seeing as she was tending to the downed mage. The other Ringleaders agreed they would meet the next morning. But on one condition: the Breaker must be well enough to speak.

Disgruntled, Jack headed back to the saloon and collected Emmaline. The disapproval on her face almost made him feel bad about the whole thing. Almost.

"Why did you do that?" she asked as they walked to their home on the outskirts of town, rubbing her arms in the cooling night air.

Jack didn't reply for several minutes. He collected his thoughts as he listened to the steady sound of their footsteps and shrugged off the chill of her eyes on him. "I have my reasons."

Her hair whipped around in the silver light of the moon as she shook her head. "Well, it was rude. You've never acted like that to anyone new before."

No one like that has ever set foot in this town before. Jack kept that thought to himself. He knew it sounded petty and dramatic. Mages of varying ability called Itude home. They were all dangerous in their own way. But not like *that.*

"I said I have my reasons." He heard her huff a frustrated breath. Jack didn't like getting into spats with his daughter.

Emmaline was all he had, and it hurt his heart to cause her distress. But he wasn't willing to tell her more. Not now.

She said nothing else to him for the rest of the night. That was fine with him. It allowed him to avoid questions he would rather not answer. She continued the silent treatment the next morning, stomping out the door to school without so much as a glance in his direction.

Jack rubbed the short bristles on his chin. He hadn't slept well, troubled by the Breaker's presence in his town. The morning cup of coffee only did so much. He dressed and then headed out to Headquarters.

He was the last to arrive, but that was by design. Jack wasn't sure he could contain himself with minimal people around to keep him off the kid. He ambled into the back room where they held their meetings. Everyone was seated, awaiting his arrival. The injured mage sat between Nadine and Vixen, the skin around his left eye an ugly purple. His nose was crooked and swollen, a crust of blood flaked around his nostrils. When he recognized Jack, fresh panic flooded his face.

Vixen leaned over and whispered something, and the kid settled. Jack glanced around the room and found an empty seat. He slid into it, slouching.

Raven Dawson, his hair the same color as his namesake, rose from his chair as Jack seated himself. Raven was young, a handful of years older than the kid mage. The difference was that Raven was charismatic, full of savvy, and had stealthy magic that he firmly controlled.

"Now that we're all here, let's get this started." Jack didn't miss the fact that Raven's knives were sheathed at his hip. Raven was young, but he wasn't a fool. He had taken Jack's warning about the Breaker to heart. "To put everyone on even footing, we'll begin with introductions. I'll start." Raven cleared his throat. "Raven Dawson, one of Itude's Outlaw Ringleaders."

Great. Introductions. Jack was ready to ship the Breaker out of town and they wanted to introduce everyone and play tiddlywinks.

"Nine Lives Nadine, Ringleader and Healer," Nadine offered. She traced the vivid white scar that laced down her right cheek. "In case you're wondering, this would have killed anyone else." Jack noted that the young mage blanched at her words.

"Vixen Valerie, Ringleader." Vixen leaned back in her chair, smoked glasses perched jauntily on the bridge of her nose.

"Kur Agur, Ringleader." The Theilian was the second-scariest looking resident of Itude after Clover. Like the Knossan, he had the vague suggestion of a humanoid body. He stood on clawed paws, his body covered in a thick grey-yellow pelt with black guard hairs trailing down his back. His head was that of a wolf, from the upright ears to the tapered muzzle full of gleaming, pearly fangs. As a Theilian, he was supposed to be able to shift into a full lupine form, but Jack had never seen it. Rumor had it that Kur was under some sort of curse that prevented the shift.

All the same, Kur's snarly visage was frightening. It didn't escape Jack's notice that the Breaker looked at Kur with less fear than when he looked at Jack. *Good. You should be afraid.*

All eyes fell on Jack. Right. They wanted him to play nice. He could do so, within reason. "Wildfire Jack. Ringleader." He kept his voice low and gravelly. The kid's face turned another shade of pale. Jack hadn't thought it possible.

Then everyone's eyes rested on the Breaker. The kid's gaze fell away from Jack. There was a tremor in his voice as he spoke. "Blaise Hawthorne. From Desina." He looked like he was desperate to say more, but was too afraid.

Jack didn't miss the way the other Ringleaders shifted in their seats at the mention of Desina. They were all aware of the news he had brought of the Salt-Iron Confederation's advance into the nation.

Vixen leaned forward, taking off her glasses and setting them on the table. Everyone else was very, very careful not to catch her eye as she turned to look at Blaise. "It's good to meet you, Blaise. Tell us why you came to Itude."

Aside from Kur, everyone sitting in the room had magic, and Vixen was actively using hers. Jack frowned. The other Ringleaders must have agreed to the use of her magic before he arrived.

Vixen's ability was vision-based, but one would almost swear it was auditory, with the way her voice lilted and charmed as she spoke. She was so calming and welcoming that everything she said sounded like a good idea. And as long as she had her listener's undivided attention, they took the bait. Jack glanced at Blaise. She had him hook, line, and sinker.

When the young mage spoke, his voice was steady and devoid of emotion. He was in her thrall, and that spoke to the level of his exhaustion. Vixen was good, but it normally took her longer to work someone under her spell. The kid's mental defenses had to be shattered.

Blaise spoke of how the Salt-Iron Confederation had come to his home to capture him—to use him and his magic. He detailed his headlong flight and saving Emrys. To his credit, Blaise omitted his run-in with Jack.

But by the same token, Blaise painted himself as a victim. And now Jack was the asshole for punching him in the face. The kid had dropped a *tree* on his pursuers—he said so himself. He had little control over his magic. He was *dangerous*.

Once Blaise finished speaking, Vixen slipped her glasses back on. The young man blinked in a daze as the spell dissipated.

Raven rose again. "One responsibility of the Ringleaders is to ensure the safety of the town. We're charged with approving any new mages who wish to join us. We appreciate you telling us your plight, and we'll hold a vote on it in a moment." He made a tiny gesture with one hand, Vixen's cue to clear Blaise from the room.

Vixen dutifully moved Blaise elsewhere and rejoined them for the deliberation. When she had taken her seat, Jack glowered at them. "I don't know why we have to talk about it. He can't stay here."

Raven pulled out one of his knives and fidgeted with it. "I don't get it, Jack. Usually, you're eager for us to have more mages to bolster our defenses. Why not this one?"

"You got cotton stuck in your ears? He's dangerous. He has no training."

Vixen drummed her fingernails against the table. "With all due respect, you're the only one sitting here who had any formal training for your magic. All the rest of us had to teach ourselves."

Jack scowled. He didn't need a reminder of what he was or what he had lost. As far as he cared, the difference between an outlaw and maverick was splitting hairs.

"And," Raven added, "If you're thinking about it from a power level alone, he's no more a threat than you or Butch."

Jack curled his lip at mention of their resident Necromancer. That wasn't even the same thing. "The difference is *I* have training. And Butch has his damn ethics. We're safe by comparison. That kid doesn't even know which way is up."

Kur twitched an ear, thoughtful. "I will agree with Jack that the man poses a threat. The scent of his magic makes me twitch. But by the same token, I would not be comfortable throwing him out to the elements. He looks like a lost pup."

Damn wolves. They were always protecting the ones in their pack they saw as vulnerable. Jack had hoped Kur would consider the town as the thing to protect in this case. That had been a miscalculation.

"Breakers are bad news." Jack dredged his memory. "The last one on record caused an avalanche that buried a town. There's a *reason* the Confederation ended their line."

"Spare us the history lesson," Vixen said with a roll of her eyes. "And a Stonemage having a temper tantrum could do the same."

"I'm inclined to vote in favor of the mage who got punched in the face by one of our very own Ringleaders," Nadine said wryly.

She gave Jack a penetrating look meant to shame him for his behavior. *Not gonna work.*

Raven nodded. "Jack, you're the only one here who has any problem with this mage. That leads me to believe the issue is more with *you* than him. Unless anyone else has more to say, we'll take the vote."

Rage smoldering in his chest, Jack went through the motions of casting his *"nay"* vote. He couldn't believe they were voting to let the Breaker stay in their town.

That kid was going to be the end of them.

CHAPTER SEVEN
Rider

Blaise

"*I*'m sorry. Jack's an asshole, but he rarely greets newcomers with a fist to the face." Vixen walked companionably beside Blaise. The meeting had adjourned, and she'd brought word that the Ringleaders voted to allow him to stay in town.

After last night, he wasn't sure he *wanted* to stay in Itude. Exhausted and dismayed tears prickled his eyes, further irritated by the throbbing pain in his bruised and swollen face. Having his face smashed in by an irate outlaw was the last thing he needed.

But Blaise still grappled with the yawning emptiness of the question: where else could he go? He didn't want to ask Emrys to take him anywhere else—though the stallion hadn't seen what happened to him yet.

Blaise nodded at her words. Bullies were nothing new. He

wished he could say it was the first time he had ever taken a punch. Unfortunately, it ranked up there as the most forceful and competent punch. And with his luck, it wouldn't be the last.

He wished it hadn't happened when he thought things were looking up.

"Are you okay? I can take you back to the clinic if you're not up to it," Vixen offered, scrutinizing his face.

Blaise hadn't come across a mirror yet, and he was almost afraid to. "I'll be okay. I just . . ." He trailed off, at a loss for what to say.

"That's real tough, what happened to you with the Salties," she said, guiding him down the street past the bank. "You're not the only one here who's run from them. Lots of mavericks here." When he said nothing, she continued, "But Itude is safe. And everyone here does their part to chip in. We'll get you figured out and get a job for you."

"I may be able to help with that."

Vixen steered him around, and Blaise looked *up, up, up* at a hulking, horned figure. His vision was a little blurry from the punch, but it looked an awful lot like a cow walking upright. Maybe the irate outlaw had hit him too hard.

"Oh, howdy Clover," Vixen said brightly. "Blaise, this is Clover —she's a Knossan. She runs the Broken Horn Saloon." She pointed up the street to the ill-fated saloon from the previous evening.

A Knossan? Blaise had only read about the part-bovine, part-humanoid race. And her name was *Clover*? He stared up at her. "Howdy?"

Clover gave him a patient look. "I need a dishwasher. My current staff struggle to keep up." She tipped her head. "I can offer you room, board, and a fair wage."

What? She was offering him a job? That had never happened before. Hope stirred in his chest. But first things first. "I don't know if you'd want me with my magic."

The smooth hide on her shoulders rose in a bovine shrug. "Tell me how it works, and we'll figure out a way to work around it.

Don't know that you can be worse than some of my regular customers."

Blaise furrowed his brow. She seemed to have a sense of his magic, even though he hadn't told her what it was. Did she know? "Um. Wearing gloves provides a barrier from my magic." He hazarded a guilty glance at his bare right hand. How was he going to afford another glove?

He heard a swish and realized she had a tail. "Gloves? Excellent, I can get just the thing from the mercantile." Clover turned to Vixen. "He can have one of the guest rooms. If you take him to the Broken Horn, Hannah can show him where to go."

Vixen gave the Knossan a little two-fingered salute. "You got it, cowgirl." She said it fondly, and in a manner that made Blaise suspect it was something few others could get away with.

Clover looked at Blaise. "If you're up to it, start tonight. But Jack rang your bell, so it's not urgent. I'll have the gloves ready."

Blaise nodded, watching the Knossan clop down the street toward another storefront.

Vixen nudged his arm. "C'mon. I'll take you over to Hannah, and you'll be in excellent hands."

BLAISE DISCOVERED THAT MOST OF THE PEOPLE IN ITUDE WERE polar opposites to Jack. Hannah was of a similar age to Blaise, and she had an infectious smile.

"You have no idea how excited I am by the prospect of not staying up until the wee hours of the morning washing dishes!" Hannah exclaimed as she stomped up the stairs.

It was late morning, and the saloon was empty. Blaise saw a lone figure wiping down some tables, but Hannah didn't stop to introduce them. She took Blaise to the top of the staircase where five doors lined the landing. Hannah pointed to each door. "That's Clover, Wildfire Jack's daughter Emmaline, Abe, me—"

"Wait. Hold on . . ." Blaise quailed. Wildfire Jack's daughter?

Hannah nodded, eyes widening as she realized the cause of his distress. She paused outside the room she had indicated for the teenager. "She only uses it occasionally, when Jack is out of town working."

Blaise cocked his head. "What does he do?"

Hannah blinked, surprised by his ignorance. She waved one hand in a circle. "You know. He's an *outlaw*. Goes out to find stagecoaches to rob. That can keep him away for days at a time."

"Oh." Blaise wished he could kick himself. He should have known.

She continued down the short hallway, moving to the last door and thrusting it open. "This room is for you." She beckoned for him to follow her inside. "I have to tell you that before Clover got a hold of it, this was a house of ill-repute. Sorry in advance for the decor."

Blaise tugged at his ratty shirt collar, looking around the small room. Silky red sheets covered the bed, along with a quilt. Blaise leaned over to inspect the embroidery. His face flamed when he realized the embroiderer had created tiny scenes of men and women in the throes of passion. He turned away, facing a chest of drawers with a lace doily on top. Blaise made a conscientious decision to not look at the doily.

Hannah coughed, glancing at the quilt. "We, um, never come in here. I forgot about that, and I'm sure Clover did, too. Knossans don't see things the same way we do . . ."

Blaise rubbed the back of his neck. At least he wasn't alone in his embarrassment. "It's fine. It'll beat the cave I had to sleep in the other night."

His words cheered her, and she grinned. "I guess so! Well, I'm sure Clover won't mind if you redecorate. She's not attached to any of the stuff in these rooms, far as I know."

Blaise glanced around. "Did you redecorate your room?"

Hannah rolled her eyes. "Oh, sweet Faedra, yes. It was awful. I won't ever tell another soul what painting was in *my* room. I dropped it off the side of the cliff."

He hadn't even looked at the painting over the dresser. Blaise hazarded a glance and then regretted it. A gilded plaque beneath it that read *"Orgy of Pleasure"* spoke volumes. "I like that option. That would be an uncomfortable number of people staring at me while I sleep."

Hannah giggled, and for the first time since he had arrived in Itude, Blaise felt like things might not be so bad. Out of principle, he took the painting down from the wall and turned it around.

"Do you have any belongings?" Hannah asked once the awkward artwork was no longer a source of distraction.

Oh. Right. Blaise pursed his lips. "I did. I don't know what happened to them." He had lost track after Jack's fist had been introduced to his face.

"Stop by the clinic—Nadine may have it. It's two doors down from us." She pulled a key out of her pocket and handed it to him. "Here—key for this door. You should stop by the mercantile to pick up whatever you need."

Blaise sighed. "Thanks, but I can't afford anything right now."

She flapped her hands at him. "Don't worry about that. Go on. Get." Hannah turned and hurried off, heels tapping on the floorboards.

BLAISE TOOK HANNAH'S ADVICE, AND AFTER LOCKING UP HIS ROOM, he checked to see if his go-bag was at the clinic. He caught Nadine packing a black medical bag. She glanced up as he tapped on the door.

"You have good timing. I was about to leave to check on a poor sod who got chewed on by a chupacabra at one of the outlying ranches last night." Nadine tipped her chin to indicate his go-bag, resting beside a clean white cot. "Let me check on you before I go. How are you feeling?"

Blaise shrugged, wondering how much she wanted to know. Hopeless. Fatigued. Heartbroken. And that didn't even touch the physical pain.

Nadine pressed her lips together and made a humming sound. "Sit on the cot." He followed her direction, and she snagged the leg of a short stool with her foot, pulling it over. Nadine's nimble fingers probed his tender nose. "I need to straighten this while I can. I should have done it last night, but you were bleeding like a stuck pig."

Nadine wasn't exaggerating. Blaise's nose had bled and bled, ruining his clothing. Some thoughtful citizen had donated a second-hand shirt to him. Blaise's pants had traces of blood, but they weren't the same spattered horror as his shirt had been.

Her practiced hands settled over the bridge of his nose. Blaise bit his tongue as the pressure of her fingers flushed out a fresh wave of intense pain. Then warmth flooded the abused cartilage, and he heard a soft crunch as Nadine used her magic to realign it.

"That should help. Let me see that shiner now."

Blaise fought the urge to cower as she examined the bruised flesh around his left eye. Nadine paused, pulling back to look at him. "Something wrong?"

"No." His racing heart exposed the lie.

The Healer assessed him with cool eyes, moving in to continue the examination. This time, she moved with caution, as if she were trying to calm a frightened animal.

"Here's some advice. Don't lie to a Healer. We can feel the tension in your muscles and the fear in your pulse." Nadine drew her hands away. "Am I right in thinking you didn't like my hands near your face?"

He nodded.

The Healer sighed, settling back on the stool. "That's normal after what Jack did to you." Nadine studied him, thoughtful.

"You're not a fighter by nature. Yet you have old, healed injuries. Cracked ribs. A broken hand."

She could tell all that about him with her magic? The injuries were testaments to how much his age-mates had despised him for what he was. After those experiences, he was shy of touch or anyone getting too close. He didn't know how to explain, so he shrugged.

Nadine crossed her arms, angling her head to get him to look her in the eye. "Anything you want to talk about?"

"Not really."

She ran a hand through her short hair. "I respect that. Oh, and you should know I took the edge off that blistering sunburn. Be sure you wear a hat from now on."

Blaise blinked. He had forgotten about the sunburn. He rubbed his left cheek and found that it didn't have the roasted sensation from two days ago. "Oh. Thank you. For everything."

Nadine waved it off. "It's my job. I'd better get to that ranch."

Blaise collected his go-bag and headed out. Nadine followed along, stowing her medical bag on the back of a strawberry roan pegasus. The roan gave Blaise a curious look, ears pricked forward.

<There you are.>

Emrys swooped down from above, dirt billowing as he back-winged and landed nearby. The stallion folded his wings and trotted over. <Your face didn't have spots before. Why do you have spots?>

"Bruises." Blaise gingerly touched the skin below his eye and winced. "Wildfire Jack punched me."

The pegasus swished his tail, agitated. <What? Why would he do that to my rider?>

Blaise shook his head. He didn't want to go into it. "Don't worry about it." Then Emrys's words gave him pause. "Wait. What do you mean your *rider*?"

<I picked you, obviously.>

Had the outlaw hit him harder than he thought? Blaise rubbed his tender cheek. "I don't understand."

Emrys flipped his velvety nose in Nadine's direction as she set off with her pegasus. <Many stallions without a flight of their own pick a rider, usually a mage. It's always been that way, ever since the first outlaw mage set foot in the Untamed Territory. At least, that's the story passed down from mare to foal.>

Blaise blinked. "Oh."

<We're a good team.> Emrys stomped a forehoof, as if declaring something made it so. The pegasus prodded Blaise with his muzzle, his next words uncertain. <We are, aren't we?>

Maybe Blaise wasn't the only one in need of a friend. He reached up and gave Emrys's cheek a pat. True enough, he and Emrys may have perished in the Gutter without each other. "We are. Let me put this bag in my room at the saloon. Then can you show me around?"

<Of course.> Emrys followed him over to the Broken Horn, his mental voice radiating contentment.

With his meager possessions stored, Blaise came back out and walked beside Emrys. Itude was smaller than Bristle. Blaise noticed it still had many of the same amenities. Every building had an outhouse a suitable distance behind it so that people could take care of their necessaries. Emrys told him a bathhouse and a laundry were located on the northeastern side of town, in the shade of the massive wind-pump.

Blaise shaded his eyes, peering up at the spinning blades. Exhaustion had kept him from noticing it sooner. It was larger than any Blaise had seen before, the bulk of the structure made from whitewashed stone.

"What's it do?"

<Pumps water from below to the cistern and livestock trough. I don't know how it works. It's the oldest building in town.>

Blaise nodded. He couldn't imagine how long it had taken to build the wind-pump. It looked like a true feat of engineering and —he presumed—magic.

Emrys took him to the mercantile. Blaise gave an appreciative sniff with his newly healed nose. The diner next door had amazing smells wafting from the open door. Down the same street, he saw a bakery, hardware store, greengrocer, and dry goods store.

"How long has Itude been around? I didn't even know it existed."

The stallion snorted. <Hmm. I'm not sure. That would be a better question for a human.> He nudged Blaise with his nose. <Go into the mercantile and get what you need. Ellie and Gus run it—they're good people.>

Blaise trotted up the steps to the mercantile. A smattering of customers browsed the wide assortment of goods. A little girl begged for candy from one of the colorful jars beside a window. Blaise looked around, overwhelmed by the amount of merchandise.

"Hello! You look like someone in need of assistance." A short, sturdy woman with brown hair pinned up in a messy bun hurried over to him. "You must be our newcomer who has Jack's tail tied up in knots!"

Blaise blinked in surprise, then nodded. "Er, yes?" Word traveled fast in Itude.

The woman introduced herself as Ellie Pembroke. She pointed to her husband, working behind the counter and ringing up another customer, and introduced him as Gus. That done, she looked him up and down, clucking her tongue.

"Child, I'm guessing you came to us with little more than the clothes on your back, is that right?"

Not even that. The clothes on his back had been too bloody to save. "Um . . . that's the gist of it. I have a bag of a few things but . . . not a lot."

Ellie tapped her fingertips together. "As I thought. That won't do, not at all." She ducked behind the counter, returning with a pad of paper and pencil. "Let's brainstorm. Tell me what you think you need, and I'll give you my suggested additions."

This was not what Blaise had expected. He rattled off the few
things he knew he needed (clothes, new gloves, a razor, comb and
brush, maybe a new hat). Before he knew it, Ellie had filled the
page with her florid handwriting.

She gave him a kind smile. "No offense, but you look a little
out of your depth." She tore the paper out of the notebook and
handed it to him. "We have some items here. I made a note of
where you can go to get the ones we don't have."

Blaise looked over the long list, his heart sinking. "I don't have
any way to pay."

Ellie waved a dismissive hand. "Here in Itude, we take care of
each other. Don't worry yourself about that. We'll open a line of
credit for you. Once you have some funds, you can pay it down as
you're able."

Here in Itude, we take care of each other. Blaise felt an unexpected
prickle in his eyes again. Someone cared. Someone was *kind*.

"What happens if someone skips town without paying?" Blaise
blurted out, curious.

The laugh-lines around her mouth puckered as she grew serious. "Oh child, you are new as a day-old calf, aren't you? No one
would dare skip out on their debts from any folk in Itude. No one
wants one of our Ringleaders hunting them down."

The skin around his eye throbbed a painful reminder. Point
taken. Blaise nodded. "Makes sense. I appreciate the help."

Pleased, Ellie nodded and hummed a contented tune as she
helped him gather the items on the list. Before Blaise knew it, she
had a wooden crate full of items.

Ellie peered out the window and noticed the pegasus waiting
outside. "Oh! Is that Emrys? Can't let him wait out there without a
treat." Ellie hurried over to a colorful jar of candy and pulled out a
striped peppermint. She excused herself and spryly skipped down
the stairs to the stallion, holding the candy in her extended palm.
Blaise watched as Emrys's delicate lips plucked it from her hand.
No wonder the pegasus had called her *good people*.

She came back inside and set up an account in his name and

listed the items and their prices. Blaise watched as she pulled a yellow piece of paper out from beneath the one she had written on. "This is your copy."

Blaise took the paper from her and regarded it with curiosity. "Never seen anything like that before. Is that magic?"

"Oh." Ellie's smile was gentle. "Ditto paper. Nothing magic about it. It's imported here from Thorn. Not sure where it comes from before that."

He folded the copy down into a square and tucked it into his pocket. Ellie passed the list of items he still needed back to him, then directed him to see Jasper Strop, the knocker who ran the dry goods store.

When the afternoon drew to a close, Blaise was the proud owner of almost everything on the list. He had a new hat to keep the worst of the sun at bay, a smart new dark blue duster, and several matching bandannas. He had a few changes of clothes, a hairbrush and comb, pomade, and most importantly a replacement pair of leather gloves.

Blaise was uncomfortable about the amount of money that he owed the Pembrokes and Jasper Strop. But they didn't seem at all bothered by it, so he let the concern slide. He stowed his new purchases in his strange little room. Happy that his nose was feeling better, and that he had some possessions to call his own, he went downstairs to see if Clover wanted him to start work.

CHAPTER EIGHT
Breakfast, Interrupted

Blaise

*C*lover's ears flicked in surprise at Blaise when he made his way down to the ground floor of the saloon. She was buffing the wood on the bar to a soft luster, and she set aside her cloth at his approach.

"I didn't think you would be up to starting today." She moved out from behind the bar. "Are you sure you're well enough?"

Blaise shrugged. "I may as well start now. It'll take my mind off . . . things."

The Knossan gave him a considering look, then led him into the small kitchen in the back. Blaise felt more at ease. The man he had spied earlier was at work in the kitchen, tending to something that smelled like a stew.

"Abraham, this is our new dishwasher, Blaise. Abe is the cook." Clover clopped past the older man to the washstand.

Blaise nodded to the cook. Abe glanced over his shoulder and gave a salute with a wooden spoon. "Howdy."

Clover picked up a pair of gloves and slapped them against the rough palms of her hands. "Rubber gloves from the mercantile." She held them out to Blaise.

He accepted them, pulling off one of his new leather gloves. The rubber was a strange barrier against his skin. A weird, squeaky sensation. He tugged it on, twisting his wrist and flexing his fingers. His magic prodded the new material, but that wasn't anything new.

"Will those work?" Clover asked, watching him with interest.

"For a while," Blaise replied, replacing his right leather glove with the other rubber one. "The test will be to see how long they last."

Clover seemed content with that answer. "Let me know when you need more. The evening rush will be here soon."

She wasn't kidding. Hannah came down for work, tying an apron around her waist as she blew into the kitchen. When Blaise looked out the door a few minutes later the saloon had a full house. Cheerful music emanated from the floor as the pianist came in to play, and a steady flow of dishes circulated into the kitchen for Blaise to wash.

The evening was a blur, which was a relief to Blaise. It left him with little time to think about all that he'd lost, which was his inclination anytime he had a quiet moment. Abraham cooked, Hannah took orders and delivered food, Clover kept the brew flowing, and Blaise washed the dishes. The rubber gloves felt odd on his hands, but as the night wore on, Blaise grew used to them. He was so caught up in his task that Abraham nudged him partway through their shift, pointing with meaning at a plate of food he had left nearby. Blaise smiled his thanks and took a quick break to eat before going back to work.

"Wouldn't reflect well on me if you collapsed your first night on the job," the cook commented.

Blaise knew he looked haggard. His time on the run hadn't

been kind. He made a note to do something about his unkempt hair and beard tomorrow.

It was well after midnight by the time Clover shooed the last customer out of the Broken Horn. Hannah carried back the last dishes, blowing out a weary breath.

"My dogs are barking." She set the dishes down for Blaise and wiggled her left foot with a groan. "Survived your first night working here, I see."

"It's not over yet." Blaise picked up one of the plates.

"I'll dry," Hannah volunteered, picking up a towel as he washed.

The sound of hooves on the wood floor announced Clover's arrival as she came in from the bar. She surveyed the kitchen. "Where's Abe?"

"Snuck up to bed already, as usual." Hannah used her wrist to swipe a lock of damp hair from her eyes.

Clover sighed. "Should have known." She watched them work for a moment, then scrutinized the dishes Blaise had washed. The Knossan nodded her head. "You did well, Blaise. Not a speck of dirt on them."

Blaise winced. "I should hope not."

Hannah laughed. "What Clover means is we're not used to a dishwasher doing a good job."

That seemed terrible to Blaise. Clean dishes, pots and pans, and utensils were important. Clover helped put away the remaining dishes. When they finished, they stumbled up the stairs to their rooms. Blaise was so tired that he had no difficulty falling asleep in the uncomfortably decorated room.

When he awoke the next morning, light filtered in through a tiny window above the bed. Blaise sat up, disoriented. The last comfortable place he had slept in had been his own bed at home. His face throbbed, reminding him of his situation in a strange counterpoint to the soft sheets.

Blaise sank back onto the cotton-stuffed mattress and pulled the covers over his head. His face hurt. He was still tired, and he had aches in muscles he hadn't known existed. He wanted to go home. But he couldn't go home. The knowledge settled on his chest like a weight, and for a moment he almost couldn't breathe. Anxiety and the yawning expanse of his unknown future clawed at him. The warmth of his magic flowed over his palms, and out of reflex, he clenched them into fists to try to call back the power. It was of no use, though, and his magic threaded its way into the sheets.

"*No*," Blaise hissed, panic rising. He didn't want to ruin the sheets so soon, hideous as they were. He sat up and folded his hands into his lap before too much damage was done. The fabric looked worn but didn't have any holes. Yet.

He rubbed the side of his face, cringing as his fingers ran across the untamed beard growth. Blaise took deep breaths to calm himself. As tempting as it was to hide in bed all day, he had vowed to make himself presentable. Reluctantly, he dragged himself out of the tangle of obscene bedsheets. He turned on the mage-light perched atop the dresser.

He pulled out a set of fresh clothes and changed. The simple, familiar task was an anchor to normality. Blaise found a hand mirror in the top drawer of the dresser and pulled it out.

"Sakes alive," Blaise murmured, angling the mirror from left to right to see both sides of his face. He'd known he looked bad, but he wasn't prepared for the reality. The lid of his left eye was an impressive shade of purple. The bruise extended down his cheek and into the scruffy beard that had sprouted during his time on the road. His nose was puffy, but at least it was straight. He didn't recognize the face in the mirror. It couldn't belong to him.

But it did. He tucked the mirror back into the drawer. He needed to do something about that. Tame his beard, comb his hair, and maybe he would feel more like himself.

A sharp knock on the door interrupted his thoughts. "Morning, Blaise! Me 'n' Clover are going to the diner for breakfast, if you want to join us," Hannah called.

The mention of food made his stomach rumble. That was

tempting. It was a good idea to eat first and then take care of everything else.

He cracked the door open. "I'll come."

Hannah beamed at him, looking like she hadn't been ready to drop only hours ago. "We're going now if you're ready."

Blaise ran the new comb through his hair, then headed down the stairs. Hannah and Clover waited for him by the door, and a sense of camaraderie filled Blaise. It was a foreign sensation after everything he had been through—people waiting for the simple act of sharing a meal with him.

And neither Hannah nor Clover cared about what he was.

HANNAH'S OLDER SISTER, CELESTE, AND HER WIFE, MINDY, WERE the proprietors of the Jitterbug Diner. Hannah admitted to Blaise in a low voice that as much as she loved her sister, she couldn't bear to work for her. She had opted to take her talents to Clover at the Broken Horn. Blaise felt a stab of jealousy that she lived so close to her sibling. He squelched the thought as Mindy handed him a menu.

"If you don't know what to pick, I can pick for you." The young woman's yellow eyes danced with amusement. "My magic is never wrong." She bustled away to give them a few minutes alone with the menu.

Blaise glanced at Hannah. "What sort of magic is that?"

She set her menu down on the white tablecloth. "We call it Hospitality. Mindy can pick the best dish for any customer to enjoy just by looking at them. Without fail."

"And it can change from day to day. If you come see me tomorrow, it may be something different, hon." Mindy swept back over to their table. "Did you make your choices?"

Clover and Hannah placed their orders. Blaise glanced at the menu, then handed it back to Mindy. "Surprise me."

She saluted him with the menus. "Challenge accepted."

It wasn't long before Mindy came back bearing a tray laden with griddlecakes, sausages, bacon, and eggs. She made a return trip with a variety of syrups, jellies, butter, coffee, sugar, and creamers. Blaise's stomach growled eagerly when he saw the spread. Maybe there was something to her magic.

Clover and Hannah tucked into their food. Blaise's face was sore, so he took his time. He was certain one of his teeth was loose. Despite the pain, the food was excellent. He thought it was odd there weren't any fresh-baked items, though. He asked Clover and Hannah why that was.

"Oh, the town baker had black fever about a month ago and up and died," Hannah explained with a grimace. "Bakery's been empty ever since. Celeste will whip up the occasional cake or loaf of bread, but she doesn't like it as much as making other things."

"And Abe tried to make a loaf of bread once. It was a brick." Clover shook her head.

Blaise tapped a finger against the table. Should he tell them? After everything he had been through, he didn't think he could handle disappointment or scorn. Baking was the one skill in which he had any confidence. He didn't want to risk it. Safer to say nothing at all.

Hannah carried most of the conversation at the table, at ease as they talked about a wide range of topics. Blaise decided she'd had a lot of practice from her work as a waitress. She had a way of keeping the conversation flowing without delving too deeply into uncomfortable topics. She asked him a few things about his past that he could answer without too much angst or embarrassment.

They had almost finished their meal when the bell over the door jingled, Wildfire Jack striding through cloaked in determination. He surveyed the occupants of the Jitterbug Diner until his eyes settled on Blaise.

"Oh no." Blaise debated hiding under the table. He didn't think the table would stop a resolute outlaw, though.

Hannah gave him a confused look, then her eyes widened when she saw Jack. "Um, Clover?"

The Knossan didn't so much as twitch. Blaise figured she had no reason to worry since she outweighed the outlaw two or three times over. She also hadn't been the recent recipient of a punch in the face from him.

"Howdy, Jack." Clover was serene and unruffled as Jack approached their table. She took a sip of her coffee.

"Ladies." Jack nodded to Hannah and Clover. "Pardon my interruption." He turned, stabbing a finger at Blaise. "You. Out at the stables in five minutes. We're going to have a *talk*." His ice blue eyes pinned Blaise to his seat.

Blaise stared at him, pulse racing. Things had been going so well. *Of course* Jack wanted to talk to him. Probably with fists or guns or whatever his horrible magic was.

The corners of Jack's lips twitched, an acknowledgment of Blaise's terror. But instead of saying anything to lower the tension like a compassionate person might, he pivoted and stalked to the door.

Hannah waited until he left, then squeaked, "Um, Clover, is he going to kill Blaise?"

Blaise wished he could curl into a ball and hide. "Did you have to say that out loud?"

Clover laughed, a deep sound like rolling thunder. "Jack may wish you dead, but he wouldn't have you go to the stables if that were the case."

Blaise lifted his head, frowning. "Why?"

"I know Jack. Anytime he goes to the stables, it's to be held accountable. His pegasus and yours will not tolerate reckless behavior again."

CHAPTER NINE
A Little Sugar

Jack

Jack leaned against the top rail of the paddock, watching a pair of donkeys snacking on the flakes of hay a stable hand tossed over the fence. Zepheus was nearby, pretending to browse the dry vegetation on the outskirts of town. It was a ruse. The stallion had cleaned out his bucket of oats and sweet feed, chased down by sugar water. The pegasus was like a blasted hummingbird.

When Zepheus raised his head with ears pricked, Jack knew that the Breaker was approaching. He didn't budge from his place. Out of the corner of his eye, Jack noticed the Breaker's black stallion stride up beside Zepheus. Jack turned to frown at the stud. So what if the kid had freed him from a snare? Didn't mean the pegasus owed him any allegiance. Didn't change the threat he posed.

But for whatever misguided reason, the young stallion liked the kid and had picked him as his rider. And Zepheus had relayed to him that Emrys wasn't happy about the punching incident. *Too bad.*

It didn't matter, though. Jack had decided that since no one else saw things his way, he was going to feed the young mage enough rope to hang himself. Then matters would be out of Jack's hands.

Boots scraped the dirt. Jack looked back and saw the kid walk up, head bowed. Jack had to admit, part of him thought he wouldn't come. No doubt Clover had told him it wasn't optional.

The young man said nothing as he approached. He leaned against the fence, one of the fuzzy donkeys ambling over, curious about the newcomer. Jack pursed his lips when he saw the young mage offer the donkey a sugar cube.

"Your pegasus will be jealous." Jack tilted his head toward the two stallions. They were pretending to graze again, tails twitching to shoo away flies, wings fluttering with the motion.

"I have some in my pocket for him, too." Blaise kept his focus on the donkey. He scratched the little equine behind one of its long, shaggy ears. It leaned into the motion with a blissful sigh.

Jack blew out a breath through his nose. He shifted to face the Breaker, one hand braced against the fence. "I don't like that the other Ringleaders agreed you could stay, but it's something I have to live with now. I wanted to make some things clear."

Blaise kept his eyes averted, shoulders hunched. He gave a tiny nod, the only sign that he'd heard Jack's words.

Damn, but it felt like he was haranguing a day-old kitten that didn't know any better. But Zepheus had said it himself—even kittens had claws. "Itude is *my* town. I've worked hard to make it a safe place for the people who call it home. I'm watching you."

Blaise turned to him, and for a moment Jack anticipated a fight. But the kid's bruised face crumpled, eyes watery with the tears he was holding back. "Do you think I *want* any of this?" He held up his gloved hands. "I *never* wanted this. Never wanted magic, *especially* this magic. It's taken *everything* from me. I don't have a home anymore. Family. I have *nothing*."

Jack narrowed his eyes. Somewhere deep in his iron-clad heart, sympathy stirred for the kid. He knew how it felt for everything he loved to be stripped away. But that was different. He wasn't the same as this mage. Not at all.

"You have a home. Clover gave you a room at the saloon."

The Breaker shook his head. "That's a roof over my head. Not a home."

He didn't clarify, but Jack understood what he meant. Home wasn't where you bunked. It was having a place where you belonged, surrounded by people you cared about—and who cared about you. Blaise needed to find that somewhere else. Not in Itude.

"I'm sorry about the thing with your gun." Blaise's voice was so soft that Jack almost didn't hear. "I'm sorry if that's why you hate me."

Jack snorted. "Don't think I'll ever forgive you for that, but the gun itself is not why I have a problem with you."

Blaise wiped a tear from one eye. "Then why?"

"You're dangerous. You have no control. A mage with no control gets other people killed. Especially with magic like that." Zepheus raised his head, paying close attention to their exchange.

"Then teach me," Blaise said, almost begging. "I've never even met another mage like me. No one has shown me how any of this works."

Jack turned away, shaking his head. "I can't teach you. You'd piss me off, and I'd kill you, and that would be the end." *But that's not why. Can't let you or anyone else discover why.*

"Then . . . then I'll find someone here who will." Blaise swallowed, an edge of determination in his voice.

Jack pushed his hat up, thoughtful. So the Breaker wanted to learn to control his magic. Jack liked to consider himself a fair man, as far as outlaws went. He could hate this kid but still be fair. At least until he had reason to drive the Breaker from town. "Try

Vixen. Her magic isn't the same as yours—gods, no one else breathing today has magic like yours. But she probably has some concepts that will work for you." Yeah, the more he thought about it, the more Vixen seemed like the best match.

Blaise raised his eyebrows like he hadn't expected Jack to offer him the slightest bit of help. *Yeah, look at me. I can make nice sometimes, too.*

"Oh. Thanks." The kid shifted, uncomfortable.

Jack was about to tell the Breaker to get out of his sight, but then he remembered the other reason he had summoned him. "One more thing." Blaise's eyes shifted to him, full of trepidation. "When you told us about the Salties chasing you from Desina, you mentioned they had a commander with a unicorn. What was the man's name?"

Blaise chewed his lip, considering. "Gaitwood, I think."

"Shit." Jack slammed his open palm against the fence rail.

Blaise turned in surprise, his fear lost for a moment. "You know him?"

Jack bared his teeth. "Yeah. We have a history." He would not go into that history. Not here, and not with the Breaker.

The younger man shifted his weight from one foot to the other, indecisive. It took him time to gather his courage to speak. "My mother attacked them. The soldiers."

Jack whistled, impressed. That took gumption. "Did she, now?" The kid hadn't mentioned that in his little speech with the other Ringleaders. It hadn't been relevant.

"I think . . . they wanted her, too. She told me I couldn't let them capture me. But they have her. Or . . ." He trailed off.

Or they killed her. Jack knew the unspoken words. He didn't think Blaise wanted his thoughts echoed aloud. "She's gone, at any rate." Jack kept his tone neutral, not meaning any harm by the words. It was a reality. A reality he was well aware of.

Blaise splayed his arms across the fence rail, resting his chin against the wood. "Why did you want to know about Gaitwood?"

"Needed to verify some information from one of my sources."

Jack wasn't going to tell the kid that it was bad news to have Gaitwood so close to the Gutter. That wasn't his concern. If Jack had
his way, Blaise would be long gone before Gaitwood was any
threat. Jack glanced at the kid's ramshackle countenance. "You
look like the south side of a northbound mule. Barber's up the
street." He hitched his thumb over his shoulder.

Blaise nodded, stepping down from the fence. He looked
relieved by the dismissal. Jack stayed put as his footsteps receded.
Zepheus ambled over. <You should carry sugar in your pockets
for me,> the stallion suggested.

"You heard, huh?"

<Oh yes. All of it,> the palomino confirmed. <You should be
nicer to him.>

Jack grunted. "I was nice. I told him to see Vixen about his
magic. And I didn't punch him again, even though it's tempting."

<We have got to work on your people skills.> Zepheus sighed.

"My people skills are fine. Everyone else just needs to work on
their me skills."

"WILDFIRE JACK!"

Jack paused, one foot on the bottom step leading up to the
Ringleader Headquarters. In the space of a week since his chat
with Blaise, he hadn't seen anything to call the kid on—yet. Clover
kept him apprised of everything related to the saloon. According
to Vixen, Blaise took his suggestion to heart, and he had asked her
to help with his magic. She agreed, and they met regularly. Every
time someone stopped him on the streets, Jack hoped for some
minor bit of news he could leverage against the Breaker.

Jack kept his expression neutral as he turned to face Hank
Walker, Itude's postmaster and a part of Jack's spy network. To be
sure, he trusted the man about as far as he could throw him. But

Walker's magical talents made him a valuable asset. Not just anyone could travel across great distances in a short time using the natural network of plants.

"Howdy, Walker." Jack crossed his arms as he addressed the postmaster. "News for me?"

Walker fidgeted, nervous. "From Desina."

Desina. Jack motioned for Walker to wait. He hurried up the stairs and poked his head into HQ. It was empty. "Come on up."

The postmaster followed him inside. Jack led him to the meeting room, shutting the door behind them.

"What did you find?"

Walker's forehead puckered. "First, confirmation of what you already know—Desina has joined the Confederation. They're rounding up all the mages they consider worth a damn and taking them to the capital. From there, they're going to pack them onto steamers to Izhadell."

Jack scowled. Depending on the flavors of mages they found, putting them on steamers was a poor choice. Did they have enough salt-iron to keep their magic at bay for a long trip? No new salt-iron veins had been struck, as far as he knew. The mages with the strongest power wouldn't be ready to be bound to a handler for some time, which made the restraints a necessity.

Jack already knew most of the information Walker provided, except for the bit about transportation. "What else? Do you know how many mages they took in?"

"Ah, the last count was two dozen. But I know there's a small group of mavericks evading them. The Salties are pissed, from what I heard."

Jack perked up. "You made contact with the mavericks?"

Walker shook his head. "Not yet. Last I found out they were in Morton, but then the Salties plowed through."

Striding over to the window, Jack leaned against the frame, thinking. With the tides turning in Desina, he needed to proceed with caution. "Are you familiar with the name Gaitwood?"

The postmaster straightened. "The politician or the soldier?"

"Both. Either. Doesn't matter."

Walker scratched his head, thrown by the question. "I know *of* them."

Jack scuffed the floor with the heel of one boot. "I need you to do what you can to intercept any missives between them. Bring any information you find to me."

The postmaster's eyes widened. Out of respect to his profession, Jack generally avoided having Walker tamper with the mail. Especially mail that wouldn't normally route through Itude, one way or another. But now that Jack knew Lamar was close, he needed to tread carefully.

"That may be a tall order," Walker admitted with reluctance.

"Why?"

Walker spread his hands. "Couriers handle military correspondence, rather than the normal means."

Damn. Jack grumbled to himself. As far as he knew, no one in his network had any ins with the couriers. The Black Market was due back in less than two weeks. He might have to wait that long to pick Slocum's brain. If anyone knew a courier or a way into their confidence, it would be him.

"Fine, scratch that," Jack relented. "I want you to keep your eye on those mavericks and let me know if they reach an extraction point."

Walker considered it. "I'll try. But it will take some time. Can't use all my magic hunting for them if the town still wants me to do my day job."

It was tempting to tell him that the postal service could go to Perdition as far as he cared. But businesses and townspeople relied on the mail. Itude was cut off from everything else—as much as Jack could keep it, and mail was one of the few means of communication they had. It was a lifeline.

"Mail still needs to flow," Jack agreed. "But keep searching."

"Understood." Walker turned and headed for the door.

CHAPTER TEN
Practical Magic

Blaise

A month had passed since Blaise's chat with Jack. Their paths crossed—it couldn't be helped in the small town—but at least Jack didn't punch him again. But anytime he was near, the outlaw watched Blaise. Waiting for him to screw up so Jack could throw him out of town.

"You can't let him play mind games with you," Vixen told Blaise one afternoon as they sat at a table in the saloon. Blaise stared uneasily through the plate-glass window as Jack spoke with someone outside the bank.

Blaise fell into a routine, and part of that included magic lessons with Vixen several times a week. It was a slow start—Vixen had her own duties to attend to. Blaise was thankful for the time she spared. Clover allowed them the use of her saloon as their practice area. Each time they practiced at the saloon, the Knossan found an excuse to tidy things up around their vicinity.

Blaise scratched at his close-cropped beard. "I can't help it."

Vixen removed a shot glass from a serving tray stationed on a nearby table. Grinning, she set it down in front of him. Then she picked up a mug and took a long drink. Not for the first time, Blaise wondered if she'd agreed to work with him at the saloon as long as the free booze kept flowing.

She wiped a drop of foam from her lips. "If there's one thing to know about Wildfire Jack, it's that his favorite thing in the world is to scare the piss out of someone. Am I right, Clover?"

The Knossan looked up from the pitcher she was drying. "That is the highlight of his day."

Blaise sighed. Every time he sat down to practice with Vixen, if he caught sight of Jack, things went wrong. And the blasted outlaw had a penchant for appearing outside every time he practiced. It was like he knew what Blaise was doing and wanted to sabotage him.

The thing was, Blaise was no stranger to bullies. But Jack was a league above any provincial bully from Bristle. Something about the man terrified him to his very core. It was hard to shake.

"Hey Clover, you're sure we're good to use this set of shot glasses?" Vixen asked, gesturing to the grouping on the serving tray.

"Yes. They're chipped, and I have new ones on the way."

Vixen motioned to Blaise with a flourish. "Have at it."

Blaise picked up the shot glass. His gloves were off, and the smooth glass was cool to his touch. It was strange to not feel the glass through rubber gloves.

Vixen wanted him to focus on gaining a level of control over his magic. She said once he had that figured out, they could do more. But they had to start with the basics.

Blaise gritted his teeth, concentrating on the glass. His aim was to *not* break it. That was so much harder than it sounded. Shot glasses stood up to heavy use, but they were still glass. Glass was fragile. His magic didn't do well with fragile things. Blaise didn't know why they couldn't start with a sturdier target. Like a horseshoe. Or a boulder.

But Vixen insisted on glass. She reasoned that it would benefit him in the long run to go from hardest to easiest. So far, all Blaise had to show for it was a trail of a half dozen broken shot glasses, courtesy of Clover.

His hands itched. Sweat trickled down his forehead. A crack split the side of the glass. "I can't do this." Blaise's shoulders sagged with defeat.

Vixen took the glass from him before it could shatter, tucking it into a burlap bag. They both knew from experience that the glass wouldn't stay in one piece much longer. "Right, let me think." She pushed her glasses up the bridge of her nose. "When you're nervous or upset, your magic grabs the bit and runs. Is there ever a time when you *can* control it? Where it doesn't . . . do what it does?"

Blaise rubbed the back of his neck. "Yes." But after all he had been through, would it still work? It had been so long since he had done anything besides wash dishes in a kitchen.

"Well?" Vixen leaned forward, expectant.

"I . . . I used to bake. That was the only time I never had to wear gloves at home." Blaise's voice was soft and reluctant, expecting Vixen to laugh at him.

Vixen cocked her head, looking intrigued. "Really? Are you any good?"

Am I? Blaise asked himself. He wasn't sure what to say, so he shrugged.

Vixen traded a look with Clover. "Can we use the kitchen?"

The Knossan flicked an ear as if listening for something. "I don't see why not."

Blaise didn't know what Vixen had in mind, but he rose from the table and followed her into the kitchen. Abe was already preparing the evening menu. He gave them a curious look when they entered.

"Let's clarify some things." Vixen looked around the kitchen, getting her bearings. "Is it just baking, or cooking too?"

Blaise thought about that. The kitchen was his domain—relaxation flowed over him as soon as they walked in. His father had done most of the cooking at home, but Blaise had helped. And he hadn't worn his gloves then, either. He didn't lose himself in the joy of it the same way as with baking, but he didn't destroy anything, either.

"Cooking should be safe, too," Blaise told her. "Baking is the sure thing."

Abe grunted, pulling out a bowl and a bag of cornmeal. "Was planning on making cornbread tonight. Have at it."

Blaise's eyes lit up, but he glanced at Vixen to see if that was something she had in mind. She waved him on. "Go ahead. I'm curious to see if you can do it with gloves off. If you can, we'll try something while that bakes. And it'll be a bonus if you can make it taste less like rocks."

"That happened one time. *One,*" Abe muttered.

Blaise ignored their exchange, getting to work. The tension oozed out of his muscles as soon as he had the bag of cornmeal in hand. He sifted it and made dough after combining it with boiling water. Abe watched for a moment, then shoved the other ingredients to his side of the countertop. Lard, salt, brown sugar, and a cake of yeast. The familiar pleasure of working with his hands in the kitchen consumed him. Blaise was disappointed when he had to stop to allow it time to rise.

Vixen gave a low whistle when he set the bowl aside. She moseyed over to inspect his work area. Not a single bowl or utensil had any signs of wear outside normal use. "You weren't kidding."

Blaise rubbed his hands together. They were gritty from the cornmeal, but it was like a balm for his soul. "I've missed this."

Vixen lifted her chin, studying him for a moment. Then an impish grin crossed her face. "Catch!" She flung open her hand, a shot glass arcing through the air.

He didn't even think about it; he reacted. Blaise saw the projectile flying towards him and he reached out and caught it with both hands, cradling it against his chest. He stared at Vixen with wide eyes.

"Think about what you just did." Vixen pointed at the countertop where the batter was resting. "Not on the thing in your hand."

Blaise shifted his weight from foot to foot, the small glass feeling heavier in his hand with each passing moment. Then a thought occurred to him that made him forget about the glass. "I didn't grease the pan and get it in the oven to warm."

Vixen raised her eyebrows, then laughed, amused by his priorities. "Do that. Then I want you holding that glass until you're ready to put your cornbread in the oven."

Blaise sighed, setting down the shot glass on the counter as he found a cast iron pan. He prepared it and put the pan in the oven. When he picked up the shot glass, he realized it was still in one piece. He had expected it to shatter into a thousand tiny pieces.

But it was pristine, aside from the wear of Clover's customers.

"Huh." Blaise turned it over in his hands. He didn't feel itchy, either. He looked up at Vixen. "How am I not breaking this?"

She shrugged. "I'm not an expert, but I think you just lack practice and confidence. That means a lot of your problem is in here." She tapped the side of her head. "When you do what makes you happy, you expect your magic won't mess up. You don't have that expectation for the rest of your day-to-day, though. You become a self-fulfilling prophecy."

Blaise winced. That sounded accurate. But her idea sounded a lot simpler than reality. He fervently wanted his magic to not destroy his life. But he had always had a low level of confidence in that actually happening.

Vixen rubbed her hands together with glee. "So this is what we're gonna do. Every practice from now on, we're going to meet in this kitchen. You'll bake something first, and we'll go from there."

Blaise nodded, setting the unbroken glass down beside the dough. "It's worth a try." Even if it didn't help his magic, at least he would get to do something he loved.

AFTER THAT, BLAISE DIDN'T MIND PRACTICING WITH VIXEN. THE kitchen's windows faced away from the town square, so Blaise never saw Jack. That alone was a boon, but the opportunity to bake as a calming outlet was the biggest help.

During the second week of their practice in the kitchen, Blaise discovered that Clover had started to stock more items for baking. Abe ceded half of the workspace as well. However, the cook was overall lazy and enjoyed having someone else do his work so it didn't mean much. Blaise still worked every evening washing dishes, so his days were full.

As much as he loved baking, it was his newfound control over his magic that thrilled him. It was tenuous at first, and Vixen started him small. First, they just focused on holding something and not breaking it. After he had success with the shot glass, she and Clover brought in a wider array of items: porcelain figurines, ceramic beer steins, mirrors—every session something new.

The effort paid off. Clover challenged him to wash dishes one evening without the rubber gloves. Blaise wasn't sure about it, and he told Clover as much.

"Try it. I'll not take anything you break out of your pay," the Knossan said with a swish of her tail.

How could he tell her *no* after that? Blaise tried and surprised himself, ending the night without a single broken dish. His hands were pruney from the dishwater, but otherwise, nothing was the worse for wear.

His successes restored his sense of self. Blaise hadn't realized how low he felt since fleeing his family, but looking back, he saw he hadn't been in a good place. He had been adrift and heartsick. But now he had a routine and purpose. He enjoyed practicing with Vixen and working with Clover. Some days, Emmaline hung out with Clover while Blaise practiced. He didn't particularly like that, though Emmaline was harmless compared to her father. She liked to sit and talk with the Knossan while Blaise mixed dry ingredients or convinced his magic to not break whatever random object he was holding.

One afternoon, Emmaline watched him put a pan of bread into the oven, and she frowned. "Vixen, why don't y'all just use the bakery for this?"

The Knossan twitched with surprise, and Vixen made a soft sound.

"Out of the mouths of babes," Clover murmured. But she was nodding, and Blaise straightened up, paying close attention. Itude's bakery had sat empty for months. Blaise thought about it whenever he passed by.

Vixen rocked on her heels. "We'd have to ask Jack. He owns that building."

Blaise winced. *Of course, Wildfire Jack would own that building.*

Emmaline bounced to her feet. "No one's using it. We'd have a town baker again." Her eyes gleamed mischievously.

Blaise frowned. Was she trying to annoy her father on purpose? He knew the antics his own sister pulled back home were meant to aggravate without causing damage. He wanted to tell Emmaline *no*, but the words didn't come. Working in the bakery in any capacity was too tempting. It had always seemed so far out of reach. Now Emmaline placed it in front of him on a platter.

"Clover better be the one to do the asking. She has the best odds out of any of us to convince him," Vixen reasoned. "Your stuff is good, Blaise. If Jack agrees, we could have the rest of the Ringleaders and the Business Association hold a vote to see if you could lease the bakery. What do you think?"

Blaise almost collapsed in shock from her words. That was

beyond anything he could have hoped for. "Okay." *Okay? Just okay?* He knew he was capable of more words than that.

Clover chuckled. "In that case, I'll ask. I think you're right that I'm the best one to broach this topic. As it is, he won't be thrilled with me."

CHAPTER ELEVEN
Outmaneuvered

Jack

"Not just *no*, Clover. *No way in Perdition*." Jack glared at the Knossan, not caring that she towered over him. She'd tricked him, and he wasn't at all happy about it. And to make matters worse, this was the third time she had asked him. *Ridiculous.*

When she invited him to see her at the Broken Horn, he was suspicious. Vixen was nowhere in sight, and Jack had the vague idea that this was the usual time the Breaker practiced with her at the saloon. Emmaline confirmed as much. But it wasn't unusual for Clover to request a word with him, so he agreed.

Clover leaned against the bar, flicking an ear back at the voices coming from the kitchen. She gave him a disapproving look. Jack knew they could hear him in the kitchen. He didn't care.

"You're not being reasonable." Clover pulled a bottle from

beneath the bar and poured Tanglefoot into a mug, pushing it over to him. "The bakery is not making you any coin sitting there empty."

I'd rather have it sit there empty than have that mage squatting in it. Jack took a swig of Tanglefoot, savoring the burn in his throat. "I said *no*. I thought I made myself clear."

She lowered herself, bringing her head down so she looked him in the eye. "Why won't you give him a chance? You gave *me* a chance."

Jack set down the glass, meeting her gaze. "That's different. You were little more than a calf. And you . . ." He faltered, annoyed she had him thinking about that.

Clover couldn't smile—her lips didn't work the same way as a human's. Her equivalent expression was a slight tilt of her head, ears pitched forward—as she was doing now. "You're the big tough outlaw with a soft spot for the broken." Clover's voice was quiet, not carrying beyond Jack's ears.

Damn her. The mage wasn't a broken thing—he was a *Breaker*. Jack knew he was being stubborn, but that didn't matter. He was trying to keep everyone who mattered safe. It infuriated him that none of them saw that. It was like trying to keep a gaggle of chicks from the side of a cliff.

When he said nothing, Clover lowered her muzzle. "He's worked at the saloon for two months now. Guess how many things he's broken in his shift during that time?"

Jack frowned. "I don't know."

"Two glasses," Clover said, her dark eyes serious. "And those weren't even his fault. That happened a night you weren't around, and a brawl made it as far as the kitchen."

Jack grunted. "So you're saying it's *my* fault he broke those glasses?"

Clover snorted at him. "That's not what I said at all. *Hannah* has broken more things over that span. Blaise is vigilant, even before he practiced. He's had to learn to be that way. You should give him a chance. Let him try to get that bakery up and running. Faedra knows, this town could use decent fresh bread."

Jack drummed his fingers on the bar. He didn't understand their fascination with Blaise. Clover and Vixen had fallen for his woe-is-me ploy far too easily. But they were right. The bakery served no purpose as an empty building.

And Jack would be Blaise's landlord, which would add a layer of discomfort to the young mage.

"Fine, Clover. You win. If the Ringleaders and Business Association agree, he can lease the bakery on a trial basis."

Cheers erupted from the kitchen. They *had* been listening. Jack scowled. Clover inclined her horned head, an innocent twinkle in her eyes.

Blaise

THE NEXT MORNING, BLAISE FOUND HIMSELF BACK AT THE Headquarters—under different circumstances than his last visit. This time, the Ringleaders weren't the only ones in attendance. Most of the town's business owners were there, seated in wooden chairs that creaked as they settled down. Clover sat atop a stump designed to accommodate her bulk. She lowered her horns to Blaise in a greeting. Celeste and Mindy from the Jitterbug sat nearby and grinned at Blaise. Ellie Pembroke gave a friendly wave and gushed about how excited she was for him.

Jack was there too, lower lip curled as if he'd eaten something sour. From what Blaise had seen, *disgruntled* seemed to be the standard mood for the outlaw. He was pretty sure Jack didn't know how to smile.

"Thank y'all for coming!" Vixen Valerie bobbed her head as she took her seat. The Ringleaders sat in a row at the front of the room. Blaise sat with the rest of the Business Association, the chairs laid out in neat rows.

"My kingdom for fresh bread on the regular," Celeste mumbled, earning an elbow in the ribs from Mindy. Monty Fromhold, the ice mage who ran the icehouse, chuckled.

Raven Dawson rose from his seat, his gaze sweeping over the gathering. "Clover has raised the proposal to allow the use of the bakery to Blaise Hawthorne on a trial basis. Jack has generously agreed." Blaise saw a few gazes wander to Jack, and the indistinct murmur in the room proved that most noticed how *generous* Jack felt about it. "The town charter dictates that the Ringleaders and Business Association hold a vote to agree on the addition of any new business or lessee. Blaise, if you're still wanting to go forward with it, we'll hold the vote on that now."

Blaise nodded, still not quite believing that if the vote went his way, he would have a bakery to work out of. He felt a tingle in his hands, an early warning that anxiety was tugging at his magic. *Breathe.* He curled his hands into fists, focusing on the rough leather of his gloves.

"All right, Ringleaders, all in favor?" Raven raised his brows as he looked at his cohort. He raised his own hand, as did Vixen, Nadine, and Kur.

Jack glowered. "Abstain."

Raven cocked his head, a lock of black hair falling into his eyes. "Unusual, but . . . moving right along. Members of the Business Association, all in favor?"

An enthusiastic chorus of *"aye"* and raised hands rumbled through the room. Blaise had the full support of the Business Association. His heart hammered in his chest. It was almost hard to breathe, he was so surprised.

"You have a bakery!" Vixen crowed when the meeting ended, running over to Blaise and swooping him into a hug.

He blinked, going rigid in her arms. No one outside of his family had ever hugged him before. Vixen didn't seem to notice and gave him a sound thump on the back. Clover plodded over and patted him on the shoulder when Vixen peeled away.

"I guess so," Blaise mumbled.

"Lease. It's a lease," Jack growled, glaring at them from his chair.

Vixen put out her hand. "Not talking to you right now, Mr. Abstain. That was lower than a snake's belly."

Jack rose, reaching into his pocket. "I could have voted nay and scuttled the whole thing." He fished a key out, then held it out to Blaise. "I'm still watching you."

Blaise took the key, lifting his chin in defiance. He would not let Jack steal his joy. "I'd be surprised if you weren't."

THE BAKERY'S INTERIOR WAS PAINTED A PALE YELLOW THAT reminded Blaise of melting butter. He liked it immediately. The hue made him feel optimistic, as if his life had turned a corner. He mentioned it to Hannah and Emmaline, who were helping him organize the bakery.

"Yellow is Daddy's favorite color." Emmaline sat on a multi-colored rag rug spread across the hardwood floor painted in a motif of alternating black and white squares. She sorted through a box of gadgets. "What's this? And this? And this?" She held up three items for his inspection.

Blaise grimaced. Figured that Jack would paint the bakery his favorite color. The exterior boasted the same color, though with white trim that reminded him of the outlaw's palomino. He cast a glance at the items Emmaline showed him. "Pastry jigger, hand mixer, and—I think that's garbage." Whatever the last gadget was, the metal was so warped from its original shape, the damage rendered it useless.

"Right." Emmaline dutifully tossed the unknown item into a

sack set aside for trash and moved the other two to a counter. More utensils and dishes lined the counter, all in need of a thorough wash before use.

The interior of the bakery was more of a challenge than Blaise had expected. He didn't know if the last baker had been careless or if it was because of the disuse, but it was a mess. Blaise needed to inventory everything, if only to know what he had on hand. Then he would make a detailed list of replacement items needed.

Someone had left the flour unsealed, and weevils had gotten into it. Blaise scrunched up his nose, putting the flour aside. The sugar was in better shape, sealed in an air-tight container. He discovered a tin of salt hidden behind the sugar, along with lard. Blaise made a face when he realized mice had gotten into the lard container. He chucked it into the trash. It was rancid, even without the mice. *Might have to get a cat.*

The oven was in excellent condition. Blaise bent down to get a better look at it, whistling with appreciation. The words *Argor Metalworks* and the outline of a mountain peak were embossed near the bottom. Argor boasted some of the best metalworkers on the continent. Whoever purchased the oven had bought the best that was available. And then would have had to transport it a long distance at a considerable cost. Had Jack done that?

"I hope someone looks at me someday the way you're looking at that range." Hannah grinned as she looked back at him from where she nested a set of bowls.

Blaise shook his head, chuckling. "Sorry. I just . . . wow, this is something I never thought would be possible."

Emmaline moved a container of wooden spoons to the 'to be washed' pile. "You can make eyes at that oven all you want if it means you'll make cinnamon buns."

"And cake," Hannah agreed.

"And cookies," Clover said, ducking down to get through the doorway. She carried a sheaf of paper in her hand and offered it to Blaise.

He wiped his hands on a towel, taking the paper from her. "What's this?"

"Something I remembered from my past." Clover watched as Blaise read over the paper. It was a recipe. "When I was a calf, they tasked me with helping in the kitchens at—" She shook her head, tail swishing with sudden agitation. "That part doesn't matter. But it didn't occur to me the recipe was unusual. Not until I came here and realized it was uncommon. I wrote down what I remembered."

Blaise hadn't seen her handwriting before. Her strokes were severe and sharp, with few curves. But it was easy to read, and he admitted he hadn't seen a recipe like it before. He thought it would work, though—if he had all the ingredients on hand. Blaise tapped the last item in the list. "Is that the same as baker's chocolate?"

Clover leaned over to see what he was pointing at. "Semi-sweet chocolate? No. But if you want to make this, I will have the Pembrokes special order some." Her tongue stuck out as if savoring the taste of an old memory. "This is the one thing I miss from . . . my old life."

As curious as he was, Blaise didn't ask. Emmaline and Hannah clammed up, feigning absorption in their tasks. Blaise nodded. "I'd be honored to try your recipe, Clover. Thank you."

She dipped her horns. "I will leave you to your work. I'll stop by the mercantile and see about the chocolate."

They waved goodbye to the Knossan. Hannah opened the small utility closet, peering inside. She used an old rag to whisk away a cobweb and then pulled out a broom. "Are you going to run this place all on your lonesome once it's in shape?"

Blaise looked around. He hadn't thought that far ahead. Jack was only allowing him to use the building on a trial basis. But there was no doubt the bakery would be popular—curious towns-people were already peering inside, asking when he would open for business. Blaise wondered if Jack had any inkling how eager the townsfolk were for the bakery to open.

The outlaw must know. From what Blaise saw, there was very little Jack didn't know about what was afoot in "*his*" town.

"Maybe. I'm not sure. Never done anything like this before." Blaise sat back on his heels. If the bakery was busy, it might turn into more than he could manage on his own. That would be a problem.

"Well, even if you don't get someone right away, you might want to consider bringing on an apprentice or something," Hannah advised as she swept the floor. "That's what got us into this mess in the first place. The last baker refused to let anyone learn from him and then he up and died."

"Which is a shame, because his cinnamon buns were amazing," Emmaline lamented.

Blaise chuckled. "I'll keep that in mind. Thanks, Hannah."

"If you think you need help, I wouldn't mind working here." Emmaline's voice was soft, tentative.

What? Blaise winced. Wildfire Jack's young daughter working *here* with him? That sounded like a recipe for disaster. Hannah's broom came to an abrupt stop, her eyebrows raised as she glanced from Blaise to Emmaline and back again.

"Please consider it." Emmaline closed the cabinet she was looking through and got to her feet, dusting off her knees. "I don't get to do much but sentry duty, and not even that often. There's so much I don't get to do."

Blaise cringed. She didn't say it, but he could hear it in her voice: *There's so much I don't get to do because I'm Wildfire Jack's daughter.* Blaise had been shackled with limitations by his magic. She was hobbled because she was her father's daughter.

But that didn't mean he liked the idea of her working with him. It meant he could sympathize.

"I don't know . . . don't you have school?"

"Only three days a week," Emmaline shot back, eager. "And those days I could come by before school. And after. If you needed me."

Blaise studied her for a moment, then looked at Hannah. She

shrugged as if to say, *your funeral*. Blaise pursed his lips. He asked himself the dangerous question: would Wildfire Jack be more likely to kill him if he let his daughter work at the bakery, or if he upset her by telling her *no*? Both options were terrible. "I'll consider it on one condition," Blaise relented with a sigh.

Emmaline grinned, pressing her hands together. "Thank you! You won't regret it! What's the condition?"

"Your father has to agree."

Her face fell. "That's just topping."

Blaise grunted agreement. That about covered it.

CHAPTER TWELVE
Fragility

Jack

Jack stared at his daughter, hardly believing the absolute bosh coming from her mouth. Did she think he had fallen off Zepheus and hit his head?

"And I'll make sure all my chores are—"

"No."

Emmaline stopped in surprise, green eyes wide. "But Daddy, I—"

Jack held up his hand. "No. I said *no*. I will not allow my *daughter* to be a part of that Breaker's cockamamie scheme. Bad enough he's bamboozled the rest of the town."

Maybe it was time to clean the young mage's plow again, to remind him not to trifle with Jack's family.

Zepheus was out on patrol, so his pegasus wouldn't be around to interfere. Jack angled past his daughter, pushing open the front door and trotting down the steps. He would check the bakery first. Hopefully, the Breaker was there and not at the saloon. Clover wouldn't be too happy at what he had planned, but he would deal with the Knossan later.

He heard a muffled exclamation as Emmaline figured out what was afoot. He heard the sharp staccato of her boots. "Daddy! Stop! Please *don't*." She came running up alongside him, tugging at his right arm.

Jack shook her off. "It's for your own good, Emmaline." She clawed at his arm again, but he was moving faster. She broke into a jog to keep up with his ground-eating strides. The bakery wasn't far, but he had to get by the stables, which could pose a problem.

"Oby!" Emmaline called, and the beating of massive wings heralded the arrival of her spotted stallion. With a grumble, Jack checked over his shoulder. At least the black stud wasn't anywhere in sight.

Emmaline pulled herself onto the stallion's bare back as Oberidon trotted in front of Jack. The stallion squared up and spread his wings, blocking Jack's path.

"Out of the way, Oby."

"Daddy, I'm tired of you treating me like I'm a little kid," Emmaline said, her voice low and full of righteous anger. A distant part of Jack's brain registered that she was channeling his attitude. "Have a row with me, I don't care. But don't take it out on Blaise."

Jack's fists clenched at his side. "He needs to know his place." A few citizens had stopped what they were doing to stare at the spectacle. Jack shifted his glare to them. "Shoo! Go on, get!"

The gawkers hurried off. Over the edge of Oberidon's wing, Jack saw the door to the bakery was open. Jack set his jaw as the Breaker strode into view.

"Emmaline, everything okay?" Blaise asked.

Jack growled to himself as Emmaline looked over her shoulder and shook her head. Blaise walked to the edge of the boardwalk in front of the bakery, leaning against the wooden support of the awning. His ungloved hands were in his pants pockets.

"Emmaline will not be working with you," Jack snarled.

Blaise's mouth pressed into a thin line, but he nodded. "All right, then."

"It's *not* all right." Emmaline slid off Oberidon, pivoting to look between them. The spotted pegasus maintained his position, keeping Jack clear of the bakery. "It was *my* idea, Daddy. Not Blaise's. So if you're going to be mad at someone, be mad at me."

Jack scowled. Didn't she understand he *didn't* want to be mad at her? He wanted to protect her.

Emmaline wasn't finished. "And I'm not a little girl anymore. You keep treating me like . . . like I'm a fragile doll! But I'm not. And I want a chance to learn new things away from *you*." She waved her arms in a descriptive circle.

He winced. Was he doing more harm than good, trying to keep her safe? She didn't know what the world was like beyond the Gutter. She had been so little the last time she had been anywhere else. Damnation, Emmaline was so much like her mother. He had to be careful. If he didn't give her some rein, eventually she would break free, and he might never see her again.

Jack bowed his head, thinking. She was growing up before his eyes, and he had to acknowledge that. The next words pained him to say. "Give me a few minutes to talk about the arrangement with the Br—with Blaise."

Emmaline raised a brow, and Jack's heart jumped. *She has my hair, but I'll be damned—everything else about her is Kittie.*

"You mean *talking* like normal people, or *talking* like punching him in the face? 'Cause there is a difference, and I'm strongly opposed to the second one," Emmaline drawled.

Jack snorted. "You have my word. I won't punch him in the face without good reason."

Blaise rested his head against the wooden support. "I'm doomed."

Emmaline glowered. "Daddy!"

Jack sighed. What did she want from him, a miracle? "I promise I won't punch him in the face for the next five minutes."

She gave a sharp nod. "Get talking." Emmaline nudged Oberidon with her knees, and the pegasus headed back to the stables.

Jack watched her go, then turned his focus back to the Breaker. "I don't know why she wants to be involved with your baking nonsense."

"With all due respect, sir, it isn't nonsense," Blaise replied, still leaning against the support.

Jack walked closer, annoyed that the young man didn't cower in the slightest. "Be that as it may, Emmaline has other things she needs to keep her mind on. And *you* are a distraction."

"I'll remind you, *she's* the one who had the idea. She was the one who asked if she could help organize the bakery." Jack heard a tremor in Blaise's voice. *Good.* He wasn't actually as confident as he was pretending.

"You don't understand—"

"But I do," Blaise cut in, and Jack was just as surprised as Blaise looked by the interruption. The Breaker plowed on, like a horse with the bit clenched between its teeth. "I know how it feels to be in her place. Told that she can't do certain things because of who and what she is. Do I really want her working with me? No, because I know it'll bring your wrath down on me like a hammer if the slightest thing goes wrong. But I'm at least willing to give her a chance because everyone deserves a shot at happiness."

Jack crossed his arms. The *nerve* of this kid to lecture him. By the same token, Blaise had a point. And that really got up Jack's dander. He wanted to stick to his firm *no*. But he also wanted Emmaline to be happy. *Damnation.* Jack let his arms hang loosely at his sides, stepping onto the boardwalk. He was so close to the Breaker now, it would be a simple thing to attack. He had made a promise, though. And Blaise had done nothing to warrant it unless Jack counted the fact that he was still breathing. "Emmaline's all I have left in this world."

Blaise nodded. "I figured as much. You can't protect her forever. You can try. But eventually, she'll end up like me."

"A maverick opening a bakery?" Jack asked dryly.

Blaise chuckled, a sound that surprised Jack under the circumstances. "Hopefully not exactly like me."

Jack turned, peering through the plate-glass window at the interior of the bakery. It had been in rough shape after Bart's untimely death. Jack hadn't wanted to bother setting it to rights. He grudgingly realized that the place was in better shape than the last time he had looked inside—better than he could have done for it himself. Items clustered together in neat piles, the floor freshly swept. It looked like someone competent had been at work.

"Emmaline has a target on her back because she's my daughter," Jack said after a moment of assessing the bakery. "Whether she has magic or not, that will be the case until my dying day. All the young-uns in our town train to defend themselves. But she's pushed harder than the rest—because she's mine, and she must." Jack didn't know if the Breaker understood, but the young man nodded as if he did.

"It's good you're letting her learn to take care of herself. I wish I had that chance," Blaise remarked.

Remorse seeped through the kid's tone. Jack frowned. *Don't trick me into thinking you're a broken thing. You're still dangerous.* "I'll let Emmaline work with you. Two days a week to start." Jack rocked on his heels. "But if you do anything to harm her, I'll make that punch in the face seem like a love tap."

Blaise rubbed his jaw, and Jack felt a grim satisfaction at the sight of a bead of sweat on the kid's forehead. "Understood."

In a flurry of wings, Oberidon touched down on the road in front of the bakery. Emmaline looked at them expectantly. "Time's up. Did y'all behave?"

"I stuck to my promise, if that's what you're asking," Jack told her. "Two days a week, Emmaline. That's what you get."

She crowed as she jumped off Oby's back, punching the air with her fists. The sheer joy of it made Jack's face crack into a brief smile. He liked to see Emmaline happy. She raced over and plowed into him, wrapping her arms around him so fiercely he staggered under her enthusiasm. "Thank you!" She rested her head against his shoulder, and for a moment his irritation melted away.

Then he remembered Blaise's presence. He pulled back from his daughter. "I'll be watching. And if I see anything I don't like, this tomfoolery ends."

Emmaline's face fell, and Jack almost wanted to take back his words. *Almost.* But he didn't. She nodded to him, then stepped over to her pegasus.

Jack sighed. Why did he feel like he was still pushing her away? Figuring out how to interact with his daughter was becoming harder and harder. And he hated to admit it, but he couldn't blame *that* on Blaise.

CHAPTER THIRTEEN
Free Market Pegasi

Blaise

*B*laise learned many things while getting the bakery up and running. First, running a business was a lot harder than it looked from the outside. It took two weeks to get the building ready to open from its original state of disarray. Second, he discovered that he—much to his dismay—had to become one of the dreaded *"morning people"*. Gone were the days of lingering in his bed until the sun's glare woke him. It made working his shift at the Broken Horn difficult. But he didn't want to leave Clover short-handed.

With the bakery, his days began before the sun was even a suggestion on the horizon. He moved his belongings from the uncomfortably decorated room at the saloon (he had never found time to redecorate) to a loft room situated over the bakery. On the plus side, the new living arrangements meant he didn't have to go very far after stumbling out of bed each morning.

Every day began the same. He pulled on clean clothes, then covered them with a white smock and cap. For the agreed-upon two mornings each week, Emmaline joined him at the outrageous hour, and despite her wide yawns, she never complained. She rubbed the sleep from her eyes and listened as Blaise explained how to build the fire to heat the oven.

Blaise had to relearn how to build the fire himself—he was rusty from months out of practice. He had thought getting fire-wood would be problematic. It pleased Blaise to discover that, although Itude was in an arid area, the town had steady access to firewood thanks to the local Greenmage, Uriah Jackson. Jackson lived on one of the area farms, and Emmaline helped Blaise make his acquaintance and work out the details of a steady firewood delivery. Jackson, a pleasant older man boasting a halo of frizzy grey hair and the grit of permanent dirt beneath his fingernails, was much obliged.

While the fire blazed to life in the oven, Blaise demonstrated how to mix the dough for bread, knead, and shape it into loaves on a sturdy wooden table. When that job was complete, they set them near the oven's warmth to rise.

Emmaline was a quick study. Her attention never flagged as they moved from one task to the next. Once the bread was in the oven, Blaise showed her how to prepare the other items he planned to bake. Through trial and error, he found it worked best to bake cakes or pies after the loaves of bread were removed from the oven.

The final recipe of the day was Clover's cookies. He had to admit that Clover was right about how delicious they were. They were chock full of melty deliciousness with the addition of the semi-sweet chocolate.

When Blaise officially opened the bakery on a crisp autumn morning, he underestimated the popularity of his business. The response gobsmacked him. As far as he could tell, everyone in Itude was in line at the door. Even Jack.

Blaise blew out a nervous breath. Emmaline was beside him, and she fidgeted with the end of her ponytail as she peered out. "Ready to open?"

Blaise licked his lips. He glanced at his bare hands, afraid they would betray him. His magic lay quiescent below the skin, calmed by the morning's baking. "May as well."

Soon the murmur of customers filled the bakery, accompanied by the sweet, yeasty aroma of fresh-baked bread that fell over the building like a warm blanket. Blaise stayed busy as Emmaline gathered up orders and took payment. He tried not to glance up as the line wove through the bakery. The hum of voices was constant and worry seized him.

These people were here for *his* bakery. What if they liked nothing he made? What if something went wrong? Panic smoldered, causing his stomach to clench. His palms itched.

No. He closed his eyes and took a calming breath. Focused on the dust of flour coating his skin. Vixen said he was getting *good.* He could control the magic. It belonged to him. He was the master. Not the other way around.

"Blaise? You okay?" He heard Emmaline's boots tap on the floor as she shifted in his direction. Blaise nodded, eyes flitting open as he shot a glance over his shoulder.

Wildfire Jack stood at the counter, cold eyes moving from the display case full of fresh-baked goods to Blaise and back again. Watching. Judging.

Blaise swallowed. The magic settled down in his hands, going dormant. He lifted his chin. "I'm good. Was just thinking about something."

Emmaline handed her father his order. Blaise had half a mind to wish Jack would choke on it but banished the thought. That wasn't kind. He decided that taking the high road was the better option when dealing with Jack. Besides, Jack *would* blame him if he choked on his food.

By the end of the morning, he and Emmaline were bushed. Almost everything they had prepared for the morning sold. Emmaline dragged a chair over, sitting down and pulling off her boots. "If every day is like that, you're gonna need more help."

"That's the truth." Blaise slouched in a chair. Besides his feet hurting, he had a headache from worry.

"I might know someone," Emmaline said, cocking her head. "Nadine's son, Reuben. A few years older than me."

Blaise tipped his head back and groaned. "I don't need the town Healer wanting me dead."

Emmaline laughed. "Nadine likes you. I think."

Blaise tapped his fingers against the countertop, considering. It couldn't be any worse than Jack. "I suppose it wouldn't hurt to ask."

The next thing he knew he had a second employee. Reuben was gangly, taller than Blaise and still growing into his body. He didn't have any magic, and it pleased him to help at the bakery. Anything was better than learning medicine from his mother, he said. Turned out, Reuben was squeamish. Blaise didn't blame him.

They settled into a routine. Emmaline cast a spell only a daughter could get away with—she convinced Jack to let her work at the bakery daily. She reported to Blaise that her father said the food was *"decent"*, which she translated as *"pretty darn good"*. Blaise couldn't decide if Jack liked their baked goods or if he was just adamant about keeping tabs on them. He stopped by the bakery every morning for bread or a donut.

As far as Blaise could tell, everyone in town enjoyed the items from the bakery. But the pegasi were their biggest fans, because of their famous sweet tooth. Every morning, Emrys and Oberidon stood outside the window at the back of the bakery. Blaise discovered the stallions were taking orders from the other pegasi. Emmaline or Reuben would fill a bag with their order and hand it to them through the window. Most mornings, both stallions ended up with a bag to carry back to the stables.

"They're paying for that, right?" Blaise asked, rubbing at his forehead as he watched Emrys trot off.

"Yup," Emmaline said with a grin. "Your Emrys has the banker move the amount from his or Oby's account to yours each day. And the banker moves the funds from the other pegasi accounts to Emrys's and Oby's."

Blaise furrowed his brow. He still thought it odd the pegasi were interested in money, but they seemed invested in the idea. "Wait. Are Emrys and Oby making *money* off us?"

<We charge a delivery fee,> Emrys said, indignant. His voice was distant—likely almost back at the stables.

Blaise shook his head. Would wonders never cease?

THE BAKERY HAD BEEN OPEN FOR A MONTH WHEN CLOVER INVITED Blaise to sit with her at the bar before the start of his shift. "I am letting you go." She rested her arms atop the expanse of wood, her thick fingers threaded together.

Blaise's eyes widened, and his stomach clenched with worry. Had he done something wrong? Clover straightened, laying one of her enormous hands on his shoulder, a reassuring gesture. "Not because you do a poor job, but the opposite." Clover gestured to the pristine kitchen counters. "Between your work at the bakery, practice with Vixen, and your shift here, you are running yourself ragged."

Blaise's shoulders slumped. He didn't want to admit it, but she was right. His last few sessions with Vixen had been abysmal. Whatever progress he had made slid backwards as he stumbled through each day fighting off exhaustion. "I don't want to leave you short."

Clover lowered her horns, an acknowledgment. "We'll be fine. It's your turn to take care of yourself and your fledgling business."

He stared at the woodgrain of the bar as he tried to come up with excuses to stay. Excuses that hid the truth of the matter. "I enjoy working with you." And he *needed* to fill his days and evenings. It meant less time to be alone with his thoughts. Was he exhausted by his schedule? Yes. But he preferred that to the alternative.

Clover laid a hand on his shoulder. "You are one of the kindest humans I've met—and you do not know what a compliment that is, coming from me. If it makes you feel any better, you can help a few times a week. But you've dropped weight from when you first came into town, and that is odd since you work at a bakery."

Blaise glanced down at his slender belly. His arms had gained muscle tone from all of his work, but he kept so busy he didn't eat much. When he ate alone, dark memories burdened him. Things in his life that he couldn't do anything about; couldn't change.

"Okay, Clover," Blaise agreed, his voice soft. Conflicting emotions warred within him. Rest in between his obligations would help. But it would also allow too much time to think. Clover's unwavering brown eyes watched as he slid from the stool and gave her a half-hearted wave.

Blaise slipped out of the saloon at the time he would have normally started his shift. Vixen waylaid him, lurking just outside the door.

"Howdy, Blaise. Let's go." She jerked her head, encouraging him to walk with her.

He took a step back, surprised by her sudden presence. "Where are we going?"

The red-haired outlaw grinned. "Practice. I heard you have time on your hands."

Blaise shook his head. "That's not a good idea."

Vixen tilted her head to one side, hands on her hips. "It's the best idea. Let's go break something."

"Wait. What?" He scowled. This was contrary to the normal focus of his lessons: preventing his magic from doing any harm.

"It's the natural progression of things." Vixen steered him

toward the bakery, his safe place. It was quiet in the afternoons—
Blaise closed up shop after lunch since he worked early mornings.
"You've spent too much time not using your magic. Time to focus
on *using* it."

"But I don't want to," he protested as Vixen shouldered open
the door.

She tut-tutted as she covered his preparation table with a cloth
he hadn't even noticed she had tucked beneath her arm. "You said
you wanted to learn control. This is part of that. Hang on." Vixen
slipped out the door, boot heels tapping as she jogged around to
the back, reappearing a moment later with a crate filled with
different objects. The sly fox had come prepared.

Wrapping paper crinkled as Vixen pulled a cracked blue and
white porcelain teapot from the top. "You've spent so long pulling
the magic back in, you gotta learn how to push it out when you
need to." She rested the teapot on the table between them.

Blaise eyed the teapot like it was a rattlesnake. "I don't know
when I'd ever need to."

She leaned forward, ginger hair brushing the top of the teapot.
"Oh? How 'bout the time you ran from those soldiers? Seemed
mighty helpful then."

Blaise's gut clenched, and he dropped his gaze. Pinpricks of
stress knotted the back of his neck. *Not that.* Nightmares of that
day still haunted his dreams. "It was an accident."

Her silver eyes twinkled, fierce. "Confederation *soldiers* were
after you. They weren't planning to invite you for afternoon tea,
ninny."

Blaise put his elbows on the table, resting his chin in his hands.
"I know. I know that. But it doesn't make what happened *right*.
Those soldiers—they were someone's son. Maybe a husband or
father. Who am I to take that away?"

Vixen shook her head, sorrowful. "You can't be so nice. That's
going to end up getting you hurt. Or worse."

He appreciated what she was trying to do. He understood. But
that didn't mean he liked it. His desire to not hurt others set him

apart from those soldiers. Vixen was an outlaw, and he couldn't expect her to understand. "My magic has hurt enough people. Does yours hurt people?"

She gave him a considering look. "It can, depending on how I use it. It's all in the intent, Blaise. Did you intend to kill anyone?"

No. "I just wanted them to stop chasing me. To leave me and my family alone." *And I failed at even doing that.*

Vixen tapped her index finger against the teapot. "Right. And what happened because you couldn't control it?"

He gritted his teeth, tightness growing in his shoulders and back. Blaise could almost hear the sickening sound of the massive oak crashing down. "I probably killed someone."

She snapped her fingers. "Exactly. If you'd practice, you coulda done it without squabashing anyone."

What? Blaise blinked, shaken out of the conversation by the unfamiliar word.

Vixen laughed. "Means killing."

Blaise made a face. *That's colorful.* Then he refocused on what she'd said. "Wait. You're saying if I practice breaking things *on purpose,* I can use this curse of mine with more forethought?"

"You got it." She grinned. "It's like learning to shoot a gun. At first, your aim's gonna be off, and anyone near you is in danger. But afore long, you can hit your mark."

"Terrible example, since I've never shot a gun."

Vixen rolled her eyes. "Surprised Jack doesn't give you grief over that alone."

"He's not aware yet. And I'm better off if you don't tell him."

She canted her head. "I won't tell him so long as you break the things I brought here. On purpose."

Resigned, Blaise ran one thumb against the edge of his trim beard. "Hope you realize how ridiculous that sounds."

Unabashed, she shoved the teapot closer to his side. Just to be difficult, he was tempted to give the teapot a hard knock against the edge of the table. But Vixen wouldn't let him get away with such a childish move. Besides, she made a good point. It would be nice to have options beyond dropping unexpected trees on people. "Okay, but give me an idea of what to expect. How does it work for you with your magic?"

Vixen settled back in her chair. She wore her signature glasses, but pulled them off briefly before settling them back on the bridge of her nose. "My glasses serve the same purpose as your gloves. It dampens the effect of any magic I don't keep under wraps." She pursed her lips, thoughtful as she puzzled out how to explain it to him. "Being a Persuader differs from being a Breaker. I'm trying to work on minds, not physical things. For me, it's eye contact."

"Oh. So for me, it's skin contact." Blaise drummed his fingers against the table.

Vixen nodded. "Right. And magic has rules. I can't control anyone's mind, even though that's what most people think I do. I don't. What I *can* do is push my ideas and perceptions onto them. Suggest things. Make them think we're best friends. I can get people to relax and talk about things they may not otherwise say. But I can't make anyone put a gun to their head and pull the trigger, unless they already had some notion of that floating around in their head."

Blaise gaped. Her magic was daunting. She didn't mean to spook him; she was just laying out the ground rules of her magic. His magic had rules, too. "Okay."

"Far as I know, all mages share one rule: you can only hold so much magic at one time, and when you use it, it can take a while to replenish. Use too much too fast, and you run dry." She slanted her keen gaze at him. "Your magic ever run low?"

Blaise snorted, shaking his head. "Not even sure what that would feel like. You?"

Vixen chewed on her bottom lip. "Once. When I escaped. Had to use so much, I ran out. Makes you feel exhausted, like a nap and a good meal are the best idea." She picked up the teapot and thrust it over to him, punctuating the end of her sentence. "Enough of that. Let's try this."

He took the teapot from her, holding it gingerly. He had questions. From who—or what—had she escaped? Judging by the jut of her jaw, he wouldn't discover more on that topic today. Was it possible he wasn't the only one in Itude plagued by dark thoughts?

"Well? What are you waiting for, moss to grow over us?" Vixen asked.

Blaise's forehead wrinkled, focusing on the cool smoothness of the teapot. His magic swam beneath his skin, like fish beneath the glassy surface of a pond. Blaise sat there for a moment, marveling at the sensation of magic pooled, waiting for his command. No longer leaking from him with abandon. It stayed put, obedient as a hunting hound, ready to let fly. Blaise hadn't thought it possible.

Vixen cleared her throat, reminding him she was waiting.

He called on his magic, and it rose to the surface. Too much. More than necessary. And it was *fast* as a striking rattlesnake—too quick to call back. Blaise felt it flow from his fingers and into the porcelain, washing over the teapot. His fingers scrabbled, trying in vain to call some of it back.

The teapot imploded into a fine powder, crumbling through his hands like sand. Blaise pulled his hands apart, shaking off the grit. His heart pounded a furious rhythm in his chest.

Vixen's jaw hung open. "You didn't break it. You *squabashed* it."

Blaise winced. "Is that good?"

She eyed the remains of the teapot, skeptical. "Mmm. Looks like another aspect of your control needs work."

Blaise sighed.

CHAPTER FOURTEEN
Second Chance

Jack

"Wildfire Jack, sir! A moment, please."

<Ignore him or stop?> Zepheus flitted an ear backward at the sound of Hank Walker's voice. The stallion arched his neck as he awaited Jack's answer.

Jack gritted his teeth, biting back a curse. He had spent the morning making preparations for the run he and Zepheus were about to take—a stagecoach loaded down with Confederation gold was in striking range. Jack and Kur had moved a transport wagon into position, and the Theilian was waiting for him to make his move. The stagecoach wasn't going to rob itself.

"May as well stop," Jack groused, hoping this wouldn't take too much of his time. At his command, the palomino pivoted, stirring up a whirl of dust that blew into the postmaster's face, spurring a coughing fit.

"What is it, Walker?" Jack crossed his wrists over the pommel of his saddle, the reins loose in his hands.

Walker jogged up, eyes squinting against the dust. He huffed and wheezed from the exertion. By Jack's guess, the postmaster had at least ten years on him, which put him at roughly a half-century old. It must have been a ghastly time. Wrinkles lined his pudgy face. Walker wasn't wearing a hat, and the late morning sun beat down on his bald pate, the breeze whipping his wisps of grey hair about.

Walker held up a bundle of rolled papers in one hand and offered them to Jack. "Got some new bulletins for you. And . . . you told me to keep an ear out. See what I could find out about the Confederates."

That captured Jack's attention. He slid out of the saddle, patting Zepheus's neck in a *pay close attention* signal. Walker was the only mage in town the pegasi didn't like. As useful as he was for a spy, Jack wasn't foolish enough to dismiss the pegasi's misgivings about him. Zepheus's head dipped into a relaxed position, but he kept one ear swiveled in the postmaster's direction.

Jack scanned the street for anyone who might eavesdrop. Itude was full of nosy gossips. One of the ranch hands from the neighboring farms swaggered out of the barbershop, heading across the street to the stables. Gus Pembroke opened the door to the bank, pausing long enough to give Jack and Walker a polite nod before going inside. Once the immediate area was clear, Jack turned back to the postmaster, holding out his hand. "Learn something about the situation we spoke of before?"

Walker offered the bulletins to him. "I did. I found them. They're near the border of Desina and the Tombstone River. Going to get hemmed in by the Salties before too long."

Jack narrowed his eyes, thinking. At times like this, he wished he had a clearer idea of how the postmaster's magic worked. Jack knew he could transfer inanimate objects between points—that was how the bulk of their mail got to its destinations. "Can you bring them here?"

Walker shook his head. "No."

Zepheus's head jerked up as if annoyed by a fly. <That may not be true.>

Jack stroked the stallion's mane. As much as he'd like to call Walker on his bullshit, it was difficult to do so. No two mages were the same, even if they shared the same magic. Jack had no hope of knowing all the rules that bound Hank. There was the possibility that Hank had tried that move before, and it hadn't gone well. Might not be worth the risk.

That made rescue more challenging. But it was still on the table. "Who're the mages?"

"Two women and a half-grown boy."

Jack's pulse quickened. *Two women.* Could one of them be her? He wanted to ask what they looked like, but that would seem like a ridiculous question. What did it matter, in the grand scheme of things? *It matters to me.* Even so, he held back the question.

Instead, he gave a firm nod. "Right. Once I'm ready to make my move, I'll need you to rendezvous with them, to get them to stay put, and then place a marker. Can you do that?"

"Shouldn't be a problem," Walker agreed.

Jack studied him. Something in the way the postmaster acquiesced with calm assurance jarred him. Walker was one of his more reluctant operatives, and Jack often had to follow up with him for updates and information. "Not a problem?"

Walker shifted his weight but stood his ground. "I have my own reasons to want this to work out."

"That so?" Jack glowered, suspicious.

The postmaster cleared his throat, eyes wide in alarm. "You misunderstand. My brother. I'm doing this for my brother."

Jack's shoulders eased. "What's he look like? You think he's in Desina?"

"Desina or Mella," Walker clarified. "Joshua looks like me, but five years younger."

Jack inclined his head in acknowledgment. "I'll keep an eye out."

The postmaster blinked in surprise. "Appreciate it."

Jack nodded, and Walker took it as a dismissal and stepped away. That was fine by Jack. He watched the postmaster walk back to the post office, then shook his head as he considered his next steps.

Zepheus arched his neck. <That man makes me twitchy.>

"You 'n' me both." Jack hated that his most reliable informant was one who he didn't fully trust. So far, Walker hadn't fed him any worthless information. And if the postmaster knew what was good for him, he never would.

With Walker gone, Jack unrolled the bulletins and paged through them. They were bits of mail intended for other recipients but pilfered by Walker at Jack's direction. Technically, as a postmaster, doing so would get Walker into a heap of trouble. But as long as no one else knew, Jack didn't care. Information was vital.

It was the usual stuff. The bulletins sent through the mail to the field commanders were generally ripe with inconsequential information, and when Walker could scrounge them up, Jack mined them for what little he could. There was one in this batch, carrying news of disturbing weaponry advancements that the Salt-Iron Confederation's engineers were developing. Rapidfire guns? Flying vessels called *warbirds*? He grimaced.

A sheaf of updated Wanted posters fell away from the back of the bundle. "Wonder how much I'm worth now." Jack skimmed through them, disappointed. Nothing new for him. Some faces were familiar—outlaw mages he had tried to recruit, but who had eventually set out for other towns. The last poster was a *very* familiar face, however.

A poor sketch of Blaise stared back at him. The words *Wanted Dead or Alive* framed the top of the kid's portrait. Below it read: *For the Murders of Two of The Confederation's Finest.*

"Huh," Jack murmured, scratching the bristles on his chin. "So the kid really killed somebody." He was always pleased to read about the Salties losing any of their number, but this news conflicted him. He still didn't trust the Breaker's magic, even if he was training with Vixen.

<Should I head back to the stable and get untacked?> Zepheus interrupted his train of thought.

Jack pulled out his pocket watch, flipping it open. It was nearly noon. Tempting as it was to lay the groundwork immediately to look for the mavericks, Jack also needed to do his part to keep Itude financially stable.

"Nah. It would take time for Kur to bring the wagon back anyway, and he'll need to attend the meeting I'm calling." Jack felt around in his pocket and found his yellow bandanna, taking it out and tying it around his face. His fingers fumbled with the knot as he thought about the mavericks.

Zepheus nudged Jack with his nose. <Don't set yourself up for disappointment. You know the odds are good Kittie won't be one of them.>

Jack scowled. "Don't care. I'm going to keep trying until I find something. Until I find her," he corrected himself.

The palomino bobbed his head. <And I will be by your side until you do.>

Jack couldn't help but think that most of the time, he didn't deserve Zepheus. He rolled the bulletins up and tucked them into the saddlebag for safe keeping. Then he put his foot in the stirrup and swung into the saddle.

"ARE YOU OUT OF YOUR ALL-FIRED MINDS?" JACK SHOULD HAVE known that the easy agreement of the other Ringleaders to his plan was a bad sign. Nothing was ever simple. It was a miracle that Jack even managed to convene a meeting the next morning without argument.

Despite serving as the informal spymaster for Itude, the other

Ringleaders always analyzed any information he brought to them. Jack didn't mind that part—it was shrewd, to be sure. Keeping Itude safe was Jack's priority and the way he saw it, the more eyes on that goal, the better. However, he preferred that they agree with him when he had strong opinions on the matter at hand.

Everyone was receptive to his idea to rendezvous with the fleeing mavericks in Desina and bring them to Itude. If the Salt-Iron Confederation was coming, they could use every bit of magic in their arsenal. But with Confederation soldiers in Desina, they were hesitant to send anyone into the nation. Every single qualified mage in town had a bounty on their heads. The price of failure was high.

And the other Ringleaders, to Jack's utter amazement, thought it was a good idea to send the *Breaker* along with him on a mission.

"He's from Desina," Raven reasoned, rubbing his fingers over a golden coin. Before the meeting started, they had divvied up the haul that Jack and Kur had brought in the previous day. "He may know things we don't."

Jack ground his teeth. "Then consult with him. Don't send a greenhorn along with me." Sure, he saw the logic in sending along someone familiar with the country. But why did that someone have to be Blaise?

"It's a good chance to see what he is made of," Kur Agur said, his tone infuriatingly reasonable. "It's a common practice among the Theilians to send new pack members on an easy hunt. Builds their confidence and fosters working relationships." He bared his fangs in the semblance of a smile for emphasis. "And if the Salt-Iron Confederation is truly as close as you have heard, this may be the last easy hunt."

"We're not hunting a sick antelope—which I doubt Blaise could do. Sending him with me will only slow me down and put us both in danger." Jack crossed his arms.

Vixen drummed her nails against the table, drawing everyone's attention. "Do you even know what he can do? 'Cause *I* do."

"I do, too." He pulled the *Wanted* poster out of his pocket and unfolded it, tossing it across the table to her.

Vixen picked it up and smoothed it flat, scanning the words before looking up at him. "Everyone in this room has blood on their hands. You could choke a river with yours."

That was the truth. But Jack wasn't the one on trial here. He had proven his dedication to Itude many times over. "I don't want him dropping a damn tree at the wrong time."

Vixen scoffed. "Here I thought you knew everything—but it seems you don't. That maverick has *control* now. Leastwise, more than he did when he first got here."

Jack snorted. That didn't take much.

Raven studied the map of Desina on the wall, hands clasped behind his back. "Jack. What if we made a deal?"

Now that was interesting. Jack lifted his chin, considering. "Depends on the deal."

Nadine, who had kept her opinions to herself, hissed. Jack glanced at her—she had some idea of what Raven was all about. "I told you that's hardly fair."

Jack bit back a growl. Damn the lot of them. They must have discussed this and left him out of the loop. But if Nadine didn't like it.... He smiled. It was something that would give Jack an edge.

Raven ignored Nadine, turning to Jack. "It's no secret you hate Blaise. You've been trying to run him out of town from the start, and to be honest, it's irritating the rest of us because you're itchy as a shaved cat." He stalked closer, laying his hands flat against the table. "Take Blaise along with you. If it doesn't go well and you still want him gone, then we'll arrange for him to travel to Asylum."

Jack's brows flew up. That was . . . well, he hadn't expected that. There must be a catch. "I'm listening."

"If it goes well, then you have to stop harassing him. It doesn't make the rest of the Ring look good when you're baiting him and no one else can see why. His magic has caused no problems. His bakery is popular."

My bakery, Jack groused, but kept it to himself. Blaise was just using his building. But that was beside the point. "And if I don't?"

Nadine took over for Raven. "Then I hate to say it, but we'd have to ask *you* to leave town."

He flew up from his seat, slamming his palms against the table so hard they stung. "You can't do that. I brought this town back from *nothing.*"

The other four Ringleaders met him with calm expressions. Raven shook his head. "It's in the charter. The one *you* agreed to years ago."

He growled, frustrated. But then he had a thought. It was a gamble, but the odds were weighted in *his* favor, not Blaise's. Jack had a lot more savvy than Blaise.

Jack settled down in his chair. "Fine. I agree." He paused, looking at Vixen. "If his magic gets me killed, I'm telling Butch to raise me just so I can haunt you for a few years."

She met his words with a mischievous grin. "Don't worry your pretty head about that. He's gonna be solid."

Jack canted his head, doubtful. That remained to be seen. "Then you should probably tell the kid what we're doing, Vix. He's like to piss his pants if I tell him."

CHAPTER FIFTEEN
Just Outlaw Things

Blaise

laise stared at Vixen, jaw gaping. "You can't be serious."
The fire-haired outlaw had stopped by the bakery before the normal practice session, and Blaise, Emmaline, and Reuben were cleaning up after a busy morning. Reuben pretended not to eavesdrop and continued to work, but Emmaline stopped sweeping and set the broom aside when she heard her father's name mentioned.

Vixen took a bite of the cookie she had bought before dropping the news, savoring the flavor before speaking. "You're a mage, Blaise. And you have considerable magic. This will be an excellent test. It doesn't get much easier."

"That's not . . ." Blaise wasn't sure how to explain it to her. The mission she proposed was far outside the realm of things he was comfortable trying. "I didn't come here to use my magic and do . . . outlaw things. Can't I just bake in peace?" He kept the whine out of his voice. Mostly.

Vixen nibbled on her cookie. "Mmm, this is good. And this isn't an outlaw thing. We're not asking you to rob a stagecoach, though I guess we could arrange that if you'd rather."

"*No!*"

She grinned, pleased to have tugged his tail. "This is to help people. Maverick mages. People just like *you*, from Desina. They're probably scared out of their minds. You know a thing or two about that, I reckon."

Blaise frowned. Blasted Vixen, playing on his empathy. Of *course*, he knew what that was like. He tried to forget, but he never would. It was too raw, too personal.

The potential to help others in the same predicament appealed to a tiny sliver of his persona. But not if it meant going with Wildfire Jack.

"I don't see how I'd be any help if things got ugly," Blaise reasoned. "I can't shoot a gun."

"First off, if Jack plays his cards right, this won't get ugly. Only Raven is better at sneaking around, and that's 'cause of Raven's shadow-hopping magic. And if things turn sour . . . well, Jack's seen more than his share of fights. He's a hard one to bring down."

Blaise glanced at Emmaline, who was paying close attention. She grimaced at the mention of her father in fights, her eyes troubled. It was probably difficult, having a father who always flirted with danger.

"And if that happens, someone with more experience should be along." Blaise didn't want to be responsible for anything happening to Emmaline's father.

Vixen waved a hand. "It won't. They'll be close to the border, so it should be easy." Her expression sobered. "Everyone who lives here learns to defend Itude, Blaise. *Everyone.* This is a simple way to start."

Judging by her tone, Blaise assumed the decision was made, regardless of his feelings. He didn't like that, but there was no way around it—aside from flat-out refusing. He wasn't sure what the repercussions for that might be. It would be easy for them to force him to leave. And that would be heartbreaking, after he had worked so hard to carve his little niche with the bakery.

No, he couldn't let his dream go so easily. There was no telling what else lay out there for him if he left Itude.

"I'll do it," Blaise relented. "Does Wildfire Jack know, or am I going to end up with another black eye for my troubles?"

"He knows," Vixen confirmed. She didn't say it, but by the slash of her brows, Blaise surmised Jack wasn't happy with the arrangement, either. Curiouser and curiouser.

"I wish he wouldn't go." Emmaline's lips puffed out with concern.

Vixen gave her an encouraging look. "It's going to be easy-peasy, Em. It'll be no more than two days—they'll have the pegasi. And you know Zeph won't let anything happen to your daddy, either."

Blaise groaned. He had forgotten about the pegasi. Flying was not one of his favorite things, despite Emrys's best efforts. Then he thought about what she had just said—two days. "The towns-people won't be happy if the bakery is closed for two days."

Vixen gestured to Reuben and Emmaline. "You sure? You seem to have two very capable folks working with you."

Blaise frowned. She had a point—both teenagers were quick studies, and even though Reuben wasn't as confident as Emma-line, he wasn't bad. Their inexperience wasn't an excuse. The crit-icism would tear them down, and he appreciated the hard work they contributed. Vixen had backed him into a corner he couldn't get out of without making them look incompetent. That was not only unfair; it was untrue.

And then he realized something else. Vixen was clever. Emma-line had latched onto her words, too, and she bounced on her feet, distracted from her father's mission.

"We can do it, Blaise! Might have to ask for an excuse from

school for those two days—but it shouldn't be a bother. Right, Reuben?" Emmaline elbowed the older teen.

Reuben blinked, Adam's apple bobbing with uncertainty. "Um, right?"

Blaise scowled at Vixen, who returned it with a wide-toothed smile. She looked like she had won a game of Wild Dragon. "I'm fine with it if Jack and Nadine agree."

"They'll agree," Vixen said sweetly.

He rubbed his forehead. "When do we leave?"

"Tomorrow morning."

Damn.

"DON'T FORGET TO—"

"Sweep out the embers after I take out the last loaves of bread. I know, I know." Emmaline flung a flour-covered hand over her shoulder, a shushing motion if Blaise ever saw one.

"We got this. Go be a hero." Reuben grinned as he ran a fresh cleaning cloth across the top of the display case.

Blaise shook his head, feeling anything but heroic. He would rather stay and hide in the bakery. This business of taking part in a rescue—risky or not—wasn't for a baker like Blaise. Strange enough to think someone like *Wildfire Jack* would go to anyone's rescue.

To be fair, Blaise suspected that in some ways, the outlaw was softer than he let on. Not that Blaise would ever tell him so. Offhanded things Clover had said in the past made Blaise think he had rescued her from an unpleasant situation. She didn't speak of it often, but she was steadfastly loyal to the man. Even if she had to knock sense into him on occasion.

If that were the case, Wildfire Jack would keep his eyes on the outcome and not give Blaise as much grief as he might otherwise.

At least that was what Blaise hoped. He turned to gather his bag, but a tiny form on the windowsill caught his attention. He leaned over, curious. It was a doll, no longer than his thumb.

"What's that?"

Emmaline pursed her lips, ducking her head with embarrassment as she dusted her flour-covered hands on her apron. "Daddy gave me that when I was small. I keep it with me whenever he leaves. Makes me feel better."

Further proof that Wildfire Jack wasn't as hard-boiled as he pretended to be. Blaise was glad for that. Emmaline deserved kindness from her father. She didn't speak about him often, but from what Blaise could discern, her relationship with her father was strained. He imagined it was difficult to be Wildfire Jack's daughter. Maybe even harder than being Wildfire Jack's hated enemy.

"Shake a leg, before Daddy comes looking for you. Not a good idea to start the day on his nasty side." Emmaline flourished a rolling pin in his direction, a mocking threat.

Blaise grimaced. She was right. He strode across the checkered floor and picked up his travel bag from the base of the steep stairs that led to his loft. He paused, checking to make sure he had everything. Blaise wore a long-sleeved shirt, denim jeans, and sturdy boots. His dark blue duster was slung over one arm, his hat on his head, and a bandanna in his pocket. Earlier that morning, he had tucked a canvas sack with leftovers from the previous day into the travel bag. A full canteen sloshed in the same sack.

With his check complete, he headed out to the stables. Blaise discovered Emrys and Zepheus waiting for their riders in the stable yard, both tacked and ready to go. It was normal to see Zepheus saddled. Emrys was a different issue. Blaise didn't own a saddle or bridle.

Blaise walked over, noting the fine tooling on the rich mahogany leather of the saddle. He ran a hand over it, admiring the star-shaped basket-weave pattern that a talented artisan had embossed on the leather. Blaise hadn't seen an outlaw saddle up close before, and he noticed how the design differed from a normal saddle to allow the pegasus to have full range of motion for their wings. The skirt at the front of the saddle slanted back at an angle, and a breast collar complete with wither strap to prevent the equipment from fouling the wings secured everything in place.

A pair of flight goggles hung from the saddlehorn, the brass fittings winking in the early morning sunshine. "Where did this come from, Emrys?"

Emrys craned his neck to look at him, the metal pieces of the matching hackamore that graced his head jingling with the movement. <I bought it. Figured we needed a proper kit.>

"*You* bought it?" Blaise asked, bewildered.

<I bought it.> The stallion sounded smug. In the morning light, tiny starbursts of silver gleamed on the bridle.

He didn't have time for further questions. Zepheus shifted his posture as Wildfire Jack came around the corner, saddlebags perched on his shoulders. The outlaw's eyes settled on Blaise, and he saw a brief sign of chagrin.

"Surprised you showed up," the outlaw said, giving voice to his thoughts. "There's room in your saddlebags for anything you might need to add." He dumped one saddlebag into Blaise's arms.

"Good morning to you, too. And I'm here because this town gave me a second chance, so I figure I'll help however I can." Blaise took the leather bag, not hazarding a look at Wildfire Jack's face. Judging by the weight, one side of the pack was already full. Curious, Blaise peered inside and saw a pair of first aid kits. He heard the gentle slosh of alchemical potions and pulled them out, checking the labels.

"Why do I have two?" Blaise asked, holding up the kits.

The corners of Wildfire Jack's lips pulled back in irritation. "Put those back. We may need them for the mavericks if they're injured. And you have two because my bags are already full. Extra cartridges."

That drew Blaise's attention to the outlaw's new gun belt, the cartridge loops full all the way around his waist. The sight made him uneasy, but he tamped down his nerves. No doubt Jack was trying subtle intimidation. "My mother was an alchemist, specializing in medicinal potions. I was checking to see what we had."

Jack gave him a considering look. "And what do you think?"

The question surprised Blaise, and he almost dropped a vial—which would *not* have inspired any confidence. "Um." He wrapped the vial in its protective cotton wrapping and tucked it into the kit, surveying the array of potions as he did so. Pleased, he noted that he was familiar with everything in the kit. There were potions to treat injuries from burns to cuts or breaks. But there was something missing. "It looks good. I would add Faedra's Embrace. Mom always kept it on hand in case we needed it."

Wildfire Jack canted his head, and Blaise realized the outlaw was unfamiliar with the potion. "What's it do?"

"Helps stabilize patients with critical injuries." Blaise relished feeling competent about a topic other than baking. "One of our neighbors had a horrendous accident with his thresher last year." Blaise shuddered at the memory of Jethro Whitt's arm entrapped in the thresher. He could almost hear Jethro's wail and the drip of his blood on the sheaves of wheat. "Anyway, Faedra's Embrace was the only thing that kept him around long enough to get freed and taken to the doctor in town."

Wildfire Jack raised his brows. If he was wondering about the wisdom of letting a Breaker anywhere near an accident of that magnitude, he didn't mention it. Blaise couldn't help but wonder —if he could have controlled his magic then, could he have freed the man sooner? Something worth thinking about.

"Might be worthwhile to have around. Side effects?" the outlaw asked.

Blaise chewed his bottom lip, thinking. He knew the benefits of most of the potions, and their contents. Side effects were another matter—and every potion had something. The miracle of alchemy balanced out in that it wasn't always pleasant. He thought back to Jethro's accident. After they had loaded him onto a wagon and stabilized him, he wouldn't stop talking. Blaise didn't know a lot about Jethro, but he recalled that the older man was usually quiet. That was out of character enough to be an effect from the potion.

"I don't remember all of them, but I think compulsive talking is one."

Wildfire Jack wrinkled his nose in distaste. "I'll see if the mercantile has it and then pray we don't need to use it on anyone. Wait here."

Blaise repacked his saddle bags, adding his items. The outlaw had packed a canteen of water and a bag of food that included hard biscuits, dried strips of meat, and fruits. Blaise thought the fruit might be emergency rations for the pegasi.

Jack returned a few minutes later, handing the red vial of Faedra's Embrace to Blaise. He packed it in the first aid kit with the others, nestling it into the protective cotton wrappings. That done, he looked up, up, up at Emrys's tall back. His stomach lurched.

"Hold up." Blaise glanced back as Wildfire Jack strode over. He scrutinized the saddle and tugged at the girth. "Some pegasi are jokers. They suck in air when you tighten the girth. Then when you mount, the saddle slips and you go face down in the dirt. Sometimes that doesn't happen until you're airborne."

<I wouldn't do that!> Emrys snorted, stamping a rear hoof in offense.

The outlaw shrugged, and Blaise didn't know if Emrys had broadcast to him as well or if he understood the stallion's body language. "Don't want anyone accusing me of foul play before we leave town. You're welcome."

Blaise winced.

Jack made the same check of Zepheus's saddle, though Blaise suspected he only did it for show. He swung into the saddle but didn't ask the palomino to go anywhere. "I've arranged for a couple of colts to come along. We'll make better time if everyone is mounted. They were getting saddled with loaner tack last I saw."

Blaise nodded. That made sense. The sooner their rescue party got back to Itude, the better.

A few moments later, two new pegasi trotted up. The first colt, Rhoxio, reminded Blaise of a magpie with his black and white coloring. The other colt, Icoron, was a beautiful sorrel with a flaxen mane and tail, and a large white star between his eyes. They whinnied at Blaise with recognition.

<Cookies?> Rhoxio asked, nostrils flared as he drank in Blaise's scent.

<Greedy colt,> Emrys snorted, pinning back his ears.

Blaise chuckled. "I'll make sure you get some when we come back to town. Stop by the bakery the next time I'm there and I'll get some just for you."

The two colts bobbed their heads, delighted at the prospect. Jack shook his head at their antics. "I'm the lead on this mission. If I give an order, you follow it. Understand?"

At first, Blaise thought Wildfire Jack was speaking only to him, but Emrys and the two colts dipped their muzzles in agreement. Blaise winced at his oversight. He needed to remember that the pegasi were equals in Itude.

Zepheus minced forward as Wildfire Jack continued. "When we get close to the rendezvous point, I'll go first. Zeph and I will come back to you when it's all clear. Any sign of trouble and you get somewhere safe. We can handle ourselves. Can't do that and babysit y'all, though."

Blaise frowned, but said nothing. What was the point of him going along, then? Blaise wasn't spoiling for a fight—quite the opposite—but he didn't want to be useless baggage.

Wildfire Jack studied them, and Blaise realized the outlaw would much rather do this all on his lonesome than with a mage he hated and two half-grown colts. But that option was off the table. Jack shook his head, Zepheus spinning beneath him. "Let's ride."

CHAPTER SIXTEEN
Unhappy Reunion

Jack

<'I'm flying low,> Zepheus warned Jack as they dropped
down into a canyon.

Jack scowled. Between the bandanna protecting his mouth and
the fierce wind whipping his grumbled words away, there was
little chance the stallion could hear his annoyance. But Zepheus
could read his mood and detect his displeasure without hearing
anything.

It wasn't a point worth arguing. For the sake of their strategy,
it was sensible to stay low. Potential enemy look-outs kept their
eyes upward for outlaw threats. Standard operating procedure for
Zepheus and Jack was to either stay so low that they could pass
for a horse and rider, or so high that they were mistaken for a bird
of prey. Jack preferred height, though that presented its own set
of challenges. It was exhilarating to swoop down on his prey like a

falcon.

For this trip, they had too many unknowns. Emrys could handle the height, but his rider was another matter. And Rhoxio and Icoron would have a harder time with high altitudes. Zepheus didn't tell him much about the life of a wild pegasus, but Jack was an astute observer. He had seen pegasus flights out in the Untamed Territory, and the youngsters seldom flew at the high altitudes the adults weathered. They had some growing into their gangly bodies to do before they were proficient enough.

And Blaise . . . well, he definitely wasn't ready. The way he clutched the saddle horn, knuckles white as lilies, when Emrys took to the sky was deplorable. If he ended up staying in Itude, Jack had to make sure he dropped such behavior. It was downright embarrassing.

Zepheus kept the lead, though he slowed so the colts could keep up. They were still adjusting to the drag caused by their tack. It was harder to fly with saddles but no rider, Jack reasoned. A rider, at least, could help minimize the blow of the wind against leather. He had tied up the stirrups on their saddles as much as possible, but it was still a lot for them to get used to. They were stalwart little colts, though. He liked them.

Once Zepheus reached the rim of the canyons that gave the Gutter its name, he turned to the east. It would have been more direct to keep a southeastern path, but Jack didn't trust the simplicity of it. If something was simple, it was predictable. He hadn't made it this long by being predictable.

The other pegasi followed as they hooked to the east. This path would take them to the area where the Gutter transitioned to the Untamed Territory. Zepheus turned again, the Tombstone River a dancing ribbon off to Jack's left. Their destination wasn't too much further. The Tombstone arced into a lazy bend where it intersected the Desinan border. That was where Jack expected to find the first of the waypoint markers.

The palomino dropped altitude and touched down on a bluff overlooking the river. The other pegasi circled overhead like massive buzzards, awaiting instructions from Zepheus. Jack scanned the nearby tree line as his pegasus trotted up to it, searching for a telltale pop of color.

There it was. Anyone else might have thought it just an unfortunate scrap of cloth lost from its owner, but Jack had worked out a color code with Hank Walker. The cheerful blue strip of calico fluttered in the breeze.

"West." Jack nudged Zepheus with his knee, and the stallion took to the sky again. A short distance later, Jack spied the next marker. Orange. They shifted and headed south. Jack lost the trail of markers and called a break for lunch on a bluff overlooking the river. Blaise's face was tinged with green from the flight and he didn't say a peep during the quick meal. That suited Jack just fine.

After lunch, Jack was re-energized and had no trouble finding the next marker, though the color was cause for concern. Red. Jack bared his teeth. Red meant they were close—and *proceed with caution*. Salt-Iron Confederation soldiers were in the area.

"Tell 'em to come down but keep quiet and low," Jack murmured to Zepheus.

The other three pegasi came to the ground, clustering around Jack and Zepheus so they formed a square. Blaise's face was green, and he still held onto the saddle horn for dear life, but he didn't look like he had vomited. *Yet.* He was thinking about it. Jack smirked.

"I want y'all to go back and wait at the orange marker. Zeph and I will check things out, make sure everything is right before calling you to come get the mages." Jack shifted in his saddle. He debated telling them what the red flag meant but discarded the idea. Much as the Breaker annoyed him, Jack didn't need him losing his mind with worry right now. "We're in hostile territory, and we don't need any undue suspicion. You know what that means."

By Blaise's puzzled expression, he didn't know what it meant. But the pegasi did, and that was what mattered. All pegasi had the ability to hide their wings when a situation

demanded it—a crucial adaptation for their survival. Jack
watched as their wings faded from existence, making them look
like four normal horses. It was a discomfiting sensation,
knowing that Zepheus should have wings, but he couldn't see
them. The best part of their trick was that they weren't just
invisible—they vanished completely. If Jack ran his hand over
Zepheus's shoulder where his wings sprouted, it felt like the
shoulder of a normal horse.

Blaise made a little gasp when the pegasi did their trick.
"What?"

Jack grinned. Emrys must have told the kid something because
his expression cleared.

Time to get down to business. Jack laid a reassuring hand on the
revolver strapped to his pommel holster. It was one of many
weapons around or on his person. "If you hear any sounds of
trouble—gunshots, shouts, anything—or if I don't come back at
all, go back to Itude. Don't come after me."

Blaise frowned. "With all due respect, I'm here to help."

Jack spat on the ground. "And I'm here playing schoolmarm
making sure nothing happens to any of your fool heads." He
wouldn't tell the kid, but he had a grudging respect that he wanted
to help. It was more than Jack thought him capable of—unless his
brand of help was baking a cake. Truth be told, Jack wasn't sure if
he would want even a seasoned outlaw beside him on this
scouting mission. The more people involved, the higher the risk.
With knowledge of the soldiers in the vicinity, Jack almost had a
mind to call off the rescue mission.

But he couldn't. Not if it meant a chance to find Kittie.

Blaise pulled a silver pocket watch out, checking the time.
"Thirty minutes."

Jack's train of thought derailed at the Breaker's words. "Thirty
minutes what?"

The younger mage patted Emrys's neck. "That's how long we'll
wait before we follow you in. As I said, I'm here to help."

Jack ground his teeth at the impertinence. How dare this—

<Thirty minutes.> Zepheus twisted his head to look back at him. <Or I don't lift a hoof.>

Infuriating, that's what the lot of them were. Jack glared at Blaise and gave a stiff nod of agreement. "Thirty minutes." He whistled to Zepheus, and the stallion spun, whisking into the copse of trees before Blaise said another word.

Jack kept his head on a swivel, surveying their surroundings. Autumn had the region in her grasp, the forest floor carpeted in flame gold leaves. The skies overhead were clear, and the temperature was crisp. Everything worked in their favor so far. Jack was determined to keep it so.

A black strip of cloth hung from a tree branch on the deer trail ahead. Zepheus slowed, sniffing the cloth. <Walker.>

Jack pursed his lips. *Black.* It meant they were close. He pulled down his bandanna, then removed his flight goggles and hung them from the saddle horn. Normal folk wore bandannas, but not flight goggles. If he ran into anyone, he wanted to project the illusion of normalcy.

But just in case, he pulled out a sixgun and tucked it into his belt for a quick draw.

He clucked his tongue, and Zepheus ambled forward, ears pricked and attentive. Ahead, Jack saw motion as the underbrush parted, a grey shape moving through it.

Zepheus paused, ears flicking back and forth with indecision. <Something isn't right.>

Jack froze in the saddle, straining his senses. Silence descended over the surrounding woods.

That was *wrong.* The utter absence of sound stood out in sudden stark contrast to the birdsong and chittering of squirrels from moments earlier. It was as if someone had wrapped a heavy blanket around the area, muffling everything. Gooseflesh shivered across Jack's skin. He was familiar with that magic. *A Dampener.*

Jack opened his mouth to yell at Zepheus, but nothing came out. He tugged at the reins and nudged the palomino with his knees, but Zepheus was already backing up in alarm. Trees and low-slung brambles hemmed in the stallion on either side, making it difficult to turn.

Instinct and years of training had a sixgun in Jack's hand in an instant. But the lack of sound was utterly disorienting—Jack hadn't realized how much he depended on his ears for information until silence cloaked him. Dark shapes moved through the underbrush and Jack targeted one.

He felt helpless, torn. Should he shoot? What if it was a maverick, thinking he was a threat to confuse and defend against? He kept the form in his sights, vacillating. Damn, he didn't want to shoot a friendly.

Pain lanced through his right shoulder. Without the benefit of his ears, he didn't realize immediately that they had shot him. But Zepheus smelled fresh blood, and the pegasus telegraphed his outrage and fear with his quivering body. Jack aimed at the grey figure, but his right arm wouldn't obey his command. Clumsy and slow, he switched hands and fired with his left, but the shot went wide.

<Hold on.> Zepheus surged forward, head snaking. He locked his course on the person in grey, and Jack knew the stallion intended to trample them. That was fine. Best option since his gun was useless.

The stallion never made it. Jack's stomach lurched as Zepheus staggered—*what, why?*—and pitched forward violently. A normal horse would have gone down, crushing its rider beneath its bulk, but pegasi were made of sterner stuff. Zepheus's wings fluttered back into existence, correcting his precarious balance. But wounded as he was, Jack couldn't compensate for the hard bobble. He flew over the stallion's shoulder.

The world spun around him; the air whooshed out of his lungs as he hit the ground rolling. Agony bit at his shoulder like a terrier shaking a rat. Jack struggled to gather his wits. He was face-down in detritus, dirt in his mouth, lungs burning for air. His useless right arm crumpled beneath him, and his left hand was empty of the sixgun, which he'd lost during the fall. His fingers scrabbled, searching for one of the other revolvers he had squirreled away.

Something ground against his spine, keeping him down. Jack might have screamed at the pain, but there was no way to know with the dampening field surrounding them. Fingers twined around the hair at his crown, tugging his face out of the dirt. His vision swam with the sudden movement.

The cool muzzle of a revolver pressed against his temple. Jack spat out dirt, vision sharpening as the haze caused by his fall fled, banished by his seething outrage. All he saw were boots. *Right. Who do I need to kill?*

The boot pressed against his back lifted and then surprised him by kicking him in the ribs, just under his gunshot wound. Jack's vision exploded into stars of agony and he tried to scream, tried to curl into a ball to escape the torment.

When the anguish settled and his eyes focused again, he saw the face of his attacker. A Salt-Iron-issued revolver pointed at his head. Jack knew the hawk-nosed features of the blond man holding the gun on him well.

Lamar Gaitwood.

Gaitwood made a gesture with his hand, and suddenly the disconcerting hush fled. Jack heard birds chirp and the sound of Zepheus snorting with barely contained fury.

"If you attack my soldiers, your outlaw gets a bullet in his head," Lamar told the stallion. "I've been told your kind are smart, so if you give a shit about this man you *will* behave."

Jack groaned. *Gaitwood.* Gaitwood was here. He should have turned back at the sight of the red calico. Walker had warned him. But Jack hadn't thought they would be so close. And he hadn't thought it would be Lamar Gaitwood, of all the damned Salties.

Zepheus lowered his head, his ears pointed forward to show he would keep his peace. Distantly, Jack thought it strange the stallion wasn't trying to communicate with him.

"Get up, Jack. You don't have a choice." Lamar kept the revolver trained on him, but jutted his chin to the side, indicating the pile of Jack's sixguns. They must have disarmed him while he was on the ground, disoriented.

Jack panted for breath, withholding the anguished whimper he wanted to make. It wasn't the first time he'd been shot, but this one was bad. His shirt was slick with blood and bits of dirt and shredded leaves. If only his right arm would obey. *Damn Lamar.* Jack dragged himself into a sitting position, blood dripping to the forest floor with his effort.

"I said *get up*," Lamar repeated.

"The last time I saw you I told you to go to Perdition, yet here we are," Jack wheezed, his voice sounding foreign to his ears.

Lamar laughed, a bitter sound. "Oh, Jack. I missed you. We had such good times tearing up the countryside, hunting down mavericks and outlaws."

The muscles in Jack's jaw tightened. He wanted desperately to get up, to fight off Lamar and his soldiers and get out of there. His eyes slid to Zepheus, noting the coil of salt-iron rope looped over the stallion's neck. Small wonder the stallion hadn't spoken to him. He couldn't even fly with that rope on him. There would be no help from him, though Jack knew the stallion would fight by his side if it came down to it.

The odds weren't in their favor. Five more soldiers strode through the woods to back Lamar. Their number included a woman who Jack pegged as the Dampener. She moved with the calm assurance of someone who enjoyed messing with people. Jack knew the type because *he* was the same.

"What do you want with me, Lamar?"

Lamar spat at the ground. "You should know. We worked together long enough." He stalked in a tight circle around Jack. "Oh, but that's right. You're worthless after our last encounter, *traitor.*"

Jack bared his teeth. That was low, even for Lamar. But then, he never did like to fight fair. "I've been called worse things by better people. Let's settle this like men. Twenty paces."

Lamar scoffed. "I'm not stupid. I know even with a bum arm,

the legendary Wildfire Jack could still outgun me in a fair fight."
He gestured to a pair of soldiers, and they stepped closer. They
reached down and jerked Jack to his feet. "No, we're—"

He stopped when the Dampener's eyes widened. "Commander. Someone's coming!"

Lamar aimed an inquisitive look at Jack. "Did you bring
friends? You should have told me. I like company."

Jack coughed, the coppery tang of blood thick on his tongue.
Pain radiated through his body, and it became more difficult to
focus with each passing second. But he couldn't stop, not now.
Had to bluff his way out of this. "Be afraid, Lamar."

Lamar's eyes flicked to him with interest. "Do tell."

"The Breaker's coming, and he's going to grind you under his
boot."

Avarice lit Lamar's eyes. "*Breaker*? Oh, Jack." He laughed, the
sound resonating and chilling Jack to the core. He had miscalcu-
lated. "Maybe I'll let you live after all. All these years later, and
here you are—still doing the work for me."

"Fuck you."

Lamar Gaitwood, former friend and now bitter enemy,
addressed his small force with asperity. "Williams, bring up the
dampening field again. Screen the pegasus from view if you can."

"Aye, Commander."

Two soldiers dragged Jack behind a bush. The world around
him rocked with the quick movement. He tried to shout a warning, but no sound came out.

He squeezed his eyes shut, trying to fight off the pain. Black
tentacles of unconsciousness threatened to pull him under. He
had to stay awake. Had to fight back. Couldn't let Lamar get
Blaise.

The Breaker had escaped him once. He wouldn't be so lucky a
second time.

CHAPTER SEVENTEEN
He Had It Coming

Blaise

*B*laise walked in a circle around Emrys, relieved to stretch his legs after the time he'd spent tense in the saddle. Only luck had kept the contents of his stomach in place until Jack and Zepheus trotted off. Emrys had politely looked away as Blaise found a convenient shrub to vomit behind.

The curious colts hadn't been so sanguine. They approached with nostrils wide, ears pricked with questions until Emrys warned them off.

Blaise took a sip from his canteen and swished it around in his mouth before spitting it out to clear the sour taste. Then he drank deeply, chasing the water down with a piece of bread to settle his stomach. Blaise leaned against the bough of an oak, enjoying the shade and the pleasant weather. He took a calming breath, listening to the sounds of calling birds and the distant murmur of the river.

He was back in Desina. Miles from home, but still in his homeland. Blaise thought he would feel *something* when he came back. Longing. Or sadness. But cool detachment washed over him, like it had been a part of someone else's life. He missed his family, and he always would. Perhaps he had come to grips with their loss and had sealed the pain away, like a surgeon cauterizing a wound.

Blaise vowed that someday he would find out what happened to them. And if he had the chance, apologize for what he was. What he had unleashed on them.

Emrys nudged his shoulder, interrupting his thoughts. <Something's wrong.>

Blaise screwed down the lid on his canteen, moving around to the stallion's side, securing it back in the saddlebag. "What is it?"

The pegasus shook his mane. <Hard to explain. It's more of . . . an absence.>

Blaise's brow furrowed with concern. He pulled his pocket watch out. "It's been forty-five minutes. We should check it out."

<Wildfire Jack didn't seem inclined for us to follow,> Icoron reminded them, lifting his head from grazing. Wisps of grass poked out from his lips.

Oh, Blaise knew. Risking Wildfire Jack's wrath wasn't at the top of his list. He thought about Emmaline, humming as she worked at the bakery with a tiny doll sitting nearby. Emmaline, whom Blaise would have to face if her father didn't make it back home. The outlaw was a bastard, but Emmaline didn't deserve that.

<Well? > Emrys faced the woods, ears pricked.

"We'll go a short distance." They didn't have to go far. Just far enough for Emrys to know that Jack and Zepheus were okay. No problem.

Rhoxio snorted, a half-eaten clump of grass falling from his mouth. <We'll come, too.>

Blaise rubbed the side of his face, not bothering to dissuade the colts. He doubted they would listen to him. He put his left foot into the stirrup and swung into the saddle, his thighs and calves outraged that he had the audacity to mount up again so soon.

Mockingbirds darted from tree to tree. Emrys followed the trail Zepheus had taken. The underbrush scraped against the stallion's sides and Blaise's legs as they delved deeper. Blaise thought they must not be close to any towns or farms. Some trees were pecan, their branches heavy with this year's crop. If they were closer to a town or farm, he would expect industrious harvesters to keep the ground passable.

Blaise scanned the area ahead, searching for any sign of Jack or Zepheus. His shoulders were rigid. How far had they gone? He hoped Emrys would hear them soon.

Emrys kept to a cautious walk, brambles grasping at his mane and tail. Blaise had to duck below branches, and others he had to lift overhead with his gloved hands. He had considered not wearing his gloves but was glad he had. They were sturdy protection.

Both colts had their ears pinned back with unease and shied at the slightest provocation. Blaise asked Emrys to stop, and he turned to the young pegasi. "If you're scared, follow the trail back and wait for us at the marker."

Rhoxio shook his mane. <We're sorry. We'll try to be brave like you.>

Blaise gave a tight-lipped smile. *Brave?* That didn't describe him. Terrified. Worried. Those were more accurate. He turned back around in the saddle so that Emrys could continue onward.

His magic rose, startled by a sudden, strange sensation that swept over him, like cotton stuffed in his ears. Emrys's head rocked back in alarm. The world shifted into muted chaos. Emrys lunged forward. <Look out!>

The stallion's mental command was deafening in the silence. Blaise was too slow to heed it. He never saw the tree branch that swept him from the saddle. One moment he was astride Emrys, and the next he was flat on his back, the wind knocked out of him.

He gasped like a fish out of water, hoping he didn't end up trampled by the colts.

<Blaise, you have to—> Emrys cut off abruptly.

Blaise's eyes widened. He rolled to his side, thorns scratching his face. What would interrupt a pegasus's mental speech? Was Emrys dead? He tried to get up, but something came down hard on his chest, his breath whooshing out again. A dark-clad foot pinned him down. *What?*

In a sudden rush, the world came alive with sound. The colts squealed, Emrys screaming a challenge. An unfamiliar voice cursed.

"Get him up!"

Oh, no. No, no, no.

He knew that voice. It haunted his nightmares. Lamar Gaitwood grinned down at him as one of his men grabbed Blaise, twisting his arms behind him as he hauled him to his feet. Bruised muscles protested, and Blaise huffed in pain. He tried to ignore the agony—it could be handled later when he understood the situation.

Zepheus's flaxen tail was visible through a cluster of saplings. Emrys, Rhoxio, and Icoron froze in place, ears pinned back as they stared at something. Blaise followed their gaze.

Lamar Gaitwood had his revolver out, Wildfire Jack in his sights.

Blaise almost didn't recognize the crumpled man at first. The hale and hearty outlaw who had left them behind to scout was motionless on the forest floor, dark blood spreading across the autumn leaves. His skin was ashen, eyes closed. Blaise had thought the surly outlaw was larger than life; indomitable. Wildfire Jack would never be so vulnerable.

"This is what we're going to do." Gaitwood's tone was matter-of-fact as he kept the muzzle trained on Jack. "My men are going to tie you up, and then we're going to have a pleasant walk through the forest. If you do anything I don't like, your friend dies."

Blaise clenched his jaw. *"Friend* is a stretch, but fine." He grunted as a soldier wrenched his arms behind his back, using a rope to bind his wrists. Blaise's heart thudded like a drum at the unfamiliar touch, and he wished he could squirm away. He kept his eyes on Jack, willing the outlaw to get up. To fight. *You can't seriously leave this up to* me.

But he didn't move. If not for the uneven rise and fall of his chest, Blaise would have thought the man dead. One of Gaitwood's men led Zepheus over, and Blaise narrowed his eyes at the familiar glittering rope looped around the stallion's neck. The same sort that had snared Emrys before. Now Blaise knew what had interrupted Emrys's warning. The salt-iron ropes hobbled the pegasus's magic.

Two soldiers draped Jack's limp body over Zepheus's saddle, securing him with mundane rope. Zepheus stood as still as a child's pony, twitching ears and furtive glances belying his worry. Gaitwood moved behind Blaise, revolver still out. Blaise stared straight ahead. He didn't particularly want to see a gun aimed at him.

"Start walking. Follow the horses. We'd prefer to bring you back in one piece."

Blaise plodded along in the wake of the colts. He kept his head down, turmoil eating at him. This wasn't supposed to happen. How had things gone so wrong? The mission was supposed to be simple. Easy. Not this.

He had come so far, done so much. And yet, it had resulted in his capture. Frustrated tears pricked the corners of his eyes.

Gaitwood kept pace behind him. He was quiet for the first ten minutes of travel, but eventually, he spoke. "You've probably missed your mother. Won't it be nice to have a family reunion?"

Panic gripping him, Blaise froze, and then regretted it as the muzzle of the Commander's revolver prodded his back. He didn't turn around. "Where is she?"

Gaitwood chuckled. "Back where she belongs. On a train to Izhadell by now, I imagine."

Blaise's stomach clenched as Gaitwood prodded him forward. Izhadell was half a continent away. Was that where they would take him, too? He wanted to ask about his father and siblings, but doubted Gaitwood would freely offer the information. Blaise kept his mouth shut.

He thought they would walk for longer, but after about an hour they came upon the remains of a camp. Near the ashes of a fire, a single tent was visible. Tethered horses grazed nearby, only looking up at the approach of the pegasi. No other soldiers were in sight, aside from the ones who had made the walk back to the camp.

This couldn't be all of Gaitwood's soldiers. Six was a small number, an intimate number. Gaitwood had gambled at taking them by stealth, and it had worked.

The soldiers pulled Jack from Zepheus's saddle, depositing him on the ground at the outskirts of their camp. The outlaw still didn't move, his face slack. Gaitwood stalked over, prodding him with the toe of his boot. When Jack didn't respond, he gestured with one hand, and a silver cage hummed into existence around the injured man.

"He's hurt. He needs help." Blaise gritted his teeth.

Gaitwood strode over, coming so close that Blaise flinched. "Oh no, I hurt the poor outlaw." Gaitwood clutched a hand over his heart. "There's no mercy here, boy. The Dollmaker's a washed-up outlaw. The only kindness that awaits him is a noose."

A chill crept down Blaise's spine. Zepheus angled a hind hoof, ready to kick anyone who came close. The stallion had heard, and he was angry. But he was helpless, just as Jack was.

Gaitwood stepped away, lifting a hand to gesture at Blaise. A similar silver cage coalesced around him. "That was a pretty trick you pulled the last time we met. I'll admit, I've never seen anyone hit the bars of my trap and live to tell the tale, much less break through." He canted his head, thoughtful. "I wouldn't try it again if I were you, though. Salt-iron bindings are nasty."

The Commander joined the other soldiers, who had secured

the pegasi to a picket line with the salt-iron rope. A soldier came over and stood watch while the others prepared the evening meal and gathered wood to start the fire. Blaise closed his eyes, the familiar scent of smoke a balm for his tattered nerves.

Head bowed, Blaise watched them from the corner of his eye. His stomach rumbled. He was thirsty, but they didn't bring him anything. He should have listened to Rhoxio—should have gone back to Itude for help. Even better, someone more proficient should have come along with Wildfire Jack. Vixen would have been an excellent choice.

Blaise chewed on his bottom lip. *Vixen's not here. I am.* Even with his hands tied behind his back, he was the only one capable of getting them out of there.

Because he was a *Breaker*.

He thought back to his conversation with Vixen, about using his magic for a purpose. If ever there was a time, this was it. But how?

He listened as Gaitwood instructed a soldier to serve as a messenger. "Bring the jail wagon. We'll reinforce it with salt-iron when it arrives. I don't want to take any chances."

Blaise's eyes widened. The soldier rode off, leaving Gaitwood with five, including the man himself. Jaw set, he realized there was limited time to act. The soldiers laid out their bedrolls for later, planning to spend the night there.

His shoulders throbbed from the way his arms were wrenched behind his back. Long sleeves and gloves protected him from the worst of the salt-iron, but small patches of skin above his wrists were growing raw and irritated. Blaise exhaled a frustrated breath. The metal leeched his magic away, bit by bit. How long until the salt-iron rendered him useless? He had no idea.

He summoned his magic, welcoming the familiar itch as it rose to his palms. Blaise angled his hands until he could grasp a strand of rope with his fingers. He had no way to wrest his gloves off, so he planned to let his magic eat through the leather.

Blaise stayed still as he allowed his magic to break down the leather, and as time wore on, the guard on watch grew bored. Wildfire Jack was still unconscious—Blaise refused to think he was any worse off than that. He kept his focus on his magic, struggling to ignore the bite of salt-iron against his skin.

Silently, he thanked Vixen for all of their practice sessions. He hoped to make her proud.

By the time the soldiers sat down to eat, Blaise had a big enough hole to touch the rope with his bare skin. He worked his thumb against the braid, biting back a hiss when he touched metal by accident. His magic rose in agitation. It was almost sentient in its own way, angered by the salt-iron. He let it work through a few strands of the rope, then reined it back when the soldiers moved around the camp.

As the sun set, Gaitwood retired to the tent. The lone female soldier took the first night shift, and she settled against a nearby tree, her glittering eyes intent on her caged prey. The hungry look in her eyes bothered Blaise. She reminded him of someone with something to prove. She would not be a lax guard. That was unfortunate. Blaise needed someone sloppy.

The lambent moon rose overhead, casting the clearing in silvery shadows. Nearby, the fire crackled and snapped as it grew low. The woman fed the fire, and it hissed back to life, adding its golden light to the night. Blaise waited for the woman to settle back down into her place, watchful. He kept still as he sent his magic against the rope again. If she suspected anything of him, she would have to get closer to see what he was doing.

Eventually, she swapped with another man, who yawned, unenthusiastic about being roused from his slumber. He grumbled about caged outlaws not going anywhere. A wisp of hope unfurled within Blaise.

The soldier's head lolled against his chest as he relaxed against a nearby pecan tree. Blaise observed him for a few more minutes, then let his magic eat through the last strand. The rope fell away, and Blaise grabbed it with one hand before it could clatter to the ground. He stifled a relieved gasp and gently discarded the rope.

Sure that the guard was asleep, Blaise brought his hands around to the front and massaged his wrists, wincing at the skin blistered by the salt-iron.

The pegasi pricked their ears, attentive. Blaise lifted an index finger to his lips, hoping they understood to stay quiet. Emrys bobbed his head. Blaise scooted closer to the silvery bars. The last time he had broken Gaitwood's cage, it had shattered in a dazzling light show. That would draw too much attention.

This was a time for subtlety and control. Blaise swallowed, quailing. It terrified him that he might not have what it took. But his friends were counting on him. Vixen thought he could do it. *I can do this.*

With a calming breath, he peeled off his ruined gloves. The corner of his mouth quirked as he realized this was the first time he had tried to destroy his gloves on purpose. He shook his head at the thought, then reached out and wrapped his right hand around a single bar.

The last time he had come across Gaitwood's trap, he had plowed through it like a bull. The contact was brief but fierce, like breaking an egg. This time was different. He held the construct of Gaitwood's magic in his hand, and he could *feel* the malevolence in it. Blaise didn't understand the magic of the trap, but he knew it was cruel. And if his magic wasn't as powerful as Gaitwood's was, he would succumb to it.

Blaise's hair stood on end as he sent his magic into the bars of the cage. It flooded the construct, learning every facet. Blaise saw the essence of the magic that made up the cage. It hung suspended around him like twinkling stars. It was almost beautiful. Blaise clenched his jaw. Wicked magic didn't deserve to be beautiful.

He sent his own magic against it, small amounts dripping from his hand. Blaise ate away at the construct, like the persistent tug of water eroding a riverbank. He released a little more magic, and it flowed out, consuming the trap until it winked out of existence. No great blast of light or sound. It simply ceased to exist. Nothing stood between Blaise and freedom.

He rose from the ground, listening for any hint of movement or awareness from the soldiers. Nothing. Icoron stamped a hoof, impatient. Blaise slipped over to the pegasi, moving as quietly as his bruised and sore body would allow.

He sidled in front of the four equines, pitching his voice low. "It's not much of a plan, but here we go: I'm going to free all of you first, but it's important you don't move from here until I get Jack. Can you do that?"

The four heads bowed.

"Good. Once I get him loose, if you can come over and help me get him out of here, that would be appreciated."

Zepheus bumped him with his muzzle. Blaise decided the palomino was volunteering.

Blaise slipped in between Emrys and Zepheus. The sheer size of the stallions would make it difficult for the soldiers to spy him if they realized he was missing. He freed Emrys first, since the black stallion knew what to expect. Blaise wished the colts weren't there. They were skittish and scared out of their minds, and that wasn't a good combination.

Blaise gripped the rope the soldiers had laced tightly around the stallion's neck. They had secured it to the horn of the saddle which annoyed Blaise, but he left it alone for the time being. He could take care of that later. A thrill of satisfaction coursed through him when the last strand tore free.

<I'm going to give that rope a good stomping later. Thanks,> Emrys said, the muscles of his neck quivering. <I'll help keep the colts in line when you free them.>

Blaise nodded his thanks. One less thing he had to worry about. He turned to Zepheus and repeated the same magic.

The palomino sighed as the rope fell away. He craned his neck down, his broad forehead close to Blaise's head. <You have my gratitude. When Jack is free, get him on my back. If you need us to provide cover while you free him, we'll do so.> Zepheus eyed the two colts, including them in the mission. They shifted nervously.

Blaise nodded to the golden stallion, feeling a little better that he wasn't going it alone. He freed the two colts, their hides twitching as the salt-iron ropes fell away. Blaise was afraid they would flee. But even in their terror, they held their ground.

<Listen to me,> Zepheus said. Blaise stood still, deciding that anything Jack's pegasus had to say was worth listening to. He had a lot more experience with these situations. <We'll stand here *quietly* while the Breaker frees Jack. No snorting. Do not so much as lift a hoof. If the Salties raise the alarm, that is when we move. Fight them like you would battle a murder of chupacabras.>

Three other heads bobbed in agreement. Blaise decided not to ask about the logistics of that last statement.

Blaise crouched down and eased, slow and silent, toward Wildfire Jack's cage. The campfire was dying down to embers; the full moon overhead lit his path. The soldiers were dark lumps in their bedrolls, the nasal sounds of snoring the only sign of life. The sentry dozed by the tree, a rifle propped beside him.

In the cage, Wildfire Jack turned onto his side with a soft moan. Blaise froze. It was the first movement he had seen from the outlaw in hours. His face was ashen, his chest dark with blood. His glazed eyes locked onto Blaise's in the moonlight. The injured outlaw's lips twitched as if he wanted to say something.

Blaise settled beside the cage. Wildfire Jack's chilly eyes stayed on him as he wrapped both hands around the bars. Blaise kept his focus on the cage, feeling the slide of Gaitwood's magic against him. He had used more magic tonight than he had ever used before, some of it siphoned away by the salt-iron. Vixen had warned him about the repercussions of draining his magic. He didn't know his limits.

Gaitwood's magic pushed against him, every nerve in Blaise's body on fire as he braced against the power. He made a soft grunt, pausing when he heard a soldier yawn behind him.

Blaise halted, hands still on the bars. He felt like he was trying to prop up a wall that would otherwise collapse and crush him. Out of the corner of his eye, he saw a dark outline untangle from a bedroll and get up, walking groggily toward a tree. The soft rustle of clothing followed, and then the splash of the man urinating. Blaise's heart pounded as he made a silent supplication to Faedra to send the drowsy soldier promptly back to sleep.

Dry leaves crunched beneath boots. The man was back at his bedroll. Blaise saw him kneel, but then he paused.

"Huh?" the man muttered, lethargic. "Thought there were two."

His voice woke the sentry who cursed softly. Apparently, he hadn't been planning to fall asleep.

"Commander!" the sentry squawked.

The pegasi whistled a challenge, the night descending into confusion as they unfurled their shrouded wings. Zepheus charged to Blaise, wings extended. Emrys and the two colts barreled toward the soldiers who were grabbing guns as they disentangled themselves from their bedrolls.

<Free him. NOW!> Zepheus commanded.

If only it were that simple. Blaise ducked his head, sweat beading his brow. He felt the shock of Gaitwood's magic butting against his own. *I don't have time for this.*

"Close your eyes!" Blaise said, hoping that the pegasi with their sharp ears would listen and obey.

He gathered all the magic he could and slammed it into the bars.

The cage exploded in a corona of light. The soldiers' horses squealed in terror. Jack groaned; the soldiers cursed and howled. Gaitwood was one of those voices, but Blaise didn't know what he said because he was focused on the outlaw.

Zepheus knelt. Blaise studied Wildfire Jack, trying to figure out the best way to get him onto the pegasus's back. There was no gentle way to do it. He put his hands under Jack's arms and dragged him into the saddle, blood smearing against Blaise's shirt. Zepheus flinched as an agonized squeal answered the retort of nearby gunfire. Blaise wished he could see how Emrys and the colts were doing, but there was no time.

<I'm going due north.> Zepheus spun and bolted. Blaise didn't know how, but Jack somehow kept his seat, slouched over the pommel like a rag doll.

<Go, go, go!> Emrys came up behind him fast. Blaise turned and ran, staggering as a bullet whizzed past him. He heard another devastating whinny but didn't look back.

Emrys raced by his side and slowed. Blaise didn't stop to think as he shoved a foot in the stirrup and lunged into the saddle. The stallion dashed off before he even had his seat, surging through the forest. Blaise glanced back, thinking he saw one of the colts behind them. He hoped it was the colts, and not the soldiers.

"Can you fly?" Blaise gasped for breath once Emrys slowed to a trot.

<Not yet. Still drained from the rope.> Emrys's sides heaved like a bellows.

"Are they going to come after us?"

<Without a doubt.> The pegasus sighed. <But it will take them a while to regroup. Rhoxio broke their horses free and scattered them. And with any luck, I broke Gaitwood's arm. And maybe some ribs. I can only hope.>

"Wait, you did?"

<He had it coming.> Emrys snorted.

Blaise couldn't agree more.

CHAPTER EIGHTEEN
Faedra's Embrace

Blaise

The eastern sky blushed with the pastel pinks and yellows of dawn when Blaise and Emrys finally found Jack and Zepheus. Rhoxio trotted along behind them, his gait uneven and eyes ringed with white. Icoron hadn't survived the fight. Blaise didn't ask Emrys for details. Not yet. He couldn't stomach any more grief.

It took them longer to find the outlaw than Blaise liked, because Zepheus hadn't traveled true north as he'd said. They had made it across the border to the fringe of land between the Gutter and the Untamed Territory. Jack sprawled beneath the scraggly limbs of a mesquite, the slight rise and fall of his chest the only hint that he lived. Zepheus stood over him, the palomino's saddle and sides splashed with dried blood. The stallion's wings were ragged with feathers missing, and a deep gash seeped blood on his flank.

<Sorry. Chupacabras.> Zepheus's mental voice was faint with exhaustion.

Rhoxio shied away and Emrys flung up his head. <Here?>

<A mated pair. I fought them off. But Jack dismounted, and he can't get back up.> The golden stallion nuzzled the fallen outlaw.

Blaise swung out of the saddle and knelt down beside him. "Jack?"

The outlaw's eyes fluttered open. But he said nothing, and that worried Blaise.

<He should be dead. He's bled out so much. How is he not dead?> Emrys asked Blaise.

Blaise figured the man was too stubborn to die. But he didn't want to jinx them. Blaise had never seen a wound like Jack's before, and he hoped to never see it again. The outlaw's clothing was black with dried blood, and fresh red gore oozed from the wound at his shoulder. Blaise brushed a hand against Jack's forehead. He was feverish, and Blaise didn't know if that was good or bad.

<Try the first aid kits?> Zepheus nosed at the saddlebags behind Emrys's saddle.

"Oh. Right." Blaise rose and went to Emrys's saddle, hoping that the soldiers hadn't removed them. They had taken all Jack's weapons and ammunition. He breathed a sigh of relief as he tugged a kit from the saddlebag, along with a canteen. Blaise was light-headed and exhausted from using his magic, not sleeping, and not having eaten since the previous day. He took a sip of the water, his parched tongue savoring the taste. Food would have to wait until after Jack was stabilized.

Blaise pulled out the kit. Despite their headlong flight, everything seemed whole and accounted for. Blaise opened the metal box and found gauze, adhesive plasters, dressing, bandages, sutures, and the cotton-wrapped alchemical vials. He wasn't sure where to start.

<Clean the wound first,> Zepheus directed him.

He spread a spare bandanna on the ground beside Jack and laid out the kit's contents. There was so much blood and blood-caked debris it was challenging to see what was what. Blaise followed Zepheus's direction, peeling back the clothing to reveal Jack's injury. His clothing had twisted during the scuffle, tattered bits digging into the wound. Blaise found a small pair of shears in the kit and cut off Jack's sleeve and as much of the shirt around the wound on his shoulder as he could.

Zepheus was a competent instructor. It made Blaise wonder how often the stallion had observed moments like this—not only with Jack, but others. Zepheus had him make a dressing for the wound and then secure it with surgical tape. With that task complete, Blaise did his best to clean up the area around the injury. Mostly he succeeded at smearing blood to new locations.

He found the outlaw's theurgist tattoo, arcane sigils inked onto his bicep in a dusky blue. Blaise didn't mean to stare, but he couldn't help but look as he cleaned away the crusted blood. He worried at his lower lip. If he hadn't escaped, he would have borne one of those tattoos, too.

"Can't . . . stay here."

Blaise winced, pulling his gaze away from the tattoo at the sound of Jack's faint voice. "What?" He studied the outlaw's face, eyes shut and lips still. "We should send Emrys back to get Nadine. Or someone who can help. I don't think—" *I don't think you'll survive being moved.* He didn't like Jack, but he didn't want to say the words out loud. They were horrific.

<The chupacabras will come back with the rest of their murder. And Gaitwood will not give up so easily. He'll come.> Zepheus arched his neck, stamping the ground with a hoof.

Blaise sighed, mopping at his face with one hand. He was tired and scared. Managing a crisis like this wasn't part of his skill set. He wished another functional adult would wander up and take control of the situation. The pegasi watched him, expectant.

Jack was no longer bleeding, but he wasn't out of the woods. Blaise sorted through the potions in the kit and pulled out the red vial of Faedra's Embrace. He didn't want to give the potion to Wildfire Jack. Blaise recalled his lack of enthusiasm for the side effects.

But then again, side effects didn't matter too much if you were dead.

<Jack would rather die in the saddle than in a hangman's noose.> Zepheus lowered his muzzle, sniffing at the vial.

"I'd rather no one die, but I get your point." Blaise held up the potion, swirling the vial as he checked the color and consistency. Wouldn't do any good to administer the wrong potion. It was true to the colors he recalled—a deep violet at the base, shifting to a sparkling crimson above. He uncorked it, and the rosy scent met his nostrils.

Blaise glanced up at the palomino. "If he gets mad at me later—"

<I swear he will not harm you ever again. Give him the potion.>

He raised his brows at the hefty promise. What would Jack think of that? The fact of the matter was, for the outlaw to have an opinion, he had to survive. Blaise raised the wounded man's head so he wouldn't choke on the potion and gently pried open his mouth and poured it down.

"It'll take a few minutes. If it even works." Blaise sat down criss-cross as he waited. The pegasi kept vigil, monitoring their surroundings for danger.

A half-hour passed before Jack's eyes fluttered open, his gaze locking onto Blaise. The outlaw coughed, flecks of blood on his lips. "Did you just pour shit into my mouth? Because my tongue tastes like shit."

"And he's back," Blaise muttered.

Zepheus nickered, lowering his head to inspect his rider. Jack scowled, trying to sit up. He groaned with the effort and only got as far as propping one elbow beneath him. Lips pulled back from his teeth in a rictus of pain, his eyes slitted in frustration.

"Do you need help?" Blaise asked.

Jack's lips closed into a thin, angry line.

Blaise ran a hand through his hair, belatedly realizing he had lost his hat somewhere along the way. Most likely yesterday in his fall. *Great.* "I know you hate me. But you said yourself we can't stay here. Let me help." Did the outlaw resent him so much that he would rather die than have his aid? That stung. Or was it simply foolish pride? He didn't understand what went on in Wildfire Jack's crazy head.

The outlaw said nothing. Zepheus rumbled, and Jack lifted his left hand into the air. Blaise clasped it and gently wrapped an arm around Jack, helping him up. The injured man trembled with the effort. He wouldn't get very far under his own power. Zepheus and Blaise worked together to get the outlaw into the saddle.

"Can you fly yet?" Blaise asked the pegasi.

<Not yet. And even if we could, Zeph shouldn't fly with Jack.> Emrys's ears flicked back as a haunting cry echoed in the distance. <We need to go. The chupacabras will be here soon.>

Blaise glanced at Jack, then climbed into the saddle. Every muscle in his body hurt, but he was thankful he was in better condition than Jack. The outlaw was pale, the reins slack around Zepheus's neck as he clutched the pommel with his left hand.

The pegasi broke into a trot, holding an easy pace that even limping Rhoxio could maintain. Zepheus changed his gait to a rolling stride that protected the outlaw from the jarring of a regular trot.

After an hour, Jack seemed more alert, though his wound was still grievous. Faedra's Embrace kept his pain checked.

"Do you know what it means?" Jack asked suddenly.

Blaise didn't think Wildfire Jack was speaking to him at first. He assumed he was talking to Zepheus. Then the outlaw cleared his throat, and Blaise realized his eyes were on him. "Sorry, what?"

He wanted Jack to be okay, but he didn't want to talk to the outlaw. That only led to trouble.

But he had taken Faedra's Embrace. *Oh, no. Wildfire Jack's going to chat, and he's going to kill me later when he tells me something he shouldn't.*

"The tattoo on my arm. You saw it."

Blaise swallowed. "Oh. Um, no, I'm not sure what you're—"

Jack laughed, the cackle reminding Blaise of the times at the saloon when some poor sod had one too many drinks and found everything hilarious. That was a sound Wildfire Jack never made. "You're a terrible liar, Breaker. I'm drugged on whatever swill you gave me, and I can still see that."

Blaise shook his head. "I gave you Faedra's Embrace so you would stabilize enough to ride. One goal I have for this trip with you is to not die, so please stop talking. It hurts when you punch me in the face, and I'm scared of what you may do when you get your hands on a gun."

Jack spat out a bloody glob of phlegm. "Guns. Bastard got my guns." He sounded more baffled by it than angry—which Blaise found strange. Another side effect. Jack frowned as he struggled to recall his train of thought. "The tattoo."

Blaise rubbed his face with his hand. "Zepheus, can you stop him?"

<Sorry, his mind is hazy, and I can't get through.> The pegasus was apologetic.

Wonderful. Just wonderful.

"I was a theurgist."

Blaise pinched the bridge of his nose. After his narrow escape from Gaitwood, he really didn't want to hear any more about the Salt-Iron Confederation at the moment.

Heedless of Blaise's opinion, the drugged outlaw blundered on with an unstable grin. "That's the mark of a theurgist. All of 'em have it, but they're supposed to be red, not blue. If Lamar got you, you'd be getting inked with one." He coughed, and Blaise winced in sympathy at the grating sound. "Mine's special, though. The last time I tangled with Lamar, he did a little something to me. You wanna know what?"

Blaise shook his head. He didn't want to know. Not at all.

Jack's pale visage warped, becoming savage. "Bastard burned out my magic. *My friend burned out my magic.*"

Blaise felt like a hammer struck him between the eyes. Jack didn't have magic? And Lamar Gaitwood was his *friend?*

"You . . . you don't have magic?" Blaise couldn't take back the question once he'd uttered it, but he wished he could.

"No." Jack's voice was small and defeated.

They rode in silence for a few more minutes. Blaise picked apart what the outlaw had said, boggled. He was an outlaw *mage.* Everyone said as much. Even Jack. Had the potion scrambled his brain and caused him to think he didn't have magic? Jack was terrifying. He *had* to have magic.

<He doesn't. Not anymore,> Zepheus confirmed.

Blaise thought about that. The outlaw put on a bold front, projecting a larger-than-life image. Tough. Indomitable. And to be sure, he was. And he did all that without the trademark magic the outlaw mages were renowned for. No wonder he was perpetually in a foul mood.

"Wildfire Jack?"

"Just call me Jack."

Blaise blinked, surprised. "I'm sorry they took your magic from you. I didn't know that could happen."

Jack stared into the distance between Zepheus's ears. "I thought it was the worst feeling in the world. But it wasn't. Not compared to my biggest loss."

Blaise's eyes widened. "I don't want to know."

"Tough luck. That shit you gave me has me gabbing, and you're going to listen. If I don't make it, I need you to tell Emmaline. Promise me."

Blaise's heart sank.

"*Promise me.*" Jack's voice was dangerous. With the potion dulling his pain and clouding his judgment, he was unpredictable.

But there was also an edge of fear, as if Jack worried he might not make it.

"I promise."

Jack calmed and exhaled softly. "Give me a few minutes to catch my breath. Talking is hard. But I'll tell you."

CHAPTER NINETEEN
The Gift of Gab

Jack

Jack felt a pleasant disconnection from his body, like nothing below his head existed. He figured his legs clung to Zepheus's sides out of sheer stubbornness. The reins dangled in his hands, which seemed to move and twitch of their own accord. He had only pin-prickles of sensation from his neck down, but it was probably a blessing. Jack remembered enough to know Gaitwood had shot him, and it had been ugly. Really bad. Buried with your boots on *bad*.

Zepheus was trying to speak to him, but the words were muffled and made little sense. But his ears worked—he heard the pegasi's hoofbeats and Blaise's words fine. A tiny part of his mind was alarmed and angry, but the blissful sensation of talking outweighed it. Yeah, talking was good. It was cleansing. It was the best.

His mouth felt like it was full of cotton, and his tongue tasted like death, but that didn't fetter the need to speak. "I'm not from these parts," Jack began once he felt rested enough to speak. "To be sure, most of the folks in Itude aren't from here, either. Anyone with magic is an outlaw or maverick. Those without are outcasts."

"But we're called outlaws as a group." Blaise sounded tentative, like he was expecting the gift of a punch in the face.

Jack smirked. "Makes us sound scary. The bad guys." Yeah, Jack knew without a doubt that *he* was one of the bad guys. He had the blood on his hands to back it up. Blaise gave him a puzzled look. The kid was too scared to ask questions. Wasn't he lucky that Jack was in a chatty mood? "You think everyone in Itude is bad?"

Blaise shook his head. "Not now. But before . . . well, we're told that outlaws are scary. So a town full of outlaws sounds like an undesirable place." The Breaker ran a hand down Emrys's silky neck. "I was wrong."

Jack snorted. "I still don't regret punching you in the face on your first day." Zepheus twisted his head to look back, a move Jack assumed was a warning. It was convenient that he couldn't hear the stallion. "Aren't you going to ask where I'm from?"

"Do I have to?"

"Humor me. I'm the one who bled out."

Blaise sighed. Jack felt a warm fuzzy feeling at needling the kid. "Where are you from?"

"Izhadell."

At the word, Blaise straightened in the saddle, as if on alert. "Isn't that the capital of Phinora?"

"It's where this whole damned Salt-Iron Confederation business started." Jack leaned to the side and spat on the ground. He tasted blood on his tongue. *Should I worry about that? Nah. I'm good.* "Never met my father. I—"

"Wait, you're telling me everything from the very beginning?" Blaise interrupted, dismayed.

Jack glared at him. "Shut your piehole and listen."

"As I was saying, I was raised in Izhadell by my mother—never knew my father." Maybe it was a side effect of the potion—a hallucination, perhaps. As Jack spoke, the scenes came to life before him like he was in the audience at the theater. Maybe his entire life was flashing before his eyes because he was dying. *Whatever.* He went with it.

The white clapboard house rose from the ground before him, surrounded by a picket fence. A tow-headed boy tussled with a playmate in the front yard, shoving handfuls of leaves down the other's shirt.

"In Phinora, Trackers are sent out regularly to hunt for new mages. I'd just turned ten when the Trackers came through our part of town, leading a unicorn." The scene unfolded before him. His younger self still played with his friend—Robbie, that had been the other kid's name. They dove into a pile of leaves and tossed them up into the air, watching them rain down as they laughed. Both boys froze as the moon-white unicorn approached, horn shining like a beacon. "My mother screamed when she saw the unicorn come up to me and dip its head."

In his vision, Robbie looked at young Jack like he was a demon straight out of Perdition and bolted away, crying for his mother. That had been Jack's first sampling of the fear magic could impose on another. And he had liked the power it gave him.

Blaise stared at him. "You didn't know you had magic until then?"

That was an interesting question. Jack had thought about it before and always came to the same conclusion. "I didn't know what magic was like, to know it was any different from . . . just being me. There was a strange tingling in my fingers whenever I played with some of my toys, but I thought that was normal. Thought it happened to everyone."

The Breaker nodded.

"That was the day everything changed. My mother was furious —and I was excited. She didn't want to give me up." Jack's mother wept before him, her tears shining diamonds. Jack hadn't understood her sense of loss, not back then. But he did now.

"Kids in my neighborhood used to play theurgist and outlaw." Jack chuckled at the memory, then regretted it. The metallic taste of blood was thick in his tongue. Should he worry about that? That was for later. "I thought I was top shelf for being the first of my age-mates to get pegged as a mage. They took me to the Golden Citadel, and I thought life couldn't get any better."

Blaise frowned at the unfamiliar term. "What's the Golden Citadel?"

"The Golden Citadel—" Jack coughed, and then shook his head, touching his throat with one hand.

Blaise called a halt. Jack heard Zepheus in the distance again, but he still didn't make sense. Blaise pulled out a canteen and helped him drink. The water was sweet and refreshing as it went down, and he wanted more.

"Sorry," Blaise winced. "Zepheus says I shouldn't give you too much. It might make you worse."

"Zepheus is an asshole."

The stallion stomped a rear hoof, tail flinging from side to side with annoyance. Blaise wiped his forehead. "This is the weirdest day ever, which is kind of depressing in the grand scheme of things." He gave Jack a scrutinizing look, his lips tense as he scanned the dressed wound. "You were saying about the Golden Citadel?"

Right. The pegasi started forward again, and Jack fell back into the tale. "It's a big place outside Izhadell. Former fortress, maybe. Somebody with more money than common sense had it painted gold. Gaudy as all get-out." In his vision, a soldier accompanied young Jack up the well-maintained road that led there. It was sunset, and the building reflected the light so it glowed as if it were magic. And to a young boy, it was.

"The Cit—that's what we called it—became my home. They didn't allow my mother to visit. It bothered me at first, but there was so much to see and learn that it soon seemed like a small thing." Jack clenched his teeth. Stupid young Jack.

"The geasa?" Blaise asked.

Jack frowned. That was a word he hadn't heard in a very long time, and even in his drugged state it was odd to hear it from the Breaker's lips. "How do you know that word?" The geasa wasn't widely known. Few theurgists knew the proper name for the specialized binding that tied them to their handler.

"Um . . ." Blaise backpedaled. "The tattoos are magic, right? But most Phinorans don't like magic because it's against their morals?"

Jack snorted. "Most of the tattoos aren't infused with the geasa. They're simply a way to mark someone as a mage. As a *tool*." Old outrage rose to the surface. "And even then, someone with the most mundane of magics must enter an indenture to earn their freedom." That was a farce. How many mages attained that goal? So few it was laughable. "But mages with powerful magic, or *interesting* magic . . ." The outlaw paused, casting a glance at Blaise, who fit both of those categories as surely as Jack had. "Those poor sods have a tattoo applied with special ink to bind them to a handler. *That's* the geasa."

Blaise blinked, his mouth forming a small *o*. "I see." He fiddled with the reins. "What's your magic, if you don't mind my asking, since you're so chatty?"

"Not my magic anymore," Jack reminded him, the bitterness of his words a sharp slap in the face. "Ritualist. Effigest, to be exact."

Blaise blinked at him. "Huh?"

Of course, the kid didn't know what that meant. Jack snorted. Time to use his favorite explanation that caught people off guard. "I make dolls."

"Um, what?" Blaise looked at him like he was unhinged. Maybe he was. Jack wasn't sure. For all he knew, he was unconscious in the dirt somewhere and this was a fever dream.

"Effigests specialize in making figures to represent someone —we call them poppets or effigies. I could make one out of whatever I had on hand—dry grass, fruit, clay, almost anything. They're more potent if I had a personal item from whoever I intended to cast on, but I could still be successful without." That was more than the angry Jack in the corner of his mind wanted to tell Blaise, but he reasoned this was all information the Breaker would need to tell Emmaline if he died. It was important.

"What kind of spells?" Blaise asked.

"Whatever I intended. I was strongest with spells meant to help someone. I could heal people. Give them more strength or endurance. But I could hurt people with it, too. That was the real power they wanted from me." Jack gritted his teeth, his face stony as he remembered the first time he had used his magic to take a life. "I could make people sick or wounded. Even die."

Blaise stared at him nervously.

"Once they found out I was an Effigest, they assigned me to a mentor—this crazy old one-eyed woman named Nora. She was creepy and strange, would talk to her poppets. But she was smart and knew what she was about, so I learned from her because I didn't have any other choice. Nora taught me how to make poppets and effigies, and it was the craziest thing—but I found out I loved to make them." Jack saw an image of Nora hunched over his younger self, guiding him as he pieced together a poppet from a corn husk and rags.

"When I finished learning with her for the day, I took scraps to my room so I could make more. But I wasn't just making poppets for practice. I was making dolls, and I gave them to all the new children that came into the Cit. Most of them were younger than me. Scared. So I breathed magical words of peace and hope into dolls I gave to those kids." Jack closed his eyes, shutting out the image of himself handing out the dolls.

"Awful nice of you," Blaise hazarded.

"In the Cit, they don't train up their theurgists to be *nice*," Jack growled. "They took every doll they could find from those kids. Tore them to shreds before their eyes to make them cry."

Blaise sucked in a breath. "That's cruel."

Jack allowed himself a satisfied smile. "I found out later they did it for good reason. My magic *worked* on those kids. And they didn't like that. Not one bit." He stared through the twin arcs of Zepheus's ears.

"What happened?"

Jack glanced overhead at a circle of carrion birds. *I'm not dead yet, boys.* "What you'd expect. They beat me for my insolence after Nora found me making more tiny dolls to give away. Then they threw me in a cell with salt-iron shackles for a week." His stomach wrenched at the ghost-memory of the metal blistering his skin as it sapped his magic. "They made the message crystal clear: we tell you when you get to use your magic."

Blaise shook his head. "You couldn't fight back?"

Fight back? The Breaker had no idea how laughable that concept was. "I was bound to my asshole handler Reynolds by the geasa at the time. Factor in the salt-iron shackles and it's impossible."

The Breaker made an uncomfortable sound of acknowledgement.

"After that, I was a model student." Jack listened to the comforting rhythm of hooves for a moment. "Once a theurgist has gone through their training at the Cit, we're sent out to work on behalf of the Confederation. They paired me and my handler with another kid about my age, but he was from a rich family. His name was Lamar Gaitwood."

Blaise's eyes widened, but he said nothing.

"Lamar had a complex about being a mage—his family followed Garus's teachings, so that put a bee in his bonnet. He became something of a fanatic, thinking if he used his magic for the glory of the Salt-Iron Confederation, Garus might forgive his impurity. But even with that baggage, we were friends." Jack looked askance. The word *friends* seemed wrong in his mouth, but it had been accurate enough. "They assigned us to bring in mavericks. Especially those who were dangerous. The dissidents. Sometimes we were assigned the occasional assassination to help with politics. An illness here, a death there." He waved his good hand, nonchalant. "I hate politicians."

The Breaker's face paled.

"I was good at it," Jack's voice was soft as he recalled the memory. The thrill of bringing down another outlaw or maverick. The heady rush of taking a life—the knowledge he had that power over someone. "Lamar and I made a devastating team. We kept at it, but all that time, I didn't realize that because of my earlier rebellion, the Salties had collected a surety for my good behavior: my mother."

Blaise watched him, eyes full of concern.

"One day, we received the orders to kill a child. She was the daughter of a family causing trouble for the Luminary, and they wanted the parents to fall back into line."

"You didn't." Blaise's tone was sick.

Jack thought back to that day, shaking his head. "I didn't. But I wasn't the one who suffered for my refusal. Lamar was furious and reported how I had botched the mission. It was then my handler showed me they had my mother." Jack trembled with momentary rage. "Reynolds made me watch as they scourged her for my misdeeds." He would never forget the flesh stripped from her back, blood oozing to puddle on the stone floor.

"Jack . . ." Blaise's eyes grew wide, horrified.

"They proved their point. Again. I behaved and did their bidding." Jack bowed his head. "Then, one day, they sent us on the trail of a female maverick. She was causing the Salties grief in Umber, speaking out against the Salt-Iron Confederation. She was wily and had avoided everyone sent on her trail." A smile ghosted his lips. "I knew she wouldn't be so lucky with us." He had been wrong. He was so glad he had been wrong.

"Lamar found the inn she was staying in and pilfered a mug she had drunk from. I had a little poppet ready and activated it by touching it to the rim where her lips had made contact."

Blaise muttered something that sounded suspiciously like, "Your magic is so much creepier than mine." Jack let it be since it was true.

"That night, we broke into the room she was staying in." He

made a long, low whistle. "She was fast. And powerful. And ready for us. She burned Lamar's casting arm before he could trap her. Her entire body was aflame, a walking bonfire. I tried to bind her with my poppet, but her fire was a shield my magic couldn't pierce. I could have shot her, but . . ." Jack grinned. She had been glorious, even more so than when he'd caught sight of her earlier in the evening, giving a rousing speech against the oppressive abuse of mages. "I couldn't. I saw her, and I saw freedom." *And love. And hope.*

Blaise looked confused. "So you let her go?"

Jack canted his head, which was a bad idea because that made him dizzy. "No. She set my poppet on fire, which pissed me off. Lamar and I had backup, and the soldiers came up to see what the ruckus was. She burned those men to a crisp, but didn't harm a hair on my head. Kittie was a sight to behold in her fury. She was absolutely the most dangerous and awful thing I ever laid eyes on."

"And you had a crush on her?" Blaise guessed.

Yes. Stupid, young Jack had a crush on her. "There's something alluring about seeing a woman destroy your oppressors. Kittie saw me gaping at her, and I still don't know why she didn't kill me where I stood. Instead, she asked if I wanted to be free." Jack took a ragged breath. "I told her I did, and with a snap of her fingers she reduced Reynolds to a flaming husk. Killing my handler shattered the geasa, and for the first time in my adult life I was free."

Blaise ran his fingers through his hair. "And now I no longer wonder why the Salt-Iron Confederation hates you so much."

Jack nodded. "And that's how I met my wife." He grinned at the Breaker's surprised expression.

CHAPTER TWENTY
Born of Despair

Blaise

*B*laise had a tough time reconciling Jack as the marrying type. He would never tell Jack, but he assumed Emmaline was the product of an indiscretion, and he somehow ended up saddled with the results. The mental image of Jack giving his icy heart to anyone was at odds with Blaise's perception of the man.

Blaise hid those thoughts. Jack's eyes glazed while he spoke, and Blaise wasn't optimistic about what that meant for them. He wasn't sure how long Faedra's Embrace would last. As long as Jack kept talking, the outlaw seemed determined to plow onward.

As much as he hated to do it, he needed to keep Jack speaking. "Didn't realize you had a wife."

For a heartbeat, an angry Wildfire Jack glared at him through fierce eyes. "I did. I hope I still do." Then the faraway look returned. "We had a good thing, Kittie and me. She was the fire of my heart. We did what stupid, young people do. We ran off and got married, and then hid because she was a known outlaw and I was . . . well, I was not only an outlaw but a traitor. Eventually, we had Emmaline."

Jack stared off at the horizon, shaking his head. "Around the time Em turned three, I regretted that the Salties still had my mother. I hated myself for it. Kittie saw it was eating me up from the inside, so we made a plan. It was a good plan, one I assumed would work.

"Kittie stayed behind with Emmaline. We had moved to Petria to be closer to Phinora. I got to Izhadell, and I used my poppets to evade the Trackers and hunters who might be on to me. It was looking good. Until I discovered that—that my mother was dead." He stroked Zepheus's mane, his voice catching.

"I'm sorry," Blaise murmured. He mused about his own mother. What would happen to her?

Jack waved his good hand, then grabbed the saddle horn when he nearly toppled over. "What's done is done. I was furious, but all I could do was go home. But when I got back to the little cabin we were renting . . ." His lower lip quivered.

The outlaw's shoulders convulsed. Blaise studied him, sobering as he realized that Jack was crying.

<He's never allowed himself to release his feelings over this before.> Zepheus's voice was solemn.

Jack's chin dipped against his chest. "I found Emmaline hiding under the bed, blankets and things pushed around her to keep her hidden. Kittie was . . . she was gone, the grass outside scorched. She . . . she hadn't left without a fight. Em was so little, and she said her mother told her to play hide and seek and to be quiet as a mouse. I don't know how long my child hid until I arrived." A tear rolled down Jack's cheek, splattering against the saddle.

A lump formed in Blaise's throat, uncertain what to say. What could he say to something like that? There were no words to serve as a balm. Jack wasn't looking for a balm, anyway. Jack wanted him to understand his past so that he could present it to Emmaline if necessary.

"I took Em, and we fled to Asylum. I had to get somewhere safe. Somewhere the Salties couldn't go easily. We came across Zeph, and we found our way to Itude. I won't give you the long story about taking over the town and my times working the roads as an outlaw. We cleaned Itude up. But I still wanted Kittie back. I had already failed my mother. I couldn't fail my wife." The glaze cleared from his eyes, replaced with determination.

Blaise nodded. He understood that.

"I had saved—I found Clover by that time, so I knew Emmaline would be safe with her. Zeph and I went to Petria to take up Kittie's trail. I thought my experience working with Lamar and my time as an outlaw made me so slick and crafty. But with that came a self-assurance that I should have checked at the border. I was high and mighty. Because I had the best intentions and my magic, I would save the day."

Blaise glanced away. "Did you find her?"

"I was certain I had her trail. Maybe I did, I'll never know. But Lamar found me first."

Zepheus gave a mournful nicker, glancing back at his rider. Not for the first time, Blaise wished he didn't have to hear this. He didn't like tragedies.

"Zeph got away by some minor miracle. But he couldn't help, not without risking himself. Lamar was furious at my betrayal. I thought I would talk him down. But then they strapped me down with the salt-iron ropes and poured a potion down my throat that stole my magic." Jack's left shoulder slumped.

"I won't soon forget that potion. It felt like every vein in my body was on fire. I thought it might kill me." He looked away. "For a short time, I wished it had. I lost my magic and any hope of finding my wife. But . . . *Emmaline*. Lamar planned to take me back to Izhadell for trial and execution. I refused to allow that. I needed to get back to my daughter."

<And that was the moment Wildfire Jack was born from despair,> Zepheus told Blaise privately.

"To this day, I'm not even sure how I escaped. I saw an opening, and I fought without magic. Wrestled a gun from a soldier, and Zepheus was close enough to come to my aid."

Blaise considered escaping from Lamar with life and limb a win. He thought about what Jack had said, and about their original reason for going to Desina. "Were you hoping your wife would be one of the mages we were looking for?"

Jack bowed his head, the tears glinting in his eyes all the answer Blaise needed. Instead, Jack asked, "Do you know why I hated you?"

Blaise blinked, surprised. That had been the last thing he expected to hear from Jack. "No."

"I can't protect against your magic. Once upon a time, I could have. The only way I can stop you now is with a well-placed bullet." Jack wasn't looking in his direction, so missed Blaise's wince. "And that scares the shit out of me. Your magic is dangerous. I thought you would tear my town apart." The outlaw opened his mouth to say more, but instead, let out a low groan. He sank forward, his good arm wrapped around Zepheus's neck as the only means to keep him from falling.

Faedra's Embrace had worn off.

"WHAT THE BLAZES HAPPENED IN DESINA?" KUR AGUR SNARLED, eyes aglow.

Blaise scrubbed at his face, fatigue dogging him all the way down to his bones. He didn't want to be here, sitting in the Ringleaders' HQ. He wanted a soothing soak in the bathhouse, a meal, and then the gentle oblivion of sleep for a few days.

That wasn't in the cards.

Not long after Jack had collapsed atop Zepheus, a sentry pegasus spied them and flew down to investigate. It was Alekon, Vixen's mount, and he sped back to town for help. Blaise assumed help would come in the form of more pegasi. Never had he imagined the fearsome sight of Clover charging towards them, her long legs covering more ground than Blaise thought possible, horned head stretched out before her. She said nothing when she slid to a dust-scattering halt; she only shook her head and snorted in distress. Clover reached up and gently pulled Jack down from Zepheus's back, cradling the unconscious outlaw against her like he was nothing more than a sleeping child exhausted from a day of play. Jack had looked fragile and vulnerable in Clover's arms, and that bothered Blaise a lot.

The Knossan sprinted back to town, taking the long trail up the east side. Blaise and the pegasi kept pace with her on the ground. Once they reached Itude, Clover high-tailed it to Nadine's clinic. The pegasi took Blaise to Headquarters at some unbidden command.

Now Kur Agur, Vixen Valerie, and Raven Dawson were asking too many questions, and Blaise was tired of it.

He told them everything, though they kept stopping him and backtracking, asking for clarification. He tripped over his own words, his head muddled from lack of sleep, lack of food, and stress. At one point, Blaise dozed off in front of them. A threatening growl from Kur woke him.

The only thing Blaise left out from his repeated recitations was Jack's long discourse with him. His brain felt like mush, but he had enough self-preservation to remember that Jack had said it was a story for Emmaline's ears. Jack had a secret to keep, and Blaise didn't want to be the one to spill it.

A knock at the door interrupted the questioning. Raven pulled it open, and Hannah poked her head in. "Hey, y'all. Sorry to interrupt, but Nadine needs to see Blaise to ask some stuff about Jack."

Blaise sighed. Not again. He wasn't ever going to get to sleep.

The three remaining Ringleaders traded looks. "Go." Raven clenched his jaw.

Blaise followed Hannah out. She kept her head bowed and stayed quiet, which was unusual for her. Her behavior set Blaise's nerves on edge. "Hannah, is Jack . . . ? Did he . . . ?" He couldn't bring himself to finish the question.

She glanced at him. "Oh. No, I don't think so. But Nadine's got her tail in a knot, and she has Reuben helping, so things aren't good."

Poor Reuben. But at least Jack was alive. For now, anyway.

He followed Hannah into the white clapboard clinic. She didn't bother to knock, just pushed open the door with purpose. Nadine leaned over a prone form covered in a white sheet, her eyes flicking to the door the only sign of acknowledgment. Reuben stood beside her, squeamish and miserable.

Hannah clapped Blaise on the shoulder and turned to leave. He stayed near the door, shifting his weight from foot to foot.

"I think I know his injuries, but you were there. How did you treat him?" Nadine's voice was crisp, matter-of-fact.

"He was wounded before I got to him. Zepheus told me they shot him, so that's what I treated," Blaise said. "If he has other injuries, I don't know."

"How long ago did it happen?"

Blaise sighed. A dull throb pounded at the base of his skull. He was bleary-eyed, and barely had any concept of what time it was. Reuben pulled out his pocket watch and showed him. *Right. I should have checked my watch.* "It's been at least twenty-four hours. Maybe a little more?" Time was a confusing concept. Everything was a blur.

Nadine released a hissing breath. "Too long, too long. How did you treat him?"

Blaise told her about the first aid kit and Zepheus's instructions (so he wouldn't take all the blame if he had done something wrong). He had done his best in a terrible situation. Nadine didn't criticize, just nodded as she listened. When he mentioned Faedra's Embrace, her eyes narrowed. "That wasn't a good idea."

You have no appreciation for how terrible an idea it was. "I didn't know what choice I had. He was in so much pain I don't think he would have stayed upright in the saddle as long as he did without it."

Nadine pursed her lips, unhappy but not arguing. "The problem with that potion is idiots never realize how hurt they are, and then they do stupid things like riding a pegasus for the better part of a day." She held out her hand, and Reuben gave her a wad of gauze.

"I'm aware." Blaise's voice was tight. "My mother's an alchemist."

She gave him an assessing look. "Well, you got Jack home alive, which is impressive."

"Is he . . . will he live?"

Nadine busied herself with a set of steel instruments arrayed on a silver tray. "He's closer to needing a Necromancer than a Healer. I'll do all I can. The one good thing that damned potion did is convince his body to not start shutting organs down." She was thoughtful as she spoke. "Actually, that may have saved his life."

Blaise released a pent-up breath he hadn't realized he was holding.

The Healer looked up at him for a moment, then stepped away from Jack. Nadine lifted a hand more quickly than Blaise's tired mind could process, brushing her palm against his forehead.

"Blazes, boy. How are you still standing? Go eat something and rest. Healer's orders." Nadine strode back over to Jack, all business. "I need to cajole Jack's brain to keep everything working and convince the gangrene to stay clear. It's going to be a long day."

Blaise nodded, stumbling out the door. Jack was someone else's concern now, and that was good. His eyelids felt like they were being pulled down by weights. He wasn't sure that eating first was a good idea. He would likely fall asleep and choke on his food.

Mindy and Celeste saw him stagger by the Jitterbug. Celeste slipped out, grabbed his arm, and steered him inside. Blaise didn't have the will to protest.

"You look like you were ridden hard and put up wet," Mindy pointed out, bringing a bowl of soup and setting it in front of him. "Eat."

Blaise blinked at the soup. The aroma of salt and chicken broth tickled his nostrils, and his salivary glands awoke. He tried to pick up the spoon, but the utensil was clumsy and foreign in his grip, so he sipped from the bowl. Despite his best efforts, soup dripped onto his shirt.

"You okay, Blaise?" Mindy asked, her voice sounding distant even though she stood at the other end of the table.

"Ugh." Blaise put the bowl down after draining its contents. He was wearing less of it than he first thought, so that was a victory. "I don't think I'm any version of okay right now."

The two women wore concerned looks, but they didn't press him for details, which he appreciated. He offered to pay, but Celeste waved him off and watched him totter out the door and head to the bakery.

Blaise hadn't expected to find Emmaline there. If he had a firmer grasp on time, he would have realized that it made sense that she would be there, cleaning up on her own since Reuben had been summoned away. She stood in the kitchen sweeping, tears streaming down her face as Blaise walked in.

"What happened?" Emmaline asked when she saw him. She clutched the little doll between one hand and the broom handle.

Blaise opened his mouth to speak, but his brain declared itself done with his antics of pretending to be awake. The familiar sights and smells of the bakery wrapped around his exhausted body like a blanket, and the next thing he knew he slumped to the floor and descended into blissful darkness.

CHAPTER TWENTY-ONE
The Apple Doesn't Fall Far from the Tree

Blaise

*T*he floor of the bakery wasn't a contender in Blaise's mind for top places to fall asleep, but when he awoke later, he noted that his body didn't care. Someone had gone upstairs and brought down his pillow and blanket. At least his head wasn't flat against the floor.

Emmaline sat on the floor across from him, arms hugging her knees. Blaise groaned as he sat up. Hardwood floors weren't comfortable mattresses. "How long have I been out?"

She shrugged, eyes red from crying. "I'm not sure. More than a day." It was dark outside, the kitchen lit by a single mage-light.

Blaise scrubbed at his face with one hand. He wasn't sure that he felt much better after sleeping. "How's your father?"

Emmaline kept her head bowed, studying her nails. "Bad. Real bad."

Blaise shut his eyes. "I'm sorry." He hoped she didn't blame him. Would she understand he had done what he could, or would she hate him for what he represented?

"What happened?" Her voice trembled with fear. Confusion. Worry.

He told her what he knew. How Jack had made him stay behind as he scouted ahead. How it must have been a trap—and that same trap had sprung on Blaise when he had gone to see what was taking so long. Her lips pressed together in a thin line when he recounted how Gaitwood threatened her father's life. He hated to tell her those things, but sugarcoating it wouldn't help matters. She deserved the truth.

When he finished, tears streaked her cheeks. Blaise wished he could help her, but he was at a loss. Then she surprised him by surging toward him, almost knocking him over as she tangled him in a hug, burying her head against his shoulder.

"Thank you for bringing him back to me," Emmaline whispered into his shirt. Belatedly, he realized Jack's blood stained it.

"You're welcome." He patted her back, awkward and tense from her sudden closeness.

She pulled away from him after a moment, rubbing at her eyes. "Sorry. It's just . . ." Emmaline chewed her bottom lip, as if debating if she wanted to continue. "I was afraid if he went alone, he wouldn't make it back."

Blaise tilted his head. Had she learned her father's secret? Jack said that no one else in Itude knew. "What makes you say that?"

Emmaline glanced away, embarrassed. "I just . . . nothing." She twisted a lock of hair around one finger. "Can I ask you something on a completely different topic?"

Blaise raised his eyebrows. "Sure."

"When did you come into your magic?" She sat back, watching him.

Completely different topic? Hardly. This was a conversation she should be having with her father, or anyone other than him.

But perhaps she was comfortable talking to him after all the time they had spent together in the bakery.

He respected that. Even if it meant delaying a soak in the tub that would ease his strained muscles.

"Well." He paused, stomach rumbling a reminder to eat. Blaise got up and sought the previous day's leftover cookies. "My magic is weird, so it's hard to say. I think I came into it early, but how much of it was just a kid being a kid and my magic doing its thing is anyone's guess. Definitely before I was ten." He found the coveted cookies and pulled the tin open, grabbing two. Chocolate chip, exactly what he needed. He held one between his lips for safe keeping and offered her one from the open container.

Emmaline plucked a cookie out. "Oh." She placed a mountain of weight on the single word.

Blaise savored the sweet rush of chocolate over his tongue. Tempting as it was to eat the whole tin, he needed to get proper food into his stomach before long. "Any particular reason you're asking?"

Emmaline nibbled at her cookie, then pulled something small out of her pocket. She opened her fist and showed him the tiny doll. "This is why."

After his hours with Jack, Blaise had a better understanding of the doll's importance. He scratched his chin, considering. What a very Jack-like thing to do—create a poppet and give it to his daughter.

"It's . . . special. And I . . ." She shook her head, cheeks blushing with a mix of frustration and embarrassment. "You're going to think this is ridiculous."

Blaise shrugged. "I break things by touching them. Try me."

Emmaline's voice was so soft it was almost difficult to hear. "I felt something when y'all were gone. From the doll."

"What was it like?" Blaise cocked his head, curious.

Tears welled in her eyes. She brushed them away with a fist. "It's hard to explain. I thought something was wrong with *me* at first. Then I realized the little doll was hurting. It hurt so bad,

Blaise, and it scared me. I felt it—all of it. I kept it in my pocket, so I could take it out, and I kept whispering to it. That it would be okay. To . . . to . . ." She chewed on her bottom lip. "*Live.*"

The hairs on Blaise's arms prickled at the supplication, filled with the unmistakable whisper of magic. The scent of ozone after a thunderstorm filled the bakery.

Blaise thought back to the sight of Jack in Gaitwood's silver cage. He had looked bad—so bad that Blaise feared he was already dead, or close to it. But he hadn't died, even when they made their escape, and Jack had looked so much worse.

Had Emmaline somehow given him a touch of healing through the poppet? It sounded reminiscent of the magic Jack had described to him. There was no mistaking that Blaise had experienced the thrum of her magic just a moment ago.

"Sorry. It sounds ridiculous," Emmaline whispered, shamefaced.

Blaise shook his head. "No, it doesn't sound ridiculous at all. Do you . . . know anything about your father's magic?"

Emmaline hunched her shoulders. "I know some of it. But he doesn't talk about it too much around me."

Discussion of magic would be a sore spot for Jack. Blaise winced. Emmaline needed to be informed. He hoped that Jack survived so *he* could be the one to tell her, not Blaise.

"I think you have your father's type of magic," Blaise said after a moment. There was no other thing he *could* say. Emmaline needed to know she wasn't crazy. She had, in fact, saved her father's life. Blaise would not tell her that, though. He couldn't prove it; he just had a hunch.

She blinked at him, owlish. "I guess that makes sense." Emmaline cupped the poppet in her hands. "What if he doesn't make it?" She sounded like a scared, heartbroken child.

Blaise pointed to the doll. "If you keep on doing whatever you're doing, I think he stands a good chance."

The smile that turned the corners of her lips was all the

reward Blaise needed. But an excellent second place prize would be a good meal in his belly—and a bath.

BLAISE CLOSED THE BAKERY FOR A FEW DAYS, JUST SO HE HAD TIME to recover from the rigors of his misadventure with Jack. It galled him to do it, but Emmaline and Reuben were scarce, and he was so exhausted he couldn't tackle the task alone.

Blaise spent most of the first day sleeping. Nadine checked on him at midday, to "make sure you're still alive," as she put it. She told him his body was likely needing time to recover after the drain of the salt-iron and the quick, successive expenses of magic —not to mention the exhausting ride back to town.

On the fourth day, when he was up and shuffling about, Clover ambled up to the bakery. Blaise hadn't seen her since she had carried Jack back to Itude. She was calmer now—Jack was out of danger. The Knossan eyed the "*Closed*" sign on the door, knocking gently with one of her gnarled hands.

Blaise let her in and stepped back as she ducked through the doorway. "Howdy, Clover."

She glanced at the empty display case, then fixed her attention on Blaise. "I wanted to thank you for saving Jack."

He bowed his head in awkwardness. It seemed like something that should have been done, regardless. "It was the right thing to do."

She snorted. "The right thing is often the hardest thing. But I appreciate it." Clover tipped her horns to the side. "You should stop by and see him."

Blaise straightened up, setting a bag of flour on the counter and opening it. "He's awake?" The last report he had received, the outlaw had been unconscious still.

"Awake and in a foul mood," Clover confirmed.

"Does he have any other?" Blaise muttered.

The Knossan flicked an ear. She didn't dispute it. "He was asking for you."

Blaise sighed. Jack was probably mad as a wet hen about the secrets he had spilled. Blaise would have been happy to coexist in Itude without seeing the grumpy outlaw face to face again.

"*Today,*" Clover clarified. By the tone she used, Blaise supposed she meant "*now.*"

Grimacing, he reluctantly closed up the sack of flour. "Guess I'll go pay him a visit."

"You do that," the Knossan agreed.

He put the flour back and followed Clover out. She trotted to the Broken Horn after instructing Blaise to head to Jack's house. Nadine had either released him from her clinic or gotten fed up with his presence there. Either was just as likely.

Emmaline met him at the door to the house, a wan smile on her lips. "Howdy, Blaise."

Blaise noticed her red-rimmed eyes, lower lip jutting out. "How's he doing?"

She shrugged. "Complaining and giving everyone who pokes their head into his room grief. The usual." Emmaline leaned closer to him, her voice softer as she added, "He's like to bite off the hand of anyone who gets too near his wound. It's been rough."

He could only imagine. "I'm sorry."

"Me, too." Emmaline rubbed at her cheek, her face pale. "He was asking after you when he woke up."

"Clover told me." Blaise rubbed his forehead. Emmaline moved aside and pivoted so he could follow her inside.

She led him to a door off the parlor where she paused before knocking. They heard a grunt, and she pushed the door open. "Daddy, Blaise is here."

Jack said nothing as they entered. The outlaw reclined on a bed, pillows placed under him to prop him up. A book with a tasseled bookmark rested on a bedside table. Funny, Blaise hadn't considered Jack the literary sort.

"Need anything?" Emmaline kept her voice neutral.

"Some privacy."

Emmaline's face crumpled, and Blaise understood what she meant about Jack's mood. He was as prickly as a spiny basilisk. Emmaline wiped a tear from her cheek and shut the door. Blaise sat down in the chair beside the bed, judging that Jack looked ill enough that if he took a swing, he would have time to get out of the way.

The room was sparsely furnished. A chest of drawers loomed in one corner and was the only other piece of furniture aside from the bed, bedside table, and chair. Atop the chest stood a doll as tall as his forearm was long, its pale porcelain finish marking it as more a work of art than a plaything. Fragile and beautiful. Dark brown hair framed the doll's face.

Jack stayed quiet, so Blaise pointed at the doll. "One of yours?"

The outlaw's gaze flitted from Blaise to the doll and back again. Was it a figment of Blaise's imagination, or did Jack's eyes soften? "Why'd you do it?"

Blaise frowned. Jack was incapable of holding a conversation like a normal person. "I don't know what you mean."

"You could have left me to Gaitwood. Not even the pegasi would have faulted you. I had one foot in the grave. But you didn't. You rescued me." Jack sounded baffled. "Why?"

Blaise wasn't sure why that was such a puzzling thing. "Because . . . " Why had he? Jack had been nothing but cruel to him. Blaise hated bullies, and *Jack* was a bully. But that didn't mean he deserved to die and leave Emmaline alone. "It was the kind thing to do."

Jack looked at him as if he had been expecting something more profound. "There are those who view kindness as a weakness."

He didn't say it, but Blaise supposed Jack might be counted in that number. "I prefer to consider it a strength."

The outlaw studied him for a moment, considering. He gestured to the porcelain doll, wincing as the movement bothered his injuries. "Kittie."

Blaise blinked, thrown off his train of thought again. "What?"

"You asked if it's one of mine. It is. That's Kittie."

"Oh," Blaise said, then gaped when his brain made the connection. "*Oh*. Your wife—wait, you remember us talking?" He swallowed and scooted his chair the tiniest bit away from the bed.

Jack's eyes crinkled with something like amusement. "I knew what I was saying, even if I was delirious and wouldn't shut my trap."

Blaise blanched. "I won't tell anyone what you told me."

"I know." Jack's voice was matter-of-fact.

"Wait. You do?"

"Yeah." Jack sighed. "I've treated you like a cow patty from the start, and I shouldn't have. You've been nothing but discreet about our first meeting, and I've held it against you."

"I'm really sorry I made your gun explode. I didn't . . ." Blaise felt his pulse race as he thought about it. "I didn't mean to."

The outlaw's gaze roved to the porcelain doll, his lips pressed together in a thin line. He still looked pale and drawn. "Can't say I'll ever forgive you for that. Kittie gave me that revolver." Blaise sank back into his chair, dropping his gaze. "But you proved me wrong. You got control over your magic. If you hadn't, there's no way we'd be alive to have this conversation now."

Blaise realized that, in his cantankerous way, Jack was praising him. It was an unfamiliar sensation to receive praise for his magic —especially from Jack. Maybe he was dreaming. That would make more sense.

"What I'm trying to say is you're welcome in Itude. You saved my life. Back when we were best of friends, I don't think *Lamar* would have saved me." Jack's eyebrows drew together, two angry slashes.

"Oh. Thanks." Blaise wasn't sure which was more awkward: being on Jack's good side, or being hated by him. A change of subject might help. He pointed to the porcelain doll again. "Is . . . is that how you know she's still alive?" He thought about how

Emmaline had told him of her connection to the tiny doll that represented Jack.

Jack looked thoughtful. "Something like that. Before I . . ." His voice faltered, and he looked like he was about to shift into a foul mood again. He took a breath and started over. "Not anymore, for obvious reasons. But before that day, I used to cast on that doll all the time. Gave her strength. Perseverance. Love." His eyes softened. "And now it's all I have left of her."

Blaise rose, inspecting the doll. Jack pined for his wife. Blaise looked at the glossy hair—it looked so real. "Wait. Is that your wife's hair on this doll?"

For just a moment, a feral grin lit Jack's face. "I told you how my magic works. Gives me a better connection."

Blaise made a face. "That's creepy, Jack."

The outlaw snorted a laugh, then grunted in pain. Laughing was off the table, apparently. Blaise had to admit, it was nice to hear Jack laugh when he wasn't out of his mind on an alchemical potion.

"But that's how I knew I could always help her. Believe it or not, her magic was the stronger in our relationship."

Blaise massaged his cheek. "That's terrifying." He moved back to the chair and sat. "I understand why you would keep the creepy doll with you, though."

"It's not creepy; it's art. And a hobby," Jack grumbled.

Blaise chuckled, then had a sobering thought. "Have you talked much to Emmaline?"

Jack looked uncharacteristically guilty. "I just woke up a few hours ago, and everything hurts."

Blaise grunted. He suspected Jack had been short with her. Blaise didn't blame him—the outlaw had nearly died, so he was allowed some level of boorish behavior. But not to his daughter.

He took a chance and leaned closer to Jack so he could get his point across. "You need to talk to her. I think she's the reason you're alive today."

Jack's eyes widened as he took his meaning. "What did she tell you?"

Blaise shook his head. "That's a conversation for you to have with her."

The muscles in Jack's jaw clenched. "At least tell me this much: is she an Effigest?"

Blaise glanced at the porcelain doll again, then back at Jack. "She doesn't play with fire, I'll tell you that much."

CHAPTER TWENTY-TWO
The Talk

Jack

J ack wasn't a stranger to being shot. That was a fact of life as an outlaw. He had been grazed several times, shot in the arm twice, and the leg once. Those had been inconveniences more than anything. He sought out Nadine or another similarly gifted Healer not long after suffering the injuries. He hadn't been so fortunate this time.

Nadine had done her best. She had focused on keeping his organs from giving up the ghost, and he was appreciative. She had to keep some magic in reserve for others, so couldn't completely heal him. Nadine told him the rest of his recovery would be up to him. He understood, but that didn't mean he liked it.

She estimated it would take him at least two months to

recover, which he grumbled about until she pointed out that without her healing, it would take a year or more. He had been at death's door, and Nadine said more than once she didn't know how he hadn't crossed over the threshold. Jack knew but didn't tell her.

Nadine instructed him to keep to light duties. No Salt-Iron merchant thieving operations. No intelligence gathering. No leaving town at all, for that matter. That rankled him.

Jack defied Nadine in one area. He was furious about the misleading intelligence from Hank Walker, and he made an excuse to go to the post office. The postmaster was there, and he visibly quailed when Jack strode in. Walker was lucky he wasn't up to his usual hijinks. Jack wanted to throw him up against the wall and demand answers. He settled for glowering.

Walker swore he had known nothing about the ambush. He was aware the soldiers were around, but not that they were so close. He claimed they'd fed him deceptive information. Jack couldn't prove otherwise, so he let it go. That didn't mean he trusted Walker anymore.

Nadine caught wind of his transgression and gave him a piece of her mind. After that, she had him under house arrest until she gave her leave.

Blaise reopened the bakery, and Emmaline went to help him every morning. Jack still hadn't talked to her about her magic. He wasn't sure how.

Jack was a damn good outlaw. But he considered himself a piss-poor father.

Faedra knows I bungled the birds and the bees talk with her, Jack thought wryly. That had been a disaster.

He decided to talk to her about it today. He had put it off for too long. It was unusual for him to procrastinate. Jack generally preferred to take the bull by the horns. But magic was a sore spot.

The door reverberated with a booming knock. Jack frowned and rose to answer. It was about time for Emmaline to get home, but she wouldn't knock.

He discovered Clover at the door, shifting from hoof to hoof. "Clover? You all right?"

She glanced over her shoulder, her hide twitching as if irritated by an invisible fly. "May I come in?"

Jack nodded. "'Course. You're always welcome here. You know that." He shuffled aside and allowed her to duck inside. She carefully lowered her bulk onto a sturdy chaise Jack had purchased years ago. "What's worrying you?" It took something considerable to worry a Knossan like Clover.

"An outrider came to notify the town that someone with ties to the Salt-Iron Confederation is coming to Itude."

That surprised Jack on several fronts. First, he wouldn't have expected any of the Salties to give the courtesy of advance notice —not to a town full of outlaws. Second, it was akin to asking permission. The outrider could be told *no* and sent on his way. The Salt-Iron Confederation wasn't known for asking permission; they trampled and took what they wanted. Many of their entitled merchants displayed the same behavior. Was it a trap of some sort?

"Who?" Jack asked after he'd considered those angles. He had been out of Confederation lands for many years, but thanks to his network of spies, he was aware of more than the average outlaw.

"An entrepreneur from Ganland. Jefferson Cole."

Ganland. Now Jack understood why Clover was nervous. She had a grim history with the Gannish. Jack had stolen her away from one of the Gannish elite who thought it was cute to collect children of varying races.

There was something about the name that tickled the far recesses of Jack's brain. He would need to go through his sheet of references later to see if it was listed there. "Did the Ringleaders meet to discuss it yet?"

"That is why I came. Raven sent the outrider to cool his heels in the Broken Horn. Hannah and Abe are there, monitoring things, so I could come tell you. The Ringleaders are meeting without you."

Of course they were. *Get shot, and everybody acts like you're made of glass.* Jack eased out of his seat. "I'll just make my way to HQ and invite myself in."

Clover swished her tail, distressed. "Will they be upset I told you? I know Nadine doesn't want you too active."

Jack shook his head. Clover had serious abandonment issues. She didn't show it often, but she was afraid they might cast her from Itude for what she was. The Knossans hadn't allowed her back on their lands, calling her *domesticated.* "Don't you worry your horns about it. They'll be too irate at me showing my mug there to worry about who told me."

That mollified her. Her furry shoulders relaxed. "Be gentle to your body, Jack. You're still healing."

Oh, he was well aware. In fact, as he picked up his hat and put it on, a rush of pain served as a fresh reminder. Jack made a good show of hiding it from Clover, but Knossans had a sharp eye for body language. He couldn't fool her.

"I'll do my best," Jack allowed. She would have to be content with that.

Zepheus waited for him as he made his way out the door. The palomino tossed his head, giving him an innocent look.

<What? I know you too well, Jack.>

"I'm going to have to work on being less predictable," Jack groused.

<I just know what gets you all in a dander.>

"That's unfair. That's most things."

Zepheus snorted, amused. He knelt down, and Jack clambered onto his back. He hissed when his shoulder complained at the movement. Nadine was going to be mad as a hornet if she saw him riding. It was not on her list of *"light"* activities.

Clover watched him with concern until he straightened and waved her off. She nodded to him, brass nose ring flipping with the movement, then trotted back to the saloon. Zepheus turned toward town, shifting to a floating, smooth pace that didn't jar Jack in the slightest.

The savvy stallion stopped before they reached HQ to allow Jack a chance to dismount out of sight of any wag-tongues. Two townsfolk saw him, but he pinned them with one of his trademark glowers until they stopped gawking and hurried on their way.

Jack patted Zepheus's neck, then slowly walked up the steps to Headquarters. He shoved open the door, a spirited discussion resonating from the meeting room.

"Got started without me, I see."

The other four Ringleaders turned in surprise. Nadine's face colored scarlet with fury and she looked like she was ready to get up and throw him all the way back to his bed. Vixen, bless her, laid a hand on Nadine's arm and murmured something Jack couldn't hear. That didn't stop Nadine from glaring at him like she was ready to kill him if his wound didn't get him first. Jack was pretty sure he heard her mutter, "Pure cussedness."

"We assumed you were still recovering," Raven said, his voice bland, then gestured to Jack's customary chair.

"That's where he's supposed to be," Nadine grumbled.

"But you're welcome to join us since you're here," Vixen added brightly. Kur shrugged, not caring either way.

Jack gingerly sat in his seat. "I heard there's a matter for discussion." He made it a point to ignore Nadine's intense stare. Yeah, he was going to get an earful from her later.

Raven nodded, pushing an envelope across the table to him. "Yes. Information that has us regretting you're out of commission or we'd likely have known about this in advance."

Jack picked up the envelope and drew out a letter written on expensive paper, judging by the thickness and woven finish. The author used precise, ornate writing, with no misspelled words or strange punctuation. Someone educated had written this.

He scanned the words on the page. Jefferson Cole, Gannish businessman extraordinaire, humbly asked to stay in Itude for a period of up to a month, to observe the area and seek investment opportunities. Jack scowled. A month was a long time.

"No." Jack folded the letter and nested it in the envelope. He slid it across the table to Raven. "That's my vote. No damned Salties in my town."

"Are you sure?" Vixen asked. "We were thinking I might get some information from this Mr. Cole or his men."

That hadn't occurred to Jack. He was off his game—that should have been one of his thoughts, too. But that didn't mean it was a good idea or one that he even liked. "I stand by my vote. No Salties."

"I am with Jack on this. No." Kur Agur hunched in his chair, hackles raised. He was looking bitey, which was never a good sign.

Raven tapped the letter with his index finger, thoughtful. "I understand your reasoning. It's not a comfortable thing. But it would be good to learn more. We've been cut off. And I would rather us be asked for hospitality like reasonable people than have them march on us."

"We're not *reasonable people,* according to the Confederation. We're outlaws." Jack thought that shouldn't be something he needed to remind them of. Yet here he was, doing it.

"You've also brought us enough intelligence to know not everyone in the Salt-Iron Confederation sees eye to eye, Jack," Nadine pointed out.

And damn, she was right. To an extent. The nations of the Salt-Iron Confederation bickered among themselves like jealous siblings. Phinora, the eldest and grandest, thought she was better than the rest. The others sniped at her however they could. Ganland was one of the more recent additions—though not as recent as Desina—and many of the people there felt differently about magic than those in Phinora. They were much more sympathetic to it, and open to mages using their abilities to better the world (and make a profit) in new and creative ways.

Jack grunted. Damn Nadine and her logic.

"I think it's worth the risk." Uncertainty lit Raven's eyes as he spoke, though. That was good—it was healthy to be cautious around the Salt-Iron Confederation. "We'll outnumber and outgun them, at least for now. And who knows? This could give us a measure of safety if this Mr. Cole wants to do business with us."

Jack snorted. "Look at us, gettin' into bed with the Salties. Deplorable. You lay down with dogs, and you get fleas." Kur twitched an ear and snarled at him. Jack raised his hands in supplication.

Raven ignored him. "I believe the vote is three to two in favor of allowing Mr. Cole one month in our town."

Kur growled softly. *Yeah, I know what you mean,* Jack thought.

"Y'all have some faith in me." Vixen's gaze swung from Jack to Kur. "I'll have it all under control, just you wait and see."

Jack nodded stiffly. Not that he didn't believe in Vixen and her potent form of magic. He was just violently opposed to a Saltie setting foot in Itude. It was *wrong*.

But he had opposed Blaise's presence in Itude, and that had turned out differently than he had expected. Maybe he would be wrong about this, too. For the sake of his town, he hoped so.

The meeting adjourned, and Jack escaped while Vixen caught Nadine and spoke with her about something. The flame-haired outlaw gave him a sly wink. He owed her.

Jack sighed. He would thank Vixen for sparing him Nadine's wrath later. He had to focus on getting home and having The Talk with Emmaline.

Nadine's wrath was almost preferable.

"DADDY? WHERE WERE YOU?"

Emmaline pushed her schoolwork aside when Jack walked in. He did his best to hide his discomfort. The walk back had winded him, and his shoulder burned. Damned inconvenient, this business of being an invalid.

"Ringleader business." Jack hooked his foot around the leg of a chair to pull it out and sat down. He glanced at the discarded homework. Arithmetic, something she had a good head for. Jack knew his numbers and how to figure, but he felt about math the way he felt about politicians: something overall useless to him, but must be tolerated.

Emmaline raised her brows, disapproving. She had been around when Nadine gave her orders.

He didn't want to hear her sniping, and he didn't want to think about the impending arrival of a blasted Salt-Iron Confederation businessman. So he did the only other thing he could. He charged headlong.

"Blaise said I should talk to you. About magic." It was strange to say the Breaker's name. He couldn't remember if he'd said it aloud before. It made him sound more familiar, like a friend. Jack wasn't sure what he thought about that, even if the kid had saved his life.

Emmaline set her pencil down, wary. "He did?"

Jack nodded. "You . . . ah . . . do you have the poppet I gave you years ago?" It was a stupid question. A stalling question.

She plucked the doll out of her pocket, dropping it on the table. Emmaline looked from him to the tiny figure, hesitant.

"Em, what do you know about my magic?"

"You use poppets like this one. They represent people, and you have a better connection if we attach something personal to the doll."

She had paid attention and gleaned bits and pieces from him. Jack made a note to be careful around her, for she had somehow connected things he was certain he'd kept hidden. He had made it a point to not talk about his magic in front of her. Mostly because it stung to talk about something he no longer possessed. Same reason he hadn't spoken about Kittie much in front of her.

Kittie. She would have been better at this talk. Gods, how unfair that she was the one who had been taken. "Good, good." Jack leaned forward, picking up the poppet. He had primed this one by tucking a few strands of his hair beneath the doll's makeshift rag clothing. It didn't take magic to prepare a poppet, but it was required to do just about anything beyond that. He used his index finger to wiggle the doll's shirt down enough to expose the hairs. "Did you know this represents me?"

Emmaline swallowed, studying her hands before giving a tentative nod. "When you gave it to me when I was small, I pretended like it was. And then the last couple of years, whenever you left town, I kept it with me." The corners of her mouth twitched.

Jack sighed inwardly. He was a poor excuse for a father. He should have been paying more attention to see if she was coming into magic. Once upon a time, he prayed she might be normal. If she were normal, then one day she might be spared the outlaw life, the constant danger of capture. He had worked to prepare her to protect herself every other way but magically, and that was an oversight brought about by his own hubris. It was time to correct that.

"You're probably an Effigest like me." Jack's voice was soft. "I think . . ."

"Blaise said I'm the one who kept you alive."

He met her eyes and nodded. "He told me something similar. Can you tell me about it?"

Emmaline picked up the poppet and cupped it in her hands. "I kept it with me when you were gone. I thought I was going crazy, but I could feel the poppet hurting. It was so bad."

Pain haunted her voice, and Jack's heart ached. She had a deep connection to that doll, forged by years of carrying it with her. Poppets were difficult, but not impossible, to use if the target had no connection to them. That was a lesson for later.

"What did you do?"

"I was so scared. It felt like . . . it was like having you in the room with me. You were hurt, and what could I do? I whispered to it and cradled it and just . . ." Tears rolled down her cheek, and she scrubbed them away with one hand. "I didn't want you to leave me all alone. I wanted you to live. To come back to me and be healthy."

She was still holding the poppet. Warmth blossomed in Jack's shoulder, like skin bared to the sun. The pressure of magic built in the room like a summer thunderstorm. It was subtle; a normal person would have written both off as nothing to be concerned about. But Jack noticed. Emmaline had magic, was actively using it, and wasn't aware of it. The outlaw's jaw clenched in chagrin as he thought back to Blaise's uncontrolled magic. *I'm a damn hypocrite.*

He placed his hand over hers, the movement enough to distract her. The magic released, the pressure whooshing away. "You definitely have my magic. And you kept me alive." Jack rubbed the back of his head, trying to figure out where to go from here.

Emmaline pulled her hand from beneath his and released the poppet. "Will you teach me?"

What else could he say? He had taught her how to shoot a gun and survive the rugged life outside the Salt-Iron Confederation. There was no way he would deny her this. "It won't be easy, but I will."

Relief flooded her face. She feared it, he realized. Good. A mage needed a healthy respect for their magic.

"Thank you, Daddy."

She pushed her chair from the table and came around to hug him. He let her, ignoring the burst of pain from the gesture because for a moment his turbulent life calmed. His daughter had magic, but he would figure it out with her. And he was pretty sure she had just healed his shoulder a little more, which was a pleasant bonus.

CHAPTER TWENTY-THREE
A Piece of the Action

Blaise

*I*tude buzzed with the impending arrival of someone from the Salt-Iron Confederation. Blaise heard the gossip that afternoon from Ellie Pembroke when he stopped by the mercantile to pick up a few items. She was a bustling mix of curiosity and anxiety, which Blaise soon realized was the overwhelming feeling of most of the town.

He thought to ask Vixen about it, since she was the most forthcoming of the Ringleaders. He was on better terms with Jack after everything that happened, but he wasn't sure they were friends. Jack wasn't going around trying to punch him in the face, but Blaise figured he was only hampered by his injury.

Vixen was nowhere to be found. Blaise stopped by the stables to look for Emrys. It could be hit or miss finding the stallion—

sometimes he was out working sentry duty or in areas that Blaise couldn't access, grazing. But this time he found most of the pegasi stabled, and the barn had an unsettled air to it.

"What's going on?" Blaise let himself into Emrys's stall. The pegasi stalls were large enough to unfurl the full length of their wings if needed.

<No one is happy about this Jefferson Cole coming,> Emrys answered. <Raven told us to not go out on sentry duty until he and his party have arrived.> The sound of a donkey braying reached them from outside. The stallion's ears swiveled. <Peanut says they're approaching.>

Blaise gave Emrys a conciliatory pat on the shoulder, then slipped out of the stall. Other townspeople had gathered outside, though he didn't miss the fact that it was only the humans. The pegasi were the largest population of non-humans, though Itude boasted others: Clover, Kur, a family of harpies, a knocker.

Everyone present watched the road that led into town from the east—the only side of the town accessible by horseback or wagon. It wasn't long before a lead rider trotted into town, wearing the forest green and white of Ganland. Blaise released a breath he hadn't realized he was holding. He had been afraid to see the red and gold of the Salt-Iron Confederation.

Two others followed the outrider, one of them a man who sat tall and straight in his saddle, a wide-brimmed hat shading his eyes. He wore a black duster, and he looked so much like any other rider that it took Blaise a moment to realize that nearby whispers identified him as Jefferson Cole. A woman so short Blaise nearly mistook her for a child rode beside him, strands of bright pink hair wisped loose beneath her hat.

Raven, Vixen, and Nadine stepped out to greet them. Blaise was too far off to hear the exchange of words, but he saw Vixen gesture to the stables for their mounts and then toward the boarding house. There were nodding and animated gestures all around, and Jefferson Cole even shook their hands in a show of good faith. The tiny pink-haired woman stayed on her horse and surveyed the situation, her critical eyes reminding Blaise of Jack—who wasn't in attendance.

It all looked mundane from Blaise's vantage point, and he relaxed as he saw there was nothing out of the ordinary about these visitors. He had expected Cole to come with a platoon of guards to protect him and the pennants of the Confederation flying overhead. Maybe this wasn't anything to worry about. Just a regular merchant.

He went back into the stables and told Emrys as much. It didn't escape Blaise's notice that the other pegasi had their heads over their partitions, listening in.

<You may be right, but we will still be vigilant.> Emrys shifted his weight from one side to the other. <You should be wary, too.>

"I will," Blaise promised.

FOR THE MOST PART, LIFE RETURNED TO NORMAL AFTER THE SALT-Iron Confederation businessman's first day in Itude. The humans settled back into their routines, though the non-humans were ill at ease. Kur Agur prowled the streets, hackles up and fangs bared. Clover hardly left the dark interior of the saloon.

Late in the morning, the bell over the bakery's door jingled. Emmaline had already left to practice her magic with her father, so only Reuben remained to help Blaise finish up for the day. Blaise kept his attention on mixing strained honey, sugar, and melted butter into a bowl of sifted flour, content that Reuben would handle the new customer.

"Oh, this is the charming bakery I've heard so much about."

Blaise froze, then pivoted at the unfamiliar voice. He knew everyone in town—if he forgot their names, he at least recognized who was a regular by their voice. And this speaker was new, with an accent that set him apart.

"Are you the one who owns this place?" The man leaned against the glass display case, eyes on Reuben. He owned the room with his presence, standing tall in a dark grey frock coat that cloaked his form, a burgundy vest with silver accents peeking out from beneath. His head was bare, a black felt derby hat held in one hand.

"Not me." Reuben shook his head, jerking his thumb back to indicate Blaise. "I work here. Wildfire Jack owns the building, but the business is all Blaise."

The newcomer cocked his head, tendrils of hair shifting with the movement. Intense green eyes settled on Blaise. "I see. Jefferson Cole, pleasure to meet you."

"Howdy." Blaise shrank under the power of Cole's gaze. From the gossip circulating town, Blaise gleaned that Cole was rich. Which made it exceedingly suspicious that he'd come to a tiny town like Itude. Blaise had hoped to avoid Cole's attention during his stay. So much for that.

Reuben quirked an eyebrow, then took Cole's order. Blaise tried to tune out the whole transaction, but his hands were twitchy with nerves. He still practiced his magic regularly, as Vixen advised, but just thinking of the Salt-Iron Confederation renewed his panic.

"Blaise?" It was Reuben.

Blaise blinked, turning. "Oh. Sorry. What is it?" Jefferson Cole stood on the other side of the counter, a half-eaten chocolate chip cookie in his well-manicured hand.

"I wanted to extend my compliments. This cookie is phenomenal." His eyes flitted from the cookie to Blaise. "It's amazing. Almost magical. So I have to ask: is it?" Cole bit off another chunk. He licked a morsel of chocolate from his lips and sighed with contentment.

"What?" Talking with this man was as frustrating as speaking with Jack.

Cole raised the remains of his cookie. "Magical. Is the food here magical?"

No one had ever asked him that before. Was magical baking even a possibility? And if so, why couldn't that have been his magic? "I don't think so. I just know what I'm doing."

Cole regarded the cookie with a small measure of disappointment. "That's unfortunate. But all the same, it's delicious by itself. Best thing I've had in my mouth since I was home in Nera." His forehead puckered, thoughtful. "Do you sell to any outside vendors?"

Blaise's pulse raced. These rapid-fire questions were disorienting. Why wouldn't Cole just leave? He took a moment to puzzle out what the entrepreneur meant before answering. "Oh. Um, I sell bread every day to the Jitterbug next door."

Cole nodded, making a small sound of assent. "I see." His eyes scanned the case of baked goods, a covetous look flitting across his handsome features. "I'm always seeking out new investments and profitable ventures. I see—or should I say, taste—a lot of potential here." His gaze settled unerringly on Blaise, posing an unspoken question.

Blaise wasn't sure what he was getting at. "Well, thanks."

"If you ever think to expand this operation, keep me in mind." Cole picked up a box of cookies that Reuben had put together for him. "I wouldn't mind getting a piece of the action." He gave them a friendly nod, then pushed open the door and strode out.

Reuben rubbed his forehead. "What was that all about?"

Blaise released a long, pent-up breath. "Your guess is as good as mine, but no way would I work with that guy." He finally finished mixing the ingredients, but the pit of his stomach roiled with nerves and not even baking calmed it.

"Those Gannish know how to bring in the money, though, from what I've heard," Reuben reasoned.

"There's more to this life than money."

"Maybe. But it doesn't hurt."

"I HEAR COLE STOPPED BY THE BAKERY." JACK'S VOICE WAS NEUTRAL, though his stiff-legged stance and crossed arms belied the casualness of the statement.

Blaise glanced from Jack to the line of teenagers standing in a row, taking practice shots at targets placed on the little-used north side of the plateau. Jack had taken over training the younger outlaws while he convalesced, and he had demanded Blaise take part in that training. After escaping Lamar Gaitwood for a second time, Blaise wasn't inclined to tell him *no*.

"He stopped by," Blaise agreed, deciding not to offer Jack any more information than necessary. That seemed like the most prudent way to stay on the outlaw's good side. There were way too many revolvers around right now for Blaise's comfort.

"What'd he want?" Jack kept his eyes on the teens. "Stop slouching, Reuben!" Reuben yelped and straightened with a guilty glance over his shoulder.

"He bought cookies, so that'll help me pay this month's lease," Blaise said dryly. "He asked if my baking was magical. Is there such a thing?"

The outlaw rubbed his chin, contemplating. "Huh. Hadn't thought about that. I don't know of anyone with such magic, but that doesn't mean much."

Blaise sighed. "I wish that *was* my magic."

"Anything else?" Jack pressed.

"He asked if I sold to any outside vendors, so I told him I sold to Celeste and Mindy."

Jack's lips pressed into a taut line. "Hmm." Then he cast whatever he was thinking aside in favor of the trainees. "Keep a proper grasp, Cordelia! You've got the grip slipping around in your hand like a slick basilisk. Tuck those thumbs!" The raven-haired teen winced and addressed the issue.

"What's he doing in Itude?" Blaise asked once Jack finished haranguing Cordelia.

Jack shook his head. "That's what I've been trying to figure out. He told Vixen he's here looking for investment opportunities and to see the sights. I don't trust him. He's too full of himself, and he's a businessman, and I hate both."

"I'm going to split hairs here, but you could be considered both, too."

The outlaw snorted. "Shut your piehole."

Blaise clamped his mouth shut, the corners of his mouth twisting with amusement.

"He's also a Saltie which means I trust him about as far as I can throw him. Maybe not even that far." Jack angled his right foot and dug the heel of his boot into the ground.

"Seems like a lot of strikes against him. Why is he even allowed to stay in town?"

Jack grimaced. "I'm not the only one who gets to decide. Which is unfortunate."

Blaise nodded, though he knew very well the outlaw had felt the same about his presence. Before he could say anything else, Jack had the current group of five step back so that Blaise and four others could replace them taking practice shots.

Blaise sighed and unholstered the revolver at his side. He didn't like the feel of the weapon in his hands at all, and after his first nervous touch of the metal, he had quickly taken out his gloves and slipped them back on. Jack frowned but didn't argue. No one wanted a gun blowing up in their midst.

A row of tin cans perched atop the remains of a fence served as their targets. Each student had to take down five cans—or wait until Jack called their group back, whichever happened first. It was no surprise that Blaise hadn't hit a single target yet.

Emmaline was in Blaise's group, and she gave him an encouraging smile as she lined up her shot. She squeezed the trigger, her grip on the sixgun steady and flawless. An instant later, she was rewarded by the ping of a bullet connecting, the can clattering to the red dirt. She made a flourishing gesture, encouraging him to take his turn.

"Yeah, yeah," Blaise grumbled, his gloved right hand wrapped around the grip. Sweat trickled down his forehead and seeped into his eye. He shook his head to flick it away, then took aim again and pulled the trigger. The revolver recoiled, surprising him when the bullet winged the tin can he had aimed at and sent it tumbling to the ground.

"There you go!" Emmaline whooped.

"You're still winning."

She aimed at the next can in her set. "Been doing this for years. You'll get there." Her shot sent the can flying.

Jack called for a change, and Blaise was more than happy to retreat. "Wasn't completely awful. Just mostly awful," Jack acknowledged.

Blaise gave an ironic salute. "High praise. Thanks."

Jack snickered. "Next time keep your thumb against the recoil shield. Then you can put pressure against the back of the sixgun, and it'll keep it from bouncing up. Acts like a counterweight."

Blaise blinked at the constructive feedback. "Oh, thanks." He sat down cross-legged next to the outlaw. "So, do you think Cole is here after investments? He's not . . . a spy or something?"

"Everyone's a spy until I find out otherwise." Jack said it so deadpan that Blaise figured he spoke the truth.

"Did you think I was one?"

Jack snorted. "No. I thought you were a green as grass kid who couldn't wield his own magic. And I was right."

That wasn't fair. "There were no complaints when that green as grass kid broke you out of Gaitwood's trap."

"You asked, and I answered honestly." The outlaw scratched his chin. "Cole could be a spy. He came to town on day one with that itty-bitty, pink-haired woman, and then she took off, and no one's seen hide nor hair of her since. But his story checks out in that the Gannish are always looking for a profit, which makes them . . . less antagonistic towards magic than some other Salties. But in my mind, once you throw in your lot with them, you're not to be trusted."

That made sense to Blaise.

"Some other Ringleaders see his presence here as protection. If we work with them, it would make Gaitwood and his ilk look bad if they attacked. And it may even tie their hands." He said the last with reluctance, as if he also saw the wisdom of that.

Blaise rubbed his chin. He had to agree, that sounded like a compelling reason. "That would protect Itude. So that's good, right?"

Jack snorted. "Only if you take it at face value. What if it's a plot? A double-cross?"

"You have serious trust issues," Blaise observed.

"You think?" Jack grunted. "I just don't want to take foolish chances. We have too much to lose." His gaze rested on his daughter as he spoke, the afternoon breeze whipping her long blonde hair behind her. "Cole also spoke to Vixen about permission to bring a survey team here to look for something. I didn't find out what. Maybe salt-iron. Before I was . . . a few months ago I heard there were some miners striking veins in Argor."

"Wouldn't it be a problem if salt-iron got discovered around here?" The thought gave Blaise chills. He didn't know much about mining, but a lode of salt-iron near magic users was a disconcerting idea. And with how highly the Salt-Iron Confederation treasured the ore, it could quickly become a bone of contention.

Jack's mouth tugged down into a frown. "It would be a problem. But I've got my ears open, and our knocker has been putting feelers out for me."

Blaise cocked his head, perplexed. "Jasper Strop? What do knockers do?"

"They have an affinity for precious stones and metals." Jack looked like he might say more, but he left it at that. "If the Confederation sends people here and they find something like that, no one on the outside will get word of it." His voice took on the brutal, no-nonsense tone that Blaise associated with Wildfire Jack, the outlaw who tolerated no bullshit.

Right. Jack would murder them. Blaise rubbed the side of his face.

"Anyway, you're up again." Jack jerked his chin toward the line of practicing teens. Blaise groaned.

CHAPTER TWENTY-FOUR
Every Man Has a Price

Jack

"Mr. Dewitt! A moment of your time."

Jack stopped mid-stride, hackles raised at the voice. *The entrepreneur. How does he know my name?* He pivoted, schooling his face into a cool, stony expression. "The name is Wildfire Jack."

Jefferson Cole flashed a charming yet apologetic smile. "Of course, of course. My sincere apologies. If you could spare a moment of your time, I'd like to buy you a drink and discuss a business proposition with you."

I'll bet you would. Jack fixed him with an impassive look for a beat, then shrugged. "Sure." It wouldn't hurt to keep his ears open and get an idea of what the Saltie was playing at.

Oblivious to Jack's machinations, Cole made a welcoming gesture and started walking to the Broken Horn. Jack followed. It was midafternoon, and the saloon would be empty. When Cole pushed open the door, Clover was wiping down the bar. That was good. She had sensitive hearing, so would keep an ear out for signs of trouble.

Cole selected a table in the corner. Clover didn't bother coming over; she eyed them from across the bar. "What'll it be?"

"The usual." Jack scratched at his right ear as he spoke, a sign the Knossan would understand from previous dealings.

"I'll have the same." Cole nodded.

Jack concealed his smirk. He hoped Cole had a solid constitution. The greenhorn was about to be in for a surprise.

Clover ambled over with two tin mugs. The stuff inside reeked like fetid old boots and the contents of an outhouse. Prior experience proved the vile concoction was harsh enough to take paint off a building. All the same, he took a long, steady gulp. It tasted as awful as it smelled, but Jack tolerated the occasional rotgut, even though it truly wasn't his preferred drink.

Cole followed his example, and Jack chuckled inwardly—the other man didn't outright gag or spit it out. He'd seen that before, and it amused him every time. Cole took a sip, his perfect complexion taking on an interesting shade of green. He swallowed it and then politely scooted the mug aside.

"What'd you want to discuss?" Jack took another disgusting dreg, purely for the amount of discomfort it would cause his counterpart.

The businessman coughed, and for one sweet moment, Jack thought he was going to lean over and retch. Clover snorted with concern. Fortunately, for the sake of her hardwood floors, Cole regained his composure and straightened with a great deal of effort.

"I've come to your fine town in search of some investment opportunities." Clover, showing more kindness than was strictly necessary, brought over a glass of water which Cole drank with a grateful sigh. "And it's come to my attention that you own the bakery building."

Jack noted by the way Cole settled in his chair that the businessman expected him to make some affirmative reply. Instead, he took another drink of rotgut, meeting Cole's eyes as it burned all the way down.

Cole looked away first, then started again. "Do you own the bakery, and if so, would you be willing to sell it?"

"It's not for sale."

Cole frowned. Here was a man who wasn't told *no*, Jack decided. That gave Jack even more incentive to deny him. "I understand if it has sentimental value to you. I can be generous with my offer."

"As I said, not for sale."

To his credit, Cole didn't show any outward signs of frustration. Instead, he pulled a small rectangle of paper and a pen from a pocket hidden inside his pinstriped waistcoat. He wrote something down on the back of the card, then pushed it across the table.

Jack scowled, then used his index finger to draw the card closer. He flipped it over. One side was a business card, listing Jefferson Cole's address in Ganland along with a secondary office in Rainbow Flat. On the back, he had written a number. Ten thousand golden eagles. Far and away more than the bakery was worth, at least in little Itude.

That didn't matter. It was the principle. No Saltie was going to own so much as a blade of grass or speck of Itude's dust. He shrugged and slipped the card back across the table. "I don't think so."

Cole drew the card back over and gave Jack an assessing look. The businessman tapped the card with his pen, contemplative. He wasn't done with their charade, so he wrote a new number and slid it across the table.

Jack picked up the card. This time, he was the one who was surprised. Five hundred thousand golden eagles. Who *was* this Jefferson Cole, to throw around these kinds of sums as if they were naught but crumbs? Jack needed to dig into his research as soon as he could.

But damn him, that figure was tempting. Cole's strategy of throwing money at him almost worked. Jack could buy Itude ten times over—maybe more. Bribe and pay off officials in the Salt-Iron Confederation to stop looking for him. Move around the continent with the freedom bought by gold. He could use it to find Kittie.

Every man has a price, Jack cautioned himself. Cole had just found his. He kept his cool—he couldn't let the businessman perceive how much he *wanted* that, for the sheer amount of magic that wealth could make happen. As an outlaw, Jack never hurt for money; he took what he wanted. But this was on a different level.

He made a show of thinking about the offer, but in actuality, he was trying to analyze why Cole wanted the bakery so badly. He didn't like any of the reasons he came up with. First, if he knew what Blaise *was,* that would give him direct access to the Breaker. The kid loved that bakery and that would be a binding leash for him. Even if Cole had no idea what Blaise was, there was still the fact that this would give someone with ties to the Salt-Iron Confederation a foothold in Itude, no matter how small.

Jack had worked hard to make Itude appear insignificant to the Salt-Iron Confederation. It bothered Jack that this had changed, just as it bothered him Cole knew his last name.

Jack allowed himself a whistle of appreciation, then shook his head with regret that was easy to feign. "I'm sorry. And you are a man of your word—that is *most* generous. But I won't sell the bakery."

Cole stared at him, dumbfounded. "I can do better."

Damn him. "And I'll still turn it down."

The entrepreneur concluded that he had met his match. He nodded and rose from the table. "I see. I appreciate you taking the time, regardless. It's been a pleasure."

Yeah, right. "Likewise."

Cole made a dignified retreat for the exit. Jack watched him go, then thoughtfully picked the business card up from the table. Clover plodded over and peered at the figures on the card, ears pinned back in shock and her eyes white-rimmed.

"I don't like the Gannish and even *I* think you've lost your mind."

Jack chuckled, shaking his head. "It's not about the money." He paused. "Well, I'm lying. It is, but that's why this rubs me the wrong way."

Clover considered, then made a soft sound of understanding. "You think he's trying to buy his way into making you complacent?"

"Something like that," Jack agreed. He didn't want to give voice to all his ideas. He needed time to mull over them. And he had research to do. He got up but paused as he had a thought. "He eats here sometimes?"

Clover nodded. "Most evenings."

"He talk with anyone here?"

The Knossan nodded. "He is friendly with our citizens."

Of course. He was working to curry good favor. "Anything I might find of interest?"

Clover thought for a moment. "He mentions Rainbow Flat frequently. He said that is his next stop, after Itude."

That tracked with the information on his card. "Thanks for keeping an ear open. I'm heading home."

Clover gave him a gentle thump on the back as he headed out. Jack made sure Cole was nowhere in sight, then quick-stepped toward home.

Emmaline wasn't there when he arrived, which suited his purposes. He didn't want anyone seeing what he was about to do. Jack shouldered his dresser away from the wall, revealing a panel that opened with the press of his fingers. He pulled out a leather messenger bag, opening it and spreading the contents over the bed. Then he opened the top drawer on the dresser and pulled out a notebook. It listed names and numbers, but he had devised a system that made them appear meaningless to most.

He flipped through the notebook, comparing notations to some of the folded missives. Jack went through them for several hours, long enough that the natural light faded and he had to turn on mage-lights to continue his research. He heard Emmaline come in, but he called to her that he was busy and not to be disturbed. She wouldn't be happy, but he wanted to solve this puzzle.

It took some doing, but eventually he found the reference he was looking for regarding one Mr. Jefferson Cole. The handwriting sample was a match for the writing on the back of the business card.

"Gotcha, you bastard," Jack murmured, glancing from one missive to the chart in his meticulous notebook.

Malcolm Wells
>   *Salt-Iron Council Doyen Representative: Ganland*
>   *Occupation: Investor*
>   *May use pseudonym Jefferson Cole to conduct business in Untamed*
Territory
>   <u>*Assets in Rainbow Flat???*</u>

Sometime in the past, Jack had underscored the last sentence several times. The significance panned out with the business card. Rainbow Flat. That town was downright civilized compared to Itude, and from there Cole would have no trouble going back to Confederation territory. And he would take everything he had learned about Itude with him.

With this additional information, he felt validated in his conviction that Cole was a threat to Itude. "Ace in the hole," he murmured, closing the notebook and placing it back in the drawer. Now he would lie in wait to see when he could best use that information. Cole would not get the best of *his* town.

CHAPTER TWENTY-FIVE
Good Luck and Have Fun

Jack

Jack watched as the thirteen outlaw trainees—including Blaise—assembled. He tugged his hat down to shade his eyes from the sun. His revelation of Jefferson Cole's identity had him on edge, though the Gannish man had been nothing but a model visitor, much to Jack's consternation. To keep his annoyance at bay, Jack focused on training the younger outlaws, and it was high time for one of the more entertaining training activities he had devised.

Today they would blend magic and the mundane. Most of the trainees were excellent shots, but they weren't used to aiming *at* someone. Which, to be fair, was an overall good practice while learning. Aside from Blaise, none of the youngsters had seen a true fight of any kind. If trouble found Itude, Jack wanted everyone prepared.

The other Ringleaders thought him daft when he placed the order for first-generation hexguns from Ravance. Hexguns were relatively new, the invention of a talented gunsmith attempting to blend magic and bullets. They were still in development and had limited success, but they intrigued Jack, and he thought they might be fun to tinker with.

The set that had shipped to Itude came with a trial batch of ammunition. Hexguns loaded the same way as a standard revolver, but the cartridges were different. Instead of a lead or copper casing, the hexgun's round bullets were cased in flexible gelatin. Enchanted water filled the ball's interior, designed to hold a spell. From what Jack had gleaned, only two spells worked with the hexguns so far: a sleep spell and a nullification spell. Jack preloaded the hexguns with nullification spells, but also added an injection of food coloring to show when someone was struck.

Jack was pleased with the idea. He liked the opportunity to try out new technology and see how his trainees would fare in simulated combat. The other Ringleaders had reservations, but he had successfully argued it was better than letting the trainees wing each other. Nadine didn't have the time or magic for that much carnage.

The trainees eyed the crate next to Jack with interest. He drew the cover off, pulling out a bundle covered in wrapping paper. Jack peeled away the paper, revealing the hexguns. Rather than steel, they were crafted from brass, which gave them a different heft from a standard sixgun.

"Today's training is going to differ from any in the past," Jack said to the assembled group. "You'll be pitted against one another, using anything at your disposal to come out on top—including magic."

A few of the non-mage trainees quailed. Reuben raised his hand. "Um, I thought it was against the rules to use magic in town?"

Jack glared at the teen. *Give me patience with these kids.* "This is practice. My goal is for this training to be as close to an actual fight as you can get. But don't worry, no one will get hurt." To prove his point, he targeted Reuben's left leg and squeezed the trigger. Reuben yelped as a bright purple splotch appeared. Maybe that did sting a little. "No one will get hurt too much," Jack amended.

The kids traded anxious looks. Jack wouldn't let that bother him. In an actual battle, they wouldn't have time for misgivings. He pointed to the crate. "Everyone gets a hexgun. You have six shots. Make them count. If you're a mage, you can use your magic to your advantage. If you don't have magic, you had better pray that you can get a shot off before someone else gets a spell or shot on you." He paused, gesturing to the hexgun in his hand. "These are loaded with nullification shot. If you're a mage and you're hit, you won't be able to use magic for a while." Eyes widened in surprise. "This exercise will take place in the box canyon."

Jack whistled, and a moment later, thirteen pegasi answered his summons. The trainees who hadn't ridden a pegasus before looked on with expressions of excitement and wonder.

The trainees came and picked up their hexguns. Blaise was the last in line, chewing his lower lip. "Can I not do this?"

Jack quirked an eyebrow. "You know the dangers that await us outside of the Gutter."

The Breaker dropped his gaze. "I'd rather not be reminded of that."

That was too bad. "You don't get to make that choice. Not in Itude." Jack picked up the last hexgun and handed it to him. "Keep your gloves off, unless you don't want to use your magic."

Blaise heaved a sigh and removed his gloves, sticking them in his back pocket. He accepted the hexgun, tucking it into his waistband before walking over to Emrys. Zepheus trotted up to Jack and paused long enough for him to swing into the saddle.

"Let's go," Jack ordered. Everyone mounted, and the pegasi bolted into the sky, following Zepheus the short distance to a box canyon nestled to the north.

The box canyon held the tumbledown remains of the original

town of Itude. Thick vegetation choked the remnants, obscuring the streets. Several of the buildings had fallen in on themselves, though at least three were still in a condition to serve as hiding places.

Jack called for everyone to cluster around Zepheus in a circle. "Your pegasi will drop you off at predetermined locations. I'll whistle twice when it's time to start. You can form alliances if you want—that's up to you. But the game doesn't end until there's only one person standing."

Cordelia cleared her throat to get his attention. "Um, can I ask why we're doing this?"

Jack stared at her until she dropped her gaze. "Survival. The world is unfair. It's past time y'all learned how to get the upper hand." He jutted his chin toward Blaise. "Of all of you, *he* knows how to do that. No one escapes the Salt-Iron Confederation twice without learning from the experience."

Blaise looked away, embarrassed.

Jack didn't care. It was true. Blaise was, against the odds, a survivor. Whether he used his skills in this practice didn't matter. But Jack wanted the others to have a chance to use theirs.

"Pegasi, take the riders to their positions. Good luck and have fun."

CHAPTER TWENTY-SIX

Man Down

Blaise

"Jack and I have very different ideas of fun," Blaise muttered as he slid down from Emrys's back. The stallion flew to the north side of the ghost town, near what appeared to be the dilapidated remains of stores built side-by-side along a boardwalk.

The pegasus snorted. <No one has real bullets. This is a simple way to gain practice in a combat situation.>

"Doesn't mean I'll have *fun*, though." Blaise patted the stallion's neck. "Thanks for the ride."

<Good luck.> Emrys bobbed his head and trotted off before lurching into the air to join the other pegasi on a cliff overlooking the canyon.

Blaise stood on the main drag of the ghost town and turned in a slow circle, taking in his surroundings. A building with a steeple crouched at the end of the defunct, dusty road. Scrub grew up around the remains of the buildings, obscuring their facades. Blaise walked closer to one, peering through the window. The structure's roof had collapsed into the interior, sunbeams illuminating the wreckage.

Jack's piercing whistle sliced the air. Blaise rolled his shoulders, drawing a deep breath. He exhaled, forcing out his annoyance at the situation. None of the other trainees were in his view yet, but it would only be a matter of time. Blaise was reluctant to take part in this exercise, but he didn't want to be the first out. Jack wouldn't let him live it down.

Blaise slipped into the building with the ruined roof. Once inside, slanted pieces of timber proved some optimistic person had tried to shore up the roof before it fell in, but time and the elements rendered their attempts useless. Blaise skirted the worst of the debris and found a questionably safe place to wait and consider his options.

Six shots. Each trainee had six, so no one person could take out everyone. That meant they would have to rely on crossfire or allies taking out their opponents. If he teamed up with one other person, they would have twelve shots between them.

He expected the teens without magic would group up, bolstering their lack of magic with numbers. Would the other mages feel the same way, or would they prefer to keep apart?

Blaise thought about that. He would prefer to work with someone else. Maybe he could find Reuben and join forces. Reuben had no magic and wasn't a better shot than Blaise, but at least they could be hopeless together. And maybe he could find Emmaline. They would have a chance with her on their side.

That was a solid idea. The hardest part was going to be finding them and not getting shot by anyone else first.

He crept closer to the window, peering out. Skunkbush and stunted cat-claw trees provided cover, obscuring his position. Two teens scurried down the street, crouching as they ran to keep a low profile. The shrubs hindered his view, so Blaise couldn't tell exactly who they were, but he didn't think they were mages.

A pop split the air, followed by the ping of a pellet hitting a target. One teen yelped, a bright yellow splash blooming across their back.

"Damn it!" the struck girl shrieked, spinning around to see who had fired on her. Her companion dove away, scarcely avoiding another pellet that struck the ground where he had been a second earlier.

Two shots. Whoever had just fired only had four remaining. Blaise followed the gaze of the girl to the bell tower of the church. Blaise blinked, not believing his eyes. Someone stood on the side of the steeple, as easily as anyone else would stand on flat land. Another pop sounded, and the teen on the tower skated around the side, keeping their feet in contact with the surface as they moved.

Blaise squinted, trying to figure out who it was. The figure moved, and he recognized the profile as one of the young mages, Austin. What sort of magic was that? Blaise hadn't bothered to find out the abilities of the other mages in town. He considered changing that.

The trainee firing on Austin missed, but now everyone knew his position. He had the advantage of high ground, but if enough came after him, he wouldn't have the ammunition to hold them off.

Boots crunched on the ground, a shadow flickering as someone else approached Blaise's location. He held his hexgun at the ready, keeping his position close to the door. From this distance, he had a chance to strike an opponent. It wouldn't be fair, but it occurred to him that Jack wasn't trying to teach them about playing fairly today. He wanted them to think about how to survive. And Blaise had learned how to survive.

The door opened slowly. Blaise's index finger flitted against the trigger as he waited. He recognized Emmaline's blonde hair, illuminated by the bright light, a golden halo. Blaise kept the hexgun aimed in her direction, and when she noticed the glint of its muzzle, she pointed hers at him, but didn't fire.

"It's me," Blaise hissed. "Want to team up?"

Emmaline eyed him, then lowered her hexgun. "Austin's up on the steeple. Not a terrible place. I considered joining him, but I think he'd shoot me first."

Blaise chuckled. "I saw that, too. And he probably would."

"There's already three out." Emmaline settled down by the other window. "Cordelia was the first to go. Too slow to use her magic. Then two norms, Tilla and Ambrose."

Blaise nodded. Tilla must have been the girl he saw sniped by Austin. "What's Cordelia's magic? Did you see it?"

"Briefly. The shot disrupted it," Emmaline murmured. "She's a Phase Shifter—she can shift herself out of our reality to avoid damage. She looked all wavy, but then Ambrose saw her. I got Ambrose."

Blaise blinked as the explanation went over his head. *Right.* "So you only have five shots left?"

"Right."

Three mages and five norms left. Four teens were excellent shots, if Blaise remembered right. "Think we should join Austin?"

"No." Emmaline shook her head. "We'd be exposed. I—"

The door at the rear of the building slammed open. There was no more time to discuss strategy. Two silhouettes appeared in the glare of sunlight. Blaise scrambled away from his position as a pellet spattered nearby. Wood clattered as Emmaline dashed to a better position, startling Blaise with how fast she moved. She vaulted over a broken table and fired a shot at the intruders, hitting one squarely in the chest. The boy yelped.

The other teen trained his hexgun on Emmaline, who had lost her momentum and was cornered. She dove behind a chair, running out of options. Blaise glanced at the floorboards, an idea springing into his mind. He slammed his palm down against them, willing for them to shatter beneath Emmaline's attacker. His magic responded, surging into the planks. The wood was easily suggestible, creaking and disintegrating to dust beneath the boy's feet.

He staggered as he lost his footing, barely catching himself as he came down. But he was agile, and as soon as he landed, he pointed his hexgun at Blaise. The muzzle made a muted pop, and Blaise felt the sting of a pellet against his chest. Yellow paint splattered across his shirt, accompanied by a dull sensation that forced his magic to recede.

Then the boy groaned as Emmaline returned fire, turning the side of his shirt bright yellow, too.

"Gotcha, Desmond!" Emmaline crowed, shooting Blaise a guilty look. "Sorry. But thanks for the save."

Blaise waved a hand at her, getting up. "Don't mention it. Go out there and kick some butt."

Victor, Emmaline's original target, wiped dye off his shirt before walking out the door with his hands raised, showing he was out. Desmond got up, holstering his hexgun and wincing at the demolished floorboards. "Wasn't expecting that. Nice move—I hadn't seen your magic with my own eyes before."

Blaise smiled at the compliment. "You weren't so bad yourself. I don't know how you made that shot while falling."

Desmond grinned. "Mostly luck. Come on, let's go watch and see how this shakes out."

Emmaline skulked out the back door as Blaise and Desmond exited through the front. Austin was still perched on the side of the steeple, but he didn't fire on them. Blaise glanced at the bright yellow spot on his shirt.

"Everyone who's out went that way." Desmond pointed in the overlook's direction. The two-legged shapes of trainees stood by the pegasi.

"How many are left?"

Desmond squinted, counting the tiny forms. "Just four or five."

Blaise nodded. Once they reached the outskirts of the ghost town, a small game trail wound up the side of the canyon to the overlook. Outside of the town, the vegetation obstructed more of the canyon. Young ironwoods and mesquite forced them to duck under low-slung branches. Blaise skirted around them, though he still had to navigate tangles of greasebush and purple sage.

He froze at the unmistakable report of a revolver. It was close —too close. Blaise turned, pain lacing through his left arm as scarlet blood blossomed from his arm.

Jack

"WHAT IN PERDITION WAS THAT?" JACK SHIFTED HIS ATTENTION from the remaining active trainees, scanning the area. That was a real gunshot, and it was close. Too close for his liking. No one in the box canyon carried anything beyond a hexgun.

Blaise's black stallion screamed, leaping off the ledge. Zepheus turned to Jack, ears flicking with alarm. <It's Blaise. Someone shot Blaise.>

Jack cursed, turning to the trainees and the waiting pegasi. "Game's over. Oberidon, you and the other pegasi go down and get them to stop." The spotted stallion bobbed his head, popping open his wings as he dropped over the side to glide down to the canyon.

He swung into Zepheus's saddle, ignoring the hitch in his shoulder. The palomino coasted down to the scene, where Desmond was crouching over Blaise. Zepheus paid no mind to the scrub, simply folded his wings and plowed through. Emrys had already torn through the worst of it in his haste to get to his mage.

"What happened?" Jack demanded, staying in the saddle.

Desmond looked up, face pale. "Someone shot him, sir."

"Who?"

"Didn't see anyone. I'm sorry."

Jack clenched his jaw. He didn't like this. Not one bit. Blood oozed from Blaise's upper arm—probably nothing life-threatening unless an artery had been nicked. The kid probably felt like shit, but Jack wouldn't do him any good playing nursemaid when there were more important things to do.

"I'm gonna search for the shooter in case they're still nearby looking to finish the job. Desmond, help get him onto Emrys. Kralix is coming over and when he does, accompany Blaise to Nadine's clinic."

Desmond nodded. Zepheus spun, and Jack scanned the area for anything out of place. The brush was thick and would have made a shot from further away challenging. The shooter had to be close.

"Smell anything?" Jack asked Zepheus. It was a pity Kur Agur wasn't here. His nose would be handy. But Jack would lose precious time waiting for him.

The stallion fluttered his nostrils, sucking in a deep breath. <The usual. Gunpowder, as you would expect.>

"Any people?"

Zepheus snorted. <I'm not a bloodhound.>

"I'm not sorry for asking."

Jack slipped out of the saddle. If Zepheus detected gunpowder, then the shooter would have fired from nearby. Zepheus moved aside as Jack eyeballed the area from where he was standing to where Blaise had stood. Desmond was helping him get into Emrys's saddle. Jack cocked his head. Sage blocked the shot. He wished he had been watching Blaise at the time to know the path he had taken. Then Jack would have a clue about the trajectory.

A few minutes later, Jack's search was interrupted by heavy wings as Oberidon landed nearby. Emmaline jumped off, scrambling over. "Daddy, who shot Blaise?"

Jack continued to study the ground carefully. "Don't know. Trying to find something helpful, like shell casings."

Emmaline joined him in the search. The two pegasi did their

best, trying to filter for any strange scent. Though as Zepheus pointed out, they weren't the best choice for the task.

Jack asked Emmaline to look for footprints coming into the box canyon. The canyon wasn't easy to access. Someone should have seen whoever it was, and that bothered him. Itude had two citizens who traveled using unusual means. Hank Walker with his succulents, and the town knocker, Jasper Strop. Knockers were a mystic race capable of travel via mineral deposits or precious stone veins. But Jasper was so near-sighted he was virtually blind. And he didn't own a weapon, as far as Jack knew.

Hank Walker didn't own a gun, either. But he was a postmaster, with a lot more access to supplies than a knocker.

Jack knelt down by a prickly pear. He thought he saw faint impressions of boots in the surrounding dirt, but it was impossible to verify. His hunch wasn't enough proof for anyone.

"Let's wrap it up, Em," Jack told his daughter at last, dissatisfied.

She came back over, unhappy. "I wish we found a shell casing. I could use it, right?"

"Use it?"

Her eyes were fierce. "With the magic. If I had a shell casing, I could find out who did it?"

Jack's forehead furrowed. That honestly hadn't occurred to him, but . . . he didn't see why not. At the very least, if she had found a casing but couldn't deduce who had shot it, she might be able to make their mystery shooter extremely uncomfortable.

He didn't tell her that, though. He wanted her to hold on to what was left of her innocence. It would slip through her fingers like water soon enough.

"You could," he said at last. *And so much more.*

CHAPTER TWENTY-SEVEN

Allies

Blaise

*B*laise flinched at the creak of Nadine's office door opening. The quick movement jarred his injured arm, and he groaned. He was better off than prior to Nadine's attentions to it, but there was still healing to be done.

A partition blocked his view of the door, but he heard familiar voices: Jack and Emmaline.

"How bad is it?" Jack asked the Healer.

"Could have been a lot worse. If whoever shot him had aimed a little to the right, Butch would be dressing him for a pine box right about now."

Blaise used his right hand to fiddle with the grey blanket covering his legs. He didn't enjoy considering any other scenario. Being shot was bad enough. Full stop.

"His recovery won't take near as long as yours, though. I got to heal it right away. And Blaise is more likely to listen when I tell him to baby it."

Jack grumbled in reply to Nadine's criticism then asked, "Is he up to talking?"

Nadine peered around the partition. "Are you?"

"Sure." Blaise figured it was better than sitting there pondering all the might-have-beens.

Jack stalked around the partition like a hunting cat. Emmaline trailed in his wake, her mouth a small, thin line of worry. She brightened a little upon seeing Blaise.

"Hey, did you win?" Blaise couldn't help but ask her.

Emmaline stared at him, as if that was the last thing she expected him to say. Then she laughed, shaking her head. "You're ridiculous."

Jack settled down on the edge of the cot opposite Blaise's. "I called it as soon as we saw you go down. From a *real gods-damned bullet.*" His voice held a raw edge of frustration.

Blaise watched Jack for a moment and realized he was seeing the outlaw's version of guilt. He had set up his exercise so that no one would get hurt. Maybe painted a new color, but not hurt.

"Can you tell me what happened?" Jack asked. There was a silent *I'm sorry* attached to the way his voice cracked on the last word.

Blaise sighed, using his good arm to sit up. "I was just walking back with Desmond. Then I heard a shot. I knew it wasn't one of the hexguns—they sound different. It sounded close, and when I turned I realized it had hit me." He looked down at his arm, a panicky lump forming in his throat as he recounted it. He should have been paying more attention. His guard had been down.

"You didn't see or hear anything strange?"

Blaise shook his head. "No. I just took a different trail than Desmond, since he was going under the trees more than I liked. I ended up going around the brush, but I didn't notice anything unusual."

Jack sat back, rubbing his chin. "They shot you from behind. I found an area where the brush had been broken by someone, and it wasn't any of our people. I don't understand it, though. If they stood where I think they did, then someone should have seen them coming or going."

He knew Jack was right. The canyon had sheer walls, except for the trail leading to the overlook. "Any tunnels?"

The outlaw paused, as if he had considered something similar. "Not any the average person could use."

Blaise wasn't sure what Jack meant by that, but he wasn't feeling well enough to request clarification. He was ready to go home and burrow in his bed and hope that when he woke up, this was an elaborate nightmare.

"Is there any reason someone would want to hurt you?" Jack paced between the cots, the tapping of his heels accentuating his words.

Blaise bit his lip, glancing away. He had thought he was accepted in Itude, perhaps even well-liked. The citizens certainly enjoyed the bakery. "I don't think so."

The outlaw paused in his pacing, eyes meeting Emmaline's as he asked her some silent question. Emmaline shook her head in response. "If anything changes, you let me know immediately," Jack said, pointing a finger at Blaise.

Jack's words held an intensity Blaise hadn't expected. He had moved from regret to righteous fury. "I'll let you know."

"You do that," the outlaw agreed. "I'm going to make some inquiries." He pivoted and prowled out the door.

Nadine stopped Emmaline before she could follow, hooking a thumb in Blaise's direction. "Don't expect him to do *anything* at the bakery for the next couple of weeks, got it?"

Emmaline paused, shooting Blaise a sympathetic look before giving a firm nod. "Understood, Nadine."

Blaise sighed, beginning to understand exactly why Jack had been so grumpy with Nadine's restrictions.

CHAPTER TWENTY-EIGHT
A Little Light Mail Theft

Jack

The business with the shooter bothered Jack more than he let on. The Gutter and Untamed Territories were wild places with hot tempers and flying bullets, but that wasn't how things were in the towns unless something shady was afoot. The exercise in the box canyon should have been safe enough. He didn't like this, not one bit.

He had two suspects, though he doubted their likelihood. First, he stopped by the dry goods store, run by the town knocker, Jasper Strop.

There were a few reasons Jasper was on his list. As a knocker, he had the innate ability to travel from place to place via mineral deposits or veins in the land. In theory, he could have appeared in the box canyon and vanished moments later without a trace. The other reason was his family connections. As a part of his intelligence, Jack kept copious notes on his fellow citizens. Over time, he'd learned Jasper had a niece who lived in Ganland.

That was odd. The Salt-Iron Confederation wouldn't be hospitable to a knocker. Oh, they looked humanoid, but they were different enough to stick out like a gangrenous thumb. Earning their racial name from their penchant of warning miners by knocking on walls just before cave-ins, knockers were grey-skinned and shorter than most humans—Jasper only reached to the middle of Jack's chest, and he was considered tall. Their heads were larger and more bulbous than a human's, with prominent noses. Their legs were short, their arms gangly.

He found Jasper manning his store, which was quiet this time of day. The knocker smiled at Jack, an expression that reached his dark eyes. "Afternoon, Jack. What can I do for you?"

Jack liked most of the non-humans in town more than the humans, and he chafed at suspecting Jasper of the attack. But he had to be thorough. "I need to ask you a few questions. This a good time?"

Jasper's eyes widened with fear. No one was at ease when Jack came sniffing around. Many of them knew bits and pieces of his past in the Salt-Iron Confederation. Jack had never told them, but the truth had a way of getting out. He wasn't the only one with connections.

"Sure," Jasper agreed, easing against the counter. His long fingers tapped the polished wood in a nervous beat.

"When was the last time you were in the box canyon?"

The knocker blinked, owlish. "I couldn't tell you. Not recently. Nothing good there."

"Hmm." Jack browsed a display of leather gloves, picking up a pair to examine. "No good veins that way?"

Jasper shook his head. "Nothing I like. Found a phoenixeye deposit north of here." His eyes gleamed with momentary longing. Knockers collected gems and baubles, and had some they favored more than others. Jasper dabbled with jewel-crafting when he wasn't busy running the dry goods store. The fingers on his left hand twinkled with rings, the latest fruits of his efforts.

"Good to know." Jack moved to a row of hats hanging on pegs. It had been a while since he'd gotten a new hat. Might have to check into that later. But it would wait. "How's your niece?"

The knocker swallowed, and his voice was strained. "My niece?"

"Yeah. She lives in Ganland?"

Jasper stared at him in shock. "How did you know?"

Jack ignored the question, taking down a dapper little bowler and spinning it on his index finger. "You have contracts with excellent merchants. She help with that?"

He almost felt sorry for the knocker. He didn't pale as a human would when frightened. Instead, his skin turned a shade of violet, so he looked something like a purple potato. "N-no, sir. That is all my own hard work."

Jack studied the knocker. "How are you with a sixgun?" He glanced to a display of revolvers locked behind a glass case reinforced with strips of metal. He whistled with appreciation. Winking jewels and precious metals adorned two of the sixguns.

Jasper lifted his gnarled hands. "No good." He pointed his glitzy left hand to the display. "I'd rather do other things with them."

Jack nodded, looking at a little number that glimmered with a phoenixeye-inset muzzle. He wondered if that impacted the balance. Or did Jasper take that into account when he worked? "I see that. How long have you been embellishing the guns? Didn't know you'd started doing that."

The knocker's eyelids drooped with contentment, pleased with the change of subject. "I'm just learning. Started a month ago. Only completed three so far."

"Three? There's two in the case. Did you sell one?"

Jasper nodded. "Yes, but I shipped it by request of the buyer."

Jack narrowed his eyes. "Who's the buyer?"

"Jefferson Cole."

Cole. *Interesting.* Jack hadn't considered Cole as a suspect because there was no way that the Gannish man could have been in the box canyon undetected. But perhaps he had to consider other angles of the puzzle. "I wasn't aware you shipped guns out of here. How do you secure them?"

"It was the first time, so I wasn't comfortable doing it myself. I had it wrapped in linen, but I took it to the post office so Hank could help. It was a rush job, so he planned to transport it personally."

"Is that so?" If it was a rush order, it should have a receipt at the post office. "Thanks for your time, Jasper."

The knocker relaxed as Jack turned for the door. Jack cast a parting glance at him but noticed nothing more unusual than Jasper's skin returning to its normal stony color. His boots tapped as he took the steps down to the dusty road and headed to the post office.

Hank Walker was helping Celeste when Jack pushed open the door. "Hello, Jack. I'll be with you in a moment." A vein in Hank's forehead ticked with visible tension.

"No rush." Jack crossed his arms and leaned against the wall by the door. He nodded a greeting to Celeste. He noticed the postmaster's hands tremble as he set her parcel on the counter.

"Anything else I can help you with?" Walker asked with more fervor than usual.

"No, that's all. Thank you!" Celeste tucked the box under her arm and strode past Jack, waving as she exited.

Jack waited for the door to swing closed before stalking over to the counter. Hank gestured to the sorted mail behind him. "I saw nothing for you, and I think I went through everything."

"Good to know, but I'm here on town business." Jack cocked his head. "You seem nervous, Hank. Everything all right?"

"I got back from Thorn about an hour ago. You know the farther I travel, the harder the recovery can be," Hank said, faltering.

"I see." Jack made a show of looking behind the counter. The outgoing mailbox was empty, so Hank may have just finished his rounds. "Heard Jasper had you help him mail a revolver to Jefferson Cole's residence. A special piece, as I hear it."

The postmaster nodded. "That's right."

"When was that?"

Hank shifted his weight against the countertop. "Shipped out today."

"I need to see the receipt."

Hank paled. "I can't show you that unless you're one of the parties—"

Jack leaned across the counter. Didn't say a word; just pinned Hank with a chilling gaze that promised a world of pain if he didn't comply.

The postmaster broke eye contact, upset. He shifted, then pulled a pad of carbon paper from a drawer. He paged through, turning it for Jack to inspect.

Jack peered at the scrawled date and time, which was in fact that very afternoon. He pursed his lips, thinking. The time stamp would have given a brief span for Hank to act with that weapon, but it was possible.

"Jefferson Cole, eh?" Jack pushed the book back over to Walker.

Hank nodded, then came around the counter to look out the window. "But you didn't hear that from me."

"No, of course not." Jack gave the counter a hard smack with his hand, causing Hank to wince. The outlaw pivoted and headed for the door. "Thanks for the help."

CHAPTER TWENTY-NINE
Feast of Flight

Blaise

"*R*euben, that's *amazing.*"

The young man grinned, ducking his head at Blaise's compliment. Blaise sat nearby, overseeing as Reuben and Emmaline assembled and decorated a quintet of massive, three-tiered cakes for the Feast of Flight celebration. Just days after he'd been wounded, Vixen had come to the bakery to place an order for desserts for the upcoming festivities. Blaise discovered from her that the Feast of Flight was a true holiday for the outlaws, celebrating the bond of friendship forged by the first outlaw mage and pegasus. Though Nadine was adamant Blaise take it easy, Emmaline and Reuben had been eager to tackle the job.

Reuben had revealed, with a little embarrassment, that a few years ago he had spent a summer with an aunt who specialized in sugar sculpture, and he had helped with her work. Blaise set him to the task of creating decorations for the cakes, and he didn't disappoint. Brightly colored sugar pegasi rested on parchment paper, ready to be added to the cakes. Their coats were whimsical, reminiscent of a rainbow; their delicate wings, manes, and tails sculpted from spun sugar. They were breathtaking.

"Don't break them getting them onto the cake," Reuben fretted, eyeing Emmaline as she piped frosting onto a layer.

"You're worse than a mother hen," she grumbled, finishing the last flourish. "I was thinking we'd wait and put them on the cakes once we got them to the town square."

Blaise watched as they put the final touches on the cakes, though he couldn't help a pang of envy. He rubbed at the bandage wrapped around his upper arm. A week had passed since the shooting, and thanks to Nadine's masterful healing the injury didn't bother him much. Even so, she stopped by the bakery more than normal and would fix him with an assessing gaze, a silent warning to take it easy.

"It's too bad you can't ride in the parade tonight," Emmaline remarked to Blaise as she carefully packed a set of sugar pegasi in a box for transport.

"Yeah, *such* a shame," Blaise said, eliciting an amused snort from Emmaline. She knew quite well that flying didn't agree with him.

"You should still go to the stables for the preparations, though." Emmaline paused as Austin and Desmond arrived to move the cakes to the town square. She tasked Reuben with overseeing the process, then turned back to Blaise. "It's tradition for all the riders to gussy up the pegasi before the parade."

Blaise raised his brows. "I'd like to stay on Nadine's good side."

Emmaline waved a hand. "I don't mean you have to do anything. I can get Oby and Emrys ready. Just be there for Emrys. It's his first Feast of Flight with a rider."

A rider who wasn't allowed to ride him at the moment. Blaise sighed. He hadn't realized that the Feast of Flight was as important as it was. Emrys was disappointed with Blaise's restrictions and did a terrible job of hiding it. Blaise nodded. "I'll let you run interference with Nadine in that case."

"Deal." Emmaline grinned as she packed the last decoration.

Reuben pushed open the door to the bakery, a stricken look on his face when he saw Emmaline holding the packed boxes. "I'll take those, thanks." He pulled them from Emmaline's hands, nestling the boxes against his chest.

"They were fine," Emmaline shot back.

Reuben gave an unabashed grin. "I spent a lot of time on these! And besides, you need to go see to the real thing."

Emmaline rolled her eyes. "Fair enough."

Blaise followed her to the stables, and he was surprised to see others already there, braiding colorful ribbons into the manes and tails of each pegasus. Even Jack was in attendance, plaiting Zepheus's mane with cerulean. Blaise had never seen the pegasi decorated before—their manes and tails usually hung loose. He watched Emmaline select a purple ribbon from the basket and then deftly start to work on her stallion's mane.

<Blue, I think,> Emrys commented, bumping Blaise with his muzzle.

"What?" Blaise blinked.

The pegasus gestured at the basket with his nose. <Get out the blue for Emmaline to use for my braids. Or . . .> Emrys paused, shaking his head so his mane went flying. <Do you have a waistcoat?>

What was Emrys going on about? "No."

<That's unfortunate. I suppose your blue duster will do in a pinch. Yes, the blue ribbon.>

Blaise rubbed his forehead. "Why are you worried about my duster?"

Emmaline glanced over at them, catching his half of the conversation. "Emrys probably wants to match you. The pegasi aren't the only ones dressing up for the occasion."

Oh. That made sense. Blaise's cheeks warmed with a flush of embarrassment. To cover it, he bent over and pretended to sort through the basket until he found a blue ribbon buried at the bottom.

Emrys detected his discomfiture and craned his head around. <I want to match you because you are my rider. Even if you can't ride me tonight. We'll figure something out.>

Blaise nodded, stroking Emrys's neck. He needed a change of topic. "How's your magic going?" He glanced at Emmaline, watching as she artfully braided Oberidon's mane.

She paused, making a face. "Some of it's easier than others. I thought learning would be simple. Instinctive, you know?"

He understood. Some elements of magic were instinctive, but others required practice. He was glad he was over that hump. "You'll get it."

She nodded, but her lips puffed out with dissatisfaction. "It's hard. I already have to learn to shoot as good as him. Now I have the same magic. I don't know how I can live up to that." Her voice was low, so it didn't carry far.

"Do you have to live up to it?"

Emmaline tied the purple ribbon into an obnoxiously enormous bow. Oberidon looked over his shoulder, huffing with pleasure. "I'm *his* daughter. I live in his shadow. I have to live up to that."

Somehow, Blaise didn't think those were Jack's expectations. "Just do the best you can, Em."

She nodded, and their conversation stalled. In silence, Emmaline picked up the blue ribbon Blaise had selected and started to work on Emrys. She made quick work of it, and before long the pegasi were saddled for the parade.

Emmaline shoved blond hair from her eyes as she finished adjusting the last strap. "Now it's our turn to get cleaned up so we can look as good as this lot."

Blaise parted ways from Emmaline, walking back to the bakery. Emrys tagged along, declaring that he would oversee the wardrobe matters from outside.

Shaking his head with amusement, Blaise carefully climbed up to the loft and pawed through his limited selection of clothing. He found a white dress shirt with a high collar and paired it with dark blue canvas trousers, his duster, and hat. To appease Emrys, he held the items to the window to meet the stallion's approval. With Emrys's blessing, he changed and decided the pegasus was right—a waistcoat would complete the look. Something to pick up in the future. Blaise consulted his small mirror and decided he looked presentable, all things considered.

Emrys bobbed his head with approval when he returned. <You'll do.>

Together, they set off to the town square where the other riders were already astride their mounts. Emrys rested his head against Blaise's chest for a long moment before trotting to join the group of saddleless pegasi. Blaise wondered if Emrys was disappointed to be stuck with the younger colts who hadn't bonded with a rider yet.

"Must be frustrating," a familiar voice said.

Just what he needed. Blaise angled to Jefferson Cole, who stood behind his left shoulder. The entrepreneur hadn't stopped by the bakery since the ill-fated training session, and Blaise had thought perhaps he'd left town. So much for that idea. "What?"

Cole jutted his chin to indicate Emrys. "You can't ride your pegasus at the Feast of Flight." Was it just Blaise's imagination, or did he sound envious?

Blaise shrugged. "I'd rather keep my feet on the ground."

Cole tilted his head. "To each his own, I suppose." He paused. "I was sorry to hear of your injury. I hope you're feeling better."

Self-conscious, Blaise rubbed the fabric of the duster over his wound. He didn't want to be reminded of it, not here in this crowd of people. The very thought that his attacker was likely out there somewhere made him want to turn tail and flee to his loft. "I'm fine."

The other man gave him a speculative look. "Good. That's good."

Blaise nodded, keeping his gaze fixed on the column of pegasi and riders as they made their final preparations. He hoped Cole would take the hint and stop talking. He felt the other man's eyes on him for a moment, but when Blaise glanced back, he had drifted away.

Raven and Vixen led the top of the column on their pegasi, Naureus and Alekon. Jack was positioned behind them on Zepheus, with Emmaline and Oberidon at his side. Blaise almost didn't recognize Jack. The rough-and-ready outlaw had exchanged his usual clothing for a more refined fashion. He wore a long black coat over a gold Penworth vest. The white shirt beneath boasted a high collar like Blaise's, but Jack tastefully accented it with a black puff tie. Jack completed the look with a black top hat perched atop his head.

Emmaline had dressed up too, which made Blaise glad he had changed. She wore tan twill riding pants that fanned around her legs, a cream-colored camisole covered by a brown corset, and a brown derby. A thick gold necklace hung around her neck; golden bracelets clung to her wrists. Blaise wondered if those were spoils from Jack's outlawing.

Raven and Vixen's steeds surged into the air. It reminded Blaise of watching a flock of geese rise up from a pond, the way all the pegasi burst forward into the air together. The crowd around him murmured in appreciation at the spectacle of pegasi circling overhead. Blaise kept track of Emrys, alternately proud and feeling more left out than he thought he would. He had to remind himself of the way his stomach lurched during flight.

The column of pegasi landed in pairs, trotting down the street to a cacophony of cheers, applause, and whistles. The wild fanfare would have spooked normal horses, but the pegasi reveled in the attention. Tails flagged behind the stallions like banners, ears pricked forward and eyes bright as they pranced. Blaise admitted they made a stunning sight.

Everyone ended up at the town square. Planks of wood laid out atop barrels created long tables laden with a buffet, pennants and streamers fluttering in the breeze. Blaise's cakes were at the end of the line, ready to be enjoyed. The pegasi even had their own special tables set up at the festivity.

"There'll be fireworks later," Hannah chirped as she waved a greeting to Blaise. "After the music."

"I've never seen anything like this before."

"I figured when I saw you gawking. But now it's time to eat." Hannah pointed to the line forming at the buffet. "Go enjoy. I can't wait to dig into one of those glorious cakes you made."

He thanked her for the information as Emrys sidled up next to Oberidon at a table that was covered in an array of sweet treats. Blaise joined the serving line, impressed by the spread that Celeste, Mindy, and Abe had assembled. There was boiled mutton, roast beef, fried apples and bacon, goose with olives, chicken stuffed with truffles, oysters, baked apples, asparagus, green peas, hot oatmeal mush, and the cakes. Blaise filled his plate and found a place to sit.

The food was delicious, and as he ate, he reflected he had never seen so many joyful people together all at once. It was magical. It was something he had never expected to be a part of. The sense of belonging warmed him.

After everyone was sated, they moved the makeshift tables into a new arrangement to create a stage. A handful of people climbed onto it, some of the Ringleaders among their number.

Kur Agur and Vixen took their places near the front. Raven carried a fiddle and stood behind them, resting the instrument atop his shoulder. Butch the undertaker joined them with a harmonica and Nadine with a zither. Hannah and a few other young women took to the stage, dressed in short skirts with riding breeches beneath and corsets that allowed freedom of movement.

Jefferson Cole sat a few seats down, alone since most of his dinner companions were now onstage. He noticed Blaise's sideways glance and offered a friendly smile, then slid down the bench until he was closer.

Blaise still didn't know what he thought about the businessman, but it would be in poor taste to ignore him. He tipped his head to indicate the stage. "What's next?"

"Music." Cole cocked his head as the performers tuned their instruments, angling his body toward Blaise. "The dessert cakes ... were those your creations?"

Blaise glanced at the table where the last cake still stood, only the lowest tier remaining. The revelers had demolished the four others. "It's my recipe and it was made under my direction, but Nadine's not letting me do much right now. The sugar sculptures were all Reuben."

Cole's eyebrows rose, intrigued. "Is that so? You and your employees are exceedingly talented. You should be proud." He leaned forward conspiratorially. "Those cakes would stack up against the best of the best in Ganland."

Blaise blinked in surprise. "You think so?"

"I know so," Cole replied, his gaze sliding from the cakes back to Blaise. "You're looking rather delicious tonight yourself."

Blaise's face flamed at the odd compliment. He rubbed the back of his neck, uncertain about the attention.

"Is this your first Feast of Flight?" The businessman's acute eyes stayed on Blaise even as he changed the topic.

"Yes."

Cole's face lit up. "You're in for a treat. Every outlaw town celebrates, though this is my first time seeing Itude's. I try not to miss this holiday." He clasped his hands in front of him. "We don't have this where I come from."

Ganland. That served as a reminder that Cole was an outsider. Blaise made a mental note to remain aloof.

But the entrepreneur was right—it was a spectacle unlike any Blaise had seen before. He didn't know if the group had practiced together beforehand—if they had, he hadn't seen or heard them. The musicians played a spirited song, Vixen and Kur providing vocals. Vixen's voice was sultry, and Kur's was beautiful but haunting. Hannah and the other women danced along to the music, short skirts flapping and whirling about with their energetic movement.

The audience clapped and cheered along, and Blaise found himself swept up with the crowd, doing the same. His arms pebbled with gooseflesh at the harmonic magic created by the performers. He recognized it wasn't true magic, not like his. But there was an ethereal beauty to the music that made every listener feel as if they had cast a spell over the town. The entire town was filled with a warmth and revelry that made him feel more secure and welcome than he had in his life.

The group played several more songs, and before long everyone was dancing along. The dancers hopped off the stage and selected partners. Hannah made a beeline for Blaise, grabbing his hand.

"C'mon!"

His eyes widened, and he sputtered, jerking away his trembling hand. "I—no, I've never danced before. There's no way I can dance like you just did." The dancers had been so *close*. Blaise shook his head, his pulse racing. "And I just . . . can't."

"I wouldn't expect you to. I know you're hurt and have to take it easy." Hannah's face clouded at his panic, but she gave him a circumspect look and nodded. "If you change your mind, I'm around."

His shoulders relaxed at her words, and he settled back onto the bench away from Cole, aware that he had witnessed the whole spectacle. Blaise sat and sipped his punch, his nerves slowly calming as he listened to the music.

After the song ended and the musicians prepared their next tune, Cole slid down the long bench until he was near Blaise. "Are you okay? Is your injury bothering you?"

The concern in the other man's voice caught Blaise off guard. He looked into Cole's face and discovered the crinkle of his brow matched his words. "No. I . . ." Did he really want to go into that here? Not really. But it had been an awkward scene, and Blaise feared more questions. "I don't like to be touched."

"Ah, I see," Cole said, tone light. He leaned back, quiet for a few minutes as he watched the festivities. "I've known others with similar issues."

Blaise blinked. "You have?" As soon as the words left his mouth, he regretted them. He shouldn't be talking to Jefferson Cole.

The entrepreneur nodded. "Yes. I've teamed up with a politician in Ganland to try to end trafficking." He picked up his cup, swirling the contents as he spoke. "I'm friends with several trafficking victims, and I know of at least one who won't let anyone touch her. Even those she trusts."

Blaise hadn't expected that. The way Jack spoke of the Confederation painted everyone with a broad brush—no redeeming values whatsoever. Deep down, he knew that couldn't be true of everyone. "Oh." He tried to think of something else to say but failed. Blaise was too focused on the fact that here was someone who had some understanding of his peculiarity.

Cole waved a hand. "But that's an unpleasant topic. Not one to dwell on tonight." He smiled. "Have you had any further thoughts on our discussion the other day?"

Blaise was suddenly very glad for the riot of noise all around them. It made the question less daunting. "I . . . I'm afraid I must decline. I'm happy here."

"That's too bad." Cole sighed. Blaise feared the answer might upset him, but he continued to watch the dancers, tapping a foot to the downbeat. "Have you been in Itude long?"

"Only since summer." Blaise glanced away, chewing on his lower lip as he tried to think of a way to excuse himself without appearing rude.

"Who taught you to bake like that?"

Blaise frowned, puzzled by the question. "You really want to know?"

Cole smiled at him. "I do. I enjoy learning about other people. That's part of why I travel. The world is full of people with interesting pursuits. And I take it baking is yours."

"It's a better pursuit than magic," Blaise muttered.

"I'm sorry, what was that? Couldn't hear you over the music."

Blaise cleared his throat. "Um, I taught myself to bake. I've been doing it for years since—" He broke off, not wanting to get into his past. "It's calming. I enjoy it."

Cole tilted his head but thankfully didn't ask about Blaise's omission. "Impressive that you taught yourself."

"It was a lot of trial and error. And a lot of mistakes. The recipes in the cookbooks I had made it sound easier than it was at first."

Cole chuckle. "That sounds like an accurate description of life."

The musicians played several more songs, and Blaise continued his conversation with Jefferson Cole until the last notes of music faded into the night. The festivities concluded with a stunning firework show, and once the last sparks fell harmlessly to the ground, the crowd dispersed. Blaise excused himself and followed the other pegasus riders as they took their charges back to the stables, painstakingly removing the ribbons and braids so they wouldn't tangle through the night. He hovered near Emmaline, wishing that he could do more than offer moral support.

<What did you think of Feast of Flight?> Emrys asked as the last ribbon unraveled from his mane.

Blaise yawned. "It was . . . nice. I haven't felt like I belonged somewhere for a long time. But I did tonight."

Emrys sighed, content. <It's good to belong.>

Blaise agreed. It was.

CHAPTER THIRTY
Cheap Thrill

Blaise

*B*laise pushed open the door to the Broken Horn, the boisterous sounds of drinking and gambling rolling over him. He wove through the crowd and grabbed a stool at the end of the bar. Clover ambled over to him, puzzled. "You don't drink."

Blaise managed a small smile. She knew him well. "Still don't. I wanted a change of pace from the diner, though. Can I have a plate of whatever Abe is making for the special tonight? And do you have any of the raspberry vinegar switchel to drink?"

She studied him for a long moment, one of her ears flicking back and forth in thought. "I do." Clover tapped the bar before turning to call the order back to Abe.

"This seat taken?"

Blaise turned, startled to find Jefferson Cole pointing to the neighboring barstool. "Yours for the taking." He decided this wasn't the time to be choosy with his friends, and he couldn't help but recall the companionable conversation they had shared at the Feast of Flight.

Cole's mouth parted in pleasure, and he bellied up to the bar. Clover came back over and regarded him courteously, but lacking the usual warmth she showed her customers. "Will you be having the usual tonight?"

"Please," Cole replied. Clover called another order to Abe, then surprised Blaise by producing a wineglass from beneath the counter. They were used so infrequently at the Broken Horn that Blaise recalled only washing a single one in his time there. The Knossan uncorked a bottle of wine and poured it.

"I'm going to miss this." Cole sighed, picking up the glass and swirling the contents. "Knossan dandelion wine is a rare delicacy."

Blaise raised a brow. He didn't know much about wines, much less that Clover even stocked Knossan wines. Cole took a blissful sip.

"I wanted to tell you I'm leaving in the morning. But the offer still stands."

In the days after the Feast of Flight, Blaise had thought more on Cole's offer. It was a definite temptation, and if he hadn't found a place to belong in Itude, he would have accepted in a heartbeat. "Thank you, but I'll be staying here. I'm happy here."

Cole pursed his lips, forehead furrowing. He looked as if he wanted to say something, but Clover's arrival was heralded by the sound of her hooves. She slid two plates of the daily special in front of them.

Cole cut into his beefsteak and took a bite, pointing his fork at Blaise. He spoke when he finished chewing. "I understand. But I'm very serious about going into business with you. The cookies alone would be excellent sellers."

Blaise took a swig from his drink. "Why's that? I don't under-stand why anyone would buy cookies made by a maverick."

Cole's lips slid into an indulgent grin, the corners of his eyes crinkling. "They would sell better *because* they're made by a maverick. Although, perhaps for branding we'd call you an outlaw. It sounds more roguish." Blaise's confusion must have been obvious on his face because the other man pressed on. "Call it what you will—romance, prestige, a cheap thrill. There are those who will be titillated by the thought of eating something made by an outlaw. They're the same people who will only buy wines from certain vineyards or from a 'good year'. Also, the ones with the deepest pockets." He snapped his fingers as if having a revelation. "If you don't want to bake for me, maybe we could work out a licensing deal. We could market something made by another baker, but under your name—"

"No." Blaise didn't understand half of what Cole was blathering about, but he understood that much. He didn't want his name attached to anyone else's inferior baked goods.

Cole chuckled, the sound melodious and warm. "Fair enough. Is there anything I could offer that would pique your interest?"

Blaise pursed his lips, considering. Was there? He had what he wanted now, and that was enough. "I don't think so."

The entrepreneur sighed. "If you change your mind, let me know. You'd never want for a thing."

It wasn't about the money. Blaise made enough to get by—he paid his monthly lease to Jack, paid his employees, and bought more supplies for himself and the bakery. Beyond that, he didn't need a lot. But Blaise appreciated having options. "If I change my mind, you'll be the first to know."

Cole gave him a dashing smile. "Excellent. I'll be in Rainbow Flat for the next few weeks, and then after that, I'll be traveling. But your postmaster can always send a letter to my residence in Nera. The message will reach me, eventually."

Blaise nodded. It was strange to have someone take such an avid interest in his baking. Flattering, but strange.

Cole finished his meal and excused himself, saying he had to get back to his room to pack. Once the other man had left, Clover plodded back and leaned over the bar.

"He's very interested in you," the Knossan said, her tone neutral.

Blaise glanced up the stairs as Cole retreated. "He wants to go into business with me."

Clover snorted. "The Gannish always do. They dangle coins before humans like a carrot before a donkey." She regarded him curiously. "What will you do?"

"Stay here." Blaise looked over the busy saloon. He liked the people of Itude. He *belonged* somewhere, finally.

She nodded, as if he had said the right thing. "That is good. I think Itude needs you, just as you need Itude."

Her reassuring words gave him pause. Blaise wanted to ask her what she meant, but another customer flagged Clover for a refill. He watched her clop over, taking another sip of his drink. Maybe it was going to be okay.

CHAPTER THIRTY-ONE
Accusations

Blaise

The only downside of having friends, Blaise decided, was that sometimes they persuaded him into questionable life choices. Last night, for example. Emmaline and Reuben convinced him to attend the weekly dance at the town square, which extended into the wee hours of the morning. And though he didn't do more than talk to people and watch the dancers, he had enjoyed himself and stayed the whole time.

Fortunately, he wasn't alone in his exhaustion. Emmaline dragged herself in as the oven was warming. She looked just as tired, so he decided they would be a good pair. Neither one of them said much as they set about their usual tasks. It was too early, and they'd had too little sleep to even consider making coherent conversation. Maybe after coffee.

Once the first loaves of bread were in the oven, Blaise took a breather and stumbled over to the diner to grab two cups of coffee. Emmaline normally didn't drink coffee, but Mindy added sugar and cream to make it enticing. Emmaline was so tired she didn't scoff at the cup when he pressed it into her hands. She tipped it back and took a sip.

"Mmm," she murmured, appreciating the sweetness. "Doesn't taste like dirt."

"I'd never hand it to you black." His brain felt a little more willing to string together thoughts. That was an improvement.

Emmaline took another sip, then sighed as if it had made all the difference in the world. She quirked an eyebrow at him, mischievous. "Are you sweet on Jefferson Cole? I would have expected you might have an interest in someone like Hannah, but you kept to yourself last night."

Blaise froze. "What?"

She gave him a pointed look. "I saw him talking to you at the Feast of Flight. What did he call you? *Delicious*, if I remember right?"

Blaise almost dropped his cup of coffee. "He was talking about our cakes. Were you spying?"

She fluttered her eyelashes, all innocence. "I was just walking by. And he was definitely not talking about our cakes at that point." Blaise turned away, setting down his coffee and pulling out the bag of sugar. Emmaline made an exasperated sound. "What's wrong? It was nice. He *likes* you."

Blaise shook his head. He didn't want to get into his confused thoughts on the subject, not now. Emmaline couldn't understand what it was like to be scorned by everyone during his youth. He'd missed out on the formative years of flirting and relationship-building, and he had no idea how to even respond—or if he wanted to. Sex didn't appeal to him as it apparently did to others. And while Jefferson Cole was easy on the eyes, he was also the enemy.

"I can't talk about this right now," Blaise finally said, picking up the empty water bucket sitting beside the door. "I'll refill the wash water."

She gave him a puzzled look, then shrugged. "Okay. Sorry, didn't know it was a sensitive subject. Since you don't show an interest in anyone else, I thought it was nice."

Blaise shook his head as he headed to the cistern, the bucket swinging beside him. Truth be told, he hadn't minded talking to Cole at the Feast of Flight. The man had gone from intimidating entrepreneur to companionable conversationalist in such a short time that he wasn't sure what to think about it. It was like Cole was two different people.

He placed his empty bucket beneath the spigot and turned it on, mulling over his feelings as water splashed against metal. Emmaline thought Cole *liked* him? As in, was *attracted* to him? Blaise couldn't possibly see why. He just wanted to go into business together. That was all.

Once the bucket was full, Blaise turned and started back toward the bakery. He was stepping inside the door when suddenly the air around him seemed to ripple and the floorboards shimmied beneath his feet, bucking like a cavorting pegasus. Blaise lurched forward, nearly spilling the bucket's contents.

Emmaline yelped, a falling pot almost hitting her on the head. Blaise set the bucket down beside the washstand and they traded startled looks.

"What was that?" Emmaline's voice was small and unnerved.

Blaise shook his head, a rush of frightened adrenaline in his veins as he hurried to the bakery windows. One of them had cracked from the concussive force of whatever had happened. That was a concern for later. Shouts echoed outside, people rushing up the street past the bakery.

"Bloody buggering basilisks!" Emmaline exclaimed softly, peering out behind him.

A cloud of dust rose in a plume over the town to the east,

tinged red with dirt. It was close—so close that when Blaise opened the door, dust billowed into the bakery, choking them. He slammed the door shut again and scrambled up the stairs to the loft, grabbing a pair of bandannas. He tossed one to Emmaline, and she tied it over her nose in silence.

The dust cleared a little when they poked their heads outside again, though the morning light filtered through the haze. Emmaline gasped as they both realized that Itude's skyline was missing its most prominent feature: the wind-pump that towered four stories over the rest of the town.

Blaise stared, a chill racing down his spine. He had been mere yards from the wind-pump only minutes ago. *I could have been crushed.*

"We should help," Emmaline murmured, her words prodding him out of his frightening revelation.

"Let's gather up the leftovers into baskets." Blaise withdrew into the bakery, coughing at the remnants of dust in his throat. Emmaline didn't respond, eyes downcast with worry as she found clean linen while Blaise pulled out a pair of wicker baskets to pack loaves of bread and cookies. He stalked over to the oven and opened it, removing a pair of pies destined to never finish baking. Blaise didn't want to risk leaving them unattended in the oven. That done, he extinguished the fire.

They each slung a basket over their shoulders and raced out the door to join other responders surging to the site of the wind-pump. Pegasi milled around, some of them using their bulk to form a perimeter around the disaster. Parents tugged away curious children, taking them back to their homes on the outskirts.

Blaise set his basket down in the shade of the barber shop awning, taking in the heartrending sight. Itude's wind-pump had been unlike any windmill he had seen before. Not only tall, it was broad-based, constructed of stone blocks cemented together. Blaise had never been inside, but he had heard in passing that there were gears and things that made the whole thing work to pump water up from the river below to fill the town's large cistern. It was sturdy and built to last, meant to sustain the town for decades.

Now the wind-pump was in ruins. It had collapsed, tumbling like a tower of blocks kicked down by a child. The heavy stone facade had smashed through the icehouse, though it had somehow fallen clear of the town laundry. One of the steel blades—its length greater than two pegasi standing nose to rump—pierced the side of the nearby boarding house.

The Ringleaders were already on site. Clover was there, too, bracing her leathery hands against the stone, straining to tug them off the icehouse.

"Monty!" A woman wailed, running over from the houses outside the town proper. Blaise swallowed when he recognized the ice mage's wife, Eleanor.

The rest of the day was a sobering blur. Yesterday's celebration was all but forgotten. Vixen steered anyone away that she deemed unnecessary. Jack was there, though Nadine tried to send him off. He ignored her and did what he could to help. When Emmaline saw her father, she hurried over and stayed near him.

Blaise helped however he could, though Nadine kept her eagle eye on him as well. Vixen bade him come around to the back of the icehouse to use his magic to break some of the larger chunks of rubble. Donkeys and mules in harnesses appeared, and they hauled debris out of the way.

Late in the afternoon, Blaise watched Jack approach Butch, the town undertaker. He had a talent for necromancy, according to Emmaline.

"Any news?" Jack jutted his chin toward the crumpled icehouse. They were still struggling to move the larger pieces of the wind-pump off the icehouse without causing further collapse.

"Monty's not mine yet." Butch's voice was strained.

Jack's eyes slid to Emmaline, who was staring at the icehouse with determination, clutching something in her hand.

"You okay?" Blaise walked over to her, concerned about the intensity in her eyes.

She bit her lip. He realized she was holding a hastily made doll —no, a poppet—in her hand, wrapped in a light blue bandanna. "Maybe."

Blaise suddenly understood. "Your magic?"

Emmaline nodded the tiniest bit. "Doing what I can. I have him, but it was easier when it was Daddy."

Blaise blinked in surprise. "Do you know where Monty is?"

She shook her head. "No. Just . . . under there. He's bleeding and unconscious."

That was impressive. And she was bolstering him as she had her father.

"I see him!" Kur Agur howled. He and Clover led the vanguard of rescuers and moved with renewed purpose as they shifted more rubble.

Before long, a blood-covered arm poked through the wreckage. Clover pulled Monty out gently, his head lolling as she tried to support his neck. One of his legs was bent at an unnatural angle. They loaded him onto a stretcher and hauled him off to Nadine's clinic for treatment. Eleanor followed along, thankful tears streaming down her face.

Blaise felt mentally and physically exhausted. He looked up and realized it was almost sundown. They had been at their frantic rescue for hours.

Vixen spoke the words everyone had been holding back. "How did this happen?"

Jack's eyes glittered, dangerous. "I don't know. But I intend to find out."

"How will we get water now?" a woman wailed.

Everyone was quiet as they contemplated the disturbing question. The wind-pump provided the lifeblood of Itude. Water was one of the most necessary resources.

Raven glanced at the large cistern standing behind the laundry, both of which had been relatively unaffected by the disaster. "We should have enough for the next few days, but we'll have to supplement by hauling water up from the river."

"We can probably do it with donkey trains and help from the pegasi," Vixen agreed.

"Gotta prioritize rebuilding the wind-pump." This from Jack, who scowled as he surveyed the ruins, his face unreadable. "I'll send word to Charlie Creagen in Thorn and get supplies ordered." He sighed, taking off his hat to run a hand through his sweaty hair. "Won't be cheap."

The Ringleaders moved away, engrossed in discussion. Emmaline walked over to Blaise, toting an empty basket on her shoulder. "Need some help to clean up the bakery?"

He considered it, then shook his head. It would be peaceful to clean up by himself. His nerves were rattled after the long hours of rescue work. "I should be fine. I'll take the basket back and see you in the morning."

"Will do," Emmaline replied, handing over the basket to him.

He headed down the street toward the bakery, trying not to glance at the skyline that was now empty of the massive wind-pump that had so seamlessly provided Itude with all of their water needs. He hoped that it could be rebuilt soon.

Footsteps heavy from exhaustion, he almost didn't notice the folded bit of paper tucked into the door frame. He slowed, pulling it free and opening it.

We know what you did, Breaker.

Blaise stared at the words and reread it. His mouth went dry as bitter memories reared up. Not again. He wasn't responsible for this disaster.

No. No, he wasn't. He controlled his magic now—he had done *nothing* to the wind-pump. Blaise gritted his teeth, wadding the note into a ball. He shouldered open the door and slammed it behind him, the glass rattling from the force. He set down the basket and braced his hands against the table, ignoring the dusting of flour from earlier in the day.

Blaise inhaled slowly to calm himself, but it was no use. Accusations like these were supposed to be behind him. He thought they had accepted him in Itude.

<Blaise?> Emrys's mental voice called out from nearby.

He looked up and saw the stallion outside the back window of the bakery. Blaise didn't feel like talking to anyone at the moment, whether they had two or four legs. But he didn't want to push the pegasus away, so he straightened and opened the window. He said nothing, though.

The pegasus craned his head inside, snorting. <What's wrong? Are you hurt? Are you upset you never got to finish baking those pies? I'd be happy to eat them for you as-is.> His muzzle quested toward the unfinished pies.

Blaise slid a pie tin over to the stallion. "It's nothing."

Emrys nibbled straight from the tin, velvety lips smacking. <Here's a tip: don't lie to a telepath. Also, this is delicious, so thanks.>

Blaise scrubbed at his face with one hand. "Someone thinks I'm responsible for the wind-pump."

The pegasus licked the tin clean of crumbs, savoring the puddles of oozing apple filling that seeped out. <Is it true?>

"Of course not!" Blaise couldn't conceal the hurt in his voice.

Emrys bobbed his head. <So what are you worried about? And can I have that other pie?>

Blaise scooted the second pie over. "It's just the way humans work. If one person thinks I did it, others will think the same. Even if it's not true." He shook his head. "It's what happened when I lived in Bristle—why I couldn't go to school anymore. Or into town. Even if something wasn't my fault, I took the blame."

<That's stupid,> Emrys pointed out.

"It's the way it is." Blaise picked up a pot that had fallen from the wall hours ago. He glanced around at the messy kitchen. Right, he was supposed to be cleaning.

<Vixen and Jack are familiar with your magic. They'll know this is baseless.> Emrys had more confidence than Blaise felt.

Emrys didn't realize it, but that was exactly the problem. They were familiar with his magic. And in Blaise's experience, all it took was someone knowing about his magic for it to become a problem.

CHAPTER THIRTY-TWO
On the Hunt

Jack

The next morning dawned with a sunrise of fuchsia and gold reflections on wispy clouds, Itude's skyline forever changed. The wind-pump missing from the horizon made Jack even more irritable. After Emmaline left for the bakery, he headed out to the site of destruction with fresh eyes. He wasn't the only one with that idea. Kur Agur raised a clawed hand in greeting as Jack approached.

"Find anything yet?" Jack watched as the Theilian cast around the area, nose low to the ground.

Kur straightened, lips curled in distaste. "As you would expect, there are too many mixed scents. If I had a chance to cast for a scent trail before everyone arrived, I might have had more luck."

Jack nodded. It was unfortunate, but they couldn't go back and change that. He stepped over a pile of rubble, examining the base of the wind-pump that still stood.

"It makes little sense. The wind-pump was just inspected a month ago, and we found nothing. It's withstood gale-force winds. There was nothing unusual about yesterday. What changed?"

Kur twitched an ear. "An earthquake? I've never experienced one."

Jack had. He shook his head. "No. The entire town would have felt it. Damnation, the entire town would've gotten dumped into the canyon in that case." That was a nightmare to even consider.

"Hmm." Kur cocked his head, stalking around the circular base of the wind-pump widdershins.

Jack crouched down, scanning the debris trail for any clues that might tell him what caused the failure. He picked up a tiny green plant that seemed out of place among the rubble and turned it over in his hand. He had seen these before around the post office. "Do you scent anything like powder or fire? Dynamite?"

Kur tensed, the fur on his ruff rising. "You think someone would blow up the wind-pump?"

Jack narrowed his eyes.

"But Jefferson Cole is long gone," Kur argued.

Jack studied Kur's shaggy visage. "All the more reason to suspect him. Damn Salt-Iron dandy." *And more. So much more. Should I tell Kur?*

Kur ducked his head in acknowledgment. "But why would he do it? What's the motive? And furthermore, *how?*"

Jack snorted. "The *why* is not a far reach. If there's no water, it's hard to live here. If we can't live in Itude, we must go elsewhere. And a bunch of families traveling out of here would be child's play to capture." Not to mention that if anyone from the Confederation wanted to mine salt-iron in the Gutter in earnest, it would be easy to do so if Itude no longer existed. As Jack thought about it, that sounded right. With the Salt-Iron Confederation in Desina, it would be easy to move into the Gutter next.

And as a bonus, they could snap up any of the families forced to leave town.

"As for the *how*," Jack continued, tilting his head as he studied the scene, "that remains to be figured out."

Kur sneezed, then shook his head violently as if to rid his nose of whatever scent had agitated him. "I detect nothing that a normal human could have used to take down the wind-pump." He scratched behind one ear.

Jack frowned. "What do you smell?"

Kur barked a laugh. "Too many people. Grease. Blood. Something else that makes my nose tingle, but I can't place it."

"Is it magic?"

The Theilian considered. "I'm not sure what it is. Possibly magic, but if so, not one I have scented before."

Breaker, perhaps? Jack glanced over his shoulder at one of the large chunks Blaise had used his magic on the previous day to help the effort. It looked like the rest of the rubble. He kept his troubling thoughts private. Jack couldn't imagine the kid doing something like that. Even Jack would admit it was out of character. But Clover reported that Cole had met with Blaise before leaving town.

"I see the wheels turning in your head," Kur commented, leaning against a stabilized chunk of fallen wall.

Jack shook his head. "Just thinking is all."

"Will you share the trail you're stalking?"

"No."

Kur looked disappointed. "Fair enough. But remember that you must, if it will help the town."

Jack bristled. "I know what I'm about, wolf."

Kur gave him a toothy grin. "In that case, good hunting, Jack."

CHAPTER THIRTY-THREE
Parlor Tricks

Lamar

*Y*our instructions were simple. What is the delay?

Lamar Gaitwood glared at the offending dispatch in his hands. It was only two days old, courtesy of the amazing telegraph line recently completed to Ondin, the capital of Mella. Ondin was the closest city to Fort Courage, and express couriers hustled it across the remaining distance as quickly as possible. No one delayed a message from a doyen of the Salt-Iron Council to a Commander.

Lamar prepared a thousand barb-tongued retorts, but he would never send them as much as he wished to. His elder brother was a righteous asshole, but he held the leash in the family. Lamar had magic, but Gregor . . . Gregor possessed *power*.

If only Gregor had been born with magic. Lamar reflected on it often. *He* was more cunning than Gregor. He had to be, to survive in a world where he wasn't an equal because of his magic. Theurgists were useful but inferior. Real men didn't rely on pretty parlor tricks.

Parlor tricks. As if imprisoning someone in a cage sizzling with magic strong enough to lock them inside their own bodies was a mere *trick*. The only thing that soothed his pride was the knowledge of how many of the elite *normals* suffered to his *parlor trick* before they handed him his command position.

And that brought him back to his current set of instructions. Gregor wanted the Breaker alive. Lamar preferred him dead. He was troublesome, a hassle. And he had made Lamar look like a novice. And beyond that, history supported Lamar's notion. Breakers were extinct for a reason—the Confederation had exterminated the lines that spawned them. Their magic was dangerously unpredictable.

It was all because of that wretched woman in Bristle. The Breaker's mother. *Marian Hawthorne.* Lamar knew the name as soon as he had heard it. The runaway alchemist was found after all this time.

Lamar had shipped her off to Izhadell, with Gregor pleased by the alchemist's recovery. Alchemist Hawthorne thought she had been so slick, passing herself off as a simple apothecary in the little podunk town. But now she was back in Confederation hands, where she belonged. Lamar liked when everyone was in their proper place. It made things right in the world.

That made him think of Jack, who had somehow found himself in league with the Breaker. Jack, the formerly loyal Confederation theurgist turned traitor. After everything Phinora had done for him—trained him in the ways of his foul magic, fed him, sheltered him—and he turned his back on the harmony of the Confederation that they had stood for. Lamar had even given Jack a chance to come back into the fold when he had captured him years before, but the outlaw had refused.

Lamar tilted his head, considering the dispatch in his hands.

Gregor wanted the Breaker. Lamar wanted Jack to be punished. Perhaps the two were not mutually exclusive.

An idea began to take shape as he rifled through a sheaf of old informational dispatches. It would require a favor from Gregor, but the end goal would be one that his brother couldn't refuse. Getting his forces to Jack's little town would be problematic by foot. Not so from the air.

He found the page, eyes alight with avarice at the illustration with the label *Warbird*. The latest technological marvel from Cole Productions. A fast, efficient way to move troops across any terrain.

The warbird looked very much like a ship out of water, and perhaps it was. Its industrious designer had included an elaborate diagram of the vessel, and Lamar gave it a cursory look. He expected the leviathan of an airship to require magic, but that didn't seem to be the case. The article declared it to be steam-powered, taking advantage of groups of spinning blades—five on each side of the ship, encased in protective steel cylinders—to stay airborne. The hull was reinforced with magic to ward against attack.

Lamar considered it. A working prototype was in testing for use. The military hoped to create another version that would serve as a gunship eventually, but first, they wanted to see how this vessel fared.

He smiled. Lamar knew exactly what he was going to ask for. And as soon as his operative notified him that the plan to separate the Breaker from the Dollmaker had succeeded, Lamar hoped everything would be in place to make his move.

CHAPTER THIRTY-FOUR

Sorcerer

Blaise

*M*ornings in the bakery became uncharacteristically quiet. Mindy made a point to come over each morning and order the usual amount of fresh bread to use in the diner, but aside from that, there was a marked decrease in the number of regulars stopping by.

Blaise packed the bread for the diner in a basket, spreading linen over it to retain the warmth. Emmaline was in the midst of preparing a pie, and Reuben was helping one of their now-rare customers, so Blaise hitched the basket onto his shoulder. "Be right back. Going to take this next door."

Emmaline lifted a flour-covered hand in acknowledgement. "Maybe stop by the mercantile afterward. We're running low on strawberry preserves."

Blaise nodded, pushing through the door. He paused, lips

pursed as he looked up and down the street at the townspeople going about their daily lives. A line of pack mules waited outside the stables, waterskins filled to almost bursting from the river below attached to the harnesses on their backs as they waited their turn to have the contents emptied into the cistern. Wagons rattled down the street, dogs barked, and the sound of voices rang out. Everyone had adapted to their harsh new reality while they waited for the promised wind-pump repairs. Life had returned to a tentative, nervous new version of normal. Except not for Blaise.

He had been hopeful that business would pick up again at the bakery, but the townspeople were spooked. Jack and Kur had been unable to uncover the cause of the collapse—the only conclusion they drew was that it wasn't natural. And aside from the accusatory note, no one said a word to Blaise about the matter, but he could read the writing on the wall. The bakery's former regulars dwindled to only a handful. People outright avoided him.

Blaise had one hand on the doorknob to the diner when a booming voice froze him in place.

"—you can guarantee we'll stop eating here if you continue to buy from that *sorcerer* next door!"

Swallowing, Blaise dropped his hand and took a sideways step to one of the windows. He leaned over just enough to peek inside. Mindy and Celeste stood, arms crossed in defiance, in the middle of a ring of men dressed in the dusty outfits of wranglers and farmhands. A stocky, bearded man had taken point on the mob, shaking his finger in Mindy's face.

"I'll remind you, Silas, to not use such language in public. If any children were around, I would wash your mouth out with lye soap," Mindy snapped, eyes narrowed.

Silas didn't cower from her threat, but he did lose a little of his bluster. One of his fellows spoke up. "Pardon his language, Miss Mindy, but he has the right of it. Sure as the sun rises, the Breaker had to be the one to tear down the wind-pump. That, or Faedra herself did the deed, and that ain't likely."

Blaise trembled at the anonymous man's words, almost dropping the basket of bread. Heart pounding, he retreated from the window, fighting back tears as he headed back to the bakery. But he didn't go in immediately—Emmaline and Reuben were there, and he didn't think he could face them. Instead, he went around the back, to the lean-to that sheltered his firewood. He sat under the overhang, legs curled up against his chest and his face in his hands.

It was Bristle all over again, and this time he had no one to shield him from the growing tide of public disdain. Blaise rubbed his eyes with the heels of his hands, racking his brain for what to do. His life had already been endangered, and now this.

"Blaise?"

He wiped away his tears, trying in vain to compose himself as he lifted his head to look at Emmaline. "What?" Gods, why did she have to see him like this? A flush of embarrassment reddened his cheeks.

She stared down at him, her head tilted. "What's wrong?"

Blaise shook his head, unwilling to repeat the hurtful words he had heard. That would only make them more real, enhance how deeply they cut, and he couldn't bear that. "I don't want to talk about it right now. We can close the bakery early. In fact, you and Reuben can head out, and I'll clean up." He straightened, his hands braced against a bundle of firewood.

Emmaline scowled, her braid rocking gently in the chill wind. "Whatever's wrong, you can tell me. We're friends, and that's what friends *do*."

Friends. She tossed the word at him like a rescuer throwing a rope to a drowning man. Blaise desperately wanted to grab at it, wanted to be pulled from the nightmare of his life, but he was afraid if he did so, he would pull her down with him. And that wasn't fair. So instead, he looked away. "I need time alone."

"Blaise!" she protested.

His magic swarmed beneath his palms, agitated and unstable. Unbidden, it flowed from his hands and into the firewood, splintering the kindling with a piercing crack. Hissing, Blaise pulled his hands away, tucking them beneath his armpits. *"Please*, Em. I–I can't right now."

She took a step backward, the skin on her chin puckering with concern. But she didn't argue. Instead, she nodded. "If . . . if that's what you want."

"It is." Blaise stared at his feet, quivering at his loss of control.

The crunch and soft slap of boot heels on the ground heralded her exit. Blaise stayed where he was for another half hour, just to give them ample time to leave before he entered. After checking the time on his pocket watch, he rose and slowly approached the back door of the bakery. He opened it cautiously, listening for any hint that Emmaline or Reuben had stayed behind to confront him. But the bakery was quiet, and though he had told Emmaline he would clean up, they had done the job already. The kitchen area was freshly swept, not even so much as a dusting of flour visible. At least it still held the comforting scents of yeast and sugar.

Blaise sank down to the floor, his back flat against one of the cabinets. His gaze drifted from the black and white checked floor to the cast-iron pots and pans hanging on pegs to the washbasin across the room. He had thought he'd found what his life had been missing—acceptance, friends, a place to belong. But like all things in his life, it didn't last. His magic fractured everything eventually.

What could he do? Blaise swallowed, thinking back to Jefferson Cole's parting words. *"If you change your mind, let me know."* He straightened up as he reached a painful conclusion. Rising from the floor, Blaise wobbled over to grab the calendar atop the sales counter. Checking the date, he realized Jefferson Cole would still be in Rainbow Flat.

He took a shaky breath, sliding the calendar back to its proper place. *Running away again.* Blaise shook his head. No. Not running away. He was running *toward* another chance. And maybe this time the shadows of his past wouldn't haunt him. With his decision made, Blaise climbed up to the loft to pull out his old go-bag.

<YOU DIDN'T HAVE TO BRIBE ME WITH COOKIES, YOU KNOW,> EMRYS pointed out as Blaise hoisted the outlaw saddle onto his back. The stallion crunched on one of the bakery's unsold treats, tail swishing with contentment.

Blaise said nothing. His lips pressed into a firm line as he focused on the task at hand. He knew he was doing the best thing for the town by leaving, but that knowledge offered him little comfort. He had thought Itude was different, and it hurt that he was wrong.

<Will you talk to me?> Emrys asked, craning his head around to look at Blaise. <You've been silent since fetching me from the stables, and all I can read from you is sadness. I want to help.>

Blaise pressed his forehead against Emrys's neck, centering himself with the stallion's warmth. He'd waited until nightfall to coax the pegasus from the stables, bringing Emrys behind the bakery so he could prepare to leave town in relative peace. "I need you to take me to Rainbow Flat."

<Oh.> Emrys's ears drooped with understanding. <Now? Why not wait until the morning?>

The moon hung overhead, low and full. Blaise glanced skyward, then back to the cinch as he finished the final adjustments. "I don't want to explain." The thought of it made him queasy. He wasn't sure if Emmaline and Reuben would try to talk him out of it or—his worst fear—be relieved that he was leaving them. Blaise rubbed at his face, pulse racing as he thought of Jack. He would be out of the outlaw's hair, too.

"Explain what?" Clover came around the corner of the bakery, hooves crunching against the dirt. She cast an assessing look at the saddle on Emrys's back and the readied saddlebags. The Knossan tilted her head as she connected the dots. "You're leaving?"

Blaise sighed. This was exactly what he had hoped to avoid. "Yes."

She nodded. "I won't stop you."

That was unexpected. He frowned, leaning against Emrys's side. "You won't?"

"No," the Knossan replied, taking a step closer and hunching over so that she met his eyes on the same level. "I understand the path of the exile. More so than others."

Her words gave Blaise pause. Clover had never revealed her story to him, but he knew she grappled with being different. "But everyone here likes you. Respects you." *They don't blame you for destroying the town's lifeline.*

"But my life has not always been so. I know how it is to be treated with suspicion when they see you as something *other*," Clover said quietly. "There was a time when . . ." She faltered, as if trying to gather the words. "I understand how it is to be called *monster*. To be feared for what you are." Clover tipped her head to look at the stars as she gathered her thoughts, her nose ring catching the moonlight. "Do not let their words—their thoughts of who they believe you to be— define you." She lowered her head, so her rich brown eyes bore into his, insistent. "*You* define who you are by your actions."

Blaise swallowed the lump in his throat. "Does it matter if others think I'm responsible for things that I wasn't?"

Clover blew a warm breath through her nostrils. "It would be a lie to tell you it doesn't matter. It does." Her eyes held shadows of past pain. "You are the sum of many things. You are a son, a brother. A baker."

"A Breaker."

"I was going to say friend next, but yes, that as well." Clover glanced at Emrys, then back to Blaise. "This is a difficult thing. An ugly thing. But you are resilient, and like land recovering from a wildfire, you can sprout new life. Hope persists."

Funny, it didn't seem like that now. Everything was raw and

painful. He knew she was trying to be kind. "Thank you, Clover. For being good to me when you didn't have to be."

She offered him an encouraging nod. "I would do it again in a hoofbeat. Even if it annoyed Jack." Clover thought for a moment, and she flicked her ears mischievously. "Perhaps especially if it annoyed Jack."

Blaise managed a tiny smile at that. "I appreciate everything you've done for me, Clover." Blaise picked up the saddlebags and fastened them in place. "I should get going." *Before this gets any harder.* "Are you going to tell Jack that we talked?"

"Do you wish me to?"

"No."

Clover squared her shoulders. "Then I will not." She pressed a rough hand against her chest, a salute. "Remember that every storm runs out of rain." Then she turned and plodded around the corner, the sound of her hooves soon lost to the night.

Blaise swallowed, then made a final check of the tack. Every strap was secure, each buckle fastened tight. He slipped his gloves out of his pocket and pulled them on, then added a thick wool coat before shrugging into his duster. Icy winds blowing in from the north promised the flight wouldn't be pleasant. He shoved his left foot into the stirrup and swung into the saddle.

Emrys's hooves rang as he clopped away from the bakery. Blaise shivered, not from the chill that brushed against his face but from the uncertain future that yawned before him. He settled his flight goggles over his eyes, then pulled the stampede strings tight under his chin so his hat wouldn't blow off.

<You really want to do this?>

"You called for Clover to come talk to me, didn't you?"

Emrys angled a hurt look at him. <You wouldn't speak to me.>

Blaise winced. He had been unfair to not consider Emrys's feelings in this. "I'm sorry. I can't stay here anymore. You . . . you don't have to stay in Rainbow Flat with me." His teeth chattered on the last words, and not from the cold.

The pegasus went rigid, neck arching. He nearly vibrated with intensity. <That is *not* how this works. You do *not* get rid of me so easily.> Emrys fidgeted in place. <You are *my* rider and *my* friend. I'd follow you to Perdition and back.>

Blaise nodded, reaching down to pat Emrys's neck. Warmth curled around his heart at the prospect that he had Emrys by his side. "Thank you." At the nudge of his knee, Emrys turned and broke into a trot and then a lope before his wings snapped opened and the stallion hurtled into the overcast sky.

CHAPTER THIRTY-FIVE

Gone

Jack

"What do you mean, he's gone?" Jack squinted at Emmaline in the murky darkness. She was backlit by a mage-light, standing at the foot of his bed. He was an early riser, but because of her work at the bakery, Emmaline generally arose even earlier these days. She had given him an unceremonious wake-up call, barging in and caterwauling that Blaise was *gone*.

"*Gone*," she snapped, and though he only saw her silhouette, he heard the sorrow in the single word. There was a metallic clank, and Jack sat up, flicking on the mage-light beside the bed. She had dropped Blaise's key on the bedside table.

He picked up the key, turning it over in his hand as his foggy mind put together her words. "Blaise skipped town?" Jack frowned, thinking. "You sure he's not at the stables?"

Emmaline swallowed, shaking her head. "He was acting funny yesterday. And the oven is *cold*." At his blank look, she clarified. "He would have lit it by this time to get it to the right temperature. The key was left in the middle of the counter. And Oby says Emrys left in the middle of the night."

That got Jack's attention. He rose, digging out fresh clothes. "I'll get to the bottom of this." He paused, struggling to think of some way to offer her solace and reassurance. Emmaline was a lot like him, and keeping her busy might be the best thing. "You can go work at the bakery in the meantime, if you want."

Emmaline blinked, and for a moment, Jack thought she would protest. Instead, she nodded. "I think I will."

With that settled, they parted ways. Jack stalked to the stables. "Zeph!"

<You don't have to yell,> the palomino chided, popping his head over the stall door. <And if you're planning to ask about Emrys, we don't know where he went.>

Jack glared at the pegasus, hands on his hips. "You head up the sentries. Who patrolled last night?"

Two stalls down, the dust-colored head of a buckskin stallion appeared. <Oby and I were on patrol,> Naureus replied.

The outlaw frowned at Raven's mount. "And neither of you thought to ask Emrys or Blaise where they were going? What they were doing?"

<Sentry protocol is to *not* question those leaving town,> Zepheus reminded him tartly. <And Blaise is an adult, not a child running away from home.>

Jack growled to himself. That was true enough. But the Breaker leaving town so suddenly raised a slew of questions. Had he truly been responsible for the fall of the wind-pump? Was it possible Jack had been right all along? For once in his life, Jack didn't want to be right.

Itude was small, and news of such import flitted through the town like hummingbirds moving from flower to flower. By mid-morning Raven called for a Ringleader meeting, which was not unexpected. Jack was grumpy and unnerved by the Breaker's departure, and he wished a meeting could be delayed so he had more time to puzzle through things.

The other Ringleaders were deep in conversation when Jack arrived. As soon as he took his seat, Raven called them to order and didn't waste any time. He looked right at Jack. "Why did Blaise Hawthorne leave?"

Jack crossed his arms. "Are you accusing me or asking me?"

Raven snorted. "Both."

The outlaw spread his hands. "Your guess is as good as mine at this point. Guilty or scared." Jack's gut leaned toward the latter option, but his brain was another matter. Everyone knew Blaise had been at the cistern shortly before the wind-pump fell. It was difficult to discount that, even if there was no clear motive for *why*. Had he lost control of his magic, and that was the result? Or was something more sinister afoot?

"He's not guilty." Vixen's lower lip jutted out. "Blaise wouldn't do that. I've worked with him enough to know."

Kur's ears were flat against his pelt. "Innocent people do not leave without so much as a goodbye."

Jack wasn't so certain of that. The kid was awkward and didn't have the best grasp on social niceties when his nerves got the best of him. He drummed his fingers against the table, thinking. With a sinking feeling, he realized where Blaise was likely going. Clover had told him about the last conversation Jefferson Cole had before he left town.

"Shit," he growled. The other Ringleaders turned to look at him. He hadn't realized he'd interrupted Nadine speaking. Jack shrugged an insincere apology.

"Have something you want to tell us?" Nadine asked dryly.

"Rainbow Flat. He went to Rainbow Flat." Jack rubbed the stubble on his cheeks. As the pieces fell into place, he wished he could kick himself. Jack had been a fool, snookered into believing Blaise's woe-is-me plight. He had been right from the start. And Jack should have told the other Ringleaders about Cole's identity sooner rather than playing his damned wait-and-see game. "Because that's where Jefferson Cole is. And Jefferson Cole is a doyen for the Salt-Iron Council."

He thought they might respond to the news with exclamations of shock and outrage, but instead, they stared at him, puzzled. Vixen shook her head. "That doesn't make a lick of sense. I would have been able to persuade him to tell me that."

"And there are no doyens named Jefferson Cole," Raven added, though judging by the way he tugged at his short beard, he was bothered by the potential for trouble.

"That's because he's Doyen Malcolm Wells." Jack stabbed his index finger into the grain of the table, emphatic. "Somehow he maintains the front of this Cole man as well."

"How did you discover this?" Kur inquired, his eyes glowing golden with interest.

Jack shifted in his chair, uncomfortable. He recounted Cole's hefty financial proposition and the business card Jack still had in his possession. "I have dossiers on most of the eastern Confederation doyens and anyone who dabbles financially in the Untamed Territory. My records indicate they're the same person."

Nadine crossed her arms. "Jack, we put a lot of stock in your skills, but we also know your inclinations. How sure are you?"

Jack straightened, shoulders rigid at her calling him into question like that. He narrowed his eyes. "Certain enough to worry about my town."

Raven nodded, his head bobbing from side to side as he mulled over the information. "So Blaise has gone to this doyen in Rainbow Flat—and we have already agreed to allow his survey team to come here. The question is, how do we proceed now?"

"Refuse the team." Jack didn't even spare a second to think about it. It was the most sensible answer.

"Not so fast," Nadine said with a shake of her head. "Or have you forgotten the Gannish and their damned contracts? We have a contract—"

"With Jefferson Cole, not Malcolm Wells," Jack shot back.

Nadine held up her hand, her face lined with ferocity at his interruption. "I'm *speaking*." Magic hummed to life around her, a wispy aura of green sparks.

Jack glanced away, knowing full well he shouldn't piss off a Healer. Especially one as strong as Nadine. "Go ahead."

She gave a small nod. "As I was saying, I'm *from* Ganland. I reviewed that contract, and it's ironclad. Doesn't matter the name he used. It's valid, and if we break it at this point for anything less than an act of the gods, then we owe restitution."

Jack snorted. "*Restitution*. The Gannish would bleed a rock dry." But that was interesting. Nadine had never before revealed where she hailed from. Jack filed that away for later.

"They would," Nadine agreed, turning her gaze to the other Ringleaders. "And that would put us even more on the Confederation's map than we already are. So my suggestion is we allow the survey team to come and do their thing. Treat them with the same courtesy and caution that we showed Cole." She gestured to Vixen. "And you can pick their brains."

The red-haired outlaw grinned. "I can do that."

"And what do we do about Blaise?" Kur asked.

Jack levered his elbows onto the table, crossing his arms in front of him as he leaned forward. "Nothing."

Kur flicked an ear. "Why?"

"Because he won't come back here. If he does, I'll put a bullet in his brain." And Jack meant every word.

CHAPTER THIRTY-SIX
The Armor of Bureaucracy

Blaise

The flight from Itude to Rainbow Flat buffeted Blaise and Emrys with brutal cold. Flurries of snow threatened their progress, and several times Emrys had to land and continue on foot to prevent his wings from icing over. Blaise welcomed the chill—the weather echoed his bleak thoughts. When Emrys flew, Blaise was so bitterly cold that all he could do was focus on staying upright in the saddle, goggles and bandanna in place to protect his vulnerable face from the elements.

Due to the inclement weather, it took three days to travel to Rainbow Flat. Emrys guided them to a shanty each night, and together they curled up against the blustering wind. The shanties were little more than a roof and four walls to keep the worst of the weather at bay, but they provided the respite they desperately needed.

Rainbow Flat was a balm for Blaise's battered soul. It was two or three times larger than Itude, and it was pretty as a picture with the rooftops covered in a light dusting of snow, the Tombstone River running beside it sparkling like it ran with sapphires and diamonds rather than water. The buildings in the town were all smartly painted, with care taken in their construction. The townspeople investing in Rainbow Flat intended it to last.

Blaise found accommodations for Emrys at the local stable, content when they saw other pegasi used it as a base. Emrys was happy to bury his head in a bucket brimming with sweet feed while Blaise headed to the local saloon to ask after Jefferson Cole.

His arrival in Rainbow Flat was uneventful compared to his departure from Itude. In this town, Blaise was just another face, another traveler. At first, he was on edge, afraid that somehow his reputation had preceded him. But when he walked up to the bartender to make his inquiry, the man didn't so much as bat an eye. At mention of Cole's name the bartender gestured up the street to one of Rainbow Flat's two hotels. Blaise thanked him and walked to the hotel. After the minor matter of asking the desk clerk to hand off a note to Cole, the deed was done.

Cole invited Blaise to his elegantly appointed suite to relax after his long journey. He was too tired and bone-chilled to turn down the hospitality, and Blaise gawked at his surroundings as Cole asked the staff to deliver a meal to the lavish room.

They were in a sitting room, which boasted a pair of rich brown velvet-covered armchairs, a chaise with a floral design, and a desk pushed into a corner. The sitting room connected to a dining alcove large enough to hold an ornately carved oak table and four matching chairs. A closed door led to what Blaise assumed must be the sleeping quarters. The suite was larger than his bakery and loft combined.

Blaise told Cole he had thought more on the offer and decided to seek him out. He disliked the dishonesty but hoped to keep any information about his magic to himself. He wanted to be Blaise the Baker. *Not* Blaise the Breaker.

"So here I am," Blaise said with a shrug as he finished. It was a struggle to pretend to be nonchalant after the whole ugly situation. He eyed the glass of liquor that Cole had poured out for him, froth boiling around the top. He had never been one to drink, but his stress warranted it. Blaise picked up the glass and took a sip, then nearly hacked it out as the strength of the liquor kicked him in the mouth.

Cole bit back a laugh, covering his mouth with one hand. "Sorry. I didn't realize you may not have a constitution for alcohol after living in Itude. Some of the brews served at the saloon were ... unusual."

Blaise wrinkled his nose. He knew about some of them first-hand after working there. "I'm not one to drink, but it's tempting to start."

"Is it, now?" Cole asked good-naturedly. He leaned forward, eager. "So, what made you reconsider?"

Blaise coughed. Now that he was here, he felt self-conscious as he recalled Emmaline's assertion that Cole was interested in him for more than his desserts. Maybe coming here was a mistake, but what other option did he have? "I thought it might be a good time for a change." The words felt hollow and he hoped that Cole didn't see through them.

Cole, however, seemed oblivious. His eyes shone. "Let me be certain: you're accepting the offer to be my business partner?"

It was now or never. Blaise met his gaze. "Yes."

A muscle in Cole's jaw twitched, and Blaise thought he was holding in a celebration. A smile spread across his face. "Outstanding! I can't wait! There will be so much paperwork and forms to fill out, but that's the best part."

A blissful look crossed Cole's face, reminding Blaise of the awe-filled looks on the faces of the children in Itude as they looked at the dessert table at the Feast of Flight. The Gannish were a strange lot.

The businessman took another sip, then set his glass aside. "We have a lot to think about before we even get that far, though.

We'll need to locate a bakery to serve as a base of operations." He rubbed his chin. "Damn. You won't like my suggestion."

Blaise lifted his chin. "I'm not in a position to be choosy at the moment Mr. Cole."

The other man waved a hand. "Mr. Cole? No, call me Jefferson if we're to be partners." He rose from his chair and moved to the desk, pulling a rolled-up map off of it. He brought the map over to the low table centered between the couch and two armchairs, then gestured for Blaise to come closer.

It was a map of Iphyria. Jefferson tapped a finger on Ganland, in the southwestern portion of the map. "We'll do our best business if we're close to distribution lines. Ganland is a prime contender for several reasons. Number one, I'm kind of a big deal there." He flashed an indulgent grin. "Number two, it will position us closer to our potential vendors and investors. And three, as far as Salt-Iron Confederation nations go, we're geographically one of the furthest from the elite in Phinora. Especially if we work out of Nera." He pointed to the capital of Ganland, which clung to a peninsula. "I know that may be a concern considering your . . . status." His voice rose with a curious inflection, as if he wanted to ask more but restrained himself.

Blaise grimaced. "You're right. I don't like that suggestion. You didn't forget that I'm a maverick by chance, did you?"

Jefferson laughed. "No, I'm aware. And there are mages in Ganland. In the other countries, too. It's not as if you'd be the only one."

Blaise chewed on his bottom lip. Jefferson didn't know what his magic was. If he knew, Blaise doubted he would suggest Ganland. Though the way Blaise saw it if Jefferson knew then this entire plan would fall apart. "From what I've heard, I'd be the only one not tattooed and indentured and if a Tracker came across me, I would have problems."

Jefferson see-sawed one hand back and forth. "That's not fully accurate."

Blaise stared at him. "What?"

"Mmm," Jefferson gave him a speculative look. "My wealth can provide certain protections if you work for me." He roughed a hand against the velvet of the couch, making the fibers stand on end before smoothing it down again.

"I'm no one's servant." Blaise's heart pounded frantically in his chest. What if he was blowing his only chance? If Jefferson turned him down, he had no alternatives that kept him free.

Jefferson shook his head, appalled. "You misunderstand, I'm not speaking of indenture. I don't agree with that. In fact, I—" He cut himself off with a sour look. "I'd like to see it changed. What I'm saying is I have a fair hand at writing contracts. And I intend to honor what I said earlier and *partner* with you. You wouldn't be the first mage I've worked *with*. None serve me." His mouth quirked with distaste.

Blaise wanted to believe him. He really did. But this was Salt-Iron Confederation business, and that worried him. "How do you do that? I was led to believe mages aren't considered equals."

Jefferson cocked his head. "That is true. But people have to know you're a mage for that. You said you don't have a tattoo?"

"No tattoo."

"Can you keep your magic hidden? No bursting into flame or whatever it is you do?"

Oh, thank goodness he had a modicum of control now. "I can keep it hidden." It would drive him crazy, and he would have to find some way to release it at times. But he could do that now. A year ago, he would have answered *no*.

Jefferson gave him a sly smile and shrugged. "Then no one would know you're a mage. I can draft the contract as such."

"Would you be in trouble later if the truth comes out?"

Jefferson shrugged, unconcerned. "Plausible deniability."

Blaise wet his cold-chapped lips, uncertainty gnawing at him, but nodded. "Okay. But if the truth does come out later, could they force me into other service?"

Jefferson looked pleased that he was thinking this through. "Good question. If we have the proper paperwork signed and filed, no one could force you into the military or into any other servitude, unless we broke our contract. That's the wonderful thing about bureaucracy in Ganland. As annoying as it is, it's also a kind of armor."

Blaise hadn't considered that. No wonder Jefferson didn't mind the possibility of paperwork. "I think I'm going to need a little time to think on it and then ask some more questions once I've rested. Is that going to be a problem?"

"Take your time. I was planning to head back to Nera tomorrow after I finished my business dealings, but I'll gladly extend my time here. I'm not needed back home just yet." Jefferson rolled the map back up into a neat cylinder. "You look fatigued. Do you have a room yet?"

Blaise shook his head. "No. I was trying to make sure I could find you first."

Jefferson rose from his seat. "From what I understand, the suite next door is empty. I'll see if it's available, and if so, we'll put you up there."

Blaise's eyes widened. A suite? He didn't know how much that might cost, but he could only assume it would chew through the coins he had brought quicker than he would like. "That's unnecessary. I can get a different room."

"I insist. I'll cover the cost," Jefferson said with a dismissive wave of his hand. "It's the least I can do for my new business partner."

Blaise stared at him in surprise.

CHAPTER THIRTY-SEVEN
Partners

Blaise

T he massive wheel of the paddle steamer propelled the boat down the dark waters of the Tombstone, yellow and green pennants waving riotously in the breeze. Blaise watched as it slipped into the distance, headed for far-off ports. Muleshoe and then Freeport, according to Jefferson. Places Blaise had only seen on maps but which the entrepreneur seemed quite familiar with.

"Haven't seen a steamer before, hmm?" Jefferson asked as they leaned against the fence overlooking the docks.

"No." Blaise rubbed the back of his neck. "Nothing more than creeks or ponds around where I grew up, and . . ." He trailed off with a shrug. "You travel on them often?"

"Paddle steamers are the safest way to travel any part of the Untamed Territory." Jefferson said with a nod, then reconsidered.

"Well, aside from a pegasus, but they're not as good for moving merchandise."

"You know a lot about the Untamed Territory for someone who doesn't live here," Blaise observed.

A wistful expression flitted across Jefferson's face. "If I had the chance, I would."

That was interesting. Not what Blaise would expect. "So why don't you?"

Jefferson's eyes shifted away briefly. "Obligations, mostly." He cleared his throat and changed the subject. "Have you had time to consider our agreement?"

Jefferson had displayed remarkable restraint in keeping the topic at bay for the past few days while Blaise considered his options. He hadn't attempted any further flirtations, which was a great relief. But Jefferson had made it a point to spend time with Blaise each day, which had felt awkward at first but soon became almost a comfort. The entrepreneur seemed determined to keep Blaise's attention and took him to see the sights in and around Rainbow Flat. Jefferson had treated him to a night at a dinner theater and had taken him (and Emrys, who wouldn't let Blaise leave the town's boundaries without him) to see a herd of unicorns that called the prairie outside town home. Today the steamer docks were on their agenda. Blaise had to admit that the distractions were pleasant, and Jefferson made for good company, all things considered.

"I have, actually." Blaise shifted, draping his arms over the top of the fence as birds called overhead. He had thought about it so much that his brain felt like little more than mush. As it stood, he was going to run out of money within a month if he didn't figure out a solid plan. And Jefferson, with his eagerness, seemed like his best bet. "I'm willing to go to Ganland and go into business with you." Jefferson looked ready to jump with joy, but Blaise held up a finger to qualify his words. "But I want it to be an equal partnership. Whatever you get from it, I want the same amount."

Jefferson settled, lips twitching with an impressed smile. "I see you *have* been thinking about it." He considered the proposal, then shook his head. "I'm investing up front to get us started. With overheads, I'll be out a considerable amount. What about seventy percent for me, thirty for you?"

"Forgive me if I'm wrong, but I suspect you wouldn't be out living on the streets at fifty-fifty," Blaise responded as he watched a new steamer powering upstream to the town.

Jefferson gave him a sly look, then grinned. "I need to dress down." He stepped back from the fence, hands behind his back as he paced in a circle, thinking.

Blaise took a breath, schooling himself into a serious expression. He wasn't going to back down from this. "Baking is one of the few things I *know* I do well. I'm not settling for less than an equal partnership."

"I think you sell yourself short." Jefferson halted his pacing, giving Blaise a sharp look. "But I can respect that. I've tasted your cookies, and I know what we can reap from them." He walked back to rejoin Blaise at the fence, so close their shoulders nearly brushed. "I can get us a location in Nera. It will take time to get it ready. Two, three months perhaps—but that doesn't take into account the time to get a message to my associates there. You would need to wait here. Would that be a problem?"

Blaise shook his head. "There's a boarding house, so I can get a room that I can afford while I wait. And I can see if the local bakery is hiring."

Jefferson raised his eyebrows, giving Blaise an amused look. "That won't be possible."

"What? Why?" Blaise scowled. Was he going to have to rethink things?

"You're new to Gannish contracts." Jefferson sighed. "When we sign the paperwork, you'll effectively be an asset—"

"No," Blaise said so quickly he almost hadn't realized he spoke. His heart pounded. "I'm not." *I don't belong to anyone. I'm not property.*

"It's a legal term, Blaise," Jefferson said, his tone gentle.

"Nothing more. And for our purposes, it means I would rather not have you working for someone else. It could allow them a chance to learn from you, which could impact our future profit."

"Oh." Blaise glanced away, cheeks warming with embarrassment. But the problem remained that he would need to find a way to survive until he could work with Jefferson. He chewed his bottom lip.

Jefferson bumped his shoulder against Blaise's. "What's bothering you?"

Blaise shook his head, rubbing his hands together to ease the magic that responded to his tension. "It would be simpler to ask what's not bothering me."

"Yes, but that won't help matters," Jefferson pointed out. "Is it the contract?"

"No." Oddly enough, the idea of the contract gave Blaise a strange sense of security. He pulled away from the fence, gesturing to the town. "I'm not going to be able to afford to stay here if I can't work."

"Oh, is that all?" Jefferson blinked in confusion as if it were a minor problem. And perhaps to him, it was. He waved a hand, dismissive. "You'll have a stipend while you're here, of course."

"I will?"

"It will be in the contract." Jefferson allowed himself an amused smile. "So if you're still in agreement, I'll work on getting the paperwork drawn up. We can get it formalized in the next few days. I can stay another two weeks before I need to catch a paddle steamer back home."

Home. Jefferson's use of the word sent an unsettled shock through Blaise. Once again, he was without a true home. If Jefferson followed through, then Ganland might become Blaise's home. A touch of Jack's suspicion clouded Blaise's mind, and he wondered if Jefferson might somehow take advantage of him. Or lure him into a trap. Was Jefferson luring him to Ganland where he would meet his doom?

Did it even matter? Blaise was so tired of struggling.

"Blaise?" Jefferson was scowling at him with concern.

Blaise banished his concerns. "I'm fine. Sorry. I . . . I was thinking of something. You can start on the paperwork."

Jefferson smiled, the expression lighting his face with passion. "Excellent! Tonight at dinner we should toast our new endeavor!"

"Raspberry vinegar switchel," Blaise said.

Jefferson's tongue poked out in disgust. "Ugh. Raspberry vinegar switchel for you. Wine for me."

"Deal."

CHAPTER THIRTY-EIGHT
The Battle of Itude

Clover

Clover had her shotgun in hand as she trod out of the saloon's dim interior, Hannah and Abe in her wake. She twitched an ear, unsettled by the dull vibration rumbling through the ground beneath her.

"Thunder?" Abe asked, puzzled. He looked at the sky. There were clouds, but nothing that heralded a storm.

The Knossan shook her head, scanning the area. A light breeze blew from the west, carrying the acrid bouquet of machine oil.

Hannah gasped, pointing with a trembling finger. "Sweet Faedra, what is that?"

Clover pivoted to look where Hannah pointed, and she flattened her ears back at the behemoth vessel in the sky, tiny dots clustered protectively around it. "*Go.* Both of you. Run, run away as fast as you can." Clover prodded Abe in the shoulder to get him to stop gawking. The man had frozen in disbelief.

Hannah gulped. "But . . . we're supposed to fight."

Clover bowed her head. "You are outmatched by whatever that is. You do not possess magic. You are a fair shot, but war is coming. Gather anyone who can't—" And then her words were devoured by a void of silence. Startled, Clover tried to speak again and shook her head with frustration, making a shooing motion.

Hannah swallowed, then broke into a sprint after Abe, who was a sensible coward and had already started to flee. Clover didn't fault her cook. He was old, and his knees were bad. She hoped he would get to safety.

It was mid-afternoon, almost time for school to let out for the day. The children would make vulnerable targets. Clover slung her shotgun against her shoulder and trotted up the street, past townspeople who stopped to stare at the terrifying vessel that was already casting a shadow over the town square. Mouths opened in mute whimpers and sobs. A few regained their senses, running off to arm themselves. Good. Itude needed her defenders.

The schoolmarm, Julia Lincoln, had her head out the door. Small faces pressed up against windows, a mixture of curious and fearful. It was a strange thing, to not even detect so much as a titter from their mouths. But, Clover supposed, even if not for the oppressive silence forced on them, the children would still be quiet. They raised the children of Itude knowing that theirs was a dangerous existence.

Miss Lincoln opened her mouth to ask Clover something, her face pinched with worry. A little girl clung to her leg. Behind her, Clover realized that any child old enough to fight had left. Only the smallest huddled around Miss Lincoln, terrified and defenseless.

The children needed to get to safety. Clover could take some, but it was too late to flee. Their legs were too short. They could not run fast enough. Across the street, small Jasper Strop waved his arms to get her attention. He pointed at the children, then back to the dry goods store. The knocker pointed at the ground. Clover's nostrils flared in understanding. Jasper was offering to shelter some of the children in the hidden tunnel beneath his store.

Together Clover and Miss Lincoln herded the children over to Jasper. The knocker's tunnel that led to his travel-vein was short, but after he opened the hatch, he fit Miss Lincoln and ten of the children inside before hopping down and closing the trapdoor. Clover turned, left with five of the smallest children as the airship drew overhead.

No time left. Clover hunched over, hands braced against the dirt as she tossed her head to encourage the children aboard. They climbed onto her back as quickly as they were able, their frightened tears dampening her hide. Tiny hands bit into her skin, but she ignored the pain. She had to get them to safety. Picking up the shotgun, Clover lurched forward as the first bullets flew. She couldn't hear them, but she felt the concussive force as they peppered the ground nearby.

Clover surged to her feet, her bulk angled awkwardly forward so the children wouldn't lose their tenuous grips on her back. And then she ran as fast as she could to the northeast, to the trail that led away from Itude and, she hoped, to safety.

She ran and didn't look back.

Jack

ZEPHEUS TROTTED BESIDE THE PAIR OF MULES PULLING THE STURDY wagon loaded down with a pair of heavy, locked safes filled with gold. Jefferson Cole's survey team had arrived in town mere days ago, and Jack's annoyance grew every time he saw one of the foreigners wandering around. This heist with Kur had been just the thing he needed to settle his annoyance.

The job he and Kur Agur had completed would easily pay for the wind-pump reconstruction, and the outing gave him a chance to get away from town and clear his head. No doubt it would also increase the bounty on both their heads, but that was a minor matter. Jack had yet to meet a bounty hunter ballsy enough to come after anyone in the Gutter.

Besides, Jack and Kur had let the crew manning the Paragon Bank Coach off easy, even after the audacity of trying to murder the pair. They'd left the men tied to the spokes of their armored wagon, bleeding and naked, their flesh pebbling in the chill air. In the distance, the cries of chupacabras echoed. Jack wasn't heartless. Although he and Kur had disarmed the men, he left the driver's belt knife six inches out of their reach. The proximity of the chupacabras provided a strong incentive for the men to get to the knife once Jack and Kur cleared out.

They would be fine. Probably.

Fifty thousand in gold eagle coins clanked in the twin safes. It took considerable maneuvering and cunning to complete a heist with a wagon and mule team, but Jack and Kur had figured it out. The mollies Candy and Rosie were the canniest and most dependable of the mules to call Itude home. If not for Zepheus, the lady mules would be Jack's favorite creatures on four legs.

Atop the wagon, Kur stretched out his neck, scenting the wind blowing in from the west. "Machine oil. Why is the wind carrying machine oil? And gunpowder?"

"What?" Jack's gaze snapped on the Theilian. "Zeph?"

<I smell it, too.>

Jack pulled down his flight goggles and tightened the stampede string on his hat. "We're gonna take a look. Guard this windfall with your life."

Kur lifted his upper lip, displaying yellowed fangs. "I know what I'm about, human."

Jack ignored the impertinence as Zepheus broke into a lope to gain momentum to go airborne. His hooves left the ground, tucked neatly below the stallion as his wings pumped against the wind, defying gravity. Jack's vision was a blur of silvery mane and puffy clouds as he waited for Zepheus to level out.

The pegasus spotted the threat first. <Sweet Mare of Mercy, what is that thing?>

Jack tore his gaze from the ground as Zepheus angled to allow him a better view. In the distance, a massive thing that looked ridiculously like a flying ship hovered over Itude.

A flying ship hovered over Itude.

Jack's heart thundered at the sight. His daughter. His town. Tiny dots circled the ship. Griffins with riders. Itude was under attack.

Through the years, Jack had prepared for this day. Itude had moved from a susceptible town in the canyon to a stronghold overlooking the gorge, only accessible by a narrow road from the east. He made sure that everyone in town who was old enough to stand in a fight could do so. Jack had brought in all the mages he could for additional defense. But he had only planned for an attack from the ground, not from the sky.

<Jack?>

He shook his head, returning to the present. No sense dwelling on his failure now. "Let's circle back to tell Kur. We'll have him notify the ranches. Maybe some of the outlying mages can come in." *If it's not too late.*

The palomino banked and dove to the wagon where Kur waited, furry arms crossed. Jack told him the news, and his lupine face changed from annoyed to furious. He argued that he needed to get to the fight, but Jack and Zepheus would reach the town sooner. With a reluctant growl, Kur turned the mollies and sent them to the nearby Smith farmstead to give them the news.

That task complete, Zepheus bolted back into the air, not wasting a moment to ask Jack. They were both possessed with the single-minded drive to get back to town, to do what they could to fight the enemy at the door.

As they flew, Jack checked his sixguns, reloading. He had three, plus knives tucked in each boot. Eighteen shots he needed to make count because this was war and not one of his heists or gunfights. One shot, one kill.

A mile out of town, Jack thought it peculiar he couldn't hear any sounds from the airship. It hovered overhead, silent. As Zepheus drew nearer, Jack spotted a slender form at the front of the vessel, arms outstretched in concentration. *The Dampener.* Jack admired her range—it took a considerable amount of skill to exert her magic as far as she had. Not a single scream or gunshot escaped the oppressive bubble she forced over the area. He knew firsthand how disruptive the lack of auditory cues were in a fight.

"Take her out!" Jack bellowed to Zepheus.

The palomino set his course for the airship. Jack felt the palpable silence as they passed through the bounds of the Dampener's field, the hair on the back of his neck rising at the eerie tableau beneath him. The fighting must have started recently. The streets below were a mix of soldiers and armed townspeople, surreal with the utter lack of noise. There should have been peals of gunshots. Screams. Shouts.

Zepheus checked his course hard, nearly unseating Jack with the motion as a griffin swooped inches overhead, the beast's talons raking against his hat. Jack strangled for an instant as the stampede strings garroted him, but on instinct, he loosened them and his hat ripped away. Gagging, Jack touched his tender throat with one hand as he pulled out his revolver with the other. He took aim and pulled the trigger. The griffin's beak gaped in muted agony as the bullet ripped through its side, fouling its flight. It wasn't dead, but it would think twice before coming after Jack again. And its flight was so uneven its rider had difficulty lining up a shot.

With the griffin out of the way, Zepheus swooped around to put them on a new attack path. The Dampener stayed where she was, eyes closed in concentration as she kept her spell going. The more noise and people within, the more difficult the upkeep would be. Jack smirked. Courtesy of her own spell, she would never hear him coming.

<The deck is empty. Touch and go behind her, so you have a clear shot.>

Jack patted Zepheus's neck to let him know he agreed. Touch and go landings were no easy feat, but they were something Jack had all the Itude pegasi learn. It was difficult on their flight muscles, and it wasn't something he asked them to do lightly.

Zepheus's hooves touched down on the polished wood of the deck, lowering his neck and wings for a heartbeat to allow Jack a clear shot. Jack already had his revolver up, silver muzzle gleaming as he pulled the trigger, and a silent bullet sped into the theurgist's brain. The Dampener's body hadn't even hit the deck before Zepheus shoved off with his hooves, his wings creating a sound like thunder as the bubble of silence popped.

Screams and gunfire shredded the air.

<What now?>

Jack's heart was torn. He wanted to tell Zepheus that their priority was to find Emmaline. But the town was a war zone. There was no time to waste. His daughter might already be dead in the streets below.

Fury blazed through his veins. "It's time to introduce those soldiers to Wildfire Jack."

JACK AND ZEPHEUS SEPARATED AS SOON AS HIS BOOTS HIT THE ground behind the bakery. The griffins and their riders harried the pegasi defenders from the air, with several of the equines already downed. The other stallions needed all the help they could get.

Jack flattened himself against the bakery's yellow wall, a red spatter marring the paint at chest level. He glanced around the corner and saw a dead soldier on the porch, a sticky crimson pool spread beneath him.

The outlaw caught his breath, peering out in time to catch the shadow of a griffin overhead. With the Dampener down, the din of battle echoed through the town. Sixguns and rifles roared. Men and women screamed or cried. Griffins shrieked as pegasi stallions whistled their defiant challenges.

Jack stayed hidden, taking the measure of the enemy. The soldiers had the old Saltie penchant for firing high. They were far less likely to connect with their target—though those times they did, it would be ugly. The soldiers outnumbered the townspeople who had rushed out to Itude's defense. They were going to die in a battle of fire and fury, without a single chance to coordinate their efforts.

Somewhere nearby, Jack heard a baby wail and a mother shushing the infant, frantic. A soldier turned to locate the sound. Jack stepped out and shot the man in the head, then withdrew before anyone else saw him.

Sixteen shots left.

Jack leaned against the bakery's exterior, head back. He had beaten the odds before, but nothing like this. Overhead, a pegasus and griffin thrashed together, a tangle of feathers, claws, and hooves. Glass shattered, and wood screeched under pressure as they crashed into the second story of the boarding house. Jack cringed, thankful that the pegasus was a bay and not Zepheus's gold.

How could they win this?

We can't win this.

Jack's jaw clenched in grim determination. If this was the end of the trail, he was going to drag as many of them to Perdition with him as he could. The Salt-Iron Confederation wouldn't sack Itude and take light casualties. Not if Jack had a say.

He pulled out a knife, slipping it between his teeth for quick access. Jack ducked into the melee, dodging through the confused combatants. He paused, heart catching in his throat at the distant blur of long blonde hair in the hayloft above the stables. *Emmaline.* It took every ounce of willpower to not run to her. The enemy was a thick knot between his position and the stables. It would have been suicide.

Jack snaked past the saloon, ducking into the post office for a brief respite. He was behind most of the enemy forces, and he picked off a few as he moved, forever mindful of his dwindling supply of bullets. His boots were painfully loud on the wooden floor as he shut the door behind him. Jack paused and slipped the knife back into his boot, scowling at the pool of blood spreading across the floor behind the counter.

He crouched down and crept forward to investigate the legs sticking out from the other side of the mail counter. Hank Walker? Jack's revolver stayed out as he eased around for a closer look. The dead man was dressed in foreign garb, too formal for the Gutter. One of the Gannish survey team. What in Perdition was he doing on the floor of the post office with his throat slashed?

"You weren't supposed to see that."

Jack spun, muzzle pointed at Hank Walker, who loomed in the doorway with a pistol in his hand, blocking the exit.

"What are you playing at, Hank?"

"Of all things, I thought you'd approve of that." Walker snorted. "You've been walking around town itchy as a shaved cat over Jefferson Cole."

True enough, but still. "Doesn't give you leave to kill a man."

Walker shrugged. "You're one to talk. They'll die today anyway."

A chill raced down Jack's spine, rage consuming him at Walker's implication. "You *knew* about this. You son of a bitch!"

Jack moved with a speed born of betrayal and outrage, and the postmaster didn't stand a chance. He barreled into Walker, his left hand against the man's throat as Jack pinned him against the wall, right hand pressing the muzzle of his sixgun against the postmaster's temple.

"Did you sell us out?" Jack growled, eyes blazing.

Walker trembled, gagging. Jack loosened his grip enough for the man to speak. "P-please. I had to. Those . . . those bastards have my *brother.*" The heartbreaking sob at the end gave credence to his claim. That, or he was a talented actor in a high-stress moment.

"You *lied* to me." Jack's voice was a deadly whisper among the symphony of destruction outside.

Jack intended to kill Walker where he stood, but the chance never came. The door exploded inward from a forceful kick, and with a bellow, Jack hurled Walker into the trio of soldiers pushing into the building. The havoc of the postmaster spinning into the men gave Jack all the time he needed to break open the nearest window and run.

He had more people to kill. Jack bit back a curse when he found himself at the funeral parlor.

"Damn irony," Jack grumbled, noticing Butch hiding behind a pine box, taking pot shots at soldiers out the window. "You can do better than that, Butch."

The undertaker's face was pale, eyes owlish with fear. He was also a Necromancer, a terrifying force if only he would use his magic. Jack didn't know his story, but Butch had vowed to only use his unholy power in very specific situations. And this was one of them.

"I don't know if I can, Jack." Butch quivered.

Jack bit back a frustrated howl. "We've got folks dying out there. And you might be next." He flicked his eyes to his revolver. Not that he was threatening Butch. Well, maybe a little. Sometimes motivation was necessary.

Butch's eyes widened, taking his meaning. He blew out a breath, then scuttled over to a desk and pulled a small velvet pouch out of a drawer. "I need to get to the cemetery. Can you cover me?"

Jack sighed. Damn it. That was a long way and a lot of open

ground to cover. "You can't use the dead already outside your door?"

"That's not how it works," Butch said with regret.

"Damned picky magic," Jack groused.

Butch made a noise of agreement. "Least you can use your magic and your sixgun as we go."

That's a no on the magic, Jack thought bitterly. He tipped his chin toward the door. "Let's go."

Jack led the way, slinking behind buildings to provide them with cover. Most of the soldiers had convened around the town square. Jack paused—they were too close to the stables for his liking. Butch stumbled against his heels, and with a soft curse Jack crept forward again. Smoke rolled across the town, and a glance to the north confirmed that flames engulfed several of the buildings. That was going to be a big problem later. If there was a later.

A tussle of gold and brown streaked overhead, Zepheus locked in battle with a griffin. Jack held up a hand to keep Butch from trampling him, scowling at the deep slashes of scarlet on the stallion's flanks. He lifted his revolver and took aim. They were a respectful distance away, and they were moving targets, but he didn't take kindly to that beast trying to kill his pegasus. He squeezed the trigger.

The griffin screeched, releasing its talons from Zepheus's neck. The pegasus spiraled away in a burst of loose feathers that fell like leaves from an autumn tree. Jack whispered encouragement skyward, then continued onward to the cemetery.

"Jack." Butch tugged his sleeve, gesturing to a dark form off their path.

Another pegasus hadn't been as lucky as Zepheus. Jack sucked in a breath as he recognized the mortal wound on the stallion. The pegasus made pained, rasping noises. His wings were shredded to tatters, feathers loose on the surrounding ground. Blanchydas staggered to his feet, but a griffin had tangled with him and slit his belly open. His intestines were ugly ribbons spread on the gore-splattered dirt beneath him.

Blanchydas fixed his white-ringed eyes on them. <Please. It *hurts.*>

Jack cursed. Damn the Salties. There was no saving the stallion, and they both knew it. He raised his revolver.

"Wait," Butch cautioned, and rushed over to the stallion, avoiding an enemy bullet with a startled yelp. Jack waited impatiently as the Necromancer murmured to the stallion. The pegasus bobbed his head, eyes rolling in agony. Butch picked up one of the fallen feathers and tucked it into his pouch. "Do it."

Jack came closer to the stallion. "Thank you for protecting our town. May your spirit fly up to the stars singing of your heroism." He should save his bullets, but this fallen defender deserved a quick, merciful end. A lump in his throat, he lifted the revolver, placed the muzzle against the pegasus's head, and pulled the trigger.

The stallion slumped with a soft exhalation. Jack swiped at his eyes as he turned away from the scene. "Come on."

The cemetery wasn't far. Butch raced ahead and settled down among the tombstones, pulling items from his pouch and arraying them on the ground. Jack kept watch, noting only a handful of griffins remained in the air. One griffin was on the ground, snapping at two injured pegasi who had cornered it. Jack smiled with grim satisfaction as the pegasi worked together to outmaneuver the beast and take it down.

"This gonna take much longer?" Jack asked, scanning the area. The town was on fire. He coughed as the wind blew smoke into his face.

Butch didn't answer. The temperature chilled, and Jack whirled to see the Necromancer standing in the middle of the cemetery with his arms spread wide, a look of ecstasy on his face.

"Vengeful dead, come forth and defend your town!" Butch threw something into the air—dust?—and magic pulsed.

Jack had never met another Necromancer aside from Butch, and he had never seen necromancy in action. He was pretty sure if Blaise was there, he would never call Jack's magic creepy again.

The ground above the graves shattered as their skeletal occupants broke through caskets and topsoil, released to the world again. They were in various states of decay as they clawed their way out of the dirt. Their empty eye sockets blazed with an infernal light. Most of them were armed. Itude had a tradition of burying its outlaws with their weapons. And ammunition, just in case.

The dead pegasus trotted over to Butch, innards and wings dragging behind like a ghoulish wedding train. The Necromancer climbed onto Blanchydas's back, moving with a renewed grace and energy that Jack hadn't thought him capable of.

Necromancy was some freaky, scary shit.

"The dead stand with us," Butch intoned.

Jack nodded, his skin crawling as he turned his back on Butch's small force. "Then let's go take our vengeance."

CHAPTER THIRTY-NINE
The Dollmaker

Emmaline

She thought this would be easier.

Emmaline crouched in the hay hood above the stables, using the partially opened roll-away door as cover. Her heart raced in her chest like a runaway horse, her hands trembling as she took in the chaos below. She felt like a failure, hiding up in the hayloft. She was Wildfire Jack's daughter. He had trained her to fight, and here she was trying to hide like a little girl behind her mother's skirts.

But the practices and training hadn't prepared her for this. The screams of agony, the acrid smoke in the air, the shouts and impact as griffins and pegasi tore into one another. The hexgun training in the canyon had been child's play by comparison. Tears stung her eyes as she saw Gus Pembroke fall, blood spurting from the back of his head as the light left his eyes.

The breath caught in her throat, and she clutched a hand to her face. This couldn't be. This was her town. The people wounded and dying out there were friends. Emmaline didn't know if she stood the chance of a candle in a downpour, but she had to try.

The chill of rage and adrenaline flooded her body, and time seemed to slow as she slipped a trio of poppets from her pocket. She hadn't had time to run home and grab her sixgun, but she wasn't defenseless. Brow furrowed with determination, she cast around for things she could use. She pulled a thick stalk of hay from one of the nearby bales, then scooted over to the door so she could peer out.

Emmaline took a calming breath to center herself, just as her father had taught her. "Until effigy work becomes second nature to you, always do it from a place of calm," he had reminded her time and time again. An Effigest working from a state of upset was more likely to have their magic fail—or even worse, snap back and impact the caster rather than the target.

She spread out the three poppets, glancing from them to the melee below. Her range was limited, so Emmaline selected three nearby enemies. She had to be careful—Itude's defenders wove in and out of the tide of soldiers. Chewing her lip, she targeted the soldier closest to the hayloft as he lifted his rifle to fire. She jabbed the poppet she bound to him in the back with the thick hay stalk. Below her, the soldier contorted in sudden discomfort, his shot going wide and sparing Vixen what might have been a mortal wound. The redhead kicked the man to the ground, drawing her knife.

A thrill rushed through Emmaline at her success. *I can do this.* She scanned the masses and went to work. Some of her attempts failed, but none of them backfired. She tripped a soldier who had Nadine in his sights, sending him tumbling to the dusty street where Raven appeared from nowhere and ended him with a wicked slash across the throat. Emmaline lost track of the flow of time, focused on the fighting below her. Out of the corner of her eye, she saw a scarlet-clad form trot down the steps from the Ringleader HQ, but it was too far away for her to wonder about.

The battle raged on, vicious. Once, she saw a flash of gold and realized Zepheus had joined the battle. Which meant her father had, too. In between casts, she searched for any sign of him but found nothing. What if he was dead?

No, she couldn't consider that now. She worked her magic with fervor, unrelenting even as Emmaline knew she was doing too much, too fast. Despite the chilly afternoon, sweat dripped down her face. Emmaline watched as Nadine fought a soldier like a wildcat, but the older woman was tiring. She was slow, and when the soldier closed in and punched a dragonfang knife into her gut, she writhed in agony.

Emmaline screamed at the sight, then clapped a hand over her mouth. She couldn't give away her position. Hands damp with perspiration, she frantically tried to bind a poppet to Nadine, to grant her strength and healing.

Nadine pulled herself deeper onto the knife, wrapping her arms around the soldier in a macabre embrace. The soldier screeched, floundering to get away. Somehow, Nadine reached down and dug the knife from her gut and flung it away. The soldier sagged in her arms, his skin and raw red muscle sloughing away over bones that clattered out of his uniform.

Nearby soldiers, witness to Nadine's act of horror, disengaged from their combat to circle the Healer, guns aimed at her.

"Well, well, well. What have we here?"

The wooden boards of the hayloft creaked behind her. Eyes wide, Emmaline slowly scooted around on the floor to face the tall, blond-haired man wearing a pristine scarlet and gold Confederation uniform. It wasn't mussed or bloodied from the fighting, not like the others below. Shiny gold medals pinned to his left breast likely meant he was someone of rank.

"Aren't you a little old to be playing with *dolls?*" the man leered, sinking more meaning into the last word than Emmaline liked. She had the strong suspicion he knew what she was doing.

"Just . . . just hiding from the fight." Emmaline kept her eyes wide and afraid, which wasn't a stretch by any means. *You have an advantage I don't, Em,* her father had told her. *You can look like a young, innocent girl. You don't have to like it, but there're times that will come in handy. Don't forget.*

The soldier took a step closer, head cocked as if he were trying to decide if he should believe her. She prayed that he did.

"I'm so scared," Emmaline whispered. Another truth. She squeezed her eyes shut, a move she disliked because it was difficult to track him, but it lent credence to her words.

The wood grated again with his movement. Then fingers closed around her chin, jerking her face up, her eyes flying open as the soldier stared at her.

"Please," Emmaline implored, her voice a whimper. "Please don't hurt me." Her pulse raced at the very real threat of the soldier looming over her.

His clean-shaven face would have been considered charming, even handsome, at any other time. Now it was terrifying. Emmaline heard a soft click, and with sickening realization, she saw the brass muzzle of a hexgun in the man's hand. Pointed at her.

"I'll admit, you're good. But you don't fool me." He prodded a poppet with his toe. "I'd recognize those anywhere. You must be the Dollmaker's daughter."

Trembling, Emmaline held his gaze as she covertly snagged a single poppet with one hand and slipped it into her boot. She'd never heard her father called that name before, and she suspected it wasn't a compliment. She wanted to say something, anything, to defend her father. But her tongue sat heavy in her mouth, and she had never felt so helpless as his fingers tightened on her chin, the hexgun nuzzling her side.

"Your father was careless to leave these just lying around where anyone might find them." The soldier chuckled. Emmaline knew it for the lie it was. The hexguns had been stowed away in a safe at HQ.

Someone in town had tipped this man off. Someone in town

had betrayed everyone. She trembled, fury flooding through her as her mind connected the dots. Her father's near-death at the hands of the Salt-Iron Confederation. The collapse of the wind-pump. Blaise had been there for both. Blaise knew about the hexguns. Were the rumors true? Was Blaise the traitor?

"Why are you doing this?" Emmaline whispered.

The man leered, a feral grin. "Too many reasons to list. But right now? This is personal. I'm going to enjoy seeing your father suffer." The hexgun nudged her again. "What do you say we find out which sort of ammo this is loaded with, hmm?" Before Emmaline could react, he pulled the trigger, and she slumped to the ground.

Jack

WITH BUTCH AND HIS UNDEAD LEGION, JACK HAD BECOME HOPEFUL. And that was a mistake. Hope was a fragile thing, meant to be shattered.

The undead were unkillable, for obvious reasons, and their appearance in the battle as they preceded Jack and Butch in a wedge formation sowed momentary confusion and chaos as the soldiers fought an implacable force that wouldn't die. But unkill-able was not the same as invulnerable. The enemy assailed the undead (who, Jack noted, were piss-poor shots unless they were close to their foe) with blades and blunt weapons when bullets did nothing. That was fine with Jack. It allowed him the opportunity to take out a few more unsuspecting soldiers with well-timed bullets. But his supply was dwindling, and the two Confederation weapons he had come across were empty.

A screech ripped the air overhead, and Jack dove to avoid the reaching talons of a griffin. The undead outlaw in front of him wasn't so fortunate, and with a sorrowful moan, the beast lifted her into the air, skeletal legs flailing. Jack cursed as the griffin launched her over the side of the cliff.

Jack lost sight of Butch as he wove through the thinning throng of undead defenders to visit death and destruction on the enemy. Somewhere along the way, a bullet grazed his right leg—a minor annoyance, all things considered—and a knife sank into his left arm. Jack lost himself in the frenzy of battle, shrugging off the wounds for later. He fought like Butch's undead, an implacable force that nothing short of death would stop.

Or so he thought until a familiar voice rang out above the cacophony of battle. "Jack! I know you're here somewhere. Come out, unless you're a coward."

That damned taunting voice. Jack followed it through the writhing knot of soldiers, casually shooting a man here, stabbing one there. Blood caked his hands, slashes of red lacing his arms. Some of the blood was his, but most of it belonged to the enemy.

Around him, the sounds of fighting died off as the last of the defenders were defeated or surrendered. Panting, Jack stepped into a ring of Salt-Iron soldiers, weapons trained on him. Jack made a quick mental count of his bullets. One. He should have one left unless he had lost count in the heat of battle. One was all he needed.

"I'm here, Lamar, you frothy, sheep-biting pignut." Jack tightened his grip on the sixgun, eyes glittering as he searched the surrounding faces for Lamar. *C'mon. Where are you?*

A soldier tittered nervously at his insult, then cleared their throat as they realized the error. One side of the ring of soldiers shifted, and Jack tensed, prepared for action. He froze as Lamar stepped into the circle, Emmaline limp in his arms, her head lolled back.

Jack's blood ran cold, heart leaping in his chest. His mouth was dry, gaping.

Then rage slammed through him like the Wildfire of his nickname. He lifted his gun, a blur that the soldiers recognized too late. He sighted just over Emmaline's slender shoulders, aimed for Lamar's head. Pulled the trigger.

Nothing.

Lamar should have crumpled to the ground with a hole in his head. Why was he still standing?

Jack had failed. He had lost track of his bullets, the worst thing he could do in this situation. His brain froze, refusing to process what had happened.

With a taunting smile, Lamar handed Emmaline to a nearby soldier, gesturing as a silver cage coalesced around Jack, beautiful and deadly. The Commander put his hands behind his back, ambling over.

"Oh, Jack." Lamar shook his head, projecting false pity. "What happened? It's not like you to miscalculate something so basic." He slid his gaze to Emmaline's form. "Something distract you?"

Jack wobbled on his feet as the exertion of fighting, his wounds, and the psychological trauma of his daughter in Lamar's custody rocked him. He had a knife in his boot. He could throw it —but no, that wouldn't work. Nothing could get out of the trap.

"Let . . . let her go, Lamar. You have me. Take me in for the bounty." Jack's head pounded as the fight ebbed out of him. He was so tired. All he wanted was for his daughter to be safe. Then he could die knowing he hadn't failed everyone he cared about.

Lamar smirked. "As tempting as that is, I have other plans." He cast a glance around, the smoke from the fire ravaging the bakery and diner blowing over him. Lamar smiled, as black as his heart. "I'll be kind, traitor. I know you treasure this hole-in-the-wall town. So you get to stay here and watch it burn down while I leave with the mavericks."

Jack stepped as close as he dared to the bars, scanning the crowd. Heart sinking, he spotted familiar faces interspersed among the soldiers. The shock of Vixen's red hair. Raven, his handsome face purple with bruises and spattered with blood, in salt-iron shackles. Cordelia with a gun to her head. The soldiers herded the surviving magicless defenders across the square, held in a tight knot in front of HQ.

Jack closed his eyes. This was a nightmare. "Lamar. *Please.* Take me. Leave everyone else alone."

"As much as your begging is music to my ears, that doesn't work for me." Lamar shrugged, then turned away to address his surviving forces. "Get the new recruits loaded up and prepare the *Retribution* for travel." He paused, looking back at Jack. "One thing: I will commend you on the ferocity of your fighters. I thought we would waltz in, but they put up a fight despite our surprise." Lamar plucked a piece of lint from one sleeve. "Lucky for me, I made sure your Breaker wasn't here. You might have stood a chance otherwise."

Blaise? Jack's blood ran cold. Shit on a shingle. The Breaker was innocent after all.

Lamar noticed his expression and canted his head. "Do you know which way he went, by the way? He's next on my list."

"You leave him *alone,* Lamar," Jack snarled.

His old friend made a sour face. "I wish I could, but you know how these assignments go." He waved a hand, dismissive. "It is what it is." Lamar pivoted to trail behind his departing soldiers, pausing beside the man who still held Emmaline. He gave her a covetous look. "It's been years since we've had an Effigest worth a damn, Jack. Will she be as good as you, do you think?"

Jack knew better. Damned, dirty Lamar was goading him, the same as he did anyone in one of his blasted traps. Always poking at them, hoping they would slip. Jack realized his mistake too late as he slammed a hand against the bars of the cage with a ferocious roar.

The last thing he saw was Lamar's stupid grin as every muscle in his body pulsed with fire. And then everything was dark.

Clover

VERUC, THE GREAT BULL, SMILED ON CLOVER WITH FAVOR. SHE considered it a stroke of fortune that she and her load of children came across Kur Agur as she trotted down the road that meandered away from Itude. The Theilian hunched atop the driver's seat of a loaded wagon, furry arms crossed and shoulders hunched, as Clover gently lifted the children from her back and to the bed of the wagon. Clover didn't chide him for his behavior. She felt much the same way, frustrated to be away from the fighting.

Kur, to his credit, had gathered a small force from the outlying farms and ranches and led a column of loaded wagons heading to the town. Men and women who routinely traded goods with Itude came to support it however they could, armed with rifles, pitchforks, magic, and healing ministrations.

As the sun set, their group camped at the Collins place, the closest farmstead to Itude. It was a necessity, but Clover agonized at the delay. Winter's dark descended early, and it was ill-advised to travel in the consuming veil of night. This irritated Kur, too, and he paced their campsite, snapping and growling like he had an infestation of ear mites.

As soon as dawn touched the horizon, they broke camp. The wagon train lumbered toward Itude, slow and steady. The airship had long departed, but Clover supposed that might be for the best. The people responding were not fighters, but they had big hearts. They wanted to help.

As the molly mules crested the final rise, Clover hopped down to the wintry ground from her seat beside Kur. The Theilian's lips curled back, eyes glowing gold. Clover sucked in a breath, flattening her ears.

Death. So much death on the wind. The humans couldn't smell it yet, not with their weak senses. But soon they would.

She traded a look with Kur. He said nothing, only lowered his head, the fur on his ruff erect. "I will scout ahead," she told him, pulling her shotgun down from where she had stashed it beneath the seat.

Clover loped ahead of the vanguard, scanning the area as she travelled. Only a few human bodies, and those dressed in the scarlet of the Salt-Iron Confederation. Viscera and broken feathers from pegasi and griffins littered the outskirts along with their corpses. The humans were griffin riders, she supposed.

The homes outside town still stood, though a few suffered broken windows or roof damage from falling aerial combatants. Curtains twitched in a window, and a moment later a gaggle of trembling women streamed out, surrounding Clover.

"Our babies! Where are our babies?" Dirt, tears, and blood streaked their faces. They were dirty, terrified, and heartsick. Clover wanted nothing more than to reassure them, but the empty words died on her tongue.

"Five children came with me, and they will arrive soon in the wagon with Kur Agur. The others . . ." She looked towards town, squinting. So much smoke. "Jasper took them to his bolt-hole beneath his store."

Choking back sobs, the women fled towards town. Clover lowered her head and whispered a prayer to Veruc. *Please let the children be safe. Please.*

Head down, Clover trailed behind them, the biting wind coiling the stench of death around her. She paused, noting a skeletal corpse clutching a rifle. Clover snorted, head cocked in alarm until she caught a familiar scent wafting from the bones. *Butch.* The Necromancer had wielded his terrifying craft.

Bodies of friend and foe littered the streets of Itude. Blood pooled in the dirt, congealing in the chill temperature. Near the edge of the mesa, carrion birds croaked and danced around the bloating corpse of a pegasus.

Clover surveyed the gutted town. Most of the buildings on the northwest side of the square were smoldering husks—bakery, diner, mercantile, hardware store, greengrocer. The windows in her beloved Broken Horn Saloon were shot out, and part of the

roof caved in. Some miracle had spared the dry goods store, and
Clover watched as the mothers led a shivering line of children
from the depths of Jasper's bolt-hole.

She sighed, closing her eyes as she thanked Veruc. Trembling,
she opened them again and resolved to search for any wounded
defenders clinging to life. More survivors joined Clover,
including Hannah, who silently wept as she went from body to
body.

They found Nadine amid a circle of slain soldiers, though
Clover saw no wounds on their bodies. Against the odds, the
Healer somehow lived and breathed, though bullets riddled her
body and a rust-colored stain on her abdomen hinted at a
grievous wound. The farmers and ranchers arrived, and a pair
brought a stretcher and took Nadine to her clinic.

Clover straightened, gazing across the carnage spread out
before her. Her breath caught at a limp, too-familiar form face
down in the dirt. *Jack.* With a bellow of despair, she tore over to
him, kneeling beside him.

"Jack, no." Clover dipped her head in sorrow, turning him over
gently. With a gasp, she realized that his chest rose and fell. Shallow, but there. She placed a furry ear to his chest. Sluggish
heartbeat.

He lives. Barely.

Clover called for help, and moments later, Jack lay on a
stretcher, face slack and eyes closed. The men carried him to
Nadine's clinic. Clover rubbed the side of her muzzle, overwhelmed.

"Clover?"

Tiny hands tugged at her elbow. Clover glanced to the side and
saw Jasper Strop staring up at her, imploring. She dwarfed the
knocker which normally intimidated him. "Jasper, thank you for
saving the children."

He waved his hand, a *think-nothing-of-it* gesture. "The man.
The leader of the enemy." Jasper pointed to the nearest soldier in

Salt-Iron crimson and gold, to clarify. "They are going after Blaise next."

"What?" Clover blinked, trying to decipher how Blaise fit into this horror.

Jasper tugged at one of his ears. "Excellent hearing. I heard him talking to Jack. It was a set-up, Clover. They tricked Blaise to leave so they could attack." His face fell. "And now they plan to go after him."

Clover sucked in a breath, eyes wide as his words struck her like a hammer to the head. Blaise was innocent. And he was in danger.

Jasper waited as she put the pieces together, his lips pressed together with determination. His eyes glittered. "It does not have to be that way, Clover."

"What do you mean?"

The little knocker smiled, a feral grin of bared teeth. "If he is in Jefferson Cole's company, I can find my niece. I can tell her. Warn him."

Clover jabbed her horns at him. Under any other circumstances, she might have thought to consult the Ringleaders first. But aside from Kur, who patrolled the town with barely restrained fury, they were all missing or near-dead.

"Do it," she ordered.

Jasper gave her a determined nod, scuttling off to the dry goods store.

CHAPTER FORTY
A Matter of Appearances

Blaise

I want to go with you,> Emrys insisted for the thousandth time, pressing his forehead against Blaise's shoulder.

Blaise shook his head. He was having an impossible time convincing the stallion that accompanying him to Ganland—to a new life—was a terrible idea. And to be honest, he hadn't made a convincing argument against Emrys's desire. The stallion was emphatic that he would be fine hiding his wings. But Blaise feared what might happen if anyone discovered the pegasus. As much as he craved a familiar friend along on his journey, he didn't want anything bad to happen to the loyal stallion.

"I know," Blaise murmured, and together they watched a paddle steamer trundle down the river. When they made the journey to Ganland, it would be by ship. If Emrys went, Jefferson explained, he would have to stay in the hold for an extended time, unable to move around. Definitely unable to spread his wings.

Emrys declared that a stupid idea, countering that he saw no problem with flying to a better location before getting on a boat. Blaise admitted the pegasus raised a good point—flying would be preferable to spending a long, long time on a steamer.

"There's nothing stopping you from going back to Itude, though," Blaise said. He had told Emrys that before.

<And I've told you before: you're my rider.> Emrys snorted, flicking his ears back. <Company's coming.>

Blaise glanced behind them, lips slipping into a smile as he saw Jefferson striding in their direction. The businessman looked pleased with himself as he joined them, arms resting on the top rail of the scenic overlook.

"We're all official now." Jefferson grinned, eyes alight. "My local attorney checked over the documents and said everything appears to be in order. She's sending them by courier to Nera. We're officially business partners."

Emrys rolled his eyes. <I'll leave the two of you to your boring business talk.> He ambled off, tail swishing.

Blaise returned the grin. It had taken longer than expected for all the paperwork to get together once he and Jefferson had agreed on the terms. He had no idea it took so much effort to open a business. When he said as much to Jefferson, the other man had shrugged and said that it varied by country. Ganland loved paperwork so it was more arduous than others.

Jefferson sent messages to his associates to put out feelers for a bakery location that could be snapped up for a cheap price and improved. Blaise was giddy at the thought of having his own bakery. Again.

It had taken time, but he had adjusted to life in Rainbow Flat. He didn't mind staying there another few months until Jefferson gave him the go-ahead to make his way to Nera.

"I leave in three days," Jefferson reminded him, watching a flatbed ferry convey a stagecoach from one side of the river to the other. "I don't like leaving you here alone to your own devices, so I have an associate coming out here to keep you company."

Blaise eyed him. "What's wrong? Do you think I'm going to skip town now that we have a contract?"

Jefferson shook his head. "Not that. It's a matter of . . . appearances." When Blaise raised an eyebrow, he continued. "Until we're a known quantity in Ganland, if I were to send you a message here in Rainbow Flat, it may appear suspicious. Do you follow my meaning?"

Blaise glanced down at the water lapping below, trying to keep his face impassive. "You're concerned to be seen as a traitor."

Jefferson gave him a fond look, chucking Blaise's shoulder with a gentle fist. "You catch on quickly. But yes, I already get enough flack for my Untamed Territory business ventures. I have some rivals who would love to throw me to the wolves for the slightest reason."

Blaise cocked his head. "That's the first time you've mentioned that. So why take the risk of working with me at all?"

Jefferson paused, rubbing the back of his neck as if he wished to take back his earlier words. "Sometimes the risk is worth the reward." He straightened, clearing his throat as he gestured to the surrounding town. "And I enjoy taking risks. It's the reason I go out to these exotic locations and make my own deals."

Blaise tilted his head, suspecting that Jefferson was keeping something from him. He thought about pressing but decided not to. He hadn't told Jefferson what his magic was, so who was he to judge? He wished he could talk to someone other than Emrys about it. As much as Blaise loved Emrys—and he did, the pegasus was like family to him—he craved someone else not fearing his magic, but accepting it as part of who he was.

"Blaise?" Jefferson was giving him an expectant look.

He blinked. "Oh. Um, sorry. I was thinking about something."

Jefferson smiled. "As I was saying, tomorrow Flora Strop will arrive. I'll introduce you, then I'll leave you in her tender care."

Strop? That was a familiar last name, but it could be a coincidence. Blaise shook away the thought. "I'm changing hotels when you leave. We'll have to let her know." He couldn't afford the place Jefferson had him in now.

"You will not," Jefferson said, straightening as if he had taken offense. When Blaise opened his mouth to protest, the other man stepped closer, his face serious. "I have good reason for you to stay in the hotel I chose."

Blaise's forehead wrinkled. "Why?"

"Protection, among other reasons." Jefferson studied him with concern. "It's one of my properties, so I know the staff will keep you safe and well-tended."

Blaise's jaw dropped. "Wait. This entire time . . . we've been staying at *your* hotel?"

Jefferson had the good grace to look slightly embarrassed. "Obviously."

Blaise rubbed his face with one hand. "Okay. That's fine. I assume you won't charge me for the stay."

Jefferson grinned. "Oh, I will—but steeply discounted. You're welcome."

Blaise rolled his eyes. "You mentioned other reasons. What are the other reasons?"

Jefferson studied him, as if trying to decide what to say. He seemed uncharacteristically nervous and gave a small shake of his head. "It's nothing. Come on. We should go celebrate with wine. Well, that blasted switchel for you, I suppose."

"I might give the wine a try tonight."

THE RESTAURANT BUSTLED WITH ACTIVITY, AND WITH A SINKING heart, Blaise realized it was the most expensive that Rainbow Flat offered. He gave an imperceptible shake of his head as he studied the menu. It was difficult to adjust to Jefferson's casual flaunting of wealth.

"What?" Jefferson peered across the table at him. "Don't see anything to your liking?"

Blaise folded the menu and set it down. "It's not that. I just don't fit in here." He gestured to the plush, velvet-upholstered chair in which he sat.

Jefferson rested his chin on his hand, frowning. "Don't belittle yourself. You're my business partner. Of course you fit in."

Blaise shook his head. "I've signed a very large stack of papers. I don't think that qualifies me for much of anything yet."

"It does. And we need some of that wine to toast it." Jefferson flagged the server over. "Two glasses of the Umber Dolce." The server bowed his head gracefully, then strode off.

"What, I don't get to pick?" Blaise asked.

Jefferson gave him an exasperated look. "I'm not about to let you ruin this by picking some cheap wine that tastes like vinegar."

Blaise chuckled. "If I didn't know better, I'd say you're insulting my raspberry switchel."

"I would never do that," Jefferson intoned solemnly, though his mouth twitched with humor.

Blaise relaxed in the opulent chair, running his thumb over the velvet. The last several weeks in Rainbow Flat with Jefferson had been . . . nice. He had discovered that Jefferson was more than an entrepreneur—he was a comfortable conversationalist, and he never seemed to consider Blaise as anything less than an equal. And best of all, he never asked about his magic. It rarely came up in conversation. "You're right. I'd have no idea how to pick wine. So why that one?"

Jefferson leaned back in his chair. "Umber Dolce is one of the livelier wines on this menu. It will be a good starter wine for you. It has a fresh, fruity flavor."

Blaise tapped the exorbitant number beside the menu item. "And it's the most expensive."

Jefferson grinned. "You have a lot to learn. The finest bottles of wine are the most expensive."

The server returned with the wine and made a flourishing show of uncorking it and then pouring into a pair of crystal goblets. Jefferson's eyes gleamed as he watched, savoring the show. After the server finished and retreated, Jefferson lifted his glass and swirled the golden contents. Blaise took his cue and followed suit.

"And now a toast. To bright futures." Jefferson hoisted his cup towards him. Blaise let his goblet ring against Jefferson's.

"To bright futures," Blaise echoed. Jefferson took a sip, so Blaise did as well. It wasn't bad, though he had been expecting a little more on the fruity side. He could still taste the aggressive headiness of alcohol. Blaise was polite and took another sip.

Jefferson watched him, intent. "What's your opinion?"

"Um. It's different," Blaise stalled, setting down his glass.

"You don't like it." Jefferson's shoulders drooped with disappointment.

"It's not bad," Blaise amended. "Just not what I was expecting."

Jefferson rested his arms against the white tablecloth and leaned forward. "I could say the same for you."

Blaise froze. "What do you mean?"

"You're not what I was expecting." Jefferson glanced away, and Blaise realized he was discomfited, which was unusual. Jefferson drummed his fingers on the table, then looked up at him again. "We've spent a lot of time together and I . . . I care about you." He licked his lips as if they had suddenly gone dry. "In more than a professional manner."

Blaise stared at him as he wrapped his mind around Jefferson's words. He didn't know what to say to such a direct statement. His mind whirred and came up blank, his heart racing in response.

"Forget I said that. It was improper." Jefferson rubbed the back of his neck, ill at ease. His eyes darted around the restaurant like a man looking for rescue. "Where's that server? I'm ready to order. Are you ready?" His voice rose, almost feverish.

Blaise leaned forward, his brain finally catching up to the situation. "Jefferson. Stop."

Jefferson gave him a pained look, his mouth a down-turned slash.

"I'm flattered. You're . . ." Blaise pursed his lips, trying to grasp how to describe it. The best he could do was to gesture at Jefferson, then the restaurant. "You're like this. I'm not. And I've never had anyone interested in me, so I don't know how to feel about that."

Jefferson blinked. "Ever? You're kidding, right?"

Blaise rubbed the edge of the tablecloth between his index finger and thumb, self-conscious. It was a hard thing to admit that he had resigned himself to a life alone. He liked the idea of a companion, but it seemed out of his grasp. "I wish I were."

Jefferson shook his head, puzzled. "Then you've been surrounded by short-sighted fools."

Blaise's breath suspended for a split second at Jefferson's words. "What?"

"I'm serious. Look at that strong jaw beneath the rugged beard. That long bit of hair above your brow that sometimes falls into your eyes." Jefferson grinned as he added, "The way your eyes narrow when you think I'm being ridiculous."

"I'm doing that right now, aren't I?"

"Yes," Jefferson deadpanned.

Blaise shook his head, hoping his cheeks weren't aflame with embarrassment. "I've enjoyed my time with you. I don't know if I share your feelings. This is new to me." His stomach writhed with indecision. This was uncharted territory. No one—man or woman—in Bristle would have him after the disasters of his youth. And now the opportunity stared him in the face in the guise of a bronze-haired, green-eyed man who saw none of Blaise's faults.

Jefferson reached across the table, laying his hand atop Blaise's. Not claiming or grabbing, but reassuring. It took all of

Blaise's willpower not to startle away from the touch. "Take all the time you need." Jefferson drew his hand back.

Blaise swallowed, caught off guard by the enormity of the situation. Jefferson could have anyone. "Why me?"

"Why not you?"

"I'm serious."

"As am I." Jefferson's green eyes sparked. He relented, glancing around. His voice was low when he spoke. "Because you're kind. You talk to me like . . . like a normal person. Not like you're trying to groom a prized racehorse to make you rich. You're not chasing after me for my money or . . ." He trailed off, shaking his head.

"To be fair, I chased you for the chance at a bakery."

Jefferson blinked, then chuckled as he waved a hand, dismissive. "That's different. That's business, and you'll do your part." He smiled, and it was a content expression. "And you have this single-minded determination to open a bakery, of all things. You have magic, and I'm sure could do other things. But you chose that." He tucked his chin. "It's cute."

Blaise leaned back. "Let me assure you that baked goods are a serious business."

Jefferson's smile widened into a grin that reflected in his eyes. "That's what I'm counting on. Businessman, remember?" He pointed to himself.

Blaise relaxed. This differed from anything he had ever imagined, this comfortable banter with someone who found him attractive. The server circled around and took their orders, and when she hurried off, Jefferson picked up the conversation as if he hadn't moments earlier rocked the foundations of Blaise's world.

"I know you're from Desina. You told me that much. Which town?" Jefferson asked as he picked up a slice of bread and buttered it.

Blaise cringed. He hoped Jefferson didn't plan to delve too deeply into his past. "Bristle." When Jefferson nodded, he asked, "Do you know it? It's not a large town."

"I've never been to Bristle, but yes, I know it. If I travel by boat, we usually stop at the ports in Sable Point and Gulfton before making the longer trek across the Gulf of Stars to Nera." Jefferson sank his teeth into the bread.

Blaise seized the opportunity to learn more about Jefferson, especially since he couldn't pose another question without being rude while chewing. "You speak of Nera often. Is that where you're from originally?"

Jefferson shook his head, swallowing the bit of bread before answering. "I was born in Seaside, and most of my family is still there. Do you know anything about the Fortune of Majority? It's particular to Ganland."

Blaise's forehead puckered, quizzical. "No."

Jefferson settled back in his chair. "They prize business acumen where I'm from. The Fortune of Majority is a tradition that most families take part in. When a child turns eighteen, they're gifted a hundred golden eagles to spend as they choose." His eyes glittered with the fervor of a distant memory. "The new adult can spend it however they choose. Save it, invest it . . . or spend it on frivolous things."

Blaise cocked his head. "It's a test?"

"Exactly." Jefferson nodded.

"So what did you do?"

Jefferson coughed and glanced away, embarrassed. "I, ah . . ."

Blaise smiled. He thought he had Jefferson figured out. "You spent it on frivolous things, didn't you?"

Jefferson swung his head back around, meeting his gaze with sudden intensity. "Not exactly *frivolous*." He brought his right hand up from beneath the table and pointed to the ring he wore on his index finger, holding it out so Blaise could see.

The ring featured a large cabochon-cut dark red stone; a garnet, Blaise guessed. The precious stone was set in a golden enamel bezel accented with tiny diamonds that winked in the light. He was no jewelry appraiser, but Blaise knew he was looking at top-of-the-line craftsmanship.

"I made some investments and then cashed them all in to buy

this—and yes, I'm well aware that seems frivolous. But I assure you, it's not. Did I spend the investment money on new ventures like any sensible young Gannish man would do? Absolutely not." Jefferson shook his head, rueful. "But this opened doors for me. Would you believe a year after I bought this ring, I quit my job working for my father, traveled to Rainbow Flat, and invested in my first hotel?"

The server brought out their meals, and Blaise waited to reply until she had left. "If anyone else said that, I wouldn't believe them. But it's you so I do."

Jefferson smiled, and this time it was the satisfied expression of a hunter reminiscing on a fine hunt. "That was eleven years ago. I like to think I've done well for myself since then."

Blaise opened his mouth to respond when the front door to the restaurant blew open in a great gust of wind, a petite form hustling inside. The doorman yelped at the sudden intrusion.

"You need a *reservation!*" the hostess hissed urgently as the invader ignored her, shucking off a rain-dampened oilskin great-coat and tossing it over the hostess's extended arm.

A courier? Blaise wondered, tensing as he watched. The stranger scanned the restaurant before their eyes settled on Jefferson, moving with speed and purpose in their direction. Blaise clenched his fists, alarmed. His palms itched as his magic rose up, ready.

"Relax, I know her," Jefferson murmured. He waited as the small woman claimed an empty chair from a nearby table without so much as asking, butting it up beside their table. "Flora, good to see you. Wasn't expecting you until tomorrow."

Blaise blinked. So this was Flora Strop. She was nothing like he expected. Flora was short, the tip of the cheerful pink bun of hair atop her head coming no higher than the middle of Blaise's chest. She wore scarlet-framed glasses that reminded him of Vixen, giving him a brief pang of homesickness. Blaise thought she wasn't fully human—if he had to guess, he would say she might be half-knocker, which made sense if his guess about her

last name was correct. But that wasn't something he was prepared
to ask.

"Something came up, and I had to rush," Flora replied, then
clapped her hands. "What's a girl gotta do to get some service
around here?"

A harried server came over, offering Flora a wine goblet and
pouring out a sampling of Umber Dolce. She lifted the glass in a
salute of thanks and sipped, releasing a pent-up sigh as she closed
her eyes in bliss. As she enjoyed her refreshment, Blaise realized
he had seen her before—for a brief time on Jefferson's first day in
Itude. Afterward, she had vanished, never seen in town again.

"Mmm. Good vintage. That hits the spot." Flora's eyes shot
open, reinvigorated. "So which do you want first? The bad news,
or the worse news? Also, is this the place that has the oysters in
that creamy sauce? I could go for oysters."

Blaise's mouth ran dry, and he traded a worried glance with
Jefferson. Somehow retaining an air of calm, Jefferson flagged
another of the staff down and ordered oysters for Flora before
answering. "I'm assuming the news should wait until we're no
longer in polite company?" He gestured with his fork to encom-
pass the restaurant.

Flora tilted her head, considering. "Hmm. After oysters, then."

DINNER DIDN'T SIT WELL IN BLAISE'S STOMACH AFTER FLORA'S
arrival. Jefferson attempted to eat, but Blaise noticed the develop-
ments bothered him, too. Only Flora attacked her food with vigor,
eating like she had been starved for days. She asked Jefferson if he
was going to finish his trihorn fillet and promptly claimed it when
he pushed it over to her.

Afterward, they retired to Jefferson's suite. As soon as they entered, Jefferson hightailed over to the bar and poured out a finger of whiskey for himself and Flora.

Blaise sat in an armchair, perched near the edge with his hands clasped, consumed by alert apprehension. With a sigh, Jefferson eased onto the side of the chaise nearest Blaise, setting his whiskey on a coaster on the low table. They waited as Flora peeled off her boots with a groan, flexing her stockinged feet as if they ached. Then she produced an oilskin-wrapped envelope from a carrier Blaise hadn't noticed strapped to her back.

She pulled a smaller white envelope out but didn't offer it to Jefferson. Instead, she pointed it at Blaise, her eyes narrowed to dangerous slits. "I have questions for you. First of all, how dare you?"

He blinked, unbalanced by her query. "What?"

Jefferson uttered a frustrated sound. "Flora, don't. Please." He cast a furtive glance at Blaise before settling his pleading look on the pink-haired woman.

Flora frowned, turning her pique on Jefferson. "Of all the mages in the world, you had to find a *Breaker*?"

The blood rushed from Blaise's head. No. No, no, no. He closed his eyes, pained. *Not again.* Why did this always happen when he found some place he might belong, someone who didn't hate him?

A firm hand latched onto his, warm fingers twining together. *Reassuring.* Jefferson. Blaise trembled. "It doesn't matter." Jefferson's breath warmed Blaise's ear, voice gentle. But he was wrong. It *did* matter. It always ended up mattering.

Flora sighed. "Ignoring all the history—"

Blaise's eyes flashed open, indignation overcoming his panic. "History doesn't define who *I* am." Flora gave him a side-eyed, skeptical look. "I'm more than just a Breaker." He squeezed Jefferson's hand, warmth blooming when the gesture was returned.

Jefferson reluctantly released Blaise's hand. "I agree with that, and as far as I'm concerned it has no bearing on this conversation." He refocused on Flora. "Tell me your news. And try to do it in a way that won't insult my new business partner."

Flora blew out a huffing breath. "Fine, but I think you'll find he *does* have bearing on this conversation. I have three news items, and they range from bad to horrible to awful. Which do you want?"

Jefferson raked a hand through his hair. "I don't even know where to begin."

With a shrug, Flora offered him the envelope. "Then start here."

He took the proffered envelope, pulling a small pocket knife out to slit it open. Jefferson drew out the letter, eyes scanning the page before he fully unfolded it. His jaw tightened as his teeth ground together. Without a word, he passed the letter to Blaise and took a long gulp of whiskey.

Full of misgivings, Blaise opened the page and read. By the second sentence, he understood why Jefferson required a stiff drink. The author of the letter claimed that Jefferson's Gannish survey team in Itude was slain by *"the bloodthirsty outlaws"*. In retaliation, they sent a force from Fort Courage out to *"bring the guilty to justice"*.

The letter was dated several days ago. Maybe the attackers hadn't arrived yet. "They . . . they wouldn't have killed your survey team, Jefferson. We have to warn them."

Flora gave a tiny shake of her head. "The letter is misleading in more ways than one. It was penned the same day as the attack."

Jefferson drained his glass and rose for a refill. "How did you discover this?"

The pink-haired woman's eyes went steely. "First-hand information." She lifted her glass, a silent request for more. Blaise hoped her metabolism could keep up with it.

"Your uncle?" Jefferson poured out golden liquid for her. He paused, glancing at Blaise. "Can I get you something? Water?" Blaise shook his head.

"My uncle," Flora confirmed. For Blaise's benefit, she added, "Jasper Strop."

Ah-ha. He pressed his lips together. "I thought your last name was familiar."

Flora waved a hand, warding away distraction. "This is important. Uncle Jas survived by hiding in his bolt-hole. He heard things, Jefferson." She crooked a finger at Blaise. "Gaitwood's next target is your boy here."

Gaitwood. Blaise shuddered involuntarily.

Jefferson pinched the bridge of his nose. "First off, he's not my boy. *Business partner.* I know it doesn't roll off the tongue as well, but there it is. Second, why would he want Blaise? They were fed the same history lessons we were. The Salt-Iron Confederation line dictates Breakers are bad news. The normal response to a Breaker is . . ." He trailed off, eyes studying his whiskey as he swirled it in the glass. Flora helpfully completed the thought by slashing her index finger across her throat.

Blaise blanched.

"Not helping," Jefferson growled.

"*Lamar* Gaitwood doesn't care for him, far as I can tell," Flora clarified. "*Gregor* Gaitwood is a different story."

For the first time since the world-shaking conversation began, Jefferson was thunderstruck, as if Flora had punched him in the gut. "Why does *Gregor* Gaitwood want a Breaker?"

Flora smiled, devoid of mirth. "That's the question of the day. The one I can't figure out." Her eyes slid to Blaise. "Why would someone like that want you?"

He leaned back in the chaise, scratching at his beard with one hand. "For starters, I don't even know who you're talking about. If it's not obvious, I'm unaccustomed to people wanting me for anything." *Except Jefferson.* Strange as it was, that thought offered a moment of comfort. An oasis in a desert of despair.

Jefferson and Flora traded glances and came to a silent decision. Jefferson rubbed his chin, thoughtful. "Have you heard of the Salt-Iron Council?"

Blaise winced. "The Confederation wasn't discussed in my home. My mother . . ." He shook his head, closing his eyes as he took a breath.

Jefferson set his whisky on the table and then sat down beside Blaise on the chaise lounge, leaning forward so his forearms braced against his knees. "It's fine. Short answer: every nation in the Confederation places members called Doyens on the Council. The number of positions vary by country. Phinora, Ganland, Canen, and Petria have three district representatives, while Mella and Umber only have two. Desina and Argor don't have representatives yet, as the Council won't be in session to admit them for another few weeks." Jefferson watched Blaise to make sure he was following along. "Gregor Gaitwood is a Doyen for Phinora. Does that make sense?"

Blaise chewed on his lower lip. "Yes, but I don't know why he'd want me." He paused, thinking. "Except . . ."

"Spill it," Flora growled.

"Be nice." Jefferson gave Blaise a reassuring look. "Will you please tell us? It may be important."

He didn't want to tell them, didn't want to relive that day. Blaise bowed his head. Jefferson was right—it might be important. In a whisper, he told them of his first encounter with Lamar Gaitwood and his mother's gambit. And then he spoke of his second brush with the Commander, when he found out his mother's fate.

Flora scratched at the arm of her chair. "Something to do with her then. She a mage?"

Blaise shook his head. "Alchemist."

Jefferson's eyes widened, and Flora groaned. "That's almost worse. What's her name?"

"Marian Hawthorne."

She tipped her head, considering. "Not familiar with that name. But I'll do some digging, see what I can find out." Flora swallowed, her eyes hooded with regret. "And now the last bit of news, which I don't think either of you really registered because the human brain can only process so much dragonshit at once."

She sucked in a breath. "Lamar Gaitwood *already* attacked Itude. He sacked the place and took the surviving mages back to Fort Courage."

Blaise stared at her, his mouth so dry he wished he had taken Jefferson up on the offer for water. He clutched the arm of the chaise, so focused on Flora's words that he didn't notice the tell-tale itch in his palm as his magic responded to his distress. The wood beneath the velvet made a thunderous crack as his magic assaulted it, and an instant later Blaise held the sagging arm onto the chaise. He closed his eyes, hating himself for his failure to control it.

"Leave it," Jefferson murmured, shaking his head. "It's just furniture."

Flora muttered something Blaise couldn't quite make out, but he suspected it wasn't flattering.

"I should have been there," Blaise whispered.

Flora snapped her fingers. "That's the thing. Lamar specified he *didn't* want you there." A wicked smile played on her lips. "Something about your presence made his odds of winning unfavorable."

The hairs on the back of Blaise's neck stood on end, chilled. He had thwarted Gaitwood twice. From what Jack said, Lamar Gaitwood wasn't a stupid man. He was canny. Which meant he was crafty enough to force Blaise out of Itude before he went on the attack. Blaise shook his head as white-hot rage coursed through him. But the sensation only lasted a moment. It didn't serve him to be angry around Jefferson and Flora. Anger could wait.

Flora watched him, head cocked to one side. "I see all these emotions crossing your face, and I don't know if I'm more concerned that you're not collapsing the building around us or that you're just sitting there like a fly landed in your soup."

"I can control my magic," Blaise muttered. "Getting mad right now won't solve any problems." He took a shaky breath. "I . . . I should go to Itude. There must be survivors. They'll need help." His stomach lurched as he connected what had befallen Itude with the people he cared about. Jack. Emmaline. Reuben. Clover. Hannah. Vixen. So many more. It was easier to think of Itude as a unit—it was less personal. But as he thought of the individuals, he felt sick.

"There are survivors," Flora confirmed. "But I don't know that you should go there." She glanced at Jefferson, imploring. "He can't go there, not if Gregor wants him. It's too close to Courage. He needs to go far, far away. Thorn or Arbor. Even Highhorse if they'll allow it."

Jefferson's smile was sad. "Blaise has my support to do whatever he thinks is best." He touched Blaise's arm. "You didn't leave under the best conditions. I'm assuming this changes things?"

Blaise exhaled. "I suspect Gaitwood set me up."

Jefferson nodded, grim. "I agree with that assessment." He reached for his glass, draining the last dregs of whiskey. "Allow me to recap what we know. Flora, correct me if I miss anything. One, Gaitwood has made sure my survey team is out of the picture. Two, Gaitwood wants Blaise, but we're not sure why. Three, they attacked Itude. Did I miss something?"

"Lamar took the surviving mages with him, back to Courage."

Blaise's heart raced. So many of them had fled to Itude to escape that fate. He clenched his fists. This couldn't stand.

"I'm going back to Itude," Blaise said, voice soft. "I'm going to help the survivors, and then I'm going to get back the mages that were stolen."

Flora gave him a speculative look. "Don't get me wrong, I like where you're going with this, but you and what army?"

Blaise was done running away. "I may not have an army, but I don't need one." He refused to meet Jefferson's worried eyes. "I'm a Breaker."

CHAPTER FORTY-ONE
It's Complicated

Blaise

*E*mrys tried to ignore Blaise at first when he came to the stable, but the stallion didn't hold out long when he sensed the palpable anger rolling from him. The raspberry tart Blaise had snagged from the hotel room service as a peace offering didn't hurt, either.

Once Blaise explained the news, the pegasus was full of righteous fury. <We should go now,> Emrys demanded, his neck curled in a tight arch and every muscle in his body tense. <There's no time to lose.>

Blaise shook his head, laying a hand on the stallion's shoulder to quell him. He felt much the same way, but it would be dangerous to leave now. It was dark and cold; the moon was hidden by clouds heavy with the promise of snow. "We have to wait until morning, if the weather holds."

The stallion hung his head. <We should have been there.>

Blaise nodded, threading his fingers through Emrys's warm mane. "We can't change the past. We can only respond."

They stood in companionable silence for a few minutes. The stable was quiet but for the soft sounds of some of the other occupants snoring or shifting around their box stalls. It was a quiet, safe place in a world that was anything but.

<What will Jefferson do?>

Blaise leaned against Emrys, brushing dust from his glossy neck. "He . . . ah, he has his own obligations. Jefferson leaves for Izhadell tomorrow." Izhadell, where Blaise's mother might be. "But he's sending his associate with me, Flora Strop."

<Strop? I know that name.>

"Jasper's niece."

Emrys snorted. <Jack's going to have kittens when he finds out.>

Blaise chuckled, then stopped as his blood ran cold. He didn't know Jack's fate. The surly outlaw was a survivor. Surely he had survived with wits and raw cussedness.

<Don't count someone out too soon,> Emrys cautioned, following Blaise's trail of thought.

He nodded. No sense worrying about Jack or anyone else until he had a better grasp of their fate. If the weather held, in two days, he might know more. Blaise sighed, releasing those worries for his future self.

"I need to get back to my room to rest. See you in the morning." He filled Emrys's bucket with a late-night snack of sweet feed before letting himself out. Blaise left the stable with Emrys's contented crunching in his wake.

He trudged down the hotel hall, tired but consumed with the manic energy of anticipation. As Blaise turned down the hallway to his suite, he saw Jefferson carrying a burlap sack into his room. He paused, dropping the bag just inside the door before closing it as Blaise approached.

"I thought you'd be asleep by now."

Blaise shook his head. "I was with Emrys. It's going to be hard to sleep tonight."

Jefferson's green eyes intensified. "Do you want to talk?"

Did he? Blaise wasn't sure how to bleed off the nervous energy —not even using his magic would take the edge off. He was angry and distressed, determined and ready to take action. Blaise had hoped time with Emrys would help, but it only stoked the fire.

"I'm sorry I grabbed your hand earlier," Jefferson murmured, his own hands threaded together over his middle. "That was thoughtless of me."

The unexpected apology shook Blaise out of his worries. "Oh. I didn't mind it, actually." If anything, it had been the thing he had needed in the moment—someone stalwart beside him, unshaken by the news of what he was.

Jefferson stepped closer, tentative. "All the same, I should have known better." He sighed, running a hand through his hair. "And we don't have to if you don't want to. But this path you're going down will not be an easy one for us to reconcile." Was it Blaise's imagination, or did Jefferson sound hurt?

Blaise bit his lip. He liked Jefferson and didn't want to leave him on a sour note. He unlocked the door to his room and tipped his head toward it. Jefferson blinked in surprise but didn't hesitate to follow him in.

"I can't allow what Lamar Gaitwood did to go unanswered." Blaise dreaded the words coming out of his mouth. They sounded like they belonged to someone else.

"I understand." Jefferson met his eyes. "And as I said earlier, I support you." He sat down on the edge of the bed, sighing. "Do you want me to cancel the contract?"

Blaise blinked, startled. All thoughts of business ventures with Jefferson had fled his mind long ago. "What?"

Jefferson pursed his lips. "Do you want me to cancel the contract? Our partnership. I can do that." The way he said it made

Blaise think Jefferson desperately wanted him to say *no*. But that was madness.

Blaise paced the short distance to the dresser, staring at his reflection in the mirror that hung on the wall. "I just want to be a baker. But I don't think I get that choice."

A smile ghosted Jefferson's lips. "You always get a choice." He exhaled a pent-up breath. "I can leave it as-is?"

Blaise swallowed. "I saw the clause about death breaking the contract."

Jefferson's eyes frosted over. "Don't you die on me." His voice grated with unexpected ferocity.

Blaise sat down on the bed beside him. "I just don't know what's ahead of me."

Jefferson's eyes softened. "Isn't that the thing about life, though? None of us know that. We can only go forth and choose to live with courage."

"I don't feel very courageous," Blaise admitted, glancing away. He wasn't dauntless or quick-witted like Jack.

"You don't know it, but you already live with courage." Jefferson tilted his head, smiling. "Look at you. You're a *Breaker*, and you've made it this far. Your life is extraordinary."

Blaise raised his eyebrows, dubious. "I don't know that I'd call it *extraordinary*." But the simple act of speaking with Jefferson was so calming that the next thing he knew, they talked into the darkest hours of night, voices soft and companionable.

BLAISE GRUMBLED AS THE FIRST RAYS OF SUNLIGHT PIERCED THE lace curtains. He burrowed into the warmth of the bed, freezing when his left hand brushed another solid form. His eyes shot open, and he looked into Jefferson's emerald eyes.

"You slept," Jefferson murmured, content. He used one hand to adjust his pillow, aiming a sleepy smile at Blaise.

"I guess so." A blush raced through his skin. They were both fully clothed. Nothing had happened aside from talking. He had discovered that Jefferson wasn't afraid of him, even after he coaxed out a litany of the path of destruction of Blaise's youth.

"I think we overslept. Is Emrys going to be annoyed?" Jefferson yawned, stretching out his arms to loosen his muscles.

"Not if I bring him breakfast pastries from room service."

"Mmm. That sounds like a good idea for everyone." Jefferson rose from the bed, languid. Mussed hair and rumpled clothing added to his appeal, and Blaise turned away to keep from staring. Jefferson filled out an order card on the corner desk and hung the placard on the door. "Give it fifteen minutes, and we'll have a feast."

Blaise shook his head, still adjusting to the way that Jefferson made things happen with his wealth and influence. But money couldn't solve all their problems. It wouldn't bring back the dead or lost.

Jefferson studied his unkempt reflection. "Hmm. Let me go do something about this while the food comes." He walked to the door, then paused, uncertain. "You, ah, don't mind if I have breakfast with you?"

His hesitance was endearing. He really was attempting to not impose. Blaise cocked his head. "I didn't see how much food you ordered, but I suspect even with taking some to Emrys I couldn't eat it all myself." He rose from the bed, closing the distance between them. "I would be happy if you had breakfast with me." And wonder of wonders, it was true.

Jefferson's eyes widened in delight. "Then I won't be long. We'll make every moment count."

He hurried off to his suite, allowing Blaise a moment to decompress. What was he doing? Blaise raked a hand through his hair. Who was he turning into, this person spending time with a romantic interest? This audacious mage preparing to butt heads with a Commander of the Salt-Iron Confederation? He was becoming a Breaker.

He closed his eyes for a moment, then set to dressing for travel. Blaise traded out his rumpled clothes for a pair of fresh dark blue cotton trousers, a white button-up shirt, and a blue vest for warmth. His duster and gloves were slung over a chair back. Flight goggles, bandanna, and hat awaited him on the dresser. Packed saddlebags rested on the floor by the door.

A tap at the door announced breakfast, followed by Jefferson's return. After the waitstaff left, Jefferson eyed Blaise with appreciation.

"Everyone who turned their back on you before doesn't know what they're missing," Jefferson said as he sat down at the table, loading a plate with sausages, toast, and eggs. He gestured with his fork. "And I'm not saying that just because you look good—and make no mistake, you look *good*."

Blaise ducked his head. "They had reason to. I told you last night."

Jefferson set down his fork, lifting a hand to tick off his fingers. "Yes. Let's see. There was the chifferobe incident. The Spinning Wheel Disaster of . . . what was the year you said, 1875? The shelves you broke at the library. The rain collection barrel and the hitching post outside the general goods store at the same time—that's impressive, mind you." He grinned. "Should I go on?"

Blaise's cheeks flamed with shame, pin-prickles of doubt sharp on his skin. "Please don't."

Jefferson winced as he realized his misstep. "I'm sorry. I was trying to be flippant, not hurtful." He offered Blaise a cinnamon roll in apology. "What I mean to say is I don't care what your magic has done or may do. I care about *you*."

Blaise added the cinnamon roll to his plate, relaxing. *Jefferson doesn't care about my past. Doesn't care that I can cause disaster.* It was a strange sensation—one that Blaise could get used to.

Jefferson ate, prodding Blaise to do the same when he noticed him picking at his food. "I know you were hurt in the past. I promise to never do that, if I can help it."

Blaise blinked back tears. He wanted to believe it, he really did. He just wasn't willing to gamble on it—not with the track record of his life so far.

They finished their breakfast, making small talk. But it couldn't last forever, as much as Blaise wished they could linger. With regret, he packed a chocolate muffin, glazed donut, and strawberry tart into a linen cloth for Emrys. Jefferson watched with appreciation as he shrugged on his duster, tied the bandanna around his neck, slipped on his gloves, and settled his flight goggles on his forehead beneath his hat.

Jefferson chuckled. "Can't believe I'm letting you walk away from me looking like that."

"Like what?"

Jefferson rose from his seat. "Like an outlaw who just stole my heart."

"You're being melodramatic."

Jefferson stepped closer, eyes intense. "Hardly. But I could be, if you like."

Blaise met his gaze, something that he avoided with most people, but he couldn't help with Jefferson. His breath hitched for a moment, surprised by the importance of the permission the other man was asking. There was no telling what his future held. And here was Jefferson, offering a piece of a puzzle Blaise hadn't realized he was missing. "I'll allow some melodrama."

Jefferson closed the gap between them, leaning in, his lips questing against Blaise's. Blaise lifted his chin in response as Jefferson wrapped him in an embrace. And then he gave in to the tide of passion, returning the kiss with the ferocity of someone facing the gallows.

After a hundred years—or just moments, for Blaise had lost all concept of time—Jefferson drew back. "Ah, sorry. That was rather presumptuous of me. I didn't want to have any regrets."

Blaise's shoulders relaxed. "Neither did I."

FLORA HIRED THE SERVICES OF A STURDY, NEARLY WHITE PEGASUS
stallion by the name of Tylos. Emrys dwarfed Tylos, who
measured only twelve hands tall at the withers. The little stallion
boasted colorful wings with alternating bands of magenta and
violet.

"Hope your big beast can keep up," Flora said with a smirk as
she patted Tylos's shoulder.

Blaise glanced from Tylos to Emrys. He expected that small
Tylos might be the one to have trouble. "Why is that?"

"Because this handsome fellow is an Eskelan pegasus." Flora
adjusted the girth, making sure no feathers had been trapped
beneath the leather. At Blaise's blank expression, she added,
"Imagine a hummingbird's wings on a pegasus. That's what you
get with an Eskelan. Their wings beat forty times a second."

<And we must stop every hour so he can eat,> Emrys advised
Blaise privately, ears pinned with annoyance.

Blaise saddled Emrys, tightening the girth and buckling his
breastplate. With their path laid out before them, he wasn't in the
mood for banter. He wanted to get ready and focus on the grim
task ahead.

They completed a last round of checks. Every buckle fastened
and secure. Everything accounted for. Jefferson waited beneath
the stable's overhang as they walked out, hooves and boots
ringing on hard-packed dirt.

"You're going to miss your boat," Flora chided him.

He chuckled. "I paid them to wait." Because of course he had.
Jefferson wore a warm, charcoal grey cutaway morning coat over
his grey paisley vest. "I would tell you to be careful, but . . ." He
shrugged.

"We'll be fine." Flora waved a hand. "As long as the airship's not
at Itude we'll—"

"Airship?" Blaise and Jefferson squeaked in unison.

Flora blanched. "Uh, did I fail to mention that Gaitwood attacked the town using an airship?"

Jefferson massaged his forehead. "Gods. Gregor had the balls to send the *Retribution* out there? It's meant to be a prototype." He clenched his fists, a vein ticking in his jaw. "Blaise, a moment?"

Tilting his head, Blaise came over to Jefferson.

Jefferson pitched his voice low, so low that any passersby would have difficulty hearing it over the ambient noise of the river. "I have . . . insider information about that airship. Remember the Council we spoke of last night?" Blaise nodded. "Some members are strong proponents of air travel to tame the Untamed Territory. To loosen the grip outlaws with pegasi have over the area."

Blaise swallowed. "But the Untamed Territory doesn't belong to the outlaws. They're just allowed to stay there."

Jefferson made a helpless gesture. "I'm aware of that. But try arguing that with people who have more greed and hatred than common sense." He glanced over his shoulder, hands on his hips as indecision warred on his face. "I'm going to the gallows or firing squad if word of this gets out."

Blaise scowled, alarmed. "Word of what?"

Jefferson shoved his hands into the pockets of his coat. "My treason."

"Wait, what?"

Jefferson's face was serious, his voice urgent. "The airship. Destroy it. Use your magic. Break it."

Blaise stared at him, heart racing. He stepped back, horrified that Jefferson would ask him to do such a thing. "Why?"

Jefferson's eyes were fierce. "It's my fault the thing even exists." Before Blaise could sputter a question, he plowed on. "Originally, it was meant to transport goods across the Untamed Territory. Not soldiers. I made that clear in the contract. But the Confedera- tion Safety Act was invoked after the prototype was completed." A muscle twitched in his jaw.

Blaise glanced back to where Flora awaited him. "What happened?"

"The military seized the airship and dubbed it a warbird." Jefferson shook his head. "I shuttered my manufacturing plant in response. But now it's too late. This won't end with Itude. Don't you see, Blaise?" He rubbed his forehead. "It will bolster their confidence as a success. They'll attack the other towns. Asylum." He gestured around them. "Rainbow Flat. More innocent people will die."

And not only that, but the accord forged by the pegasi and outlaws would shatter. The other sentient magical creatures would retaliate. Blaise felt sickened as the inevitable timeline of death and destruction stretched out before him, painting the Untamed Territory and the Gutter in rivers of blood.

Blaise closed his eyes. "I wish you were telling this to anyone but me."

Jefferson chucked him under the chin. "You're the only one I would trust to do this." He stepped back, turning in a restless circle before facing Blaise again. Worry lines crinkled the corners of his eyes. "I hate to ask you to do that. I know it's not who you are."

Blaise bowed his head. "Sometimes it's not about who I am, but what I can do."

"It's *always* about who you are," Jefferson shot back. "And you're *more* than a Breaker. You have a good heart. And I'm proud to call you a friend."

Jefferson's words fortified Blaise in a way he hadn't expected. He allowed himself a tentative smile, basking in the other man's acceptance. "Thank you."

"I should head out before the captain loses his patience with my dalliance," Jefferson said with regret. He shifted, as if he were contemplating another moment of melodrama before giving Blaise a wink and striding off to the docks.

Blaise watched him go before walking back over to Emrys. Flora swung into Tylos's saddle, the small stallion fluttering his wings as she settled. Blaise mounted Emrys, and Flora stayed quiet until they trotted to the outskirts of town.

"What was that about?"

"I have to break the airship."

Flora blinked at him, stony-faced. Then she shrugged. "Okay."

CHAPTER FORTY-TWO

Tenacious Cuss

Blaise

The weather held, though the skies were frosted with clouds and the constant threat of flurries. True to Emrys's prediction, Tylos spent so much energy flying that he required hourly stops to keep his stamina up. Their progress slowed, so it wasn't until early afternoon on their second day of travel that the dead-grass prairie of the Untamed Territory shifted to the rocky sandstone outcrops leading to the Gutter.

Flora pulled a map out of her saddlebag as Tylos hungrily grazed nearby and Emrys rested with one hoof cocked. "I think if we continue the same, we can get to Itude by mid-afternoon." She peered at Blaise over the rims of her glasses. "The problem is we don't know if there will be hostiles there when we arrive."

Blaise shook his head. "The townspeople won't hurt us."

Flora gave him a pitying look. "It's not them I'm concerned about. I mean a military presence."

He winced. He had forgotten about that. "Right."

Flora pursed her lips. "When we get closer, Tylos and I should go first. If Gaitwood has men there, I have reason to be there—looking into the deaths of the survey team."

"They could try to silence you."

She bared her teeth in a smile, and the feral look was chilling. "They can try."

"Okay, then." Blaise decided not to push the issue anymore with Jefferson's tiny scary lady.

Once Tylos was reinvigorated, Blaise and Flora got back into the saddle and continued the journey. Blaise's legs were like jelly from the long day of travel yesterday—he wasn't used to being in the saddle for so long. But he pushed away the discomfort. He might fall over with barely functioning legs later, but that was a problem for future Blaise.

The pegasi kept up their steady pace, and Flora was right—they would make it there in the afternoon. Emrys promised to signal Tylos once they were close to the town. Blaise felt a thrill rush through him as he recognized the canyons and hoodoos blurring below them. He was almost home.

Emrys slowed and landed on a canyon rim. Tylos flew ahead, Flora's hair a cheerful twinkle in the afternoon sun. Blaise took a break to stretch his legs while they waited for Flora's return. If he was going to fall over, he would rather it not be the first thing anyone else saw when he returned to town.

The white pegasus flew over a nearby ridge a short time later, hovering near Emrys. "It's clear," Flora called. She wasn't close enough for Blaise to get a good read on her facial expression, and her tone was neutral.

Emrys snorted, and Blaise climbed back into the saddle. The stallion took a running leap off the side of the cliff, wings snapping out as Blaise's heart jumped into his throat. Moments later, Itude spread out before them.

Blaise peered over the stallion's side, gripping the brim of his hat as the wind threatened to knock him around. Emrys swept over the town in a wide circle, allowing time for any sentries to come out and investigate. Blaise's gut clenched as he took in the destruction below. His bakery was a burned-out shell, only the ash-covered bulk of the oven standing sentinel. The Jitterbug and mercantile shared the same fate. Other structures had suffered roof damage. Three massive dark piles huddled at the outskirts of the town—one north, one south, and one to the northeast. As Emrys descended, he realized they were piles of bodies.

A clarion call shattered the crisp air. A familiar golden stallion launched into the sky. <Blaise? Emrys? You may land.>

Still-healing slashes crisscrossed Zepheus's body. Primary and secondary feathers were missing from his wings. He likely shouldn't have been flying in such a condition. They landed, and Emrys touched noses with the palomino.

The town was painfully quiet. The normal hum of voices, the squeak of the wind-pump working, the braying of the donkeys, and the laughter of playing children were all absent. No one walked the streets. Faces peered out of windows, like rabbits afraid of a stooping hawk. Bullet holes riddled the storefronts that weren't damaged by fire. The only sounds were the drumming of pegasi hooves and the whistle of the wind.

Oberidon trotted out of the stable, ears flicking as he joined them. <You came back.>

Blaise nodded. "I . . . I did."

<I wish you had come sooner.> Oberidon hung his head so low his muzzle almost touched the ground.

The spotted stallion's dejection set Blaise on edge. "Where's Emmaline?"

<She's gone. I failed her.>

Blaise's heart hurt for Oberidon. He knew the feeling. "We'll get her back. Where's Jack?"

Zepheus flattened his ears, and the palomino's agitation filled Blaise with apprehension. Renewed hope filled Oberidon's brown eyes. Zepheus's only held desolation.

<Follow me.> Zepheus turned, leading them out of town to the rows of homes.

Itude was broken.

That much was clear to Blaise as they followed Zepheus. Flora and Tylos joined them after a brief introduction. The faces peering out of the broken windows wore mixtures of resignation and exhaustion, fraught people pushed to the edge of their existence. No one came out to greet him. They were scared. He wasn't sure if they were afraid of Blaise the Breaker or reliving the trauma of the enemy in their streets.

Zepheus led them past Jack's house, continuing on to Nadine's. The palomino provided no explanation, only stopped outside the house, rustling his wings like a sparrow coming to nest.

Movement flickered in one window, and then Nadine darkened the doorway. Blaise gaped when he saw her, recognizing her only because it was her house and who else would come out the door? Divots pocked her face, one eye swollen shut. The scalp above her right ear was bare, the skin pale and smooth, like it was newly regrown. Her left hand was a wizened mess. Despite the trauma, her undamaged eye was sharp. "You should have seen the other guy. Guys," she corrected, her voice raspy.

"What . . . what happened?" Blaise asked. Nearby, Flora pretended to not be too interested, but she kept sneaking glances at Nadine.

Nadine grunted. "Taught some boys why you don't attack Healers." She rolled her shoulders, wincing. "After they stabbed me and shot me a dozen times, I had to drain their life to sustain myself. Lucky for me, they thought I was dead."

Drain their life to . . . Blaise blinked. *And* I'm *the one people are terrified of?*

Nadine waved her good hand, inviting him in. "You can come in, but your friend has to stay out there. I've got my most critical patients here, and I don't trust anyone else right now."

Flora held up her hands, placating. "I'm not coming in, trust me. But I am going to go check on someone else." Blaise was mildly impressed that Nadine intimidated her.

Nadine moved at a slow pace, negotiating her way between tables and chairs. Some of the tables had bloodstains on them, as if they had served as last-resort operating tables. Perhaps they had.

"You shouldn't have run away." Nadine paused, bracing her good hand against the back of a chair.

Blaise bowed his head, blinking rapidly as he noticed a trail of dried blood beneath his feet. "I couldn't bear people thinking . . ."

"What? That you destroyed the wind-pump?" Her words had a bite to them, and her tension reminded him of an agitated rattlesnake. "Did you?"

He lifted his head, meeting her good eye. "*No.* But people were starting to say I did." The very thought made Blaise light-headed with panic. "And when the rumors start, no one has ever believed me in the past."

"This is a small town. There's always going to be rumormongers and backbiting." She leveled a finger at him. "And when you run like that, it makes *you* look guilty."

"But I didn't—"

"We know that *now*," Nadine cut in. Her eye glittered, dangerous. "Someone is a traitor, and it's not you."

Blaise nearly trembled with relief. He had feared he would have an uphill battle vindicating himself with the survivors.

"Zepheus said you wanted to see Jack. He's . . ." She shook her head, then gave him a long look. "He's not doing well."

A chill slithered down Blaise's spine. "How bad is it?"

Nadine didn't respond. She pushed open a door, and Blaise

followed her inside. The room might have been Reuben's, judging by the possessions tucked away on the dresser. He didn't dare ask Nadine about her son. He wasn't sure if he wanted to know.

Jack lay on the bed and appeared to be asleep. His skin was ashen, with no signs of visible wounds. His face was almost skeletal, and the arm that rested outside of the blanket was gaunt. Jack's tattooed shoulder was bare, the arcane symbols vivid against his skin.

The man in the bed wasn't the tenacious cuss who had punched Blaise in the face his first day in town. He was a shell. If the hard look in Nadine's good eye meant anything, he was dying.

"What happened to him?"

Nadine scratched at the smooth skin over her ear. "One survivor said Gaitwood had him in a trap and Jack made the mistake of touching the bars." She pursed her lips. "He knew better, but still he did it. Gaitwood baited him with . . . with . . ." Nadine cleared her throat, unwilling to complete her sentence. "They found him collapsed in the middle of the street. Clover thought he was dead, but then she saw he was breathing." She shook her head. "He hasn't woken up or moved in . . . I don't know how long. I don't know what day it is. My magic is too drained to do anything for him. All I know is that he's barely alive, and he's trapped in his own body." She closed her eyes, pained.

Blaise stared at Jack. "Has he eaten?"

Nadine nodded. "Celeste comes by daily and brings broth or whatever she thinks he'll keep down. But it's not much. He won't last much longer at this rate."

Blaise pulled a chair closer to the bed. Only the gentle rise and fall of the outlaw's chest gave proof to the shred of life left in his body. "Jack?" He studied the outlaw's face, looking for some sign of movement or comprehension. When nothing happened, he laid a hand on Jack's arm.

Magic surged across the outlaw's skin, thin as a hair. But it was there. Blaise felt it. Or rather, his magic did. Sucking in a surprised breath, he let his magic quest against the hostile power.

He recognized the magic. He had encountered it twice. Blaise had *broken* it before.

Nadine watched him like a hawk, hyperaware. "What is it?"

For Jack's sake, Blaise hoped he was right. "I recognize the magic on him. The trap is still active, it's just *on* him now instead of acting like a physical cage. His skin is a cage."

Nadine made a *tch*-ing sound. "Damn, that's sadistic enough to be something Gaitwood would do."

Blaise nodded. He thought so, too. "I . . . I might be able to break it."

Her eye cut to him like a dagger. *"Might?"*

He swallowed. Once, when he was ten, his worst bully had cornered him before school. The son of Bristle's mayor was an insufferable tormenter who considered himself untouchable. He enjoyed harassing Blaise every way he could. Charles tried to snatch Blaise's lunch away and throw it into the nearby pond so that he would have to choose between wading in after his soggy food or going hungry. Blaise couldn't take anymore. He had grabbed Charles's arm with his ungloved hand. He would never forget the sound of the bully's bones snapping as his magic roared to life. Blaise hadn't been allowed back at school after that. He was still so ashamed of the event that he hadn't breathed a word of it to Jefferson.

I have control now. He rubbed his forehead. "I broke Gaitwood's traps before, but not when they were acting as a second skin. It may behave differently." It might hurt Jack. He feared speaking it would make it so.

Nadine gestured to the prone outlaw with her mangled hand. "Do it. It can't be worse than this. He's dying."

Blaise leaned over Jack, wrapping his right hand around the outlaw's left arm. He closed his eyes to concentrate, shuddering as the sinister magic assaulted him like a thousand wriggling maggots. His own Breaker magic rallied to the surface at his call, and he opened his eyes to survey the nefarious Trapper magic. With his magic engaged, he recognized the remnants of the trap overlaying Jack like a ghost. It made him a prisoner in his own body.

Gods, Jack was alive and awake in there. He was living in a personal abyss. But not for much longer, if Blaise had a say.

He studied the magical overlay, hunting for the weakest links. As much as he wanted to slam his magic through the trap, he didn't want to risk harming Jack. With surgical precision, he found a weak strand of magic and sheared through it. It snapped as it broke, blowing loose like a strand of unanchored spider's silk. Blaise found his next assault point and sent another pulse of magic, satisfied when it came unfettered.

A moment later, the trap dissipated entirely, and the outlaw's chest rose as he took his first deep, conscious breath. Still clutching Jack's arm, Blaise's magic prodded at something buried deep in the outlaw's brain. Something foreign; out of place. Harmful. Afraid that it might be a lingering effect from the trap, Blaise let his magic shred it before pulling his power back under control. Blaise let go of Jack's arm and scooted the chair back.

Jack took another ragged breath and then coughed, a dry sound from his parched throat. His ice-blue eyes snapped opened, locking on to Blaise. "It's about damn time you got here."

CHAPTER FORTY-THREE
Secrets and Traitors

Jack

Jack didn't fear death. After days trapped in his own skin, with only his own regrets and failures for company, he longed for the respite of eternal darkness. It was preferable to the knowledge that he had failed everyone he'd ever cared about. For all his hoarding of information, he should have seen the attack coming. But he hadn't.

Jack wasn't a religious man. But he was wondering if someone with a plan bigger than his had kept him in play for a reason.

At the present moment, all that mattered was that Blaise had broken him from his waking prison, the enemy had stolen Emmaline away, his town was in ruins, and he was weak as a newborn kitten.

"Let me up, Clover," Jack growled, staring down the Knossan.

Nadine had summoned her after Blaise had freed him, muttering she didn't have the strength to hold him at bay.

"No." Clover's ears swept back, upset. "You are not well. You need rest and food, and perhaps in a few days—"

"We don't have a few days. There's an ass I need to kick before then." Jack sat up, ignoring the wave of dizziness and nausea that threatened his ability to remain upright. He didn't have time for this. His body was just going to have to get its shit together.

She placed a hand on his shoulder and prodded him back down. "I understand. Truly, I do."

Jack shrugged out from under her hand, struggling to sit again. In the same motion, he swung his legs over the side of the bed. His stomach churned, and he was in genuine danger of losing whatever they had fed him while he was out of commission. He closed his eyes, ignoring the Knossan's grumbles.

He wanted to get up. *Needed* to get up. But he was quickly realizing that, while his body and mind were free, Lamar's damned trap had sapped every last reserve of his strength. He would look about as graceful as a newborn colt if he tried to stand. And he would get an up-close-and-personal view of Nadine's floor if he tried. Defeated by his own body, he shifted back onto the bed. "You win."

"I don't want to *win*," Clover said with a snort. "I just want you well. But perhaps we can talk and plan? Strategize?"

Jack closed his eyes. Yeah, that might help. "Aside from me and Nadine, any other Ringleaders still here?" He almost didn't want the answer.

"Only Kur, and he's as grumpy as a freshly shorn grasscat. He's still mad you left him at the farms."

That sounded like Kur. The attack distressed the Theilian, and his instincts would be working overtime to make things right. That was a losing battle.

"Fine, leave Kur out for the moment. If Nadine's up to it, have her come. And Blaise." Jack relaxed into the soft pillows. Maybe laying down wasn't so bad.

Clover shifted. "Blaise isn't a Ringleader."

"No, but he's the only other mage we've got. And I think we *need* him." He stared at the ceiling, Lamar's words haunting him. *Lucky for me, I made sure your Breaker wasn't there. You might have stood a chance otherwise.* Damn it.

Clover nodded, ducking out. A short while later, Nadine arrived. She still looked like shit, but Jack imagined that was going to be her look for quite a while. He hadn't seen his own face in a mirror yet, but he assumed he shouldn't be one to talk.

She dragged a chair over and sat down, glancing at the door for any signs of others joining them. When she saw no one else, she said in a low voice, "Jack, what in tarnation?"

His eyes were thin slits watching her. Sleep dragged at his brain, telling him that maybe a meeting right now wasn't the best idea. "What?"

Her lower lip stuck out. "Kur and I put the pieces together. You haven't used your magic on any of the missions you've taken with him."

The muscles in Jack's jaw twitched. "Not sporting to use magic against those men. Hardly fair."

"And you didn't use magic in the battle. Even *Butch* used magic." Her voice was soft and dangerous. An accusation accompanied her unspoken question: why would Wildfire Jack, Effigest, self-proclaimed Scourge of the Untamed Territory, not use his magic?

Jack realized he was on the knife's edge with an angry, life-leeching Healer beside him. Nadine had a sharp mind, and he could guess the two scenarios running through it. Scenario one: Jack was a turncoat which made about as much sense as a one-legged donkey in an ass-kicking contest. But stranger things had happened. Scenario two: Jack didn't have magic. The simplest explanations were the most sensible. And correct.

Jack cursed. "It wasn't any of your damn business."

She arched the eyebrow over her good eye. The one over her

swollen eye tried to keep up but failed. "You didn't think that was something the rest of the Ringleaders should be aware of?"

He was quiet, thinking. Jack was tired, and his heart ached. This was the last thing he wanted to deal with right now. But as so often happened in life, the worst shit appeared when the outhouse was occupied.

"You don't know how it feels, Nadine. To have the magic stolen away from your flesh. The alchemical potion burning through your veins, making you wish your body would burst into flames and call the deed done." He turned to stare at the wall. "The shame of knowing what you could do, and now can't. If I told you, you would have thought less of me."

"Pretty sure they wouldn't revoke your badass card," Blaise commented, startling Jack as he pushed through the door. The Breaker pulled a chair up next to Nadine's.

Jack glared at Blaise. Damn it. At least his secret wasn't news to the kid.

"You're an infuriating cuss," Nadine grumbled, glaring at him. "But that's neither here nor there. I reserve the right to be pissed at you for a while." She shifted in her chair. "I've got other patients to attend to. What do you want? I can't be lollygagging around all day with you."

She should be taking it easy, too. Her body was just as poor as his. Maybe worse. He hadn't been shot enough to look like a patch of ground full of prairie dog holes. He didn't tell her that, though. "They set us up. All of us. Even you, Blaise."

"I know."

Jack had expected a quiet hush and shocked breaths. "What do you mean, *you know?*"

Blaise rubbed the back of his neck. "Jasper Strop overheard Gaitwood talking to you. Jasper's niece, Flora, brought the information to me in Rainbow Flat."

Jack narrowed his eyes. "Tell me more about *Flora.*"

The Breaker glanced around the room, seeking a distraction.

Jack wouldn't let him get away so easily. Blaise wised up and sighed. "She works with Jefferson Cole."

Jefferson Cole. Malcolm Wells. Son of a bat-eared harpy. Jack tried to sit up fast, wincing when he recalled what a terrible idea that was. Nadine cleared her throat in warning. So they knew about Gaitwood's treachery. That was less for him to explain, at least.

"Who did Gaitwood have working on the inside?" Nadine asked.

Jack smiled, an expression that promised future violence. Blaise looked up, meeting his gaze. The Breaker's eyes held a spark of anger and burned with questions. The young man needed answers like plants needed water. "Who?"

Exhaustion swept over Jack, and for a moment he regretted summoning them. He should've listened to Clover. But this was *important*, damn it. "Walker. Hank Walker is working with Gaitwood. Where is he? Is he still here, Nadine?"

The Healer's eyes widened. "He's recovering from the attack at his home. His leg got blown clean off."

"We got any salt-iron? Shackle him. He could still bolt, missing leg or not." Something occurred to Jack. "Has Walker heard that I'm awake?"

Nadine shrugged. "Don't know. And you know as well as I do we don't have any salt-iron. We're not monsters."

Jack snorted. "Speak for yourself."

"Is . . . is Walker the one who shot me?" Hope and dread warred in Blaise's voice. "Is he responsible for the wind-pump?"

"I don't have all the answers yet, but I want to rip them from his flesh." Yes, Jack thought, that would help relieve some stress. "I know for a fact he killed at least one of the Gannish surveyors, though." Walker had killed *Cole's* Confederation man, which didn't sit well with Jack. Something was off with that. He still didn't like Cole. Needed to tell Blaise about his duplicity.

Nadine crossed her arms. "Let me see if I have this right. Walker—who, by the way, is *your* asset, Jack—works for Lamar Gaitwood. Walker killed the survey team on the day of the attack."

She cocked her head. "Safe to assume Walker led you to the earlier ambush, tried to kill Blaise, and somehow made the wind-pump fall?"

Jack gritted his teeth. No use explaining to her he hadn't trusted Walker from the start. Sometimes a man had to work with the hand life dealt him. *Always bet on the Jack.* "That's about right. But Walker is *Gaitwood's*, not mine at this point. He admitted as much in the post office during the attack."

Nadine frowned. "He's a maverick. Why would he cross us?"

Jack shook his head, not wanting to mention Hank's brother. He didn't want any sympathy for the man. Not after all he had wrought. "Every man has a price. I need to interrogate him." Jack bared his teeth in anticipation. Walker would never cross them again.

"You'll do no such thing," Nadine contradicted, waspish.

"I will." Steel gleamed in Blaise's eyes, forcing Jack to pause his protest. The Breaker lifted his chin, daring them to deny him.

Jack grunted, deciding to leave it be. It would be difficult to terrify Walker in his current state. "Fine. But if he finds out I'm awake, mark my words, he's going to make a break for it."

Nadine tilted her head, smirking. "I wish him luck with that. Had to give him a mix of laudanum and krakenvine to get his pain manageable. He's high as a mountaintop right now."

"I think we should keep word of Jack's recovery quiet," Blaise said.

Nadine frowned. "For what purpose?"

"We need time to come up with a plan."

Hope lit a small fire in Jack's heart. "We?"

"No offense, but I don't think you could do it alone." Blaise's shoulders went rigid, as if he expected an angry retort from Jack. When none came, he continued. "I know you'll want to go after Emmaline and the others."

"And fucking kill *Lamar*," Jack growled emphatically. *Priorities.*

Nadine shook her head. "I don't see how we can. They destroyed the town. They wounded or killed everyone who can fight worth a damn. Families are already leaving for the farms or Asylum with whatever they can carry on their back."

Jack closed his eyes, pained by the news. He had worked so hard to build Itude up. The battle would be the last straw for many. And he didn't blame them.

"I'm not going to back down and let the bully win this time." Blaise's voice was soft, tinged with the promise of danger, like the strobe of lightning and rumble of thunder in a distant storm. Jack opened his eyes and really *looked* at the kid. He was tired and grungy, but he had the poise of someone who had found purpose and clarity.

"You're not a fighter," Nadine shook her head.

"He is," Jack murmured. Blaise twitched at his words, as if he hadn't expected Jack to contradict Nadine. "He fights for what's important."

"I fight for the ones I care about," Blaise agreed, resolute. "It's something I should have done sooner but lacked the courage."

And now, somehow, he had found it. Jack studied the Breaker with an approving eye.

Nadine looked from Blaise to Jack and sighed. "I'm in. Just don't expect me to pick up the pieces and put either of you back together when it's all said and done."

CHAPTER FORTY-FOUR
Absolution

Blaise

*W*hen Hannah saw Blaise, she ran up to him and enveloped him in a hug, burying her face against his shoulder. With the conversation with Jack and Nadine at the forefront of his mind, her sudden appearance startled him. She quivered, sobbing into his shoulder. Blaise reined in his inclination to dodge away, instead wrapping his arms around her in consolation.

"I'm so glad to see you," Hannah whispered, her voice cracking with emotion once she mastered her tears. "We lost so many."

Blaise patted her back, and as she rested against him, he realized how devastating the attack had been. He only saw the aftereffects—the destroyed buildings, the wounded, the bloated dead. But Hannah and the others had witnessed it with their own eyes.

Some of them had lived and fought it. And none of them would ever be the same.

"I'm here," Blaise murmured.

"Abe's dead. And Monty. Ellie. Victor." Hannah continued a litany of more names, honoring the dead. Blaise held her and listened as she dampened his shoulder with her tears and her choked words. He let her pain stir the coals of resolve in his chest. Blaise stowed each name she whispered into his heart, promising that their deaths were not in vain.

He didn't know how long they stood together, but eventually, she pulled back, her face red and eyes watery. "I'm sorry."

"Don't be. I wish I had been here to help."

She shook her head. "I'm glad you weren't. Or . . ." She wiped her runny nose on her sleeve. "What are we going to do, Blaise?"

"We're going to get them back."

Hannah stared at him like he'd spoken another language. Her lower lip trembled. "How?"

That was the question. "I'm going to figure something out." Since he wasn't sure how to approach that problem yet, he thought it was a good time to change the subject. "My friend, Flora, and I need a place to stay. Nadine told me you could direct us to some houses that are available."

"Oh." Hannah turned as Flora walked up. "Um, you want one bedroom or . . ."

"Two different accommodations would be best," Flora said, saving Blaise from embarrassment. "I'm here on business."

Hannah fixed bleary eyes on Flora, then gave Blaise a quizzical look. He shrugged. He wasn't about to explain Flora's business. Hannah gestured to a clapboard house close to Nadine's. "That one's open right now. It was . . ." She laughed humorlessly, the sound of someone who had seen horrors. "You know what? Never mind. There's some clothing in there. Might be some food. We haven't gone through every house yet. It took us long enough to —" Her gaze drifted in the graveyard's direction.

"It's fine," Blaise reassured her. "I'll take that one. It'll keep me near Jack and Nadine." With that decision made, Hannah showed Flora the house next to Blaise's temporary quarters.

"I'm going to get settled. Is there a place I can grab dinner later, or do I need to go out and hunt my own?" Flora asked.

Hannah's eyes widened, and Blaise supposed his eyes did, too. "Um. Most things are rationed right now since we depend on whatever the farms can bring up, but we have enough to fill bellies most nights. We've been holding communal meals at the town square." She looked at the ground. "Gives us a sense that we're not alone in this."

Flora nodded primly and strolled to her house. Blaise watched Hannah, concerned. She seemed on the verge of shattering. "Are you going to be okay?"

Her eyes were desolate. "I don't know. I've never been so scared."

Blaise set his jaw. Hannah didn't deserve to live in fear. She deserved happiness. Hannah was meant to be full of ready smiles and cheer. Not this frightened ghost of herself.

He placed his hands on her shoulders, looking her in the eye. "You don't have to be scared. I'm going to make sure they can't do anything like this ever again."

Tears streamed down her cheeks, but this time hope kindled in her eyes.

BLAISE AMBLED TOWARD THE TOWN SQUARE, TAKING IN THE multitude of damage inflicted on Itude as he walked to the communal dinner. He spotted a man ahead of him, hobbling along with a crutch. His right leg was missing below the knee. Blaise swallowed, the brisk wind enhancing the chill that raced across his skin at the sight of Hank Walker. The traitor.

Rage coursed through his body as Blaise quickened his steps to catch up, but he quickly mastered it. It was senseless for Blaise to be angry with the wounded man. He wasn't Jack, to wear his wrath like a duster. Blaise only wanted to understand.

Walker heard the crunch of Blaise's boots. He looked over his shoulder, eyes widening in terror as he realized who his pursuer was. He shifted his crutch and tried to sidestep, but lost his balance and tumbled into the dirt, sending up a spurt of frigid red dust. Walker rolled onto his back, moaning.

Blaise stared at the fallen man in dismay. Fear. Walker feared *him*. Blaise didn't like that; the role of a bully was the last thing he desired. Did he have reason to be upset with Walker? Yes. Did he wish him ill? Absolutely not. He took a deep breath to compose himself.

"Do you need help?" Blaise asked, approaching at an angle to appear less threatening.

Walker laid on his back, pain etched on his face. "What?"

"I said, do you need help? I'm sorry if I startled you. Didn't mean to," Blaise replied, crouching down.

Those offerings of simple kindness disarmed Walker. He blinked. "I . . . yes, I need help. Still getting used to that damn crutch."

"Must be difficult," Blaise agreed, offering his hand to help Walker up.

The fallen man trembled, staring at Blaise's hand with mistrust. Blaise kept his hand extended, face neutral as he waited. Walker's face was grey with fear and doubt, but after an uncomfortable beat he took Blaise's hand.

"I'm sorry you fell," Blaise said as he helped Walker up, picking up the man's crutch and handing it to him.

Walker's eyes were wide, spooked. Blaise wondered if perhaps he was handling the situation wrong. But then Walker nodded, acknowledging the apology. "No matter." He shifted, uncomfortable for reasons that went beyond his crippling injury, eyes darting to the town square.

"Do you need help to get to dinner?"

Walker stared at him as if he had offered to throw him over the cliff. "I can get there just fine. I have to take it slow."

Blaise nodded. "Okay. Let me know if you need help with anything." While he needed to talk to Walker, Blaise decided it was best to take his time. Nadine was right—he couldn't run. Hank's leg was gone. He would never be whole again.

He felt Walker's eyes on his back as he strode to the town square. Makeshift tables reminiscent of the Feast of Flight were spread across the lawn. Mismatched chairs had been pulled from any building with furniture that survived the battle. Celeste and Mindy served food to a line of hungry, frightened faces. Murmurs swept through the line as the survivors noticed his presence.

Mindy had a bandage over one side of her face, but she smiled, handing him a plate of food. "Blaise, we missed you. It's good to have you back. Sorry, there's no bread."

Blaise took the proffered plate. "I'll remedy that for you if I get a chance."

"That would be welcome!" Mindy said almost too quickly, and several people nearby chuckled.

Someone seconded it with a rowdy "Hear, hear!"

The laughter popped the tension like a soap bubble, and Blaise found more townspeople murmuring greetings to him. He had thought he might be treated as a pariah, but word of his innocence must have already spread. There was a general air of apology, and a handful of people clapped him on the shoulder, welcoming him back. Blaise steeled himself and accepted their brief touches. Many of the adults were wounded, and those who weren't bore the trauma on their worry-lined faces. Even the normally raucous children were subdued beside their parents.

Blaise found a table and sat, surprised when Walker hobbled over to him. "Mind if I join you?"

Curious. Blaise nodded to the empty seat. "You're welcome to it. Would you like me to get you a plate?"

Walker smiled, a real, genuine smile that reflected in the depths of his eyes. Blaise hadn't noticed it before, but Walker's eyes had always radiated sadness. "If you don't mind. It's hard with the . . ." He gestured to his missing limb.

Blaise nodded and rose to get the additional plate. As he headed back to the table, he caught sight of Nadine. Her eyes slid from him to Walker, a silent query. Blaise shrugged. He would see where the conversation led.

"Here you go. I'll get some water for us, too," Blaise said, sliding the laden plate to Walker. The postmaster watched him like he was a puzzle to decipher but seemed content.

"Can I ask you a question?" Walker asked a few minutes later, after they had each eaten some of their meal. When Blaise nodded, Walker put down his fork. "Why are you doing this? Being nice to me, I mean. Is it because I'm hurt?"

Blaise studied him for a moment. "No. It's because I don't want to be the sort of person who hurts others just because I can. There's strength in kindness."

Walker picked up his fork again, poking food around his plate. "Why did you come back? I know what people were saying about you."

I'll bet you do. Blaise somehow kept a neutral expression. "Because I'm through with letting other people's perceptions rule my life." He pushed his plate aside. "I'm not going to be manipulated anymore. And you shouldn't allow others to manipulate you."

The postmaster froze, releasing his fork so it clattered to the table. "You know. You knew as soon as you saw me."

Blaise said nothing. He crossed his arms, inclining is head.

Panic flitted across Walker's face. "What are you going to do to me?"

Blaise shook his head, thinking that perhaps he wasn't so different from Walker. Bullies came in many forms. "Nothing. We're going to talk like reasonable people. And as long as you're honest with me, you'll have no fear of reprisal."

The postmaster regarded him in silence for a moment. "Once you hear what I've done, you'll regret that."

Blaise kept his steady gaze on Walker. "I'm already aware of most of what you've done. I just want answers at this point."

Renewed fear registered on Walker's face. Blaise pulled his plate closer and took another bite of his food to prove he didn't have any ill intentions.

"How can you break bread with me and act so civilized?"

"I'm going to remind you we're lacking in the bread department," Blaise quipped to keep the conversation light. "And I can do this because I do things my own way. I want answers." He pointed his fork at Walker. "I expect answers."

The postmaster bowed his head. "Ask away."

A thrill zinged through Blaise. His gambit was working. "Tell me why you worked for Gaitwood. What would compel you to sell out all these nice people sitting around us?" He kept his voice low so it didn't carry to the surrounding tables.

Walker's eyes were tinged with sorrow. "My reason won't be worth a hill of beans to anyone else."

"Try me."

Walker glanced around, self-conscious. His voice was so soft it was difficult to hear over the ambient noise. "Gaitwood has my brother, Joshua. He's all I have in this world for family."

Blaise's breath caught, recalling his mother begging him not to get captured. He remembered Jack's mother being used to keep him in line. He kept his thoughts to himself as Walker plowed on.

"Joshua was . . . born with problems, and our parents wanted to leave him to die of exposure from the start. But I was his big brother, and I swore to help him. Protect him." A tear trailed down Walker's cheek, and he swiped at it. "He grew, but he was never right. Something in his head."

His voice broke as he continued, "Our parents sold us to the child slavers when he was five. I was ten. Too many mouths to feed, or so they said." Walker rubbed his hand over his face. "We were passed between buyers like damaged goods and eventually ended up in Umber. More shit happened, but the long story short is we ended up under Lamar Gaitwood. He thought I'd make a good spy and kept my brother as a surety for my behavior."

Blaise stared at him, aghast. His palms tingled at his slumbering anger, and he quelled his magic. "That's horrible. I'm so sorry. I had no idea."

Walker shrugged. "No one here does. I never speak about it because no one ever cares what happens to someone like Joshua."

"That ends now," Blaise vowed. "I care. Does Gaitwood still have him?"

"As far as I know. I . . . Gaitwood was supposed to take me with him after the attack. He said he would. My reward was supposed to be that I could be with my brother. But when I went to him, the bastard shot out my knee and laughed." His face clouded at the bitter memory. Small wonder Walker had betrayed the people of Itude. Betrayal had been a common theme in his life.

Blaise hadn't arrived in Itude with a plan, only the desire to right wrongs. But the seed of an idea was forming. And it gave him hope. He would nurture that plan, but first he needed more information. "Next question. Did you shoot me?"

Walker stared at his plate, guilt etched on his face. "Yes."

Blaise took a shallow breath, trying to stay detached, though he wanted to run and tell Jack he had solved that mystery. He had to sit across from the man who tried to kill him and pretend like it didn't bother him. "How?"

To his credit, Walker seemed miserable as he answered. "My last name comes from my magic—Walker. Technically, I'm a Succulent Walker. I specialize in them." Blaise nodded, feigning that he knew what he meant. "It was a simple matter to snag the revolver that was being shipped to Jefferson Cole, pop into the canyon via a prickly pear, and take a shot at you." He grimaced. "I'm not a very good shot."

Lucky for me. Blaise gritted his teeth. "Did you cause the collapse of the wind-pump?"

"Yes."

"How?"

Hank Walker rubbed his face with one hand, and at that single question seemed to age another ten years. He wasn't a young man. If Blaise had to guess, he thought he might be in his fifties. "Potion. Alchemy potion Gaitwood gave to me."

Blaise's mind whirled as he thought back to everything he had seen his mother work on through the years. She specialized in medicinal potions, but he knew she dabbled in other areas. Potions that Blaise suspected a normal alchemist would have stayed away from. Since he was stuck home for so many years, he had pored through her notes and alchemical recipes when boredom struck. He couldn't replicate her craft, but he had intimate knowledge. "What's the potion called? And what does it do?"

"Breaker's Touch." The older man stared down at his plate. "Slow-acting corrosive potion."

Goosebumps pebbled Blaise's arms. *That's my mother's recipe.* He felt ill with the new knowledge, but he had to keep his stoic act together. He drummed his fingers on the table to stall as he thought. Inside, he was shaking. *The plan. Back to the plan.*

"Are you familiar with the layout of Fort Courage?"

Walker stared at him, thrown by the change in questioning. "Um. Sort of. I know certain parts of it."

Blaise latched onto that, setting aside the painful suspicions about his mother. Walker had inside information on Fort Courage. This was a promising start. "Do you know where Gaitwood has your brother?"

Walker nodded. "They give him busywork, usually around the stables. He's good with horses. Why?"

Blaise leaned in closer to the postmaster, conspiratorial. "What if I told you we're going to get him out of there? Him and our people that Gaitwood kidnapped? Would you help me?"

Hope shone in Walker's eyes. "Without hesitation."

CHAPTER FORTY-FIVE
Necessary Deceptions

Jack

"*N*o."

"But—"

Jack slammed a fist against the table in raw frustration, cutting Blaise off with a menacing glare. It was infuriating enough the Breaker vowed Jack wouldn't deliver his particular brand of punishment against the traitor. It didn't matter if Blaise's manner of gentle interrogation produced results. Walker needed to be held accountable for many wrongs, and including him as a lynchpin in a delicate operation was ill-advised at best and fool-hardy at worst.

Nadine's good eye was closed, as if their argument gave her a headache. Kur Agur refused to sit, instead stalking from one end of HQ's meeting room to the other like a caged animal, hackles raised. The Theilian, at least, seemed to side with Jack on the matter.

"The man *sold us out.*" Jack's voice was calm, reasonable. See? He could play nice, too. "What's stopping him from handing us over to Gaitwood, pretty as you please?"

"Gaitwood has his brother as a surety."

Jack snorted. "If anything, that gives him *more* incentive."

Blaise spread his hands. "Look at him. Gaitwood *crippled* him."

Jack crossed his arms. "I don't give a shit. Lamar's shot missed as far as I'm concerned." *That asshole was always a terrible shot.*

Nadine sighed. "To be honest, it's not the worst idea in the world to include him. Let him draw a map."

Jack wouldn't trust a map drawn by Walker. Nope. He glowered.

Blaise shook his head. "A map is helpful, but won't be enough." He spread his hands, imploring as he addressed Jack. "You have every reason to be furious with Hank Walker. I won't lie. Talking to him and not getting angry was one of the hardest things I've ever done." Blaise blew out a breath. "But he didn't have to talk to me. Didn't have to come clean. And you're right, Jack. He could've skipped town. I didn't know about his magic."

Jack gave a small nod of acknowledgment. Now if only they would listen to him about *this.*

Blaise continued, tenacious. "His magic is what we need for this to work, though. He can get us *inside* Fort Courage."

What? Jack scowled, reviewing his knowledge of Hank Walker's magic. Walkers attuned to different plant life—in Hank's case, cacti. He moved himself and objects from one point to another, tethered by corresponding vegetation. Hank had outright denied it was possible to take other people with him.

Jack uncrossed his arms and leaned forward. "Enlighten me."

Blaise smiled a *gotcha* smile that Jack wished he could erase. "Hank can take us, one at a time, to Fort Courage. He told me he can move people with his magic."

"That damned liar!" Jack shoved back his chair, wincing as the brisk movement made the room swirl before his eyes. He was sick and tired of feeling sick and tired.

Blaise cocked his head, wisely not taking offense at the outburst. He waited, tapping a finger against the table. Nadine shook her head. Kur continued his pacing.

Jack mastered his temper as the room settled into place, though he wove on his feet, unsteady. Jack decided he wouldn't make a very good argument if he fell over in front of them. He sat again. "I asked him about that before. He told me he couldn't. What makes you think we can believe this?"

"Because all his life, he's been used and manipulated." Blaise's face was shadowed, as if something about his conversation with Walker troubled him. One of the truths that had unfurled.

"And isn't this more of the same?" Jack asked. He knew a thing or two about being used, and how it chafed.

"Maybe. I hope he doesn't see it that way. I think we need to take the chance unless you know of another way into the fort." Blaise rubbed his forehead, and Jack saw the mental toll this was taking on the young man. This wasn't his forte. Put him in a bakery and cover him with flour and he was in his element. He didn't want to be the one planning an assault on a stronghold crawling with the enemy. But he was doing everything possible to help, to right a wrong that was not his fault.

The least Jack could do was hear him out. He sighed. "I won't lie. I don't like your idea, not one bit."

He lifted his eyes, studying the map pinned to the wall. If Jack was the one making the plan, he would use the pegasi to fly their team in. But then the enemy would see them coming, and they lost all hope of stealth. He needed more information about how Walker could get them inside, but it was worth considering. Jack wasn't a fool. Even at the top of his game, he wouldn't last five seconds against a company of soldiers who saw them coming from a mile away.

"But I'll entertain it as a part of the plan." Jack tipped his chin. "However, because this is important, I'm asking again: what's stopping him from delivering us to Gaitwood? Surety or not, if he takes us there and betrays us again, it's over."

"A fair question," Kur agreed with a growl.

Blaise held up two fingers. "One: Gaitwood has lost Walker's trust. Gaitwood left him behind and shot out his knee."

Jack snorted. "I'm going to be the terrible person who says he had it coming."

"You *are* a terrible person," Blaise confirmed, then sobered. "And here's the second reason. Something is wrong with his brother, so no one thinks much of him. Hank was his protector. He's worried about his brother's safety, with no one to look out for his well-being."

Kur Agur paused, his furry head canted. "You offered to rescue his brother?"

Blaise inclined his head, a casual move that spoke of a poise he didn't possess under normal circumstances. Not for the first time, Jack wondered at the mantle of confidence the Breaker wore. Where had *that* come from?

All eyes were on Jack. He scratched at his forehead as he took Blaise's words into consideration. "For the record, I don't like this. I'll allow it on one condition."

"And that is?" Nadine asked.

"If I get wind of Walker betraying us, I get to shoot him."

Blaise winced. "Jack—"

"I *won't* go after him for his past transgressions," Jack cut in. "But that man has a long road to travel before I'll trust him. If he's a turncoat, I'm taking him down with me."

Blaise met Jack's eyes, unflinching. Tough for the Breaker, but Jack was unwilling to concede this point. Someone with common sense had to be ready to put a rabid animal down.

"Fine," Blaise relented, breaking their staring contest.

They discussed other parts of the plan, debating the best strategies to use. After an hour, Nadine declared that both she and Jack needed rest, and they would adjourn but resume after dinner.

Blaise trailed Nadine to the door, but Jack whistled, catching the young mage's attention. He glanced back, quizzical. Jack nodded to the chair the Breaker had vacated.

"What?" Blaise asked once they were alone.

Tired as he was, Jack had fresh concerns about Jefferson Cole's ties to their troubles. Blaise thought the man was innocent. But there was much he was unaware of. "Tell me about the woman you traveled with. Flora Strop."

Blaise pursed his lips, suspicious. "Cut from the same cloth as you in a lot of ways."

"Gonna assume you're complimenting her, then."

A small smile twisted the Breaker's lips. "Actually, yes. She's scary. Tough. Loyal." He stopped there. Jack let things simmer and just watched him. "And I already told you she's Jasper Strop's niece."

"That how Cole knew Itude was more than a two-bit town?" Jack's voice was knife-edge sharp.

Blaise shrugged. "You'd have to ask Flora."

Jack nodded. He would when he didn't feel so damned tired. Not that he would tell anyone that he wasn't fit as a fiddle. "You go into business with Cole?"

"I did." Blaise met his eyes, a dare to chastise him for the move. "What else could I do?"

Jack wanted to say *anything but that,* but that was a lie. "You could have stayed. You could have not *run off* with your tail tucked between your legs."

Blaise chewed on his bottom lip, his veneer of confidence eroding. "I can't change the past. But I'm here now."

And that would have to be enough for now. Jack didn't want to pull the rug out from under Blaise with his information, but he hoped it would guard him against future pain. "There's something you need to know about Cole."

"I know you hate him."

Jack made a frustrated sound. "This isn't about my likes or dislikes. Believe it or not, this is *me* looking out for *you.*"

That got Blaise's attention. He fidgeted with his fingers, rubbing his hands together, unsettled. "What?"

"He's not who he claims to be."

The Breaker's face paled, hurt in his eyes. "How do you know this?"

Jack paused. He expected Blaise to say *that's not true!* Or anything else to refute it. But he didn't. The Breaker suspected Cole had hidden something from him, and he had steeled himself.

"You're aware I deal in information. When Cole was here, he offered to buy the bakery—"

"What?"

Jack sighed. "He offered to buy the bakery. I refused to sell. He gave me his business card, and it jogged my memory. It took me a while, but I did my research. Jefferson Cole is a front."

Blaise closed his eyes, pained. "Who . . . who is he?"

Damn, Jack didn't want to tell him. He didn't want to stomp all over Blaise's hopes and dreams. But he would do him a disservice to leave him ignorant. It was dangerous to not know. "Salt-Iron Council Representative for Ganland by the name of Malcolm Wells."

Blaise's eyes flashed open, and he jerked like a ghost had poked him. "How certain are you?"

Jack lifted his chin. "Certain enough to tell you."

Blaise sighed, seeming to collapse in on himself before shaking it off. "Malcolm Wells," he murmured, as if tasting the name. Jack saw the wheels turning in his head, piecing things together and coming to some disastrous conclusions. "Oh shit."

"That's about the long and short of it," Jack agreed.

Blaise rose from his chair. "I have to go."

Jack disliked the tension framing the young man's eyes and the slash of his mouth. "Where are you going?"

"I have to talk to Flora."

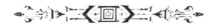

Blaise

"FLORA."

The half-breed woman turned at Blaise's voice, frowning at his firm tone. "What's wrong? Got a bee in your bonnet?"

She was on the porch of her borrowed house, sitting in a rocking chair across from Jasper Strop. The shopkeeper regarded Blaise with wide eyes.

"I should go. Shop won't clean itself." Jasper slid from the rocker, giving Blaise a respectful nod before slinking away.

Blaise watched him go, then climbed up on the porch. He jerked his chin to the rocker Jasper had vacated. "Mind if I sit down?"

Flora kept rocking. Her feet didn't touch the ground, so she shifted her weight back and forth. "I can't stop you."

She could. Blaise was keenly aware that with Jack still recovering, the pink-haired woman was the most dangerous person in town. More dangerous than Kur or Clover, which said something.

But that wouldn't stop him from this necessary conversation.

"Why did Jefferson lie to me?"

She blinked at him in confusion, her standoffishness evaporating. "Wait. What?"

"Why didn't he tell me who he is?" It took every bit of Blaise's resolve to keep his voice from breaking. Anxiety and tension roiled through him. He was tightly wound from all he had done since his return to Itude. Jefferson's duplicity chipped away at the last of his determination. Blaise bowed his head to hide the hurt.

"Oh. *Oh.*" Flora drew the word out with extra emphasis, eyes round. "Jefferson didn't lie to you. At least not the way you're thinking."

Blaise lifted his chin just enough to glance at her. "Is he or is he not Malcolm Wells?" The name was strange on his tongue. Difficult to reconcile with the man he knew.

"He is Malcolm Wells. But he's *also* Jefferson Cole."

Blaise mopped at his face with one hand, feeling the itch of his magic. He took a breath to steady it, sending it back to slumber. Blaise wished he had the time to sit down and have a good cry. He deserved it. But that would have to wait. "That doesn't make sense."

"Sure, it does." Flora slipped out of her chair and dragged the rocker closer, climbing back up. Her legs didn't touch the ground. "In this very town, you have Wildfire Jack and Jack Dewitt. Same person."

"Jack never lied to me about who he is." In fact, Blaise thought with derision, Jack had made it very clear from the start.

"Neither did Jefferson. Neglected to tell you? Sure. But he can't just go around blabbing to everyone. Defeats the purpose."

Blaise frowned. "I'm not following."

Flora sighed, bobbing her head from side to side as she considered her explanation. "Okay, first off, I need to know how many people know this information. Because I may need to do some damage control."

Any other day, those words would have unsettled Blaise. As tired as he was, he refused to allow casual promises of violence to shake him. "As far as I know, only me and Jack. And if you're suggesting you'll try to kill us, we're about to have a big problem."

She held up her hands, quelling. "I'll never hear the end of it from Jefferson if I harm a hair on your pretty head." Blaise didn't miss the fact that she failed to mention Jack.

"Jack will keep the secret. If there's one thing he can do well, it's keep secrets."

Flora gave him a speculative look. "You realize you're staking *your* life on this, too?"

Because Blaise signed contracts with Jefferson Cole, they were forever intertwined—along with Malcolm Wells. "Yes. Jack will keep the secret. Now explain."

Mollified, Flora nodded. "Right. So the first thing you have to understand is that Jeff—Malcolm is the Doyen for Ganland." She swallowed. "We discussed the Salt-Iron Council with Jefferson the other day. I trust you remember the gist of it?"

Blaise gave a stiff nod. He remembered, and the knowledge made him nauseous. Did Jefferson secretly support the atrocities Gaitwood and his men committed? Stealing mages from their homes, their families? Blaise closed his eyes, remembering discussions with Jefferson about those very points. He opposed them. But could Blaise believe that now?

"You're terrible at hiding your emotions. You should work on that," Flora pointed out.

Blaise rubbed his face. "Forgive me for having feelings. I'm listening."

"Anyway, that's what *Malcolm* does. He politics and invests. And he has to do all the political hobnobbing with snobs that comes with his position. Fancy parties and whatnot. Dreadful things. Makes me want to stab my eyes out for a change of pace."

Blaise raised his eyebrows.

"Okay, yeah, that's off topic. Sorry. All those things I just mentioned? Those aren't his passion. Well, he likes the political stuff—he *really* is trying to create change. But he enjoys travel and seeing interesting things, meeting new people. And stumbling across the occasional investment as Jefferson is icing on the cake."

"Oh." Blaise cocked his head. "But can't he do all that as Malcolm Wells?"

Flora snorted. "He could, but not the way he wants to. Doyen Wells is required to travel with a security detail." Her voice softened. "Malcolm can't do that—not while navigating the towns in the Untamed Territory without suspicion or outright battles. Don't get me wrong, I'm all for a brawl, but even I know it's unnecessary. He doesn't want to come here and be cosseted like a prized pony. His words, not mine."

Blaise frowned. "Isn't it dangerous for him to do that?"

Flora shook her head. "Not as dangerous as under his actual name. And I usually travel with him. As long as he's Jefferson Cole, playboy investor with more money than he knows what to do with, he's safe."

Blaise didn't see the logic in that. "Wouldn't that make it more likely for him to come to harm?"

She smirked. "There are some well-paid outlaws around Rainbow Flat who will do their best to make sure Jefferson Cole doesn't so much as have a mosquito look at him cross-eyed."

Blaise thought back to Rainbow Flat. Everyone in the town who crossed paths with Jefferson treated him with a mix of reverence and charitable protectiveness. Jefferson had his own outlaw protection. That made sense in a strange way. Blaise wondered how much of Rainbow Flat Jefferson owned. All of it? "How does he keep up his front? Jack figured it out."

Flora scowled. "I need to ask that cuss how he connected the dots so I can correct the oversight." She rocked her chair, thoughtful. "And I'm sorry, but I won't tell you how he does it. That's not my secret to share." Her expression bordered on sympathetic. "I doubt he wanted to mislead you. He seems to like you for some reason. But outside of Salt-Iron borders, he *must* be Jefferson Cole. Any other name and . . ." She trailed off, gritting her teeth.

Blaise nodded, relaxing now that he understood. It didn't absolve Jefferson. He still had to answer for the deception, as necessary as it was. But Jefferson hadn't done it with malice, so Blaise allowed himself a moment of contentment. He respected the need for protection.

"Thank you for telling me what you did. I appreciate it."

She gave a stiff nod. "Sure. What's next on your agenda? This place is kind of boring."

Blaise sighed. "Interested in helping with a brazen assault on Fort Courage?"

Flora grinned. "I'm always up for a little treachery."

CHAPTER FORTY-SIX
The Importance of Succulents

Blaise

*P*eople would die today. There was a good chance people he cared about would be in that number.

An emptiness had filled Blaise yesterday as he watched the remnants of the townspeople mill about, voices soft as they spoke in clusters in the town square. So many devastated citizens threw in their lot with the plan, despite the losses they had already taken. It seemed surreal watching the support team ride out of Itude, flatbed wagons loaded with medical supplies, food, and weapons.

Nadine led the support team, bolstered by Clover and Kur. The Knossan and Theilian disliked the plan; they wanted inclusion in the assault. But the plan relied on subtlety.

Now Blaise stood in the bakery's husk, his boots crunching the grit of charred wood. The loft had collapsed into the lower level, creating a tumbledown maze which he threaded through as he identified the wreckage. Anything made of cast iron had survived, and he made busywork of rescuing pots and pans, setting them in the dusty street to be reclaimed later.

The scuff of boots in the street drew his attention. Jack strode up, his movements stiff from recovery. Though, Blaise would never tell him that. He stayed outside the walls of the bakery, arms crossed.

"It's probably not safe to be in there," Jack said.

Blaise used his booted foot to nudge the remains of a cabinet out of his way. Ash flaked against his toe. "Bold statement considering where we're going today."

Amusement played on Jack's lips. "Need you in one piece for that." He glanced through the remains of the bakery's scorched walls at Emrys grazing a short distance away. "Alekon just returned and reported the support team and our ringers are in place." Jack studied him, as if the outlaw was afraid that Blaise would be their weak link.

He wasn't wrong. For all the show Blaise had put on in the last few days, he feared faltering when they needed him most. But Jefferson believed in him. His heart flip-flopped in his chest, and he shoved away thoughts of the handsome entrepreneur.

"Thanks for telling me." Blaise picked his way out of the scorched bakery, then whistled to Emrys. The pegasus lifted his head and trotted over, sweeping out his wings as he drew to a stop.

<Is it time?>

Blaise scratched the stallion's cheek. "Let's get you saddled up." While he wouldn't be riding Emrys to the fort, he was optimistic that he would have need of the saddle later.

As they approached the stable, Blaise realized Jack had been busy doing things he should have left for others. The other pegasi involved in the rescue operation waited, saddled and ready, their breath frosting the air in anticipation.

"You should have gotten me sooner," Blaise murmured.

Jack shook his head. Blaise understood. The outlaw *needed* to stay busy, as much as Blaise needed to find peace before their mission.

Blaise saddled Emrys, finding comfort in the squeak of leather and the warm scent of equine. After checking to make sure he'd fastened every buckle and the cinch was snug, he rested his forehead against Emrys's. The stallion's breath tickled his chest.

<I will not leave you behind.>

Blaise smiled, gratified by the pegasus's sincerity. "I know. Thank you."

Emrys stepped back, hooves ringing on the hard-packed dirt. He pivoted and joined the other pegasi. Zepheus shared a private moment with Jack, then broke into a lope before leading the flight of stallions into the sky.

It was hard to watch them go. Blaise released a pent-up breath. Aside from the group making the foray into the Fort, the pegasi were the second most vulnerable group. They planned to take turns conducting periodic fly-bys over the fortress, waiting for their chance to wing the prisoners to safety.

"C'mon." Jack whacked Blaise on the arm with his elbow. "Time to get *dressed*." He spat in the dust, his distaste clear.

Blaise trailed along. "How do you do it?"

Jack glanced over his shoulder. "Do what?"

"Not panic."

The outlaw was silent as they walked, and Blaise thought he wouldn't get an answer. After a moment, Jack said, "Tell me how you had those hard conversations the last few days."

Blaise shrugged. "I faked it."

Jack gave a mirthless grin. "Exactly."

Blaise blinked, puzzled. And then he understood. Gaitwood had Emmaline. Jack was still recovering, not at the top of his game. He had to rely on others—something he hated to do. Jack was terrified.

BLAISE STARED AT HIS REFLECTION IN THE CRACKED, FLOOR-LENGTH mirror. Ever the pragmatist, Flora reclaimed a pair of Salt-Iron Confederation uniforms from dead soldiers when she was doing *"intelligence gathering,"* which resembled rifling through the pile of corpses for anything she found useful. A kind soul had cleaned the worst of the gore from the uniforms and mended the damage inflicted during the battle as best they could. Wearing a dead man's clothing did nothing to bolster Blaise's confidence.

Macabre as it was, Flora's casual perusal of the dead had its uses. Her search was so thorough she discovered five of the dead were enemy theurgists, information which pleased Jack. Flora identified one of them as an Inker, based on tools the dead soldier had in his kit.

Jack's face split into a smile when Flora shared that tidbit. No one offered to tell Blaise why that was important. Instead, they moved on to another discussion topic. Their conversation ground to a halt when Blaise fractured the tabletop they were sitting at in a rare fit of pique. "Why is that important?" Blaise demanded. "The Inker?"

Jack fixed him with an expression that would have wilted him months ago but had little effect at present. "They can't move the mavericks until they're branded—not this many, at any rate. There's lots of Inkers, but most are going to be in Phinora. Gait-wood will send for the closest. Ondin, probably. It means we have time to get our people out unscathed."

The hope flaring in Jack's eyes allowed Blaise to forgive him for the oversight. Everything was on the line for him. Failure wasn't an option.

With that in mind, Blaise adjusted the collar of his scarlet overcoat, tipping his chin to inspect the shaving job Jack had forced on him earlier. It seemed like a small detail, but Flora impressed upon him the importance of a clean look. The Salt-Iron Confederation didn't allow their soldiers to have facial hair.

The cool blue eyes staring back at him felt like they belonged to someone else, an enemy. He rubbed his bare chin. *Weird.*

Flora tilted her head in appreciation when he trotted down the steps of his borrowed home. She muttered something that sounded suspiciously like "*I love a man in uniform.*" Blaise's face flamed.

Jack waited beside Flora, arms crossed, disgust etched on his face. He wore the same uniform, though the outlaw squirmed in it like he was trying to shed a second skin.

"The asshole who died in this had fleas," Jack grumbled as an explanation.

Blaise heard the lie in his voice. Jack detested wearing the Salt-Iron Confederation uniform because of what it represented to him. Everything he had escaped. And everything he stood to lose.

Flora scrutinized them, adjusting bits of their uniforms and peppering them with reminders. They both had a single revolver —another thing that galled Jack, who expected to walk into the fort armed to the teeth. Flora pointed out that this was a stealth run (until it wasn't, which they hoped was when they found their missing mages). They would lose the element of surprise if Jack's solution was to shoot everyone he came across in the face.

"All right, you'll do," Flora declared at last. "Let's go."

The trio walked to the post office. Hank Walker sat on a bench outside the damaged building, the awning overhead shredded during the attack. His crutch butted up against the bench, and a small brown satchel was nestled on his lap.

"What's that?" Jack's voice was throaty with suspicion. His hand twitched beside his holstered sixgun.

Blaise sighed. "Will you calm down?" Hank stared at them with terror, beads of sweat on his temple.

"What do you have there, Walker?" Jack repeated, insistent, ignoring Blaise. Blaise had the sudden worry an unhinged outlaw might become the biggest hitch in their plan.

Hank didn't answer, frozen in place by the menace. Jack snatched the bag and opened it, dumping the contents into his palm. Tiny plants shaped like clusters of miniature crescents, the edges of their leaves a vibrant purple, rolled into his palm. "What in Faedra's name are these?"

"M-mother of thousands," Hank stammered. "Plantlets. They'll help me move around the fort more easily. I swear, I brought them to help."

"Jack," Blaise warned, pulling a growl of authority into the word. Hank Walker was a crucial part of their plan. If he backed out, they were going to be in serious trouble.

Jack's eyes whipped up to him, acknowledging him at last. "Fine." He poured the tiny succulents into the bag and handed it back to the postmaster.

"I want a sample of one of those if we survive this," Flora said, as cheerful as if she were asking after produce at a farmer's market. "Do they have any medicinal properties?"

Hank blinked at her. "Um. I think so?"

Jack cleared his throat.

Flora waved a hand, dismissive. "We'll figure that out later."

Blaise groaned. He was a ball of stress, and they hadn't left Itude yet. "We should go." Before he lost his nerve.

Walker shook three plantlets out of the bag. "Need you each to hang on to these. If you have them, I can locate you."

Jack cocked his head, distrust in his eyes. He opened his mouth to say something, but in a rare moment of clarity, bit back his comment. Or maybe it was the fact that Blaise leaned in close and whispered, "Emmaline."

Jack plucked one of the tiny plants from Walker's hand, tucking it into a pocket. "I promise, if you pop up next to us with Gaitwood, I'll put a bullet in your skull."

Blaise selected a plantlet and slipped it into the pocket on the underside of his coat. "Please stop threatening our ride."

"No." Jack's lower lip stuck out, reminding Blaise of the times his younger brother had been on the verge of a tantrum. He decided not to point that out.

"I hate Gaitwood as much as you, you know," Hank muttered. "I want to get our friends back. And my brother."

Jack's eyes narrowed into speculative slits. Blaise assumed he was thinking no one could hate Gaitwood as much as he did. Blaise had to admit, he was probably right.

Flora tucked her plantlet away. They were ready. Blaise drew on his fake mantle of authority, hoping that one day this would be more comfortable. "Hank, review where you're going to drop us."

The postmaster took a breath. "Supply room. Located between my jump point and Gaitwood's office. Not used much, from what I saw. Plan is, I jump to my cactus at the fort, and when the coast is clear, I drop one of my babies in the supply room." He patted his satchel.

Blaise nodded and spoke up before Jack could issue any new threats. "Good luck."

Walker's wrinkled face parted in a tremulous smile, then he vanished with a soft pop.

Flora stared at the space he had occupied. "Huh. His magic works like a knocker's, but with plants."

They waited in silence, Jack shifting his weight from one booted foot to the other. Blaise spent the time with his eyes closed, practicing his calm. His hands were itching. He couldn't afford to leak any of his magic. But thinking of control made him think of Vixen, and she was among the captured, too. They were depending on him.

"Snap out of it," Jack growled.

Blaise cracked one eye open. "Need to work on your people skills."

Jack's mouth quirked, and for an instant he allowed himself levity. "Maybe people need to work on their me skills."

Blaise snorted. Hank reappeared with a pop, his sudden return startling Jack so he had his sixgun aimed at the postmaster's head before Blaise could even blink. Jack corrected himself when he realized it was Walker, lowering the muzzle and slipping the weapon into its holster. He ducked his head, which was as good as an apology as anyone would get from him.

"It's clear," Walker confirmed once Jack had his gun put away. His eyes were wide, though he seemed resigned to the fact that if he so much as sneezed, Jack might shoot him. "I'll take you one at a time."

"Me first!" Flora volunteered, excited.

"No," Jack growled.

Flora wheeled on him, her eyes twin daggers of ferocity. "Where are your manners, Mr. Dewitt? Ladies first."

Blaise feared it might come to blows between the tiny, vicious woman and the gruff outlaw. Jack stared at her, unblinking.

Flora tut-tutted. "If this is a trap, who has the better likelihood of squeaking out of it?"

Jack ground his teeth. "But it could be dangerous."

Her eyes lit up. "*Will* be dangerous. And I'll be fine." She spoke with such self-assurance that Flora left no room for doubt. Blaise worried for her sake. He imagined Lamar Gaitwood wouldn't be happy to discover a subordinate of his brother's political rival skulking around. If that crossed her mind, she didn't show it. Flora grinned at Hank. "How do we do this?"

"Link your arm in mine," Hank instructed. She did, and a moment later, they were both gone.

"Faedra's tits," Jack grumbled. "I have to be arm-in-arm with that man?"

Hank reappeared at the end of Jack's complaint. Blaise stepped beside the postmaster and linked arms before Jack could say anything. Hank activated his magic, and Blaise's stomach churned. It felt like the ground opened up beneath them, and Blaise's magic rose like a watchdog. He tamped it down, afraid to find out what might happen if Hank's magic shattered in the middle of transport.

Hank's method of travel didn't take long. Blaise blinked, and then found himself in a dim room. Flora busied herself reading labels on jars lined up on a shelf.

"If I don't make it back, Jack got pissed and killed me," Hank grumbled.

"He won't," Blaise promised. If he said it, maybe it would be true.

Hank vanished and then reappeared with Jack, the outlaw stumbling away from Walker as soon as he was able. He turned in a quick circle, assessing their surroundings with a sixgun in his hand.

"Hello. We're not dead yet." Flora waved at him. "Wow. They shouldn't just leave this stuff here for anyone wandering around to take." She pulled a small vial off a rack and pocketed it.

Hank stared at them like he couldn't believe Blaise had talked him into this. Blaise sighed. He wondered about that, too.

"You still want me to . . . do the thing?" Hank asked, gesturing to the door.

"Yes." Blaise nodded, then glanced at Flora. "Hey. Stop stealing their stuff. You were going to go scout for us."

"It's not stealing. I'm reallocating resources," Flora said, indignant. "I'm on their side, remember?"

"Uh . . ." Blaise stared at her, half-expecting Jack to have his revolver aimed at her head.

"That's what they'll think, anyway," Flora clarified, chipper. "I'll do more shopping later if I get a chance. Be right back."

Walker waited a beat, then slipped out in her wake. Blaise sat on a crate, elbows on his knees.

Jack pulled another crate over to sit opposite him. "You hanging in there?"

Sighing, Blaise shook his head. "No. I don't think I can do this." The enormity of the task before them was daunting. The chance of success seemed laughable.

"Why did you *really* come back to Itude?" Jack murmured.

Blaise closed his eyes. "Because I found a new family. You,

Emmaline, Reuben, Vixen, Clover. Even if I thought you hated me, I couldn't allow this."

Jack was quiet for a while. Blaise opened his eyes to watch him, noticing the pensive expression on the outlaw's face. "You've changed, kid."

"Not a kid."

"No, you're not." Jack agreed quickly, leaning forward. He pointed his index finger at Blaise's nose. "You're a damn good outlaw mage."

Blaise rubbed the back of his neck. "Doesn't feel like it. I should be sitting here calm and collected like you."

Jack rolled his shoulders, the golden braiding atop his uniform glinting in the low light. "Jack Dewitt is not calm and collected right now." For the barest moment, he dropped his façade, and Blaise saw the worry lines around his eyes. Then, as if donning a mask, his face hardened. "Wildfire Jack, on the other hand, is."

Blaise nodded. Jack had endured so much trauma in his life. It made sense he compartmentalized what he could when necessary. It made as much sense as Jefferson's need for an alter ego. Lost in thought, he didn't notice Jack reach out to pluck hairs from his head until he felt a sharp tug and yelped.

"Hey! What was that for?"

Jack clapped a hand over Blaise's mouth. "Shh, you're going to get us caught. And I have my reasons." He tucked the three hairs into the same pocket as his plantlet, buttoning it closed to keep the contents safe.

Blaise opened his mouth to ask, but the door opened. Jack had his revolver out. Flora poked her head in. "All clear. Let's go!"

CHAPTER FORTY-SEVEN
Fire in Her Eyes

Lamar

"Your father is dead. Your town is destroyed. Everything and everyone you ever loved is gone. *You are worthless.*"

Lamar repeated the words over and over, a mantra of suffering, as he walked in slow, steady circles around Jack's daughter. She refused to give her name, spitting in his face when he asked and yowling that she would never submit.

Stubborn. So much like her father. That only appealed all the more to Lamar. Jack would pay for his betrayal with his daughter's servitude. Everything had come full circle.

He continued the relentless chant, watching her closely for any signs of cracking. She bowed her head, flexing her arms against the salt-iron restraints that pinned her to the ladder-back chair. Her eyes watered, either from the sting of the metal or from his words, but she refused to allow her tears to fall.

A knock sounded on the door. Lamar scowled. He had left instructions not to be disturbed. He ignored it, but it came again, this time more insistent. Biting back a growl of annoyance, he stalked to the door and opened it a crack. "What is it?"

Lieutenant Smithson stood outside, clenching the arm of a man Lamar hadn't thought he'd ever see again. "Apologies, Commander. This man says he has urgent news."

Lamar gave Hank Walker a cool once-over. The maverick leaned heavily on a crutch, the empty bottom of his right pants leg pinned up over the stump of his knee. "I made it clear I'm through with you."

Walker's face contorted, a mix of fear and supplication. "Please. I have important news—news you need to know. Wildfire Jack and the Breaker are coming."

Impossible. Lamar stared at the old man, dumbfounded. No one touched one of his traps and survived. Anyone stupid enough to do so withered away, a slow and horrific death. He had seen Jack make the fatal mistake with his own eyes. But then a thought occurred to him: that damned Breaker. He'd found a way when no one else could. Gods, if only Gregor would let him kill the man.

Lamar glanced over his shoulder at Jack's daughter. Her head was up, ears straining. No doubt she had heard her father's name. Hope kindled in her eyes, undoing all of Lamar's hard work to extinguish her fire. He couldn't risk her hearing anything more that could jeopardize his progress. Lamar stepped into the hall-way, closing the door behind him.

"Wildfire Jack should be dead," Lamar said, his tone low and dangerous.

"He's not. He's coming here, and he's mad as a demon straight from Perdition." Walker gulped and added, "Sir."

Bit by bit, Hank told him what he wanted to know. Lamar reined in his annoyance until his former spy finished recounting his information.

"Lock him up with the others." Lamar waved a hand, ignoring the devastation that shone in Walker's eyes.

"But . . . but I thought if I told you—"

"That I'd take pity on you? Let you have your brother?" Lamar asked as a soldier walked over and slipped a braided salt-iron rope around the mage's arms. Walker flinched as a bead of salt-iron burned against his skin. "I'm *done* with you. I thought I had made that abundantly clear. With the shooting out your knee and all." Lamar's lips curled into an amused smile.

Walker's anguished howl echoed through his office as a pair of soldiers escorted him to the holding cells. It would have been a kindness to end the man's miserable life. Lamar didn't do kindness.

He threw open the door and crossed the distance to where Jack's daughter sat in three long strides. "There's been a change of plans. We'll have to continue your education later."

The girl fixed a baleful look on him. She wasn't broken, not yet. Lamar and his cohorts had more to do to destroy the spirit that burned so brightly in her. Her young, pliable mind had to be shattered to its core, until her fierce independence was nothing more than tatters. Lamar enjoyed a hands-on approach. She said nothing, only lifted her chin in defiance.

Lieutenant Smithson had followed him inside and scowled. "I'd be happy to teach her *respect*, Commander."

Lamar waved a hand. While Smithson's methods could be effective, the lecherous man would be a poor choice in this situation. He had broken one of the Desinan mavericks beyond saving, the poor wretch. Jack's young daughter could serve the Confederation for decades to come if Lamar took the right approach. She would make amends for her father's betrayal.

"Thank you, but no," Lamar murmured. "This one is mine. You may take her back to the cell, however. I have preparations to make."

Smithson jumped over to her. "Yes, Commander." He dragged the girl to her feet. Lamar didn't miss the way he grabbed her bottom in the process. Jack's daughter stomped on the soldier's instep, causing him to howl and stagger away.

"You bitch—" Smithson thundered, raising a hand.

Lamar grabbed his arm. "Have a care, Smithson. She is *mine* to break. Forget that and I'll have you on latrine duty." He turned to the girl. "I'll bend your will into a theurgist yet." It was both promise and threat. She spat at him, though the glob of spittle went wide. Jack's daughter was going to be entertaining.

Smithson hauled the unruly teenager away, allowing Lamar to refocus on the matter at hand. Walker's trust in him had been misguided. Lamar smiled. A pity he had already sent out a squadron, headed for Rainbow Flat. Lamar planned to ride after them once the replacement Inker arrived. He couldn't send that many outlaw mages to Phinora without first knowing they were contained. Couldn't afford any more missteps.

He hadn't counted on the Breaker coming back to help Itude. Lamar studied the map on the wall. Hank had reported the pair were riding in from the east, coming across the Deadwood River. He supposed Jack would plan some sort of ambush. His old friend was wily and hadn't escaped justice for so long by being stupid. That he was in the Breaker's company made them an extremely dangerous pair.

"Gallagher. Prepare three squadrons," Lamar barked.

Gallagher, dozing nearby, snapped to attention. "Yes sir." Rubbing sleep from his eyes, he hurried out of the room. Lamar hoped he remembered the damn instructions.

Lamar checked the guns at his side, then pulled his rifle from its place behind his desk. He settled it on his back, then headed out to the stables.

A glimpse of pink gave him pause. He knew that hair. A growl of annoyance rumbled in his throat. "*Flora Strop.*"

Cole's little shadow turned to greet him, peering at him over her glasses. "Lamar."

Damn her, not even giving him the benefit of his hard-won title. "Commander."

She dimpled. "Oh, I don't have a rank."

His fingers twitched. Blessed Garus, if only killing her wouldn't start an *incident*. "Why are you here?"

Flora's eyes widened, playing at innocence. "Mr. Cole received word of the awful killings of his people. He sent me to investigate."

Of course he had. Lamar gritted his teeth. "We retaliated against the ones who took their lives."

She squinted at him. "You did? That's too kind of you. However, since they were Gannish citizens, you won't mind if I'm thorough. I have forms to fill out in triplicate about this incident after all! I'll stop by your office later so you can sign them. But don't mind me—you'll hardly know I'm here."

Gods, the Gannish and their damned paperwork. "My lieutenant can sign them. I'm busy."

"I'm sure you are," Flora agreed, waving him off and walking away with purpose, as if she were in command of the whole damned fort.

Lamar shook his head to clear it. Later. He would deal with Cole's little crone later, if he could find a way to do so without causing a ruckus. Lamar continued on to the stables, pleased to see that the word had gone out and the horses were being readied. He found his stolid bay gelding saddled and awaiting him. Things were looking up.

CHAPTER FORTY-EIGHT
Deal Me In

Jack

Jack and Blaise studied the rough map that Flora had scratched on a sheet of paper using a charcoal pencil. Her perusal of the fort allowed her the opportunity to locate their sentry postings, and she helpfully marked them with little smiley faces. Besides sentries, the fort still had the usual complement of soldiers going about their tasks. Flora reported that some of them were preparing to ride out with the Commander. That would help, but there were still more soldiers between their location and the prisoners than Jack liked. He folded the map and tucked it into his pocket.

"Splitting up is a bad idea," Blaise said, giving voice to Jack's own concern.

"Not fond of it myself," Jack agreed. "But it's our best shot."

As far as strategy, what they had to work with was less of a plan and more of a rough outline glued together with unfounded optimism. Hank hadn't returned. Flora hadn't seen him, and the only thing that kept Jack from believing Hank sold them out was no one came to the supply closet looking for them.

Regardless of Hank's status, Blaise had promised to free Joshua Walker. Time was of the essence, so Jack proposed they split up. Blaise would search the stables for Joshua while Jack located the prisoners. It was too soon for the wheels to come off the plan, but Jack supposed he should be pleased they had gotten as far as they had.

"I'll follow after the count of twenty," Jack reminded Blaise as the younger man got up, his uniform whispering with the movement. After Blaise closed the door, Jack reached into his pocket and pulled out a tiny poppet he'd brought along. Keeping a mental count in his head, he wrapped Blaise's hairs around the doll.

At the count of twenty, he tucked the poppet back into the safety of his pocket and shouldered the door open. He stepped out into the lantern-light of the hallway, glancing around for any witnesses he might need to silence. It was empty, though voices echoed in the distance.

Out of reflex, Jack touched the holster at his side, reassured by the steady presence of his sixgun. Six shots. He had a knife in his boot, but he wanted access to more guns. He never carried less than two. Flora had told him he would look suspicious if he were armed to the teeth.

"I'm coming, Em," Jack murmured, following the hallway to a wide corridor that opened onto a courtyard.

Overhead, engines rumbled like an ever-present distant thunder. The warbird loomed over the fort, docked against a rampart that had been built to serve the purpose. Jack studied the area, committing it to memory. He wished he could take a potshot at the airship out of spite, but that would draw unwanted attention. He settled for a middle finger.

"Later you get your reckoning with the Breaker," Jack muttered to the warbird.

He got himself back on track, heading to the wing that housed the holding cells. Flora, bless her vicious little heart, received confirmation that the prisoners from Itude were still there. Jack wasn't sure what he would have done if he'd found out they were shipped off to Phinora already. Razing the fort was high on the list, though.

A nearby soldier called out a question, but Jack pretended to not hear and plowed forward. His fingers twitched, ready to pull his sixgun at a moment's notice. If any of the soldiers inspected his weapon, the gig would be up. His revolver was not their standard issue.

Jack paused as a hiss and a pop reverberated across the fort, followed by shouts. A plume of violet smoke wafted into the air. He smiled. Something was working in their favor. As much as he detested Jefferson Cole, he liked his woman, Flora. She was a proper scoundrel.

He turned another corner and slowed, listening. The telltale sounds of a card game echoed ahead—the scrape of coins on the table as money changed hands and the swish of reshuffled cards. Someone wasn't doing their job. *Now isn't that a shame?*

A puddle of light spilled from the cardsharks' room. Jack paused, studying the visible area. The hallway ahead was poorly lit. They had little care if their prisoners could see. Jack knew from personal experience it was psychologically horrifying to be imprisoned in near-dark. He bit back a growl.

Jack's well-broken boots were silent as he ghosted down the hallway. Nothing on his person rattled or chafed to betray his presence. The shadow work of an assassin was more Raven's wheelhouse, but the guards ahead were lax. They would never hear him coming.

Twenty feet. Ten feet. Then Jack was right outside the door, back flat against the wall. He listened to their banter for several heartbeats, getting a peg on how many were in the room. Three, maybe four. He had enough ammunition to take them out.

Jack stepped into the doorway, sixgun in hand. "Deal me in."

Four soldiers turned to look at him in surprise. They were slow to react, confused by his sudden appearance. *Bang, bang, bang!* Two of his shots ripped into the eyes of his targets, taking out a pair sitting side by side before they could flinch. His third target was on the move, and the bullet grazed the top of the man's head as he ducked.

The fourth soldier, the dealer, overcame his surprise and lunged to a nearby table arrayed with weapons. Jack fired a shot at him before the man could reach it, grunting in satisfaction as blood and brain matter spurted from the back of the soldier's head as he sank to the floor.

The last surviving soldier scrambled for a weapon. He found a knife and hurled it, the pommel glancing against Jack's shoulder. The knife clattered to the ground as Jack finished his opponent with a shot to the forehead.

Jack holstered his sixgun. *Two shots left.* He needed to restock and to pick up anything else that might be helpful. Keys to the holding cells, for one. He searched each of the dead men, scowling. No keys, damn them.

He turned his attention to the table of weapons. His eyebrows flew up in recognition, the breath catching in his throat. Hexguns. *His* hexguns. Shit, in all the chaos he had forgotten about them. Hadn't checked to make sure they were still there. Didn't matter. They were here now.

One hexgun lay disassembled, as if someone had either taken it apart to clean it or had been trying to figure out what made it tick so they could reproduce it. Damn. His contact in Ravance would be pissed if she found out these beauties had fallen into Confederation hands. Jack counted them. Of the original thirteen, only six were on the table.

Jack would deal with that later. He checked to see which ammunition was loaded. Four were loaded with sleep, the fifth with null. Jack picked up a sleep hexgun and shoved it into his waistband. Now wasn't the time to be choosy.

He pulled the rough map from his pocket, studying it.

Although it wasn't to scale, he wasn't far from the holding area. Jack cocked his head, straining as he caught the timbre of a voice he recognized. It was Raven, though his words were indistinct.

If Raven was close by, then so was Emmaline. Sixgun drawn, Jack left the cooling corpses behind him in pools of congealing blood. Dim lantern-light revealed the T-intersection in the hallway ahead. Cells lined the end of the hallway, the dark bars looking rough and uneven. Jack would bet his sixgun those were salt-iron bars. Raven's pale face was visible in the distance, the captured outlaw shaking his head at Jack. Jack slowed, cocking his head as he listened.

"I know someone's there," an unfamiliar voice echoed in the quiet. There was the soft click of something being engaged. A rifle, perhaps. Or one of the missing hexguns. "Who's there?"

Raven shot Jack another pleading look. "I've already taken out four of your men. I'm much obliged to make it five," Jack said.

There was a grating laugh, and a mocking voice rang out. "So you *are* an outlaw. I have one of your people lined up in my sights. Pretty little thing. Blonde hair."

Jack bit back a growl. Emmaline. He couldn't see her from where he stood, or the man who threatened her. Jack wanted nothing more than to storm around the corner and take out the threat. But he couldn't—not at the risk of her life.

Raven's gaze flicked to the neighboring cell, then back to Jack. Something he saw made him reconsider the situation. He gave Jack the tiniest of go-ahead nods.

Jack smiled. He may have had his share of disagreements with Raven, but he knew he could count on him in a pinch. He tossed the revolver to the floor, wincing at the clatter of metal on stone as it slid forward. Jack hated giving up his favorite weapon, but he had to make this seem legitimate.

"Fine, do it your way. Don't hurt the girl."

A satisfied chuckle preceded the clomp of heavily booted feet. The guard yelped as he tripped and went down hard, his balding head sliding into Jack's line of sight as he hit the ground. Jack

lunged, skidding along the dirt floor as he scooped up his sixgun.
A bright flash illuminated the dim holding area as he fired. The
guard went still as his body tumbled to a stop, blood oozing from
a hole in his temple.

"Daddy?"

"*Emmaline!*" Jack stepped over the corpse, heart pounding. Her
eyes were watery, face grimy and tear-stained. She looked like a
lost little girl, and he wanted nothing more than to crush her
against him and protect her from the world.

He scowled as he laid a hand against the bars, hissing as he
drew his fingers back. *What in Perdition?* They were salt-iron, but
he hadn't reacted to salt-iron in *years.*

"Jack? Is that really you?" Vixen interrupted his thoughts,
walking up behind Emmaline. Her eyes were glassy, red hair
mussed, and her clothing torn and bloodied from battle. Her
trademark glasses were missing.

He nodded. "I'm here to get you out." He glanced at Emmaline,
gesturing to the dead guard. "Was that you?"

She released a shaky breath, coming as close to the bars as she
dared. Emmaline cupped a poppet in her hand.

"Good girl," Jack whispered, pride warming his heart. His
brave, unyielding daughter had somehow cast a spell through salt-
iron. Not impossible, but damn difficult. Then he addressed the
rest of his captured friends. "Anyone know if this asshole had a
key?"

Raven shook his head. "If it's not on him, it may be around the
desk in there." He pointed into the guardroom.

Jack was tired of searching corpses. He cast a hopeful look at
Butch, who was in the same cell as Raven. Along with Austin and
Hank—well, that answered his earlier question about what
happened to the Cactus Walker. "Butch, can you do your thing
and reanimate him just to give me the key?"

Butch winced, his face battered. "I . . . I can't. Even if I wanted
to." He turned away, shaking his head.

"They stripped our magic," Vixen whispered, her voice shaky.

Jack's tongue dried, and for a moment buried memories threatened to overwhelm him. "Well, shit."

"That about sums it up, yes," Raven agreed wryly.

"Everyone?" Jack scowled. Emmaline had her magic . . . .

"Not the kids," Vixen answered, rubbing her face. "They think they can still break them. And Hank is a recent arrival."

Jack sighed and continued searching for the damned key. The guard ended up face-down after Jack shot him. Jack checked his back pockets first. With distaste, he turned the man over. "You better have a damn key, or I'll shoot you again on principle," Jack muttered to the dead man. As he searched, the internal timer in his head kept track of how long he had been at his mission. Every second counted. *Where is Blaise?*

He discovered the lump of keys in the guard's front pocket. Jack rose with his prize and freed the men first. Raven hobbled out with difficulty, followed by Butch. Austin helped Hank up and out of the cell.

Raven claimed the guard's rifle. Jack nodded. That was wise. And it reminded him . . . . "They got my hexguns. Need y'all to grab them from the room up ahead to the left." He tapped the grip of the hexgun poking from his waistband.

"Shit. All of them?" Raven asked.

Jack scowled. "I'm guessing so. You'll find five in the room, but only four are usable."

Once Jack unlocked the women's cell, Raven, Cordelia, and Vixen hurried to reclaim the hexguns and commandeer any other weapons they could find. Jack intended to go with them, but Emmaline rushed out and wrapped him in a hug so fierce he didn't want it to end. She buried her head against his secondhand uniform. Jack nestled his face against her hair. He wanted to hold her in his arms forever, but the cold outlaw within reminded him that time was of the essence.

Jack drew back from her and looked at Hank. "How's your magic?"

The postmaster took a pained breath. "Not good. They had me

bound with salt-iron until they got me here, and the cells are just as bad. Drained a lot of it. I may have enough to jump myself and Joshua." He swallowed. "If I can find him."

"Blaise went after him," Jack said, trying to keep the accusation out of his voice and failing. *That was your job, Hank.* The post-master hung his head, wrung out and miserable.

"What's the plan?" Raven asked as he returned with the hexguns. "There is a plan, yes?"

"Eh." Jack waggled his fingers. "More or less." The new plan was for Blaise to rendezvous with Jack at the holding cells. They couldn't delay any longer. Five men were dead. Discovery was inevitable.

Jack pulled the poppet he had made earlier out of his pocket, pressing it into Emmaline's hand. "Hang on to this. We'll need it."

She blinked with confusion. "Who is it?"

"Blaise."

Her expression frosted, her fingers tightening over the doll. "Did he betray us?"

Jack stared at her, confused. He shook his head, realizing that her harrowing experience had brought her to some startling conclusions. He couldn't blame her. Gaitwood had set up the chain of misdirection masterfully. "No. *No,*" Jack emphasized, closing his hand over hers before she cast something she would regret. "He came back. Blaise is here to help."

Emmaline's eyes were bleary with unshed tears. "Okay."

Gods, she sounded hollow, as if her very soul hurt. Jack wanted nothing more than to lash out at the ones who hurt her, but he settled himself with the knowledge that retribution was coming. *Soon.* He looked her in the eye. "We need your magic. Understand?"

Emmaline nodded.

"Are we just going to stand around and wait for them to recapture us or what?" Raven asked.

Jack snarled in frustration. Raven had a point. "Let's go."

Their group inched down the hall, slowed by the need for

Austin to support Hank and Raven's limp. Jack led the way, revolver out. He held up a hand, calling for a silent halt when he heard the shuffle of heavy feet coming toward them.

"Don't shoot," Hank called weakly. "I feel one of my plantlets getting close."

Jack glanced at him, brows raised. Walker had better be right. Jack kept his revolver readied. He would not be caught unawares. The footsteps came closer, the uneven cadence a hint it was not a trained soldier. Jack remained frozen at the head of their group, ready. The silhouette of a man rounded the corner.

"Hank? Hank, I'm here!"

"Joshua!" Hank's voice was raspy with relief. "Oh, thank Faedra you made it."

Jack pursed his lips, watching as Joshua Walker hurried over and gave his big brother a desolate look. "They hurt you. Oh, who hurt you?" Joshua wailed.

Hank shook his head. "Doesn't matter. I'll be okay. We need to go, Joshua." He held out his hand.

"Wait." Jack stepped closer. "Where's Blaise? Did someone bring you here?"

"Oh." Joshua nodded, turning to Jack with enormous eyes. "Yes. He said to tell you the soldiers were coming back already."

Jack stared at him, chilled by the news. The fort was about to be overrun with the enemy. "Shit." He turned to Hank. "Get your brother out of here." To everyone else, he said, "Follow me. We don't have much time. Keep your weapons at the ready." He reconsidered, and added for the three younger outlaws, "And your magic, if it will be useful." He led their small group down the corridor after Hank vanished with his brother.

Vixen came up on his right. "Where's Blaise?"

Jack ducked his head. "If I had to guess, making his way to the airship."

Everyone stared at him. "The airship?" Raven asked.

Jack nodded. "The plan is to break it."

CHAPTER FORTY-NINE

What Friends Are For

Blaise

$\mathcal{H}$e had feared finding Joshua Walker would be difficult, even dangerous. After parting ways with Jack, he found the stables without a problem. Most of the stalls were empty, the horses out with their riders. Blaise expected someone to stop him, question him—anything that would hinder their plan. But it didn't happen, and he discovered a man who was Hank's spitting image mucking out a stall, humming to himself.

The hardest part turned out to be convincing Joshua Walker that he was friendly and there to help. The younger Walker startled when Blaise approached, scrambling away and flinching in the manner of someone who had faced abuse. It wasn't until Blaise crouched down to make himself appear smaller and harmless that Joshua uncurled to look at him.

When Blaise pulled the tiny plantlet from his pocket and

offered it to Joshua, he won the big man over. But it had taken time—too much time—and once Blaise had convinced Joshua that he was there to reunite him with his brother and free him, Gaitwood's force was returning.

Heart sinking, he sent Joshua to the holding cells to find Jack and the others. No one around the fort would think anything of Joshua Walker wandering around. He comforted himself with that knowledge as he turned his attention to his next target.

Blaise marched out of the stables as riders returned. He kept his strides purposeful, trying to fit in. Like he belonged there. Despite the chill wind, a nervous drop of sweat trailed down from his hairline.

A distraction on the other side of the fort had many of the soldiers engaged, fighting against a plume of violet smoke. Blaise prayed that between the smoke and the need for the returning soldiers to care for their mounts, he would be unharried.

"Psst!"

Blaise jumped, whirling at the voice. He put a hand to his chest when he realized it was Flora. "What?"

She frowned at him. "Why aren't you with Jack?"

Blaise shook his head. "Hank didn't come back. I found his brother and sent him to Jack."

Flora's eyes widened. "*Oh.* Um, not to be a wet blanket, but Gaitwood's already back."

Blaise raked a hand through his hair. "I saw. I'm going to the airship."

She winced. "Alone? It's under guard." Flora pursed her lips, thoughtful. "I'll try to distract Gaitwood and his lieutenants. I can't do much for the rest. Can't have everyone sign my forms in triplicate."

Blaise swallowed. He had already scoped out the pair of guards standing atop the platform leading to the warbird's deck. The guards were Jack's purview. Fighting was his forte. But Jack wasn't there, and they were running out of time.

Flora followed his gaze, her eyes hardening. "You don't have to do it, you know. You could rejoin your friends and leave."

He could. And it was tempting. But it wouldn't end the threat posed by the warbird. The Confederation had shown they had no qualms with attacking a town of innocent people. Well, *mostly* innocent people. "It only delays the inevitable." Another attack. More death and heartache.

She surprised him, reaching up and grabbing his smooth chin in her hand. "Do what you have to do. No wonder Jefferson saw something special in you."

When Flora released her grip, he rubbed his chin gingerly. She was stronger than she looked. "Thanks."

She humored him with an impish grin before she turned and trotted off. Blaise watched her go, then looked at the rampart leading to the airship. Red and gold pennants fluttered in the breeze. He clenched his jaw and mounted the stairs. Blaise flexed his fingers, shucking off the standard-issue Confederation gloves and discarding them over the side railing.

I hope I can do this. He ascended to the first landing, pausing to summon his magic. Blaise traced a finger along the well-worn wood at the top of the stairs, power spiking into it. The wood crunched as it shredded under the magical assault, flaking and curling as if impacted with instant dry-rot. Breaker magic slithered down each step, fragmenting the wood until all that remained was a flight of stairs too treacherous to climb. Chunks of wood sloughed off to the ground below.

Getting down would be difficult. Taking a shaky breath, he decided to worry about that problem later. He had made it impossible for Jack to join him, and that was the more pressing matter.

Keeping his magic checked, he put a hand on the railing and continued up. Blaise heard a loud exclamation as someone discovered the damage he had wrought, followed by more querulous voices. He took the stairs two at a time to put more distance between himself and the soldiers below.

Blaise still didn't know how to handle the pair guarding the top. He discarded the notion of breaking the platform—doing so would cut off any chance he had of getting to the ship. He paused on the landing below, crouching to keep a low profile. What would Jack or Flora do?

He shook his head. He wasn't either of them; Blaise couldn't replicate their level of intensity in a situation like this. He had a revolver, but he had little confidence in using it in a high stakes situation.

This was why he wasn't supposed to be doing this alone. He had no chance.

On the platform above, a guard made a sharp exclamation. Blaise missed the words, but he glanced up at the familiar thunder of wings. The pegasi had arrived. He scooted closer to the side and peered down, his breath catching at the knot of outlaws in the courtyard.

Jack was at the forefront, sowing confusion by virtue of the uniform he wore. Blaise cursed softly when he realized why Jack had started the assault. The soldiers were bringing ladders and barrels over, constructing their own makeshift means to reach the undamaged section of stairs.

Jack must have found a weapons cache somewhere. He waded through the soldiers like a dragon ransacking a town, magnificent and terrible in his fury. Every move the outlaw made was deliberate, calculated. Every pull of the trigger was prioritized for the greatest impact.

A shout overhead drew Blaise's attention. "Breaker!" A bullet pelted into the wood beside him. Blaise dove as another bullet whistled by. Heart pounding, he kept a low profile. They would come for him, and then it would be over.

I can't do this.

A challenging scream sliced the air. Blaise looked up in time to see Emrys drop from the sky like an obsidian boulder. Blaise feared the stallion would collide with the platform, his wings mantled close to his sides and his neck outstretched, legs tucked neatly beneath him to cut the wind resistance. The soldiers stared at the sight, realizing too late they were the targets.

A pistol glinted as Emrys's wings snapped open to complete his stoop. His body ratcheted as he extended his hind hooves like an osprey stretching out talons to take a fish. The soldier took aim at the stallion.

"No!" Blaise screamed, racing up the stairs.

The muzzle flashed. The soldier turned toward Blaise's voice as Emrys slammed into him and his companion with the force of an avalanche. Massive hooves crunched against fragile bone. Crimson blood and viscera peppered the air as Emrys slammed them over the side of the platform to fall on their fellows below, raining down a cloud of gore.

Uncontested and panting for breath, Blaise gained the top of the platform. Emrys was already a blur in the distance, his speed and mass carrying him away. The stallion circled around, threading through the pennants atop the fortress to land on the platform, the wood groaning beneath his weight. Blood dribbled from a wound on his right foreleg.

A bullet whistled nearby, a reminder of their dire circumstances. "Emrys, you need to get out of here. You're too big a target!"

The black pegasus's nostrils flared as he sucked in deep breaths from his exertion. <I couldn't let you do this alone.>

Blaise swallowed, hot tears threatening his eyes. He had thought he was alone, but he wasn't. "You're the best." Blaise wrapped his arms around Emrys's neck, and the stallion arched his neck, lipping at Blaise's back. Blaise touched the bullet wound. "You need to get out of here before you get shot again. Can you fly?"

<I am not leaving you to do this alone.>

Blaise shook his head. "I'm not alone. You cleared the path for me." He glanced over the side of the platform, down at the fighters below. Blaise pulled away from Emrys, unable to delay the inevitable. "Can you tell the other pegasi to get them to safety? This warbird won't be in the air much longer if I have a say in it."

Emrys backed up a step, flicking his ears. <I will tell them. And I'll come back for you.> He shoved his head against Blaise's chest. <And we'll celebrate with apple pie.>

Blaise smiled, scratching Emrys's throatlatch. "Whatever you want."

Emrys turned and bolted off the strained platform, wings snapping out as he swooped over the courtyard. Screams heralded his descent as he buzzed over the heads of the combatants.

With a shaky breath, Blaise crossed from the platform to the airship's gangway. No one challenged him, thanks to Emrys. Bullets tore through the platform behind him, but it was too late. They wouldn't be able to get a line of sight on him now with the ship's bulk protecting him.

The wooden deck of the airship vibrated beneath his feet. He grimaced at the sensation but walked the length of the deck to get his bearings and decide the best location to start his work. Massive blades housed in metal spun along the sides of the ship. Was that what allowed it to fly? If he had the luxury, Blaise would like to know more about how the behemoth took to the air. But that wasn't meant to be.

The dull pressure of a tension headache pounded in the base of his skull. Blaise frowned. Had the stress gotten to him? Maybe. He felt strange, as if his magic were being leeched away, like the time Gaitwood had him in salt-iron shackles.

With a sinking feeling, Blaise realized that parts of the airship were forged from salt-iron. That was an added difficulty he hadn't accounted for. The salt-iron would make his task more difficult, but not impossible. The Confederation wouldn't want to render their own theurgists useless after a flight on the ship. How did they manage?

Blaise sat down on the polished wood of the deck. The added drain on his magic made his work urgent. When he touched the ship with his palms, his magic bloomed to life.

He nibbled his lower lip, puzzled at what he discovered. Against all odds, the airship had magic, too. Magic and salt-iron coexisting in one terrifying leviathan. Blaise was no expert, but that seemed impossible. How had they done it? And how was he going to break it?

The magic sluiced over the warbird like a second skin. Blaise sent out tendrils of his own magic, feeling it trace along the lines of the ship, following the grid of the enemy's enchantment. Not attacking—not yet. Simply questing, gathering information. The magic armor didn't extend to the metal propeller blades. He had found the salt-iron.

Blaise wondered if there was a way to avoid the blades. There were so many of them. Their proximity tugged at his magic, and he already felt the drain. He shrugged away the sensation, flattening his palm against the wood once more.

His magic painted a clear picture of how the airship's protective sorcery functioned. He couldn't see the details—he could never replicate whatever the spell was. But his Breaker magic identified multiple spells layered over the vessel, woven together like a failsafe. If one failed, another would kick in to keep the ship from harm. As far as he could tell, they were purely defensive. Smart, Blaise decided. Nobody wanted a massive airship falling out of the sky. Normally, anyway.

A single spell overlaid the others, and it was more aggressive than the rest. It actively probed Blaise's magic. He frowned as he felt the ghost of a tickle against his shoulder. His shoulder? He startled as he realized the magic was searching for a theurgist's tattoo. That was how the Confederation kept their mages from being drained by the airship. It identified friendlies by their tattoo.

He shook his head. Blaise didn't know how someone convinced the salt-iron to play nice with the identification spell. But that wasn't his concern. He needed to crack through the magic armor. Fast.

From what Blaise could decipher, the spells kept hostile magic from destroying the ship. It made it resistant to mundane weapons like cannonballs, too. The identification spell kept the workings below it from being breached. Whoever had designed this had been meticulous.

"Hmm." Blaise cocked his head, still probing. The theurgists intended to make the ship impervious to magic. That didn't mean they had succeeded. He was a Breaker, and this was his specialty.

I can *do this.*

Blaise's only concern was the sheer size of the spells. And once he had made it through those, he still needed to crack the ship like an egg. That was going to take a lot of strength and a lot of power. And it was being leeched.

"For hating magic, they sure packed a lot into this monster," Blaise grumbled. He settled down to work, hoping his friends below were either still holding the line or winging their way to safety.

He laid both hands against the deck and closed his eyes, concentrating. The identification spell was child's play for his magic, ripped apart with the ease of punching through a spider's web. There was an audible pop as it broke. One down, too many more to go.

The protection spell was the real challenge, as he'd suspected. Blaise strained his magic against it, like a mouse struggling to break a boulder. The wind carried the acrid stench of gunpowder and the sounds of fighting. He didn't have time to dally with that spell. Blaise hammered his magic against it, relentless. His head throbbed, and his hands were raw as if he were physically scrabbling against the enchantment. His magic told him he was making progress, but it was so infinitesimal Blaise quailed that he had met his match.

Shoulders hunched, breathing hard, he threw everything he could at the protective working. His muscles ached with the effort, and he understood how Nadine's body had held up to such abuse—her power had converted her own flesh and blood to magic, to restore her. Blaise felt his body doing the same, only it wasn't to heal his body. It was to destroy the airship.

The protective sorcery shattered with a resounding boom. The wood shuddered beneath him. Blaise's eyes shot open. Now he only needed to slice through the other spells. *Right. No problem.*

With a hiss, a silver cage slid into existence around him. Confusion clouded Blaise's mind. *How?* He didn't see Gaitwood—oh. Heart pounding, Blaise saw the Commander standing on the rampart across the courtyard, arm extended.

He couldn't break the trap *and* the spells on the airship. It would be a challenge for his ebbing magic to complete even one of them.

Blaise didn't think twice. He slammed his palms down against the deck, spiraling the last dregs of his magic into the thrumming wood.

CHAPTER FIFTY

Vengeance Incarnate

Jack

Jack was in his element. Blood coated the front of his uniform, though he appreciated the fact that the scarlet fabric made it difficult to tell. He could respect a practical color choice.

The rescued outlaws fought around him, creating a unified front of bullets, flying fists, and bladed weapons. Courtesy of Flora's map, Jack had led his group to the armory first, where they laid claim to more weapons. And then, to further sow chaos, Jack had Cordelia torch the armory. Her phase-shifting ability proved handy—she set the fire and skulked out without so much as a worry.

Smoke billowed behind them as fresh cries of dismay met the new development. The smoke would hinder the pegasi's vision, but the benefit of destroying the enemy's access to weapons

outweighed the risk. Determined, Jack wove through the courtyard toward the stairs to the rampart. He ground to a stop,
dismayed.

Blaise had already come through, and he had made sure no
one could follow him. *Stupid kid. How are you going to get past the
guards, bake them a cake?*

A pegasus screamed overhead. Jack cursed, shoving Emmaline
out of the way as a pair of pulped corpses splattered to the
ground. He swiped gore from his cheek, his lip curling in disgust.
Damn Emrys.

"Where's Blaise?" Emmaline asked, eyes wide, her face tinged
green at the sight of the mangled soldiers.

Jack pointed up. He narrowed his eyes as a soldier leveled his
rifle at them, casually shooting the man with one of his newly
acquired revolvers. "Time for the extraction," he called to the
group. It was just as well; they would be overrun soon if they
didn't get out

Heads bobbed in acknowledgment, though everyone was still
locked in combat. Jack ducked under a swinging saber, Emmaline
kicking out his attacker's knee and driving the man down to the
ground with a ferocity that made Jack's heart pound. *She's the spitting image of her mother.*

He hoped Zepheus was close. Gold flitted in the sky above,
and Jack filled his mind with thoughts of *get us outta here.*

<On it.> Zepheus's mental voice was a whisper, proof the
pegasus was at his broadcast limit.

The courtyard was a riot of activity. The soldiers not engaged
with Jack and his group gained a foothold on the rampart stairs.
Jack growled as soldiers swarmed up the structure.

"Send Austin!" Emmaline yelled over the din. Jack frowned,
not following her train of thought in the heat of battle. "He's a
Skater. He can just run up there!" Emmaline pointed to the rope
and wood gangway that led from the platform to the airship.

Damn. She had a good idea. But doing so would trap Blaise.

Emrys circled above the airship, his challenging cries echoing through the courtyard, answered by the whinnies of the other approaching pegasi. The stubborn black stud had the Breaker's back.

Jack pulled his knife from his boot, ducking over to Austin and shooting the teen's newest opponent in the face. Austin blinked at him in surprise as Jack shoved a blade into his hand and pointed. "Get rid of that gangway, then get out of here."

Austin's eyes widened, then he nodded and ran to the side of the rampart. He made an incredible sideways leap, his boots clamping down to the brick as he skated his way up the facade, dodging bullets as he went.

Jack turned his attention from the Skater as the first pegasus landed in the courtyard, Vixen's Alekon. The bay stallion screamed, strafing over a group of soldiers, knocking several over. His hooves kissed the dirt for a heartbeat as Vixen vaulted into the saddle in a perfect touch-and-go. Alekon's wings created a wind so fierce it blew a soldier back.

One by one, the other pegasi came in for pick up. Jack worried that Raven and Butch would have difficulty, but the Necromancer could hustle when the situation warranted it. Despite his wounds, the battle invigorated Raven, and he mounted his pegasus quick as a wink. Cordelia followed, and then Austin, who had left the gangway a drooping, useless tangle.

And then only Jack and Emmaline remained. The surrounding soldiers kept a respectful distance, many of them out of ammunition and humbled by the unforgiving hooves of the pegasi raining down on their fellows. Jack and his daughter had a healthy supply of weapons. Jack wasn't afraid to menace anyone who looked at them the wrong way. Most of the soldiers focused on attempts to get to the Breaker, alone and vulnerable atop the airship. Soft targets were always more appealing for cowards.

Oberidon lined up for the maneuver, speckled wings steady as he descended. "If it's safe, circle until you know—" Jack started, then paused when he heard a familiar voice.

Emmaline was already hurtling onto her stallion's back when

Jack turned and fixated on Lamar Gaitwood. The Commander stood atop the undamaged rampart opposite the warbird, arm outstretched.

"Daddy, no!" The wind of Oberidon's departure blew away her protest.

Rage consumed Jack, spurring him on as he stalked across the courtyard, inevitable as the chill of winter. Emmaline must have worked magic on him because the exhaustion from his recovery had faded, replaced with a swiftness and agility the men who tried to get in his way couldn't match. Jack was a living wildfire, racing from one man to the next, snuffing out lives with cold indifference before his enemies had the opportunity to react.

A solitary soldier, no older than a boy, stood at the bottom of the stairs, knees knocking together in terror, eyes wide at the trail of death in the outlaw's wake.

Wildfire Jack stared. He smiled. A wet stain spread across the front of the kid's pants. He ran.

Jack shot up the stairs like a bullet, intent on his target, unerring. He didn't think twice about what he was doing. Jack only saw the man who threatened everything he loved, everyone he cared about.

<Jack!> Zepheus was frantic. <Jack! We have to go. Jack!>

The outlaw shook his head as he reached the final landing before the top. He was almost there. Lamar would pay for his treachery. Across the courtyard, metal and wood groaned like an abused accordion.

<Jack, STOP!>

He couldn't stop. He wouldn't stop until Lamar was *dead*, damn him thrice to Perdition.

Zepheus slammed into the railing ahead of him, a shower of wood splintering from the impact of his hind hooves. Jack slowed, growling as the stallion's left wing brushed against his chest for a beat before the pegasus swept by, circling around.

The airship wailed again, and out of the corner of his eye, Jack saw the entire vessel shudder, the midsection beginning to buckle as if it were being squeezed by a giant hand.

Lamar screamed something unintelligible. *Lamar.*

<If you kill Lamar now *you will die*, crushed by that airship!>

Fuck. Jack blinked at Zepheus's cold assessment. The damn stud was right. Already the airship was listing, and before long it would slam bow-first into the rampart where Lamar stood.

<Touch-and-go,> Zepheus advised him, swooping around.

Jack stepped back and crouched to give the pegasus room to maneuver. It was all up to Blaise.

CHAPTER FIFTY-ONE
Together

Blaise

*H*ands braced against the wood, Blaise poured everything he could against the warbird. He ignored the pulsing hum of the magic trap surrounding him, keeping the knife's edge of his focus on breaking through the spells woven around the vessel.

Blaise hoped he was close. He was so tired. As he sank down against the deck, his mind drifted as his forehead rested against the grain of the wood. *Maybe I could just take a quick nap . . . .*

The echo of gunfire nearby reminded him he didn't have the luxury of rest. His body was being consumed from the inside out by his magic. And the ship was still leeching away the little he had to give.

Speckled wings zipped in the periphery of his vision. Blaise frowned, struggling into a sitting position as Oberidon banked overhead. He lifted his head, the wind tousling his hair as power seeped into him. It was like the first cup of coffee in the quiet peace of the bakery, waking him up to the possibilities of the day. Blaise closed his eyes as another wave of strength flowed through him. It was a ghost of the joy of togetherness from the night of the Feast of Flight, before his world had cascaded into disaster.

His eyes flashed open as magic suffused him, granting him renewed resolve. *We take care of each other.*

He was alone and vulnerable on the deck, trapped in a silver cage. Blaise smiled. He wasn't truly alone. Overhead, two pegasi circled, waiting as Emmaline poured her magic down on him. Her spell spoke of the belief the townspeople had in him, and it was like they stood on the deck beside him. Solid, reliable Clover, who could carry Jack like a baby. Hannah, with her ready smile and unerring positivity. Growly Kur Agur, who would stand and fight for the weak. Wildfire Jack, who had become an unlikely friend.

"We'll do this together," Blaise murmured.

Bolstered, he sank his magic into the hull, but this time with the seed of an idea. He thinned his magic into long tendrils, wrapping them around the airship like krakenvine claiming a tree. Emmaline continued to feed strength to him, and Blaise pushed more into his vines. He had seen vines break through wood and stone before. Not everything required force.

Unlike in nature, his vines didn't take time to grow. They writhed around the warbird, tightening his magical grasp. He pushed his magic, forming barbs like on a living krakenvine, hooking them into the enchantment. The protective spell reacted to the threat, recoiling. The barbs of Breaker magic snagged and shredded the working.

The airship keened as its protections were ripped asunder, leaving it vulnerable. Breathing hard, Blaise grinned.

<Blaise! You have to get free,> Emrys warned, coming to ground on the deck. His glossy hide twitched as he was sapped by the salt-iron, and he took off again quickly before it could do more damage.

Blaise bowed his head. The last of the power from Emmaline was fading, and he still needed to break the airship. Taking out the spells wasn't enough. Emrys swooped overhead, hanging stationary for an instant as he pumped his wings backwards.

"Thank you for being my friend." *For believing in me.*

Blaise poured the last of his magic into his vines, crushing them around the hull as Emrys winged away, whinnying in frantic denial. Emrys battered at his mind, desperate. But Blaise pushed him out as the deck started to buckle beneath him.

His muscles trembled with the effort of sitting up. The ship lurched, and Blaise's hands scrabbled for purchase against the wood. The airship listed to the port side, then shimmied starboard. Metal squealed, and lumber splintered as his magic ripped the ship apart, sending it spiraling toward the opposite rampart where Gaitwood stood, gaping.

And then the deck dropped sideways. Blaise struggled to stay away from the bars of the cage, but the force of gravity was inevitable. He slid against the deck, flailing as he struck the perilous trap.

His magic spent, there was nothing to protect Blaise. Darkness washed over him as the wreckage of the airship ripped through the fort.

Jack

EMRYS'S HEARTBREAKING WHINNIES SPLIT THE FRIGID AIR. JACK SAT in Zepheus's saddle, shoulders hunched. Emmaline, astride Oberidon, brushed tears from her eyes. They stood on a ridge due west of Fort Courage, far enough inside the boundaries of the country of Mella to be problematic if anyone cared to come after them.

But the mangled airship, that destroyed a good portion of the fort as it went down, distracted the enemy.

Jack was silent as smoke rose from the fort in the distance, mingling with dust motes stirred by the impact of the airship. He squinted as he watched Emrys fly over the fort, the stallion searching for his rider with single-minded determination. Emmaline clutched the poppet with Blaise's hair in her cupped hand. She was pale and exhausted after pouring everything she had left into the effigy.

"Feel anything?" Jack asked.

She swallowed, biting her bottom lip. "No. It's like . . . he's not there."

Neither of them wanted to say aloud what that likely meant. Jack balled his fists. *Damn it, the kid wasn't supposed to die.* The outlaw hung his head, comforting himself, knowing that at least Blaise knew they had succeeded. His friends were safe. Emmaline was safe. And he had guaranteed the cursed airship wouldn't bother them. Victory had never tasted so bitter.

"Let's head home," Jack said, nudging Zepheus with his knee. He cast a final look over his shoulder, knowing he should be satisfied by the defeat of his enemy. Instead, the piercing stab of loss suffused him.

Oberidon followed Zepheus into the sky. Together, the palomino and the spotted stallions convinced the black pegasus to join them, and they flew homeward to Itude.

CHAPTER FIFTY-TWO
A Minor Setback

Blaise

*D*arkness enveloped him.

Blaise assumed he was dead. But being dead shouldn't have so much pain attached to it. Dull aches and sharp pains washed through his body, unrelenting. He tried to move an arm, confused when the request didn't register with his limb. Where was he? Why was it so dark?

Then he *remembered*. Panic seized him, and if he had command of his body, he would have been sick at the memory of the airship shattering beneath him, the deck twisting and lurching as he fell into the wicked silver bars—

No. He forced the memory down, trying to master the horror as he had mastered his magic. *My magic.* Blaise recalled the utter emptiness, nothing left to give; feeling his body convert his own flesh into power to continue the fight. Was he, like Jack, trapped in a living prison after hitting the cage? That was the only explanation he could devise.

Blaise relaxed into the darkness. He had no other option. This was a battle he couldn't fight. Even if he could, he was so tired. He slipped in and out of wakefulness, his dreams filled with angry voices talking over him. They sounded distant, and he didn't bother to decipher their words. A corner of his mind recognized one voice, but he was so deep in the darkness it wasn't worthwhile to figure out who it belonged to.

He felt a jarring sensation when he was alert—as if he were being moved somewhere. That was a positive sign; with luck, he wasn't buried under a pile of broken airship. Idly, Blaise wondered if his magic would come back. Would it shatter the barrier of Lamar's magic? Or was he trapped in the depths for the rest of whatever time he had left?

His aches and pains receded. How much time had passed outside of his prison? He remembered how Jack looked, wasting away from the days of his imprisonment. Blaise tried not to think about how certain Nadine had been that the outlaw would succumb to the nefarious trap. There was no one to free Blaise.

Words and voices surrounded him again, most of them unfamiliar. But one voice remained, the same one he had tried to place before. His groggy mind grasped at the voice like a drowning man reaching for a rope. The timbre belonged to Jefferson Cole.

Blaise clung to Jefferson's voice, trying to understand his words, but failing. Jefferson spoke to him, relentless but soothing. Sometimes Jefferson spoke with others, but then he was terse, stressed. Jefferson's presence bolstered him. *I'm not alone.*

His magic came back, a slow, painful trickle. Blaise had never spent all of it before, didn't have a concept of how long it would take to replenish. Though as his magic returned, it didn't come to his call. Instead, it had a mind all its own, assaulting the spell layered over him. His weak magic attacked the trap like ants swarming a wolf.

Little by little, painstakingly slow, his magic ate away the spell.

The effort was exhausting. He regained control of his body a bit at a time; first his fingers, then hands and wrists. Encouraged by that victory, he wiggled his fingers.

"Blaise!" Jefferson gasped. "Can you hear me?"

I didn't think that through. Blaise twitched his fingers again in reply. Communication by finger wiggling wouldn't work out so well. He didn't know how to say, "Help, I'm stuck in a spell that's trapped me within my own skin."

Hope kindled in his heart as his magic continued its battle. Relief flooded him. *I'm not alone.* Once Blaise won free of the trap, there were questions he needed Jefferson to answer. But first, he had to get that far.

His awareness grew as feeling returned to his body. Someone dribbled broth and water into his mouth to sustain him. Someone kept him clean and saw to his bodily needs. His eyes still refused to open, and it frustrated him not knowing where he was.

Jefferson spoke to him often. So much that Blaise might have been annoyed by it any other time, but as he drifted in and out of wakefulness, he rested in the security of Jefferson's presence.

Finally, his magic roared back with full force, lifting the veil of shadow from his eyes as it shredded the fleeing remnants of the trap. His eyes flew open as he took a great, gasping breath.

Jefferson stared at him like he was a ghost, then dropped the book he was holding onto the floor with a resounding thump. He sat in a chair beside Blaise's bed. Clean white sheets covered Blaise's prone form.

"Blaise?" Jefferson's voice quivered, as if fearing disappointment and heartbreak.

"Howdy," Blaise rasped. *Ugh.* His throat was raw like he had breathed in a dust storm.

Jefferson leaned closer, running a hand through his unruly dark hair. His face was pale, cheeks and chin covered in shaggy bristles. He looked nothing like the put-together, dapper man Blaise remembered. "I was afraid you would never come back."

Blaise swallowed. He had been afraid of that, too.

Jefferson staggered to his feet, wobbling like he hadn't stood for days and his legs were unfamiliar with the idea. "I need to tell the doctors. They need to check you—"

"Wait. Please," Blaise whispered. His heart pounded. "Where am I?"

Jefferson glanced away. "Izhadell." He licked his lips, voice edged with steel. "We'll speak after I have the physicians check on you. They were certain you were going to die."

Izhadell. Blaise squeezed his eyes shut as Jefferson crossed the room and pushed open the door, flagging someone down outside. He was deep in Salt-Iron Confederation territory. *This is bad.*

Blaise opened his eyes as footsteps cascaded into the room. A flurry of activity swirled around him, men and women dressed in white poking and prodding him, looking into his eyes and mouth, taking his temperature, and asking him rapid-fire questions.

Blaise realized he was a curiosity to them. The doctors had never encountered a Breaker. And, judging by their studious murmurs, they had never come across anyone who had broken free of a Trapper's cage on their own. And survived an airship crash (on top of him, according to one nurse who read a passage from a report detailing the effort to extract him from the wreckage).

The specialists bickered about their theories. Blaise dozed as they talked, picking up bits and pieces. They argued over the strength of a Trapper's cage and the load the magic could bear versus the weight of a broken airship. They seemed to think Lamar's cage had saved Blaise's life. Maybe it had. Blaise didn't care. All that mattered was that he was alive. And he was in *Izhadell.*

Eventually, the doctors concluded poking and prodding him, and filed out, leaving strict instructions that he was to stay in bed. The concept of walking was hilarious for someone just regaining control of his body. His muscles were mush.

Jefferson reclaimed his chair after they shut the door. "How do you feel?"

"I just fielded that question from eight different people. Did you miss that?"

Jefferson reached out and put his hand on Blaise's. "I'm the only one who *cares*."

Blaise blinked. He hadn't meant to snap. "I'm sorry. I'm scared and . . ." He wasn't sure what else to say. There were no words to describe the overwhelming mishmash of emotions.

A bitter smile played on Jefferson's lips. "You don't have to apologize." He sobered. "You're right to be scared. You broke a big, shiny airship and a very expensive fort."

A lump formed in Blaise's throat. "How many died?"

Jefferson shook his head, a tendril of hair covering one eye. He flicked it away with a finger. "Don't count the dead. Count the living. Your friends made it out."

Blaise closed his eyes. He counted the living, but that didn't absolve him of his guilt. He knew attacking the fort would end in the loss of life. Crashing an airship would, too. He had blood on his hands, blood on his soul.

"What's going to happen to me?"

"I . . . I'm handling it. Don't worry." Jefferson answered so quickly, Blaise popped one eye open to look at him.

"You're handling it? Or Malcolm Wells is?"

Jefferson sucked in a breath. He cast a furtive glance over his shoulder and leaned in so close that an onlooker might assume it was an intimate moment. "We *cannot* discuss that here. *Please.* I'm Jefferson here and now. I *have* to be."

The desperation in his voice was so raw that Blaise could do nothing but agree. Jefferson had stayed by his side for . . . he didn't know how long. He owed him that much. "I'll honor it."

Jefferson rubbed his cheek, relief slacking his muscles. "Thank you. It's complicated. I promise to explain when I can."

Blaise nodded. He was exhausted and wanted to rest again, but he was loath to succumb to the darkness so soon after clawing his way back into the world of the living. "Why am I in Izhadell?" They had every reason to kill him at the scene of the crime.

"That's complicated, too," Jefferson breathed. "There are those who want to put you on trial for your crimes. And still others want to take you apart piece by piece to discover what makes a Breaker different from other mages." His voice rose with anger at the last. "We're in the hospital at the Golden Citadel. It was the best accommodations that Doyen Wells could argue for you to be placed in that would also keep you safe and allow you to recover."

The Golden Citadel. Why was that name familiar? *Jack.* This was where the young theurgists trained. Wonderful, Blaise was deep in enemy territory, in a place frothing with opposing mages. But he also understood from Jefferson's words that the location provided a manner of safety for him, too.

"Visitors to the Cit go through a stringent approval process. They lock this place down tighter than a nun's habit. Unfortunately, the hospital wing we're in is of salt-iron construction." Jefferson jerked a thumb to the wall. Once Blaise was up to it he would have a tough time breaking free.

"Understood." Blaise thought for a moment. "Ah . . . are *you* in trouble for associating with me?"

Jefferson raised his brows. "Well . . ."

"Are you?"

Jefferson held up his thumb and index finger, pinching them together. "A tiny bit of trouble. Nothing much. Just a minor setback, really."

Blaise's heart sank. "You're a terrible liar."

Jefferson offered a brief smile, then cleared his throat. "In this case, I am. Phinora recognizes all the paperwork we signed back in Rainbow Flat differently than in Ganland. In Ganland, we were partners. Phinora . . ." He see-sawed one hand from side to side. "They consider you my charge so I may be the teensy-tiniest bit culpable."

Blaise scowled. "What happened to plausible deniability?"

Jefferson coughed. "The funny thing about that is it's less plausible and more difficult to deny when you drop an airship on a fort."

Blaise groaned.

"We'll get through this." Jefferson reached out and took his hand again. "So what if I have a few new lawsuits? That's an average day in Ganland. It's what I pay my lawyers for." He shrugged, as if it wasn't a bother at all.

It bothered Blaise a lot. "I'm sorry."

Jefferson shook his head. "Don't be."

If only it were that simple. Blaise studied the lines of Jefferson's face. "I still don't understand what you see in me."

Jefferson sat back, giving him an exasperated look. "Do you wish me gone?"

Blaise shook his head, terror gripping him at the thought of being alone. "No, no. I just . . . you deserve better."

"You're being ridiculous," Jefferson returned, leaning closer once more. "You've been around me long enough. You're aware I'm a man who knows what I want." He moved in, brushing his lips against Blaise's. Gentle, merely a reminder of his feelings on the issue. "I'll fight the entire Salt-Iron Confederation for you if I must."

Blaise stared, heart thudding. No one had ever spoken to him like that before. He swallowed, closing his eyes. He may be in enemy lands, but he wasn't alone.

CHAPTER FIFTY-THREE
Fortitude

Jack

"Hold up," Jack ordered as Zepheus swooped over Itude. The palomino slowed and turned when Jack pointed to the town signpost. Zepheus landed and trotted over to the bullet-riddled sign.

Some joker had painted the word *Fort* in front of *Itude*. Jack frowned. *Fort Itude.*

"Hope you don't mind, but it seemed right. And I enjoyed the irony."

Jack turned in the saddle. Vixen stood outside the Broken Horn, shading her eyes against the bright spring sunshine. She no longer wore her smoke-tinted glasses. Vixen had no need, with her magic stripped away.

"What?" he asked, not following her logic. *Fort* made him think of the Confederation, and that made him want to shoot somebody.

"Fortitude. Strength in adversity." She strode over, the breeze tugging at her long brown coat.

Jack raised his brows as understanding dawned. *Fortitude.* He tilted his head, considering it. Yeah, he had to admit he sort of liked it. "I'll allow it," Jack told her, gruff.

She smiled, brushing her long, red hair over her shoulder. "It also seemed like a good poke in the eye to the Salties."

Jack grinned. "When you put it like that, it does."

Zepheus dropped him off at his home. Jack ducked inside, shucking off his duster and removing his hat, hanging them on pegs near the door. Emmaline was elsewhere with her few friends who remained. He slipped into her room, removing the tiny poppet that sat on her bedside table, turning it over in his hands. Yesterday, something changed. Emmaline *sensed* him. Alive.

He planned to have her check the poppet again when she returned home. Just to confirm her findings. Jack was about to slip it into his pocket as a reminder when something happened that stopped him in his tracks. *Magic.* In his fingers.

Frozen, he stared down at his hands. He lifted his right up for closer inspection. Foolish—he wouldn't be able to see magic like a squashed bug or a clod of dirt. But he felt the unmistakable promise, like a rain-tempered breeze blowing through a parched land.

Shaking, Jack staggered to the table, pulling out a chair to sit. He dropped the poppet on the table, and the sensation subsided. Cautious, he picked up the effigy again, and magic prickled through his skin.

"*How?*"

It was nothing short of a miracle. Jack had exhausted his resources searching for a way to reverse the alchemical process that had stolen his magic. He'd reached the grudging conclusion that once it was gone, that was the end.

He had been wrong. His magic was returning. It was sluggish, coming back at a trickle, as if he had overextended and emptied his reserves. But it was there.

He closed his eyes, shaking his head. Jack had come to terms with not having magic, had finally admitted it to the other Ring-leaders. And now, like a bolt of lightning in a clear sky, it was coming back.

Jack thought about testing it to make sure he wasn't mistaken. But he held off. He needed to allow more time for it to pool, to refill his empty reservoir. Jack almost reached out and pushed his magic against Blaise's poppet, so tempted. But no, he needed to leave that for Emmaline.

He took a shaky breath as he came to terms with what this meant. Jack stared at the poppet. "How in Perdition did you do that, Blaise?"

Blaise and Jack will return in
Effigest, coming soon.

Acknowledgments

2020 was the sort of year that pantsed you, kicked you down, stole your lunch money, and then laughed at you. It was hard, exhausting, and fearful. When I needed something that I could control as the world spiraled out of control around me, I turned to writing, and thus *Breaker* was born.

In a year known for quarantine, writing could have been a lonely endeavor, but it wasn't. And for that I have many people to thank. First and foremost, the only other person who knows the original train wreck draft of this novel, Samantha Kroese. This book would not exist without her cheering me on, and for that I will ever be grateful.

Shout out to my mom group, J14 Mamas. None of you batted an eye when I told you what I was up to, and in fact you encouraged me. Some of you even powered through the beta draft! Absolute rock stars, all of you!

Big thanks to the Twitter #WritingCommunity. Yes, I was a curmudgeon who claimed I would never join Twitter. And now here I am, all the wiser for it. I've learned a lot from the combined hivemind there and made some new friends to boot.

Thanks to my team at the Katherine Tyra @ Bear Creek Library–every single one of you are amazing and I'm proud to work with you. Your curious inquiries into my writing are humbling and kept me plowing onward. And I don't know about you, but this journey has me absolutely amazed by the work I know goes into the books on our shelves.

Breaker is all the better for the time spent slogging through the beta draft by my Outlaw Mage Beta Team: Jen Abercrombie, Cara Campbell, A.R.K. Horton, S.L. Howard, Rachel Klein, Samantha Kroese, Sumi Lough, Kate Peterson, and Tara Wood. I'm honored that you would take the time to read this and help me improve my craft with your priceless feedback.

And of course, thanks to my family. My wonderful husband Kirk who was at first bemused by the amount of time I spent writing but was always supportive. To my boys, Elias and Toby, who provided their own particular soundtrack for some of the scenes I wrote. Writing with kids running around is an adventure.

Last, but certainly not least, this book would not be possible without the love and support of my parents. Look, Mom and Dad! Dream come true at last!

Soundtrack

Level up your Outlaw Mage experience with music!

Blaise's theme
Second Chance – Shinedown
Stand – Rascal Flatts
You Are More – Tenth Avenue North
High Hopes – Panic! At the Disco
The Broken – 3 Doors Down

Jack's Theme
As Good As I Once Was – Toby Keith
Shoot to Thrill – AC/DC
All Along the Watchtower – Jimi Hendrix
The Good, the Bad, and the Dirty – Panic! At the Disco
Ace in the Hole – George Strait

Jefferson's Theme
Carry On – Fun
Glad You Came – The Wanted
Head & Heart – Joel Corry
Can't Stop the Feeling – Justin Timberlake

Itude
Together – For King & Country
Roundtable Rival — Lindsey Stirling

Stay In the Know!

Visit amycampbell.info

Sign up for my author newsletter!

Be the first to learn about my new releases and receive exclusive content.

Also, if you enjoyed *Breaker,* I would absolutely be humbled if you would take a few minutes of your day to leave a review on the platform of your choice. Reviews help little authors like me gain a foothold in the publishing wilds. It's like the *Oregon Trail* out here. Only you can save me from dysentery! (Or not. Your choice, I guess.)